The Last

"Some of the best accounts of Hawaii's past have come not from scholars, but from fiction writers, able to build on the historical records with acts of insight and imagination that bring them closer to the probable truths. The Last Aloha, Gaellen Quinn's novel of Queen Lili'uokalani, is as empathetic and accurate a reconstruction of the downfall of the Hawaiian monarchy as it may be possible to get. Hawaiian readers, who already know so much of the queen's story, will be moved to see it once again so inexorably unfold. Other readers will have much to learn."

— Elinor Langer, author of "Famous are the Flowers: Hawaiian Resistance Then–And Now," *The Nation*, April 28, 2008 (www.thenation.com/special-issue-hawaii)

"The Last Aloha is a top pick that should not be overlooked."

— *Midwest Book Review*

"Gaellen Quinn's first novel explores the shifting tides of loyalty and passion in late-19th-century Honolulu. With a sharp eye for detail, and a very good ear for the cadences and tones of both the haole and Hawaiian aristocracy of that period, Quinn offers a nuanced portrait of a kingdom's final breaths, a tale of discovery and intrigue that holds the reader's interest from the first page."

— *Honolulu Weekly*

"Beautifully and insightfully written, The Last Aloha not only shines a light on a dark part of Hawaii's history, but also challenges us to see each other with our minds and with our hearts, which is the true aloha spirit. Quinn reminds us that this spirit has always been in the hearts of the Hawaiian people, giving us hope that it is within reach of us all. From the moment I viewed the cover, with its amazing painting by Princess Ka'iulani, I couldn't put the book down!"

— Q'orianka Kilcher, actress, star of *The New World* and *Princess Ka'iulani* (2009)

THE LAST ALOHA

a novel by

GAELLEN QUINN

Inspired by True Events

LOST〰
COAST
PRESS

The Last Aloha

Lost Coast Press
155 Cypress Street
Fort Bragg, CA 95437
(800) 773-7782
www.cypresshouse.com

Book and cover design by Michael Brechner/Cypress House

Cover art: "Poppies" (1890). Painted in Great Britain by Princess Ka`iulani, heir to the Hawaiian throne, at age fifteen.

Library of Congress Cataloging-in-Publication Data

Quinn, Gaellen.
  The last aloha : a novel / by Gaellen Quinn. -- 1st ed.
    p. cm.
  ISBN 978-1-935448-00-6 (pbk. : alk. paper)
    1. Young women--Fiction. 2. Uncles--Fiction. 3. Missionaries--Hawaii--Fiction. 4. Liliuokalani, Queen of Hawaii, 1838-1917--Fiction. 5. Hawaiians --Fiction. 6. Hawaii--History--To 1893--Fiction. I. Title.
  PS3617.U564L37 2009
  813'.6--dc22   2008054940

Printed in the USA
11 9 7 5 4 6 8 10

Mixed Sources
Product group from well-managed forests and other controlled sources
www.fsc.org Cert no. SW-COC-002283
© 1996 Forest Stewardship Council

FSC

"All things in this world are two:
in heaven there is but One."

— Queen Lili`uokalani, 1838–1917

One righteous act is endowed with a potency that can so
elevate the dust as to cause it to pass beyond the heaven
of heavens. It can tear every bond asunder, and hath the
power to restore the force that hath
spent itself and vanished....

— Bahá'u'lláh

This book is lovingly dedicated to
Queen Lili`uokalani
An example for her time
and for the ages

When all material resources were denied her, she
transcended the battle and made profound choices to
safeguard the spirit of aloha in her islands and in her
people, thus preserving this treasure for the whole world.

Ua mau ke ea o ka aina i ka pono.

Acknowledgments ⟶

A book like this is the culmination of many important influences, acts of kindness, and serendipitous events. I've been fortunate to have had a goodly share of all three.

Space, perhaps fate, and my faulty memory will decree that some who've helped bring this book to light will not be named. Indeed, there are likely many mysterious convergences of which I'm unaware. That said, and with full trust that in the long run, no good deed goes unrewarded and those omitted will be otherwise compensated, I wish to thank:

My mother and father, Marie and Glenn Gronquist, for their unfailing encouragement for me to "go, do, and be"; my daughters, Ruhi and Trina Quinn, who never cease to surprise me with their creativity, spirit of adventure, and good sense; their dad, Michael Quinn, for his love and reminders always to "be happy"; my sister, Karyn Dawes, for her big heart and never once refusing to grant me a favor I've asked.

My brother and sister-in-law, Glenn and Mahina Gronquist of Kea'au on the Big Island, for sharing the amazing Hawaiian family history and resources that started me on the journey to write this story, and for providing feedback to help me keep it as true to the times as possible.

Other friends in Hawaii who supplied places to stay or provided encouragement that kept the wind in my sails as I did the research and writing: Frank Haas of Kailua; Terry and Dona McVay of Captain Cook on the Big Island; Linda and Chris Cholas of Hilo; Winnie Howell and Lynn and Billy Howell-Sinnard of Kaluaaha, Moloka'i; Curtis and Gale Crabbe of Hoolehua, Moloka'i; and all the wonderful *kupuna* who shared their stories with me in the park at Kaunakakai, Moloka'i.

The knowledgeable and ever-helpful staff at the Hawaii State Archives and Bishop Museum who assisted me with materials and photos, and where I was honored and humbled to read documents like Queen Lili'uokalani's diaries and even hold in my hand some of her original letters. And the docents and staff at historical sites such as 'Iolani Palace and Washington Place for answering all my unusual questions and, in some cases, allowing me in when I didn't have an appointment or reservation. I am also indebted to the 19th and 20th century writers who documented the period of the Hawaiian monarchy.

Others who've offered encouragement along the road: John Truby, Leeya Thompson, Gabrielle Welford, Laurel Douglass, members of the Ka Lei Maile Ali'i Hawaiian Civic Club, and many more who share their time and energy to educate and bring about a new spirit of greater justice on the planet.

My professional support team: agent Nancy Ellis; Cynthia Frank, Joe Shaw, Michael Brechner, and the staff at Lost Coast Press; and Marika Flatt, Elaine Krackau and their associates at PR by the Book.

And last, but certainly not least, my writing friends, Brigid Donelan and Gayle Brandt, and also Gayle's husband, Jeff, who have stalwartly supported me in word and in deed far beyond the call of duty or friendship.

Me ke aloha pau'ole.

THE LAST
ALOHA

Prologue ———

I came to say a last prayer for you ... that you'll be forgiven. I may not get up here again. My knees bother me. And my children worry about the air-raid warnings. So maybe it's a prayer for me too. Because I don't think I've forgiven you yet.

The New England pine that the missionary society planted near your headstone is stunted. After all these years its roots still don't go deep. It just hangs on, twisted and bare. They should've planted a plumeria like the ones across the road at the Royal Mausoleum. Those branches arch high over the graves. They make it shady and cool, and the blossoms give off such a sweet fragrance. It's peaceful there; seems undisturbed by the bombs that hit Pearl Harbor.

But from here, you must have seen it all — the planes that roared over the island seeking a victory. Did it remind you of your own bygone days?

"A great churning of the world is coming." That's what she said when the first war started. How could the queen have known that so long ago? I can still see her, raising the flag, an "aloha" on her lips that made the atmosphere quiver and the earth shift. I want to forgive as she forgave. I wish everyone could.

It's quiet on this hillside now. The mountains wreathed in clouds. The wide, blue Pacific stretching to the horizon. The breeze from the Pali billows in my memory like the trade winds that filled the Mariposa's sails when I first neared these islands. It carries me back to the girl I was and to all that once had been. ...

Chapter 1 ———

The dressmaker tilted the oval mirror forward. Then she turned Laura sideways to let her glimpse the ivory silk and lace bunched at the small of her back.

"I don't want a bustle."

"But Miss Laura, it's what all the society ladies are wearing."

"A shopkeeper's daughter is hardly a society lady, Mrs. O'Grady. Besides, I detest being bound up like a market pig." Laura tugged at the fabric, and Mrs. O'Grady let it drop. "Isn't it enough I wear all these petticoats and this suffocating corset? They must weigh ten pounds."

"Now, don't you be complaining, miss." Mrs. O'Grady wagged a pudgy finger in mock reproach. "I'll bet it was that tiny waist that caught the eye of young Mr. Edwards."

"Andrew's not like that."

Mrs. O'Grady's bemusement reflected back from the beveled glass. "Don't be too sure, dear. It'd be a strange man who wouldn't steal a look at a waist like yours."

Laura gave her a wry smile. She looked down to touch the simple gold band with the tiny twinkling diamond on her finger. It was clear and true. *Like Andrew.* She glanced at the clock on the mantle. "We need to finish up. They'll be here any minute."

"Both of them?"

"We're going to see about the reception at the Palace Hotel."

The dressmaker turned Laura toward her and continued marking and pinning the soft silk. "Well, there's not a society matron in San Francisco who wouldn't be pleased to have her daughter's reception at the Palace."

Laura sighed. "I told Father it's too much, but he insists."

"Of course he insists. You're his only child. Turn to your left, dear."

Like Shepheard's Hotel in Cairo, and the Grand Hotel of Yokohama, the Palace was known around the world. Travelers who might otherwise go straight on to the Orient stopped in San Francisco just to stay there. It had a central court of white marble, and surrounding galleries that rose to the dizzying height of seven stories, topped with a vaulted crystalline roof. President Grant himself was feted there just seven years before in 1879, when he returned from Japan. Though she'd only been eleven, Laura remembered the Palace's galleries hung with flags and garlands, and the flurry of galas throughout the city, which had been so good for business.

Mrs. O'Grady stuck a few straight pins between her lips and knelt down, knees cracking, to measure a hem. "Stand up straight now, and hold still."

Laura squared her shoulders and brushed a wisp of hair from her eyes. "Father's been so preoccupied with this wedding. Everything's expensive."

"He looks quite happy to me, dear."

"Oh, he's happy enough." Laura smiled. "About 'enlarging our family,' as he calls it."

Mrs. O'Grady took the last pin out of her mouth and poked it through the silk. She patted Laura's stomach. "Your Andrew will have to get busy and 'enlarge' you. Give your father some grandchildren, that's what you need. Then you'll have a real family."

A flush tinted Laura's cheeks. "We won't be having children right away. I'm going to medical school this fall."

Mrs. O'Grady looked up at her. "And what does Master Andrew have to say about that?"

Laura cocked her head. "I made this decision before we were engaged. Whatever I do is fine with him."

Mrs. O'Grady smiled. "He does seem such a nice young man." She groaned as she stood and steadied herself against a wicker chair. "You've turned pink, dear. Is the corset too tight?"

Laura nodded.

"Face the mirror, we're almost through. Then I'll loosen it." She smoothed and adjusted the folds of the skirt. "So, are your relatives coming?"

"All of Andrew's family lives here. From my side there's only my father and me."

"No other family?"

"Just an aunt in the Sandwich Islands, but it's too far away to come."

Her father rarely mentioned her aunt. They never visited, never wrote each other. As a child, Laura had thought it was because Hawaii was on the other side of the world and it was hard for ships to reach there, like trying to sail to stars in a vast, dark sky.

Mrs. O'Grady lifted Laura's arm and pinned a final tuck in the bodice of the dress. Then she stood behind her, placed her hands on Laura's shoulders, and leaned forward so their cheeks were side by side as they gazed in the mirror at the result.

"Well, I wish your mother could be here to see you. You look so much like her." Mrs. O'Grady lifted a strand of hair that'd escaped from Laura's bun and pinned it back up. "That same beautiful fair hair and light eyes."

"Corn-silk hair and sea-blue eyes," that's what Laura's father always said. And that the colorized tintype had never done her mother justice. Well, perhaps their eyes were the same, but not the hair. Laura's had been light when she was small, but had darkened as she grew older, like aged honey.

"She was such a fine lady. Do you remember her?"

Laura's eyes met Mrs. O'Grady's in the mirror. There it was again. That same look she'd seen growing up whenever a mother was supposed to be there, but wasn't. It produced a nameless twinge that brought back the ache of loneliness she'd felt as a child. She knew people meant well, but she didn't like the sense of being pitied.

Laura shook her head. "I don't remember much."

The dressmaker patted Laura's arm and stepped back. Laura turned side to side, looking over her shoulder in the mirror to examine the cascades of lace and dainty satin rosettes.

"It's a wonderful dress, Mrs. O'Grady."

"With this fabric your father ordered from Paris, it can't help but be wonderful. Let me just check to make sure I have all the measurements before we take it off." Mrs. O'Grady bent over the cutting table to read her notes.

Laura walked to the window. From the second-story salon, she could look down on Market Street where the cable cars were running. Carriages crowded the avenue in both directions.

"I hope Father remembers our appointment. He's been so forgetful lately."

"It's busy at midday, dear. They'll be along."

The clouds that'd rolled in across the bay in the early morning still hung over the city, gray and cool. Men in dark sack suits with bowlers or top hats accompanied ladies pinched and bunched into dresses of black or gray, wrapped in coats and capes, tottering along in pointy buttoned boots or high-heeled shoes, their hair swept up under hats tied tight under their chins. They clutched their companions' arms as they balanced dark umbrellas over their heads and picked their way across the damp, bumpy cobblestone and the tracks down the middle of the avenue.

Two iron cracks divided Market Street where the underground cable ran to pull the cable cars. North of "the slot," as the crack was called, in a district of theaters, hotels, banks, and respectable businesses, Laura's father sold fancy dry goods in a shop on Kearny Street, just across from Roos Brothers Clothiers.

South of the slot sprawled the factories, slums, machine shops, and tenements of the working class. It seemed such a thin line. A few bad seasons were all it might take to cross from north of the slot to the south.

Laura traced a small heart in the dust on the window. She smiled. Only two weeks until the wedding. Then all these details and arrangements would be over, and she and Andrew could be alone together. She stooped to pick up a scrap of fabric from the floor, cleaned the dirt from her fingertip, and wiped off the glass.

Looking up and down Market, she tried to spot her father's carriage in the parade of buggies, hacks, and buckboards that passed the arched doorways of the millinery shop, the piano wareroom, and the furniture store offering auction prices. A group of people huddled under the striped awnings in front of Beamish's shirt store, waiting for an opening to cross the street.

Laura caught sight of her faint reflection in the windowpane. She recognized the resemblance to the tintype of her mother, but her memory was like that image: not quite clear or real. It was strange to think her mother had worn dresses made by Mrs. O'Grady.

Laura recalled the silence in the house after she died. And standing on tiptoe to peek into the cradle. A baby brother, so small, so pale. Her father never named him. She'd edged a finger under his elfin hand to lift it, but it lay limp and finally slid off. He was too weak to hold on.

As she got older, Laura hoped her father would remarry. She mentioned it once, and he blurted out, "Two are enough." She imagined he meant the two of them were enough and they didn't need anyone else. He wouldn't talk about the past. He just said he didn't want to go through that pain again. His eyes grew dim and he looked away, so she'd never brought it up after that.

But since Andrew had come into their lives, her father was making plans to expand the shop. He laughed more often. And Andrew was so kind to him. She loved to see them talking at the table after dinner in their apartment above the shop.

One night after Andrew left, her father confided, "That boy has a good head for business." Then he lowered his voice and said, "He's the son I never had." He was quiet a moment, and Laura thought of her baby brother lying still in his cradle.

The corset was pinching. She turned from the window and walked over to see if Mrs. O'Grady had finished. The dressmaker looked up.

"I have everything. Let's get the dress off so I can work on the alterations and the trim. Turn around and I'll unbutton you."

A bell on a passing cable car caught Laura's attention. Something was different. It started as the ordinary clang-clang that conductors rang as they started up from each stop or passed another cable car. But it didn't stop. It kept ringing. Faster and faster. And then it maddened into a frantic din. Something was wrong. There was the screech of metal on metal, a horse whinnied, then a crash, and wood cracked and splintered.

Laura and Mrs. O'Grady rushed to the window. At the corner, a carriage lay on its side, the axle broken, and the spoked wheels askew on either side of the crushed cab. The shafts that held the harness had snapped off, and the horse was on its knees on the cobblestone. The cable car had pushed the carriage aside and rolled on past to Montgomery Street, slowing to a stop in front of Gannon's Cigar Store. Men swung off the poles of the car, jumped down, and ran back to the overturned carriage while a crowd gathered at the corner.

The horse struggled but couldn't get up. *That horse. That blue roan horse.* Most people wanted bays with matching white socks to pull their carriages. Laura watched as a man was extracted from the cab. She felt oddly suspended above the scene, and everything moved in slow motion. There was no sound. There was no time. *Someday when our ship comes in, Laura,* Father would say, *we'll get ourselves a fine matched pair. But Old Blue will do us till then. Good Old Blue,"* he'd say, patting the horse's neck. A second man was pulled from the wreckage of the cab.

Mrs. O'Grady grabbed Laura's arm when the men were laid on the sidewalk. Laura turned to look at her face and felt the jolt of horror she saw there. Then she looked back out the window at her father and Andrew lying on the pavement. Her heart pounded in her ears. The street noise came up like a slap, and she could hear someone yell, "Get a doctor!"

She felt her feet turn and carry her to the door. She heard the clatter of her laced boots on the wooden staircase as she descended, sensed the rush of damp, cold air on her face when she emerged onto the street and pushed through the crowd.

"Stand back, miss." A policeman motioned her away.

Laura stiffened and stood her ground. "That's my family!"

Mrs. O'Grady came up waving her hand and shouting, "Let her through."

9

The policeman relented, and in a moment Laura was next to them. She gasped. She hardly recognized Andrew — his face ashen, jaw slack, eyes rolled back in his head. She knew before the policeman told her in a low voice, "This one's gone, miss."

"Oh, God." Laura shrunk back and covered her mouth with her hands to suppress a sob. She saw her father turn his head at the sound of her voice. She knelt by his side on the damp pavement and took his hand. Blood trickled down the side of his chin.

"May be internal bleeding," the policeman's voice said above her head.

"Oh, no … no, Papa." His hair was mussed, and she stroked his forehead to smooth it back, biting her lips to keep from crying. Her father's dazed eyes gradually focused until he recognized his daughter.

"Laura … I was hurrying." His voice was faint and he wheezed between words. "Didn't want … to be late. We made the turn, I … never saw —"

"Shhh. Don't talk now."

His eyes searched hers. "Andrew."

Laura shook her head and blinked back tears. His hopeful look faded.

"Laura …" He winced with sudden pain. Laura looked up at the policeman.

"The ambulance is on its way," he said.

"You can't stay …" Her father struggled for a breath. "… alone in this city."

Laura swallowed before she could speak and tightened her grip. "I'll stay with you, Papa. You'll be here."

"The shop —"

"Shhh, don't try to talk."

"Promise …" His voice faltered.

Laura leaned in. "What, Papa?"

"Go … to your family … to Honolulu."

Brimming tears spilled down her cheeks. "No! I don't know them. I want to stay here with you. You're going to be all right."

His eyes pleaded. "Your aunt … will take you in."

Laura heard the horsedrawn ambulance approach and people saying, "make way, make way."

The policeman leaned over and gently placed his hand on Laura's shoulder. "We're ready to transport him now. Do you have someone to bring you to the hospital?"

"I don't know." Laura looked around. Her stomach tightened. Andrew's body was covered with a sheet. Old Blue lay on the street, sides heaving. Someone in the milling crowd said, "Shoot it. Put it out of its misery."

Mrs. O'Grady stepped up. "I'll take her."

Laura nodded, released her father's hand, and rested her palm against his bloodied cheek.

"Don't worry, Papa, don't worry. I'll be there soon." She wiped her eyes on her sleeve.

The policeman helped her up. Two attendants put her father on a stretcher and loaded him in the back of the ambulance. She watched until the wagon rattled out of sight around the corner.

Then, for the first time, she saw people in the crowd staring at her wedding dress. Muddy streaks soaked the white silk. She tried to wipe them off, but only left smears of blood. Mrs. O'Grady put her arms around her. Laura pressed her face against the dressmaker's shoulder, and began to shake in short, soundless sobs.

Chapter 2 ———

July 16, 1886

In the low latitudes, where the tropic sea turns from green to brilliant sapphire, the flying fish appear. In the daytime, the ocean, sky, and fish are all hues of the same blue. At night, a fish may fly, like a moth to a flame, to strike the window of the ship's saloon, and fall to its death on the deck where it struggles, mouth agape, gills pulsing. They say the fish takes to the air to escape the jaws of predators.

Laura scrawled the last few words in her journal, put down her pen, and lifted her hand to shade her eyes. With the sun overhead, she couldn't tell which direction was east or west, north or south. San Francisco must lie at the ship's wake, more than a thousand miles back. The steamship *Mariposa* was five days out and should reach Honolulu the day after tomorrow.

The first days of the voyage had been choppy, gray, and cold. Laura stayed in her cabin, and the trays of food brought to her door were left untouched. Seasickness was the least of it. She'd walked through all the events of the past months in a haze — the funerals, the FOR SALE sign going up in the shop window, the friends coming to check on her. The week before Laura sailed,

Mrs. O'Grady had helped pack her things into a steamer trunk and sort through her father's clothes to take them to the Bowery Mission. She worried that Laura was so solemn and dry-eyed. But when Laura was finally alone in her cabin onboard ship and heard the whistle signal departure, the haze she'd lived in for months resolved into glaring clarity. She collapsed in her bunk, exhausted, and cried for three days.

By the fourth day, the air had grown warmer and the waves smoothed into lazy swells, so she ventured out for her first try at dinner in the dining room. She saw the metallic blue fish leap from the sea, and one dashed itself against the lighted window. She cringed when the chief steward carried the dying creature around for the passengers to see. But it was strangely beautiful, with shiny scales and gauzy dragonfly wings.

Later that evening she stood with a few fellow passengers, staring at the tiny phosphorescent lights around the ship's prow. Someone said the display was made by small animal organisms, but to Laura they looked like a million fireflies in the black water.

When she left San Francisco, Mrs. O'Grady saw her off at the wharf and tried to cheer her up by telling her she was on a grand adventure. She handed Laura a blank journal and told her to fill it up with all her thoughts and experiences. She wanted to read every word when Laura returned. Writing in a journal could help her sort out what happened, she said. Laura didn't feel like writing anything, but the flying fish impressed her enough to make a note.

"Are the Hawaiians cannibals, Mother?"

A boy, dressed in knee pants, long stockings, and a middy blouse with a ribbon-trimmed straw hat on his head, walked with his mother along the deck toward Laura's chair. Pretending to write in her journal, Laura listened closely to their conversation.

"I don't think so," the mother said.

"I heard they ate Captain Cook." The boy sounded hopeful.

"If they did, it was a hundred years ago, dear."

"Well, does the king wear clothes?"

The mother sighed, and shifted her parasol to better shade herself from the sun.

"Henry, please don't bother me with all these questions. I'm still feeling queasy."

"Are the people very savage?"

"Really, son, I don't know."

The woman reached over to level the straw hat on the boy's head. Laura glanced up, and the mother nodded as they passed. Laura returned the nod.

"Who do the islands belong to?"

"Henry, please, no more questions."

"Is hot cocoa made from the coco palm?" The boy's voice drifted out of earshot as they proceeded toward the front of the ship.

Laura leaned back in her chair. She didn't know the answers to those questions either. She knew nothing about where she was going. Were the Hawaiians cannibals and savages? Or were they now all Christians? Certainly her father's people would've had a hand in that. But he'd never talked about his life in Hawaii.

Laura remembered one day when an elderly lady came to the shop wearing an old-fashioned, Eastern-style Bo Peep bonnet. It was tied with a big bow under her chin. After the woman left, her father said she reminded him of his grandmother, and made some vague mention of the early days when his grandparents first arrived in the islands. He said the natives shocked those early New Englanders. Then he mumbled something about not knowing who'd had the bigger shock, and dropped the subject.

Laura now wished she'd asked her father more about his

family and his youth. Had he left the islands because he didn't like the missionary life? She'd never even asked him how he met her mother. Tears came close to the surface again. All those precious stories lost forever.

She lifted her hand to her neck and felt the ring that hung on a slender gold chain under her blouse. Three months after the funeral, the bookkeeper stopped in to have her sign papers for the sale of the shop. He'd been a rock of support, and had taken care of so many details she hadn't been able to face. Laura hoped he'd have good news, that the sale would give her enough to stay in San Francisco and enter Cooper Medical College in the fall. It was one of the few professional opportunities for a woman, even in a big city like San Francisco. She didn't see how she'd ever make a life for herself on some faraway island. They went over the numbers. The sale would only pay off the shop's creditors and give her enough money for a passage to Honolulu and a few months' living expenses. They'd been closer to the southside tenements than Laura had ever suspected.

Mr. Dooley had an envelope that contained a few of her father's effects returned from the hospital: a pocket watch with its fob, and an unusual black pearl ring on a gold chain. The hospital attendant had told him it'd been around her father's neck, tucked under his shirt. The perfect black pearl nestled in a delicate gold wreath of flowers — a flower Laura didn't recognize. She'd never seen the ring before. Why had her father kept it hidden? It was large enough to have fit his finger, but perhaps he thought such an exotic thing was out of place in San Francisco. She decided to wear the ring close to her heart, as her father had done.

Passengers were finally coming on deck to sit and read, or stroll back and forth. Two days before, rugs were needed to ward off the cold. Now the tropic air attracted people from their cabins and from the glassed-in saloon where they'd stayed warm playing cards. Laura overheard snatches of conversation. One gentleman with a large mustache was "in coffee." A young married couple disclosed to the lady sitting next to them that they were not staying in the islands, but were going on to Auckland. Two men in linen suits walked by, animated with talk of sugar exports from Honolulu to the United States.

She thought about the letter posted from Honolulu, folded in half in her handbag — the response from Uncle Stephen, her father's brother-in-law. When she realized she had no money to go to medical school, Laura acceded to Mr. Dooley's repeated request to let him send an inquiry to her relatives on her behalf. Three weeks later, an unembellished answer came back on black-rimmed stationery:

> *Our condolences on Mr. Jennings's passing. If Miss Jennings has no other means of support, she may come to stay with us.*
> *Signed: Stephen J. Price.*

Enclosed with it was a letter of credit addressed to an officer at Wells Fargo & Company on Montgomery Street, directing him to provide money for her passage if need be. An austere communication. But they were the only family she had left, and she had no other options. She'd be living a missionary life among the savages of Hawaii.

Laura's gaze drifted back and rested on the young couple still gaily chatting with the lady across from them, who fanned herself while she talked. The sun was growing warm, especially for those dressed in their dark San Francisco suits. Laura was imagining how nice the couple's life together in Auckland might be, and noticed, when he happened to look her way, how the young husband parted his hair on the left — just like Andrew used to. Unexpected tears welled up. She lowered her eyes and busied herself with her writing, concerned that she might have been staring. Fumbling with her journal, she dropped her pen. It began to roll down the deck, but she scooped it up before it could go too far, and put it in her bag. She collected her things and hurried up the promenade.

She stopped at the small salon that served as the ship's library, sniffed back her tears, and went inside. There were only two other passengers there. An aged gentleman sat at a mahogany table, two books open in front of him, making notes in a leather-bound journal. An elderly woman in an overstuffed chair read a book with a dark green cover. They looked up briefly to acknowledge her presence.

Laura nodded and walked to the heavy oak bookshelves at one end of the room, careful not to break the deep silence. There were volumes of Dickens and Jane Austen, selections by Emerson, Poe, and Thoreau, a copy of *The Last of the Mohicans*, illustrated versions of *Alice's Adventures in Wonderland* and *Through the Looking Glass*, *Uncle Tom's Cabin*, some obscure poetry, and an assortment of slightly out-of-date issues of *Lippincott's Magazine* and the *Atlantic Monthly*.

"If you're looking for books on the Sandwich Islands, I have the only two items here."

Laura turned. The old man smiled.

"There's really not much," he said. "I should be finished in a bit, if you'd like to see them."

She swallowed to relieve the lump in her throat. "Why, yes, thank you. What are they?"

He held up a thin volume. "Just a short guide with a little history of the islands since their discovery in 1778 by Captain Cook."

He set the book on the table and pointed to the other open before him.

"And this is *Roughing It*, by Mark Twain. Chapters seventy-four through seventy-eight describe the customs of the Hawaiians and some of the natural wonders on the islands. Did you know the Hawaiians eat raw fish alive?"

Laura shook her head. The old man tapped his finger on the page.

"In this section, Twain tells of visiting battlefields filled with the bleached bones of warriors. Says he picked up arm and leg bones as mementos. Of course, this was written about fifteen years ago." He turned a few pages to the front of the book. "Published in 1872."

"Is the guidebook recent?"

"It's a few years old. Here, take a look."

Laura accepted the book and flipped through the pages, noting that the distance from California to Hawaii was a little more than two thousand miles, that Captain Cook had named them the Sandwich Islands in honor of his patron, the Earl of Sandwich, First Lord of the British Admiralty, and that they were now called the Hawaiian Islands after Hawaii, the largest island in the chain, nearly as large as the state of Connecticut. That was surprising. She thought of the islands as little more than coral reefs with palm trees.

The other island names were strange — Maui, Oahu, Kauai, Molokai, Lanai, Kahoolawe, Niihau. The city of Honolulu, where her relatives lived, was on Oahu. The volcanoes on Maui and the big island of Hawaii were taller even than the tallest peaks in the Swiss Alps, and some were still active.

She saw no mention of cocoa being made from coco palms, as

the boy had wondered, and she could find no discussion of cannibals. She handed the book back to the old gentleman.

"Thank you, sir. I would like to see them later."

Laura scanned the shelves again for something to read while she waited for the old fellow to finish. A title jumped out at her. *Women's Wrongs*, Gail Hamilton, Ticknor & Fields, Publishers. She pulled it from the shelf and sat down in a straight chair opposite the elderly woman.

"First time in Hawaii?" the woman said.

Laura looked up. "Yes, ma'am."

"Are you out for a rest cure?"

"No, ma'am. I'm going to live with relatives." Laura felt uncomfortable under the curious gaze.

"I thought you might be out for a rest cure," the old woman said. "You look a bit peaked."

Laura knew she'd lost weight since the shock of her father's and Andrew's deaths, but she didn't want to talk about that.

"I was seasick on the first part of the trip, so I haven't been eating much."

The woman nodded. "Everett and I are visiting friends in Honolulu. They wrote us that the climate is excellent for restoring health. Is your family in business?"

"No, ma'am. They're missionaries."

The old man looked up from his guidebook. "The missionaries arrived in Hawaii in the 1820s from Boston. Puritan stock, a hardy group."

"Weren't they the same ones responsible for the witch hunts in Salem?" the old lady said.

Laura hesitated. "Well, I believe my relatives are Congregationalists, ma'am."

"You don't know?"

Laura searched her memory. There was an image of being a small child, carried in her father's arms into a church sanctuary where a large, shiny, oblong box rested on a table at the front. The top was open, and she was surprised when they reached it to see her mother sleeping inside, with the baby in her arms. She asked her father to wake them up to come outside to the park, but he whispered, "Let them sleep." And then he started to cry. She put her little arms around his neck and she cried too, not really knowing why.

Then people sang and prayed. A man talked, and they prayed again. She didn't know what church it was; somehow the word "Congregationalist" stuck in her mind. Then she remembered the day she and Andrew had visited with the minister at Grace Church up on Nob Hill to make plans for their wedding. It was the first time she'd been in a church in all those years.

The room felt close and hot. Laura rose from her chair. "Excuse me, I feel seasick again. Perhaps I'll come back later for those books."

The couple nodded, looking concerned.

"Have the steward make you some ginger tea," the lady said.

"And keep your eyes on the horizon, miss," the man said. "The purser told us that helps when you're feeling poorly."

Laura picked up her journal and book and went out into the fresh air. She walked up the deck toward the front of the ship, away from chatting passengers, and sat facing forward on the edge of a deck chair. Drawing deep breaths, she fought the nausea of grief she knew wasn't caused by the ship's rocking.

To distract herself, she opened *Women's Wrongs*. The foreword said Miss Hamilton wrote it in reply to a Rev. John Todd's book, *Women's Rights*, in which, based on Christian teaching, he condemned women's suffrage.

"The Mohammedan and Mormon doctrines," Miss Hamilton wrote, "are that women have no life in the next world except through their husbands. Evidently, the Christian doctrine is that they have none in this."

Reading seemed to worsen her nausea, so Laura laid the book on the chair and stood by the rail at the front of the deck. What if her missionary relatives held such views? What kind of life could she possibly have then?

The ship's crew had raised the sails on the two masts, and they billowed westward filled with the forceful breeze of the trade winds. Smoke from the ship's single stack dissipated over the unending expanse of blue sea. Laura gazed at the distant horizon as the breeze and steam power swept the *Mariposa* faster than the wind toward the islands she couldn't see. The afternoon sun sank toward the water and tinged a few high clouds ochre and rose. Forward of the ship's prow and all around, the Pacific lay, pure and lonely.

Chapter 3 ————

*L*aura arose at five o'clock the morning the Mariposa was to dock in Honolulu. The night before, she'd packed away the things she had used while onboard, and a tidy stack of cases, hatboxes, and her steamer trunk sat ready in the corner of her cabin.

It was still dark when she went on deck. She could see the Pleiades, like a string of shining pearls overhead, and the constellation of Orion on its side, low above the horizon. Gradually, the sky lightened and the stars winked and faded behind streaks of gold and crimson clouds. The sea shifted from silver to deep blue as the sun rose. A balmy breeze fluttered the banners on the masts. Laura bent over the rail, watching the ship's prow slice the sea.

Blue fish, blue sky, blue water. Nothing but blue. In another two months, I'd have been enrolled in college, a married woman, with a career to look forward to, and a family, a life of my own.

She imagined docking at Honolulu on a stark, rocky coast and being met by black-clad, angular, sober-looking missionaries who'd take her to their humble dwelling and put her to work, no doubt, ministering to savages.

If only I had medical training, I might be of some use —

She was startled when a steward walked by to announce the news that the islands were in sight. Her first glimpse of the gray, barren peaks rising on the horizon was a disappointment.

"How far are we?" Laura said. "Five miles?"

"More like twenty," the steward said. "The air out here can fool you."

As they approached land, the coastline came in view. Feathery palms lined the white sand beaches, and a few grass dwellings huddled along the shore. Lofty peaks were cleft with cool green ravines, and waterfalls misted with rainbows plunged from their heights.

The steamship passed a jagged peak with a long sloping profile that Laura could see was the front end of a broad crater. She heard a passenger call it Diamond Head, and another crater beyond it, Punch Bowl. Two extinct volcanoes, he told his companion. Then he exclaimed, "There's Honolulu!"

Laura looked in the direction he pointed, but could make out only two church spires and a few gray roofs among the trees.

The water turned emerald as they neared shore. Long waves broke over the coral reefs; the churning white surf sounded like muffled thunder. Beyond the reefs was a deep indigo harbor sheltering a forest of masts on the ships clustered around the town, which was still hidden beneath coconut, banyan, and breadfruit trees.

Laura shifted from one foot to the other, worrying. She didn't know what her relatives looked like or how to find them. When she purchased her ticket, she'd sent a letter with her photograph to her Uncle Stephen to let him know she'd be arriving on the *Mariposa*. But she'd heard nothing in return before she sailed.

They passed a barkentine, low in the water with cargo, headed east. Near the harbor, Laura stood at the ship's rail, transfixed, as bronze men rode outrigger canoes ahead of the surf, like toboggans down a hill, and fishermen dove to the coral forests below.

The captain maneuvered the *Mariposa* through the twists and turns of the narrow channel that led to the harbor. Inside the reef, two large American ironclad war vessels and a British corvette were anchored two hundred yards from the shore. Countless canoes filled with natives threaded their way across the harbor, keeping clear of the bigger ships and an inter-island steamer headed for open water.

When the *Mariposa* docked at the wharf, Laura looked down from the towering deck, amazed at the dense crowd of people on the pier who'd come to greet the steamer. Brown men and women were festooned with flowers hung about their necks and wrapped around the brims of their straw hats. They made their way onboard, laughing and smiling, speaking a musical language. The women wore loose Mother Hubbard gowns, a blare of scarlets, blues, greens, and yellows, their shiny black wavy hair unrestrained, and red hibiscus blossoms or white ginger flowers tucked behind an ear. The men sported white trousers and bright shirts, and around their necks, colored handkerchiefs, jauntily knotted at one side. As they strolled by, regarding all the newcomers with interest, Laura became aware of a blend of exquisite scents emanating from the flower garlands they wore.

A number of Chinese men with hairless faces and long pigtails milled around on the dock, evidently waiting to offload luggage. Mixed in the crowd were people whose nationality was hard to judge, perhaps half white.

The many foreign ladies on the pier were dressed in light muslin or cotton prints and white straw hats. The dark garb of American cities, with its binding and bustles and tied-tight conventionalities of fashion was nowhere to be seen, nor were the careworn, sallow complexions so prevalent in city life. Some of the ladies even conformed to native custom, wearing flowers around their necks and hats. And everyone was smiling. Men and women looked carefree and contented.

Laura scanned the crowd looking for anyone who resembled the image she had of what her missionary relatives would look like, but no one fitting that description appeared. Taking a deep breath to steel herself for what might lay ahead, she headed down the gangway to have her luggage collected and ready when her relatives came.

On the pier, she was caught up in the press and warmth of the crowd. The perfume of flower garlands permeated the air. Everywhere, piles of fruit were for sale — guavas, pineapple, papaya, green and gold bananas, coconuts, even strawberries. Farther down, strange multicolored fish and mounds of white coral were laid out. On the ground, rows of smiling flower sellers sat on straw mats, baskets of strung garlands in front of them. *Leis,* Laura heard them called.

Beyond the crowd, a group of horses stood saddled, heads drooping in the sun, and surreys waited to carry passengers to their destinations. Laura saw a few Hawaiian women, laden with flowers, swing up on horses and gallop down the street, their hair and bright divided skirts flowing in the breeze.

Laura heard a voice behind her. "Pardon, but are you Miss Jennings?"

She turned to see a girl of about twelve holding her photograph and looking up at her.

"Yes, I am," Laura said.

"Then I'm your cousin, Hannah Price."

Cousin? Laura never considered that her aunt and uncle might have children.

Hannah took the lei of yellow flowers hanging on her arm and held it up with both hands. Laura reached to receive them.

"They're to put around your neck, Miss Jennings," Hannah said.

Laura lowered her head, and Hannah slipped the lei over her neck. She straightened up and lifted the blooms to her face. The intoxicating perfume surrounded her like an embrace. Then she recognized the flowers — the same ones that wreathed the black pearl on the ring around her neck. No wonder her father had kept it as a memento. The flowers were yellow at the center, and radiated out to a soft cream at the tips. The scent was like a fragrant whisper.

"Thank you. What kind of flowers are these?"

"Plumeria." Hannah turned and waved toward the crowd. "Lizzie, Lucien … over here. I found her." She turned back to Laura. "Father had an appointment, so he asked our neighbor, Lucien McBride, to come with Lizzie and me to get you. Mother's waiting for us at home."

Hannah wasn't Laura's idea of a missionary child, dressed in her light print cotton and white straw hat, but she had a characteristic Laura had seen in her father. Laura wondered sometimes whether his Eastern reserve and measured speech had hampered his business dealings in San Francisco. Westerners were freewheeling and informal.

A smaller girl with a freckled nose, and a young man in his early twenties, clean-shaven and wearing a spotless white suit, wended their way through the crowd.

"This is Miss Jennings, our cousin," Hannah said as Lizzie and Lucien walked up.

"Please, call me Laura." She extended her hand to Lucien. He took it, smiled, and said, "Welcome to Honolulu."

Lizzie offered a lei of rose-colored plumeria. Laura bent to receive it. The little girl stood on tiptoe to slip it over her head, and gave her a kiss on the cheek, almost losing her straw hat in the process. She stepped back and looked up with a serious face.

"I'm sorry your Papa's dead."

Surprised at the sudden declaration, Laura didn't reply. Hannah gave her sister a stern look.

"Well, I am," Lizzie said.

Hannah stood stiff and still, not knowing what to say. Lizzie, arms folded in front of her, swung her body left and right waiting for the next thing to happen, whatever it might be. Lucien finally spoke, his tone soft and apologetic.

"If you have your receipts, I can see about your bags."

Laura fished in her purse, then handed the tags to Lucien. He turned to Hannah.

"You take Laura to the surrey. Tell the driver I'll be along shortly. I'll have one of the Chinamen load up the luggage."

They started toward the street, but Lizzie trailed behind. She seemed embarrassed. Laura turned to offer her hand. Lizzie hesitated, then flashed a dimpled grin, and sprinted forward to grasp it.

Within minutes Lucien returned with a Chinese man pushing a loaded cart. Lucien helped Laura and the girls into the surrey, while the Chinese man and Hawaiian driver hoisted the steamer trunk and cases into a waiting buckboard. The Hawaiian climbed into the surrey, collected twenty-five cents, slapped the long reins against the horse's rump, and clucked for it to walk on. The buckboard driver fell in behind.

On the drive up Fort Street from the harbor, Laura was astonished to see that Honolulu was like a small San Francisco of an earlier era. Downtown, the buildings and shops were of mortar and brick, lava rock, or wood front, none more than two stories tall, some with Victorian turrets, arched windows, and awnings. There were two booksellers, dry goods stores, a photographer's shop, boots and saddle shop, law offices, banks, newspaper offices, and a post office. The streets were still earthen and uncobbled, but the carriage traffic and occasional bicyclists rolled by with no trouble. They passed City Furniture Store, its sign in English, Hawaiian, and Portuguese advertising furniture and embalming services.

Away from downtown, Honolulu was a village of narrow meandering streets, trees arching overhead to cover lanes and homes in perpetual shade. The gabled houses with white clapboard fronts could have been transplanted from New England, except that wide verandahs had been added, and chimneys omitted. Every home had a garden filled with a profusion of bright flowering trees, shrubs, and greenery, many Laura had never seen — bamboo, mango, candlenut, monkeypod, coco palms, tamarinds, and white and yellow trumpet flowers. Blazing purple or red bougainvillea and passionflower vines lined the porch eaves.

There were also flourishing vegetable gardens. Laura recognized patches of peas, carrots, turnips, asparagus, and lettuce interspersed with strawberries and melons. Here and there between the clapboard houses and nestled back from the street, were tidy thatched homes where natives sat on mats in their front gardens under sheltering trees, eating from calabash gourds.

"Honolulu's a bit different from San Francisco," Lucien said, watching Laura take it all in. "I passed through there a few months ago on my way back from New York."

"You were in New York?" Laura said.

Lizzie piped up, "Lucien finished law school at Columbia University. He's going to have an office here now."

Lucien laughed. "Well, not right away, Lizzie. I'll be practicing awhile with more experienced attorneys. Then we'll see what happens from there." He turned back to Laura. "I hope you'll like it here. It grows on you."

His easy, genteel style made her comfortable. She wondered if they would be friends.

"It's beautiful," Laura said. "Much different than I thought it would be."

The driver pulled the reins to turn the horse right on King Street down to Alakea, where they turned left past the Sing-Wo Chong Fresh Bananas stand. At Beretania, they turned left again, pulled into a circular drive lined with palms, and stopped in front of a baronial two-story mansion. It was set in manicured gardens that might have rivaled some of the wealthy country estates down the peninsula from San Francisco. Laura supposed they were stopping to let Lucien off. He jumped down from the surrey as the luggage wagon pulled in behind them.

"Let me get Chun and Sing." He ran up the steps to the front door.

"Lucien's handsome, isn't he?" Lizzie said brightly.

"Shush, Elizabeth," Hannah said.

"I don't have to shush … do I, Cousin Laura."

Lizzie's inclusion of her newfound cousin in the mutiny made Laura smile, her first real smile in months. But before she could answer, Lucien, followed by two Chinese servants, was back. He offered Laura his hand to help her down. She accepted, thinking he intended for her to make a short social call on his family. As soon as she and the girls alighted, however, Chun and Sing began to unload her luggage, setting it on the ground next to the wagon. Each of them grabbing a hatbox and a strap on opposite ends of the steamer trunk, they started for the front door.

"We get valise after," Chun called over his shoulder.

Lucien asked the surrey driver to wait. Then he paid the buckboard driver, who pulled his reins to the left and started his horse down the driveway to the street. Bewildered, Laura watched the activity around her.

"Come on, Laura," Lizzie took her hand. "Mother said to bring you to see her the moment we arrived."

Laura looked up at the Victorian palace with its broad staircases, white columns, and wide verandahs on both stories. This was where her aunt lived?

Lizzie tugged at her hand. "Come on, Laura."

"I'll say my good-byes here," Lucien said. "I have to get back to the office."

Laura tried to hide her surprise. "Oh, well, thank you for your help."

Lucien made a small bow. "My pleasure. Perhaps I'll see you at the ball next week."

"The ball?"

"Yes, at the palace. The king is entertaining the officers of the USS *Alert*, which arrived a few days ago from the Far East. You probably saw it in the harbor when you came in. I'm sure the Price family received an invitation. Right, girls?"

Hannah nodded and Lizzie grinned, squirming with excitement at the very thought of it.

Laura's eyes widened. Kings and balls and palaces — just like a storybook tale. "Oh, I couldn't impose."

"Nonsense," Lucien said. "I bet Mr. Price will insist you accompany them. You're family now. Until then." He made another slight bow, climbed into the surrey and signaled the driver to go.

"Goodbye, Lucien." Lizzie waved as the surrey headed out the circular drive to the street.

She tugged again at Laura's hand, and they started up the broad staircase to the front door. Before they could reach it, it was opened wide by a petite Japanese woman in a traditional kimono.

"Kimiko," Lizzie said, "this is our cousin, Laura."

"Welcome." Kimiko smiled and bowed. "Come in. We have lunch when your father come." Her "Ls" were softly burred into "Rs."

"Is Mother awake?" Hannah said.

"Yes, go up." Kimiko motioned with her arm up the broad staircase and her kimono sleeve swayed.

Laura entered the foyer and looked around at the gleaming hardwood floors, alcove niches displaying fine oriental porcelain, and the molded ceiling where filigreed bronze lamps with frosted glass hung. It could have been a mansion on Nob Hill. They proceeded up the polished dark wood staircase and reached the landing as Chun and Sing came down the hall.

"We put trunk in back bedroom," Chun said. "We go for valise now." He and Sing headed down the stairs and out the front door.

Lizzie and Hannah led Laura toward a bedroom at the front of the house, its door ajar. She began to feel something akin to stage fright. She'd often rehearsed what it would be like to meet her long-lost missionary relatives. This wasn't the scenario she'd imagined.

"Is that you, girls?" a soft voice inquired.

Lizzie pushed the door open. "Yes, Mother. We brought Cousin Laura."

In the bedroom, a gaunt woman lay on a tall, carved bed, a light coverlet over her. Next to her, on a night table, was a tray of fresh fruit, cheese, crackers, and tea. Only one cracker had a bite out of it, and a squeezed lemon wedge rested on the saucer of the half-empty cup. The woman motioned for the girls to enter.

"Come in, come in."

Lizzie ran to the bed, and her mother embraced her. Hannah waited, then received a kiss and a hug. Laura hung back until Hannah and Lizzie stepped aside.

"So you're Thomas's child. I'm your Aunt Katherine." She patted the coverlet, inviting Laura to seat herself.

Laura sat on the edge of the bed. Aunt Katherine didn't look much like her father. Her face was a wilted flower, soft and faded. You could tell she'd been beautiful once. She coughed, raising a handkerchief to her mouth, then folded the cloth, and tucked it under the coverlet.

"Let me look at you. Why, you're so pretty. Isn't she, girls?" She turned her head to look at Lizzie and Hannah. Lizzie nodded vigorously, while Hannah just said, "Yes, Mother."

Turning back to Laura, Aunt Katherine leaned her head to one side. "I can see the Jennings look about you. But that light hair and those blue eyes must have come from your mother."

"Yes, ma'am."

Aunt Katherine held out her frail arms. "I never thought I'd see any trace of your father in Hawaii again. I'm very glad you decided to come, dear." Laura gingerly embraced her, and felt the protruding bones beneath her dressing gown. Katherine's voice whispered low near her ear. "I'm so sorry for your loss. You've had too much tragedy for one so young." Her aunt drew back, looking at Laura. "I want you to feel like this is your home, won't you?"

Laura nodded and blinked. Katherine's tenderness brought her close to tears.

Kimiko was at the door. "Mr. Price come. Lunch be served soon. He like see Miss Laura first."

"Thank you, Kimiko," Aunt Katherine said. "Girls, you go wash up for lunch. I've already eaten. I'm going to rest some. Laura, go with Kimiko to meet your Uncle Stephen."

"Thank you, ma'am," Laura said. She leaned forward, kissed her aunt's cheek, and stood to follow Kimiko out of the room and down the stairs.

At a heavy wood door off the foyer, Kimiko stopped and knocked.

"Come in," Uncle Stephen said.

Kimiko opened the door, let Laura pass, and closed it gently behind her. The scent of old cigar smoke hung in the still air. Laura crossed the sculpted Chinese carpet on the floor of the paneled library to where her uncle stood behind a wide desk. After Aunt Katherine's faded looks, he was younger than she expected, perhaps not yet forty, with the same dark hair and eyes as Hannah. He was dressed in a stylish suit and waistcoat and wore a trim mustache.

He came out from behind his desk and held out his hand.

"So, you're Laura."

Laura took his hand to shake it. He regarded her with a quizzical smile.

"What, no kiss for your Uncle Stephen?"

She didn't like his familiar manner, but he was her uncle. She leaned in and kissed his cheek, and he put his free hand on her waist for a moment.

"That's better." He released her, pulling up a chair. "Please sit down, Laura. I want a few words with you." He went behind the desk to sit in his high-backed chair. "You've met your Aunt Katherine."

"Yes, sir."

"And you see that she has consumption."

"I didn't know what it was, but I could see that she's not well."

"Kimiko takes good care of the girls, but they miss the companionship of their mother."

Uncle Stephen put on wire-rimmed glasses and leaned forward to look at a paper on the desk in front of him.

"When we got this letter from your father's accountant, I didn't think it was a good idea for you to come here, with Katherine's illness and all." He looked up. "But she convinced me it'd be good for the girls to have another young woman in the house. They're growing up now."

"Yes, sir."

"I agreed to have you here, so I want you to do your part. The accountant said in his letter that you'd been accepted to medical school in San Francisco."

Laura shifted in her chair and nodded. "That's correct." She didn't know why Mr. Dooley would've mentioned it.

"He inquired if you might continue your studies here. But there are no facilities for that in Honolulu." Stephen eyed her over the top of his glasses. "You don't look the type. How old are you?"

"Eighteen."

"It's spinsters who need a profession. You're a pretty young woman. You'll find a respectable husband." He took off his glasses and leaned back in his chair. "Until you do, I want you to be a companion to my girls and tutor them. I want them to learn all the finest graces any young society lady from San Francisco would have." He folded his glasses and set them on the desk. "You look well finished … despite your father's limited means."

The comment stung but she remained quiet.

Stephen shook his head. "That was always the way with Thomas. Anyway, a family in our position has obligations that

34

Katherine is unable to fulfill. I expect you to take her place at certain social functions and when we entertain."

Laura's heart sank. Social obligations. The very thing she'd tried so hard to avoid. Endless tea sipping and trivial conversation. Living in a grass hut would've been a welcome alternative. She responded stiffly, "I'm glad to help, sir."

"Good." Stephen stood up. "The first occasion is a ball next week. I trust you brought suitable gowns?"

"I brought one. I didn't expect to be going to formal functions." She thought of her revamped wedding dress wrapped in tissue in the steamer trunk. It was a parting gift from Mrs. O'Grady.

"You'll need at least one gown," Mrs. O'Grady said. "I've lowered the neckline, added some beaded trim, changed the sleeves, and switched the white rosettes to blue. It'll be lovely on you."

Taking it was absurd, given that she was going to live in a grass shack on a coral rock. She would never wear it. She didn't want to wear it ever again. But she couldn't reject a dress made from the fabric her father had specially ordered, so she packed it in the trunk.

Laura stood as Stephen moved toward her. She turned to go out the door. Again, he put his hand on her waist, opened the door, and guided her toward the dining room.

"You'll need more than one gown," he said. "Next week we'll have a dressmaker in to get you ready for the social season."

Chapter 4 ———

Laura sat on a cane chair in her nightgown next to the open window, listening to the delicate coo of doves in the banyan tree. It was early and no one else was stirring. A soft shower left droplets glistening on trees and flowers and the scent of wet foliage drifted up. She opened the journal on the desk in front of her to write an entry.

July 19, 1886

I've been here three days now.

She jabbed a dot at the end of the phrase and tossed the pen down. The persistent ache she'd tried to ignore in the flurry of getting settled was still there beneath her breastbone. Rubbing her chest in a circular motion, she looked at the milk-glass bowl filled with coconut-scented soaps, and the artfully arranged stalks of bird of paradise in the china vase on the bureau. Aunt Katherine had had Kimiko attend to the smallest detail to make Laura feel welcome. But her world had contracted to one room in a houseful of strangers.

She crossed her arms on the desk and laid her head on them, closing her eyes. The pressure of her forearm against her eyelids created blotches of color against a dark, shifting background.

She imagined she could see Andrew and the shining smile that had lit him up whenever their eyes met. But now that smile just made her ache all the more. And there was her father. Behind the counter at the shop, just as always, methodically ticking off items on a bill of lading. A little impatient when she interrupted and he lost count. But when she told him Andrew had proposed, he began to hum the bridal march and waltz around, an invisible partner in his arms, as if he were dancing at her wedding.

And then that terrible day.

Tears wet Laura's eyelashes, and a slim drop slid down along her nose. No. Don't think about that anymore. She pressed her eyes hard against her arm to block out the image that had begun to materialize. Think about something else. Anything else. The purple whorl on the inside of her eyelids swirled into a short, plump form, and she heard a faint, familiar brogue.

"C'mon now, miss, write. Write all your thoughts and experiences. I want to read every word when you return."

Mrs. O'Grady's encouraging smile hung in the darkness, and then, like the Cheshire cat's, faded and dissolved. Laura expelled air from her lungs in a long, low sigh. She lifted her head and rubbed her face with both hands.

"Read every word when I return? And just when do you think that will be, Mrs. O'Grady? It'll be never, so there's no use my writing anything at all."

Laura reached for a handkerchief and blew her nose. She began to close the journal, and noticed that her pen had rolled next to it. The nib touched the paper, and ink had seeped onto the open page to form a blue blot suspiciously reminiscent of the plump image she'd just seen with her eyes closed. Laura stared at it. Goose bumps raised on her arm.

"Jesus, Mary, and Joseph," she whispered, imitating the

dressmaker. "Oh, all right." She reached for the pen, her hand suspended above it. Finally, she picked it up, pulled the journal toward her, and began to write in swift strokes.

It's hard to settle into a strange house. In our apartment on Kearny Street, the cable cars went by and there was always traffic down in the street. Here, it's so quiet. I lie awake and can't stop the images in my head, so I get up and sit by the window. I talk to my father and Andrew as if they could hear me. It feels so odd to write that. But I don't know what else to do. I want to go back to my life in San Francisco, Mrs. O'Grady. I want to go home.

Laura grabbed the handkerchief to dab the tears that gathered at the corners of her eyes.

My life is so different here. This house runs on the strictest schedule — my Uncle Stephen's schedule. Every day at 6:00 a.m. sharp, I hear Sing busy in the kitchen downstairs. Precisely at 7:00, Kimiko glides down the hallway to tap on the bedroom door and announce breakfast. Then she supervises two maids who work all day to keep the house spotless — white glove spotless. And I don't suppose I have to say whom the white glove belongs to.

Chun spends mornings overseeing three Japanese gardeners who take care of the grounds and feed and groom a pair of sorrels in the carriage house. Right after breakfast, he brings the carriage around to drive Uncle Stephen to the office. He never fails to pull up just as my uncle steps out the front door.

The servants live in bungalows near the stable, but they

come so early in the morning and leave so late at night, they're never really gone. At home, we had one girl in during the week to help with cooking and housework. She left after dinner, and didn't come on weekends. Those days alone with my father were my favorites. We got up when it suited us, and took our time over breakfast. I can't get used to this regimen and someone always underfoot.

Uncle Stephen has scheduled me too. I have breakfast with him and the girls at 7:30 before he leaves for the office. Then I tutor Hannah and Lizzie in what he calls the "social graces" — how to stand, how to walk into a room, how to introduce people, how to make polite conversation. Every dull little delicacy you can imagine. I'd rather read the books in his library.

At least the girls are warming up to me. After lunch, I listen to their music lessons and play games with them. Lizzie loves fun, but Hannah's more reserved, like her father.

At teatime, I keep Aunt Katherine company. Except for Wednesdays, when I'm supposed to help her to receive callers. I never could stand making and receiving calls, wasting a perfectly good afternoon taking tea and trading gossip. Now it's one of my duties. So far, Aunt Katherine stays in her room and never comes to meals. I suppose if callers come, I'll have to entertain them on my own.

After dinner, we go to the parlor. The girls play piano for their father. He "listens" while he reads the paper. Then he gives me the next day's instructions for planning meals and managing the household — like I'm one of the servants. Not exactly the life I'd planned, Mrs. O'Grady. And I hate being dependent on him.

The cooing doves stopped. There was a flutter of wings as the birds fled the branches of the banyan. Two Japanese gardeners set down their woven baskets and began to rake beneath the tree. Laura drew back from the open window. She remembered having thought she'd be living in a grass hut, with scarcely the necessities of life, and ministering to savages. Not only had she not seen any savages, she had all the necessaries — even all the luxuries — one would expect living atop Nob Hill or on Fifth Avenue in New York. The gardeners picked up their baskets and moved on.

My relatives aren't missionaries anymore. They're rich. As rich as the people who used to come to our shop. Uncle Stephen's business is sugar exports. He heads the Honolulu office, and has a partner who oversees plantations on Maui.

I get snippets of family history from Aunt Katherine during our teas. Uncle Stephen's father wanted him to go into the ministry, but the Board of Missions in Boston began to withdraw their support when the Civil War demanded all their attention. Aunt Katherine said they couldn't maintain their congregations' interest in these small islands so far away.

The board told the missionaries to turn the island congregations over to native preachers and return to New England to be reassigned, or make their living on their own. So Uncle Stephen went into business.

Aunt Katherine said they started out in a little clapboard house downtown. By the time Hannah was born, they were able to build this mansion on Beretania Street. When the King of Hawaii went to Washington and got a favorable sugar treaty with the United States, planters who'd been doing well before became millionaires.

My aunt tires easily, and I don't want to pry, but I wish I could ask her more. Like why my father left when the missionary descendants are doing so well in Hawaii. They're very influential. Aunt Katherine says many hold important positions in the king's government.

Laura heard Kimiko padding up the stairs. She closed her journal and went to the wardrobe to get dressed for breakfast. Mrs. O'Grady's dress hung at one end, with a sky blue wrap strung around the shoulders. The wrap matched the altered sleeves — layers of soft net tulle that overlaid the lace in a puff that came midway to the elbows. No one would ever guess the dress had been intended for a wedding.

Kimiko tapped at the door. "Breakfast, Miss Laura. Mr. Price want to speak with you now."

"I'll be down in a minute."

Laura shuffled through the row of dresses. She envied the loose-fitting *holokus* the Hawaiian women wore; they seemed so light and cool, and allowed so much freedom of movement. But Uncle Stephen insisted that the women in his household always dress like proper ladies. That required a corset and corset cover, a chemise, and pantalettes. She chose a summer muslin, pulled it on, and tied back her hair with a ribbon.

At the table, Uncle Stephen was more businesslike than usual.

"We'll be having guests for dinner tomorrow, Laura, one of our newest legislators, Lorrin Thurston, and his wife, Clara. Normally, they'd make just a social call, but they're recently married and I thought it might be nice to have them in. Your Aunt

Katherine told me she feels well enough to have dinner with us, but she'll need your help supervising the staff's preparations. I've also asked Lucien McBride and his parents. They all know each other, so it's not a matter of making acquaintances. I do want a respectable dinner, however. Thurston is one of the up-and-coming attorneys in town. Do you think you can handle it?"

"Yes, sir."

"Then ask your aunt and Kimiko about the menu, and show it to me this evening."

Laura nodded. "So it'll be dinner for ten?"

"No, just eight. The senior McBrides, the Thurstons, your Aunt Katherine and myself, Lucien, and you."

"Oh, I thought the girls would eat with us."

Stephen looked at her askance. "Not at a formal dinner, Laura."

"Yes, sir."

Uncle Stephen raised his napkin to wipe his lips. "Since your arrival, a number of people have said they'd like to call. But I told them, with Katherine's condition, it'd be best to come to the scheduled at-homes. You'll meet many of them at the ball soon, anyway."

"The girls are really looking forward to that." Laura smiled at Hannah and Lizzie across the table.

"To what?"

"The ball."

"No." Stephen leaned forward over the table to sip his coffee. "They won't be going. It's too late. It doesn't start until after the dinner hour."

Hannah looked down, and Lizzie whined, "Oh, Papa."

"None of that, Lizzie." Stephen's cup clinked as he set it down on the saucer.

42

The little girl slumped in her chair, and the corners of her mouth turned down.

"Kimiko," Stephen said, "have Chun bring the carriage around."

"Yes, Mr. Price." Kimiko floated out of the dining room like a ghost.

He turned to Laura. "What did you think of Lucien?"

"Oh … well, he was very polite when he and the girls picked me up at the wharf."

"Yes," Stephen said. "Good stock. A little background so you'll know how to make conversation tomorrow evening." He lifted his cup and finished off the coffee. "His grandparents and my parents came out with the same group of missionaries from Boston. His family owns large plantations out toward the Ewa Plain. He and Thurston have the same alma mater, Columbia Law School. He's going to make a fine lawyer." Stephen smiled. "You'll like Thurston too. He's energetic. Plus, he'll appeal to your educated sensibilities."

"Sir?"

"Can't say as I agree with him, but he got legislation passed this year that allows a woman to keep her own property when she gets married."

Kimiko floated back into the dining room. "Your carriage, sir."

Stephen pushed back his chair. "I won't be home for lunch today, Kimiko." He glanced at Hannah and Lizzie. "You girls pay attention to your lessons, now. Laura, I'll speak to you about the dinner preparations when I get home."

Kimiko began to clear the dishes as Stephen headed for the door. Laura looked over at Hannah and Lizzie. Hannah was still staring at her lap. Lizzie's small mouth puckered, and a tear started down her cheek. Laura heard the front door close.

"Instead of doing lessons right away," she said, "why don't we read more of *Black Beauty*? I want to find out how Beauty gets away from his cruel master. We could take a blanket out under the trees."

Lizzie sniffed and nodded her head.

"Hannah?" Laura said.

"All right."

&

*W*hile the girls rested after lunch, Laura talked with Kimiko to arrange the menu for the formal dinner. She thought if she had most of it planned, it'd be less wearing for her aunt.

Kimiko suggested four courses and a dessert. She told Laura Uncle Stephen's preferences, and they settled on julienne soup, chicken mayonnaise, mutton chops, braised beef, and cherry compote with Neapolitan cakes for dessert. Kimiko went to speak with Sing about the menu and get the maids started preparing the silver and the crystal. Laura went upstairs to talk with Aunt Katherine.

The door to the bedroom was open, and Aunt Katherine lay on the bed, propped up with pillows, her eyes closed. Laura turned to go, but her aunt called her back.

"Come in. I'm just resting my eyes."

Laura walked to the side of the bed. "I need to ask you about the menu for tomorrow's dinner with the Thurstons and McBrides."

"Tomorrow?"

"Yes, Uncle Stephen said he talked with you."

Aunt Katherine sighed. "I told him I might feel up to it in a few days. I didn't mean tomorrow. Oh, well. If he's already invited them, I guess it's all right. It might be nice after all. Perhaps some good Hawaiian delicacies will improve my appetite."

"Kimiko didn't suggest any Hawaiian items."

Aunt Katherine turned her head on the pillow and looked out the window. "I always liked the old-fashioned dinners with fish steamed in ti leaves and lots of fresh island fruit. We'd give each guest a lei when they arrived, in a color to match their dress or suit. Stephen doesn't like it. He says all that stringing of flower garlands is a sign of a light mind." She looked back at Laura and smiled. "I gave the girls some coins to buy leis at the wharf to give to you when you arrived." She leaned forward slightly and whispered, "I didn't even ask him."

"They were beautiful, Aunt Katherine. I don't think they indicate a light mind. A light heart, perhaps."

"Perhaps. I suppose he wants beef and preserved fruits."

Laura nodded. "That's what Kimiko said."

"Go ahead with it, dear. I don't have the energy to do it differently anymore."

"Well, I could help. What would you like?"

"Not this time, Laura. You and I can plan a luncheon later on."

&

The following evening, Kimiko gave the girls dinner in the kitchen, and at 7:30, one of the housemaids herded them off to bed. At quarter of eight, the McBrides' carriage pulled up in the circular drive. As they got down from the carriage, a surrey pulled in behind, and Mr. and Mrs. Thurston joined them on the verandah at the front door.

Kimiko ushered the guests into the foyer. The ladies were

45

dressed in gowns, the men in light suits. Laura had observed members of high society in San Francisco when by chance they met in her father's shop and occasionally when she made deliveries to their homes. Their interactions with each other were like rituals. She was surprised to see their island counterparts casually treat one another like family, calling each other by their given names and embracing like cousins.

Uncle Stephen introduced Laura to the elder McBrides and the Thurstons. The McBrides were in their mid-forties, Mr. McBride beginning to gray at the temples, Mrs. McBride, still auburn and a bit portly. Mrs. Thurston, perhaps in her mid-twenties, was dark-haired and slender; Mr. Thurston, two or three years older, was as Uncle Stephen described him — like a mainspring wound tight, his handshake vigorous, his every comment punctuated by gesticulations.

Laura looked up to see Aunt Katherine descending the stairs with a little help from one of the maids. She was elegant in a dusty-rose silk, though her face looked tired.

Since everyone had arrived at the same time, rather than showing them to the drawing room, Uncle Stephen took the arm of Mrs. McBride, as the oldest lady present, and escorted her to the dining room. Lucien offered his arm to Aunt Katherine, Mr. McBride to Laura, and the Thurstons walked in together.

The dining table was a sweep of white linen, adorned with sparkling silver, crystal, and china, with menu cards on porcelain holders between each table setting. Instead of the roses that Uncle Stephen mandated as the centerpiece, Laura had placed long, deep green ti leaves in the center of the table, topped with an arrangement of red hibiscus blossoms. Uncle Stephen looked surprised. Mrs. McBride and Mrs. Thurston said how beautiful it was, and Aunt Katherine beamed. The bowl of roses sat on the sideboard.

When all were seated, Kimiko and the maids served the soup, and then, as each guest finished, discreetly appeared to take away the used dish and offer portions of the next course. The dining room was carpeted to avoid the sound of servants' footfalls.

After the initial polite inquiries into how she'd enjoyed her voyage and how she was settling in, Laura felt like an outsider as she listened to the exchange of news and gossip. Mrs. Thurston reported that their friend, supreme court Justice Sanford Dole, would accompany the king's sister, Princess Lili`uokalani, to Niihau to study some nearly extinct Hawaiian birds, hopefully to help preserve them. She added that Mrs. Dole might be going back to Maine again to care for her ill mother.

Others offered tidbits of information heard at friends' homes or gleaned from letters arrived from the United States or by steamer from the outer islands. It seemed everyone knew everyone else's affairs right down to what they paid for furniture and clothes. As dessert was served, the conversation turned to the upcoming ball.

"Will you be attending the king's ball, Katherine?" Mrs. McBride said.

"No, my dear," Aunt Katherine said. "I'm afraid my strength is not up to late nights right now. But Laura will accompany Stephen for me."

All eyes turned to Laura. She nodded her head in assent, but everyone remained quiet, and she felt the need to say something. The question she heard from the little boy onboard the Mariposa about whether the king wore clothes popped into her head.

"Yes, I was wondering… what's the king like?"

"Oh," said Mrs. McBride. "His Majesty is good-looking in a dark brown way. Quite regal in his European uniform and side-whiskers, wouldn't you say?" She looked to the others for confirmation.

Thurston interjected, "Kalakaua's got his kingly manner down. I wish I could say the same for his kingly ability."

"Lorrin, please," Mrs. Thurston said.

"You know it's true, Clara. He has an unbalanced mentality and a total inability to grasp important subjects intelligently. What's more, he's dishonest and immoral." He turned to Laura. "In the last election, he handed out gin to all the *kanakas* to get their votes."

"Yes," Mrs. Thurston said, "but perhaps we shouldn't judge too harshly, Lorrin. You know, 'Judge not —'"

"I know, I know. But for years we've been trying to counter all the tomfoolery he comes up with." Thurston held his knife in his hand, and tapped the butt end on the table as he spoke. "I'm not talking from secondhand knowledge here." He began to wave the knife around and lift off his chair, raising his voice. "His personal extravagance is bringing the kingdom to financial ruin, and he has a bent to indulge in political intrigue with a reckless disregard for honor. And with ladies present I dare not mention his personal moral failings."

Mr. McBride cleared his throat.

Thurston sat back in his chair. For a moment no one spoke. Laura decided she'd better change the subject since she'd brought up the king.

"Uncle Stephen tells me both you and Lucien went to Columbia Law School, Mr. Thurston."

Thurston relaxed a little. "That's right. Say, Lucien, when you were there, did you ever hear Professor Sumner lecture on Social Darwinism?"

"I did, indeed," Lucien said. "His philosophy is the foundation of the political science department at Columbia now."

"What's Social Darwinism?" Mrs. McBride said.

"You know, Mother," Lucien said. "Darwin's 'survival of the fittest.' Professor Sumner applies it to human society."

"What do you mean?" Mrs. McBride said.

"We have a very good example right here in Hawaii," Thurston said. "Superior species adapt, progress, and flourish. An inferior species doesn't adapt and dies out."

"You can't mean the Hawaiians, Lorrin," Aunt Katherine said.

"Well," Thurston went on, "when Cook arrived here in 1778, they estimated there were upwards of 300,000 natives. Just a hundred years later, there's hardly a tenth of that left. They can't keep up with the changing times, so they're dying out. The fittest races will prevail, just like the fittest species. It's the way nature works."

"I don't believe that," Aunt Katherine said.

Uncle Stephen turned to his wife. "My dear, you can't expect to understand in a few moments scientific concepts that Lorrin and Lucien studied for years. Ladies just aren't accustomed to such conscious cerebration."

Laura felt for her aunt, who seemed to wilt a little more at the comment. Then Katherine lifted her chin slightly and began to rise from the table. The men pushed back their chairs to stand.

"Perhaps we ladies should adjourn to the drawing room for tea, and you gentlemen can continue your conversation over cigars."

Chapter 5 ———

At breakfast the next morning, Uncle Stephen was stone-faced. A nearly new copy of *Hill's Manual of Social and Business Forms* lay next to his plate, with a bookmark sticking out. He rose to leave for the office, and slid the book across the linen tablecloth toward Laura.

"I suggest you go over the basic rules of etiquette for the dinner table. Include the girls in the lesson. Things were a bit uneven last night, and I want them to be better prepared than you were to keep conversation light. Look at page ninety-three."

Stephen walked toward the door and then turned back. "One more thing. Don't contradict my instructions. When I say 'roses for the centerpiece,' that's what I mean."

Hannah and Lizzie, eyes lowered, waited until their father went out the swinging dining room door. It flapped back and forth and finally shut before they dared look at Laura. She sat erect, her jaw set and her eyes burning a hole in the closed door. She picked up the book and let it flop open.

"Let's see what we can learn, girls. Here's the page your father wants us to look at." She read aloud in an exaggerated manner.

As consideration of deep and abstruse principles will impair digestion, never allow the conversation at the table to drift to anything but chitchat.

Laura shook her head. "I never imagined such innocent inquiries as 'What's the king like,' or 'I understand you both went to the same law school,' could be anything but chitchat."

"What happened last night?" Hannah said.

"Nothing, except people seemed to get their feathers ruffled from the most ordinary conversation. Anyway, let me continue."

Never allow butter, soup, or other food to remain on your whiskers.

"Well, at least I know I didn't do that," Laura said, "though I can't say the same for Mr. McBride."

Lizzie tittered.

Never make a display when removing hair, insects, or other disagreeable things from your food. Place them quietly under the edge of your plate.

Lizzie grimaced and stuck out her tongue.

"Stop that, Lizzie," Hannah said. "Your face might stick like that."

Never permit yourself to use gestures, nor illustrations made with a knife or fork upon the tablecloth.

"Perhaps we should send Mr. Thurston a note on that one," Laura said.

"He gestures a lot," Lizzie said. She began to sniff, then sneezed, spraying the table.

"Cover your mouth," Hannah said.

"Here you go, Lizzie," Laura said. "Here's your lesson on the next page."

Never expectorate at the table; also avoid sneezing or coughing.

It is better to arise quietly from the table if you have occasion to do either.

Laura held her nose in the air and primly touched her forefinger to her lip. She continued in a mock English accent.

A sneeze may be prevented by placing the finger firmly on the upper lip.

Lizzie put her fingertip under her nose. "What's 'expectorate'?"

"Don't spit," Hannah said.

"I think you already know the rest of these rules," Laura said.

Never pick your teeth or put your hand in your mouth while eating. Never wipe your fingers on the tablecloth, nor clean them in your mouth. Always use your napkin. Never tip back in your chair or lounge on the table. Never hold bones in your fingers while you eat from them.

As she read, she pantomimed all the wrong actions, picking her teeth, pretending to chew on bones held in her hand, then sucking her fingers, and wiping them on the tablecloth. Then she alternately tilted back in her chair and leaned forward with both elbows on the table, until Lizzie giggled uncontrollably and even Hannah smiled.

They didn't notice the knock on the front door, or that Kimiko had let Lucien McBride in. He pushed the swinging door ajar and stood at the entrance of the dining room with a bouquet of flowers in his hand, watching the frivolity. Laura, sprawled forward on the table, began to push her chair back again when she caught sight of Lucien. Her chair came forward with a thud.

Lucien smiled. "Sorry to interrupt your etiquette lesson."

Laura blushed.

He crossed the floor and held out the bouquet. "These are for you."

Laura's color deepened. "You shouldn't sneak up on people like that."

"I didn't sneak," Lucien said. "Kimiko let me in."

Laura accepted the flowers.

"My parents wanted you to know that they enjoyed meeting you," Lucien said.

"Your parents are sending me flowers?"

He cleared his throat. "They're from all of us."

Lizzie started to giggle, and put her hand to her mouth.

"If you don't mind," Lucien said, "I'd like to talk to you about last night."

"What about?"

Lucien looked pointedly at Hannah and Lizzie. "I'd prefer to speak to you alone, if that's all right."

Laura handed the bouquet to Hannah. "Would you have Kimiko put these in water, please? Then you two go up and see your mother for a while before we go on with our lessons."

The girls went to the kitchen to find Kimiko, and Lucien followed Laura to the verandah. They sat in white wicker chairs next to the railing. The gardeners had finished their work at the front of the house, and the garden was quiet.

"I hope you don't mind me being so forward," Lucien said, "but last night, it occurred to me that since you're new, you might not understand how people think here. If I can help explain things so you don't find yourself in awkward situations, I'd be happy to —"

"Rescue me?"

Lucien looked uncomfortable. "Well, no. It's just that last night, after you ladies went to have tea, your uncle made some comments about the dinner conversation. I didn't think he was being fair."

Kimiko arrived balancing two tall glasses of lemonade on a tray, along with Lucien's bouquet, expertly arranged in a blue vase. Lucien stopped speaking while she put the glasses and flowers on the table.

Laura watched him as they waited for Kimiko to depart. Lizzie was almost right about Lucien being handsome, but not in the classical sense. Still, he had something. It reminded her of...

Lucien watched Kimiko leave, then looked back at Laura.

...of Andrew.

His voice dropped. "When we came to pick you up at the wharf, I only knew you'd come because your father died. Last night your uncle told us about your fiancé."

Laura looked down and jingled the ice cubes in her lemonade, biting the inside of her lower lip. How strange that she'd just been thinking Lucien reminded her of Andrew, and then he mentioned him. She concentrated on keeping her breath slow and regular.

"I know it must be hard, but if there's anything I can do to help you..."

Laura looked up. "I guess it'll just take time to get used to everything."

Lucien nodded. "I'll introduce you around at the ball. Everyone who's anyone will be there. You can start making friends. You'll feel like a *kama'aina* in no time."

"What's a kama'aina?"

Lucien smiled. "*Kama* is child, *aina* is land. A child of the land...native-born."

Laura drew a line in the fog on her glass. "I would like to understand some things."

"Like what?"

"Like, is what Mr. Thurston said about the king true?"

"I'm afraid so. The king's policies are causing businessmen a lot of concern. Not to mention tax dollars. Thurston gets pretty riled up about it." Lucien paused. "But then, I think Thurston's been edgy most of his life. His father died when he was only about a year old. His mother had a hard time raising him and his brother and sister on her own. He doesn't come from money. He had to work to put himself through school."

Lucien sipped his lemonade. "He's very dedicated to Hawaii, though. You know, his grandparents were among the very first missionaries in these islands. If you ever get over to Kailua, on the Big Island of Hawaii, you can still see their old place. It's an old-fashioned New England-style house with a high fence around it. His Grandma Lucy was dead set against her children mingling with Hawaiian kids. She kept them inside that compound night and day, didn't want them picking up any heathen ways. They built that house halfway up the hillside, when all the natives' grass houses were down by the sea, as close together as possible."

"Do you think the Hawaiians are heathens?"

"They're pretty much all Christians now. Most of them very sincere Christians."

Laura looked out across the gardens. The sunlight filtered through the tall palms and the banyan to illuminate the beds of variegated flowers that surrounded the cropped lawns.

"And do you think the Hawaiians are dying out because it's 'survival of the fittest?'"

"That's the theory. There's a lot of evidence to support it.

Wherever white men go, it seems they become rulers. Perhaps they're destined to rule the whole world. The Hawaiians have some fine qualities, though. You'll see that as you get to know them. They just don't have any business sense in a place that's becoming a crossroads of commerce."

Lucien set down his lemonade and pulled out his pocket watch. "Speaking of which, if you'll excuse me, I have to get to the office." He stood up. "My parents asked if you and your uncle would ride with us to the ball."

"I'll let Uncle Stephen know." Laura stood and held out her hand.

Lucien took it and bowed. His soft brown hair fell forward, hiding his face. For a moment Laura thought he might kiss her hand, but he straightened up with an earnest look.

"I'd be honored if you'd count me among your friends, Laura."

Chapter 6 ———

Laura unfastened the slim gold chain around her neck. She wrapped the black pearl ring in a handkerchief, and put it in a drawer for safekeeping. There was a tap at the door.

"Mother wants to see you before you leave," Hannah said through the crack.

Laura opened the door. "Come help me."

Hannah walked in, her little sister on her heels.

"Don't follow so close, Lizzie," Hannah said.

"I want to see," Lizzie said. "Oh, Laura, you're a vision."

"I'd be more of a vision if I could get this dress closed up." She turned around. "Would you tie the corset for me too?"

Hannah slid her fingers under the corset cover, grasped the laces, and pulled them tight.

"Ooh, not so much," Laura said. "I want to be able to breathe. Okay, now button me up."

Hannah worked the tiny fabric-covered buttons through the buttonholes at the back of the dress. When she was done, Laura slipped on her satin shoes. On each toe was a small blue rosette that matched the flowers on her dress.

"Come on, Laura, Mother has a surprise for you," Lizzie said.

Laura's ample skirts swished the floor, and her heels tapped as they walked down the glossy hallway. Aunt Katherine was in her bedroom, sitting up in a chair by the window. Kimiko had just lighted the table lamp. Laura walked in, and their faces turned in the glow — one white, one Oriental — but in their eyes was the same motherly approval.

"How darling you look, dear," Aunt Katherine said. "Come here, I have something for you." Kimiko bowed and retreated. Aunt Katherine held up a necklace in both hands. It gleamed in the lamplight. "This was your Grandmother Jennings's."

Laura moved closer to the table. The necklace was a string of pearls with a large aquamarine at the center surrounded by tiny diamonds. She'd never had anything so fine.

"Oh, it's lovely," Laura said.

Aunt Katherine lifted the gems toward the light.

"The pearls and aquamarine always remind me of the sea. Your father left the pearls with me when he sailed for San Francisco. The string had broken, and they were all loose in a little box. There weren't enough to make a long necklace, so when we were able to afford it, I had them re-strung with the aquamarine and diamonds. I meant to send it to your father someday. Stephen has bought me so many pieces."

She nodded toward Hannah and Lizzie. "I have a few other items of Grandmother Jennings's for the girls. She didn't have much, really. You know they weren't going to balls back then. They were translating the Bible, printing books, and building churches." Aunt Katherine held out the necklace. "Here, Hannah, help your cousin put it on." She turned to Laura. "I thought the aquamarine would look lovely with your eyes. I had no idea your dress was trimmed in blue. Isn't that something?"

Hannah fastened the ornate clasp at the back of Laura's neck.

"Oh," Lizzie said. "Look in the mirror, Laura. It's just beautiful."

Laura smiled and walked to the full-length mirror in the corner. It was a beautiful piece. It could have been made for the dress. The dress. Her eyes began to tear. It was the first time she'd worn the finished dress. And the last time she was in it, looking in a floor mirror much like this one —

"Mrs. Price, the McBrides come," Kimiko announced at the bedroom door. "And Mr. Price waiting." Lizzie squeezed past Kimiko and clattered down the stairs.

Laura took a breath to compose herself, and turned.

"Don't forget to curtsy when you meet the king," Aunt Katherine said. "It's best if you curtsy to all the royal family."

"Curtsy?"

"You do know how, don't you?" She saw the uncertainty on Laura's face. "Hannah, quick, show Laura how to curtsy."

Hannah lifted a fold on either side of her dress, stretched her left leg out diagonally behind her, bent her knees, and bowed her head. Laura copied her.

"That's it, Laura," Aunt Katherine said. "And don't forget, after you've been presented, don't turn your back on the king. Pull your skirts to one side and back away. Oh, I wish we'd thought of this before now."

"Kimiko!" Uncle Stephen called up from the foot of the stairs. "What's taking so long?"

"You'd better go now, dear," Aunt Katherine said. "And have fun."

Kimiko moved down the hall to the stairwell. "Miss Laura coming, Mr. Price."

Laura stopped at her room to get her blue tulle wrap and her fan, then descended the staircase. At the bottom of the stairs, Lizzie stood next to her father. He offered his arm as Laura took the last step, and escorted her to the carriage in the driveway. At the front door, Kimiko put a hand on Lizzie's shoulder to keep her from following them.

The McBrides sat in an open landau, an elegant carriage with facing velvet seats for four, and a raised seat at the front for the driver and one other passenger. Hitched in the harness were a pair of black horses with arched necks and long, silky manes. The driver, decked out in formal livery, held the reins firmly, while the horses snorted and switched their tails, restless to move on.

Lucien opened the door and got down from the carriage, his eyes fixed on Laura. She looked down, embarrassed by his constant gaze. The senior McBrides exchanged a glance.

"I'll sit beside the driver," Lucien told Stephen.

He held the door while Laura lifted her foot to get into the carriage. From behind, she felt Uncle Stephen's hands at her waist, lifting her up. She pulled her skirts around her as daintily as she could, and sat facing Mr. and Mrs. McBride, offering a smile. They smiled back, but Laura felt she was being scrutinized according to some unwritten checklist. Uncle Stephen sat beside her. Suddenly aware of her low neckline, she wrapped the tulle a little more broadly across the front of her bodice.

Lucien glanced back from the driver's bench. "Everyone ready?" he said. He turned to the front and gave the driver the signal to proceed.

The black pair leapt at the touch of the rein, prancing down the circular drive and into the street. "Easy," the driver soothed them. "Easy, now." They soon settled into a slow, rhythmic trot.

"You look lovely, Laura," Mrs. McBride said. "Is that fabric imported?"

Laura nodded. "Parisian."

"Very nice," Mrs. McBride said. "Was the dress made in Paris?"

"No, ma'am. San Francisco."

As the horses trotted down the street, Laura wondered again at Thurston's dinner comments about the king causing ruination. The kingdom looked prosperous. The streets were clean, the yards of houses tidy, with flower-speckled vines tumbling over fences and low rock walls. The natives weren't quartered into a special district. Residents freely intermingled along the avenues, exchanging gestures of friendly greeting. In San Francisco, the races never mixed.

The carriage passed stately mansions, one called "Washington Place," where, Mrs. McBride said, Princess Lili`uokalani lived. She was King Kalakaua's sister, and heir apparent to the throne. Her husband, John Dominis, was the governor of Oahu.

"Honolulu has an active social life," Mrs. McBride went on. "There are wonderful court festivities, the foreign consulates entertain, and the ships' captains hold luncheon and dinner parties onboard when they're in port. Then there are riding parties, picnics — you'll have plenty to do. It's quite a feat to keep up with it all."

They turned down Richards Street past the Hawaiian Hotel, set under tamarind trees at the back of a spacious shady lawn. Laura looked up toward the cloud-covered mountains above the Nuuanu Valley and saw rain falling. But in town, not a drop fell as they drove along in the rose-tinted glow of the setting sun.

Beyond the hotel, they turned on King Street toward the palace. Laura was astonished at the magnificence of the government buildings. `Iolani Palace was three stories, with wide verandahs bordered by white Romanesque columns on two levels. Tall, arched windows lined the walls. The roof was gray tile, and at the five highest points, red, white, and blue-striped Hawaiian flags fluttered in the evening breeze.

Natives crowded around the gate to watch as carriages passed through. A few climbed the high wall to see the procession. The McBrides' driver nodded to those perched near the gate, then turned the horses into the wide circular drive bordered with royal palms. Near the front entrance, he pulled the reins and stopped his team behind a line of carriages letting off passengers.

Lucien jumped down, held the carriage door, and helped his mother and Laura step out. Mr. McBride and Stephen followed them up the stairs to the massive front door, which was inset with etched crystal panels depicting the Hawaiian coat of arms at the top and dancing Hawaiian maidens, birds, leaves, and flowers below. A royal servant opened the door, bowed, and bid them enter.

Inside was a grand hall with burnished wood floors, gas-lit chandeliers, and English vases and French statuettes in the wall niches. A polished staircase led up to the second story, where the king and his family lived. Large and varied floral arrangements were artfully placed about the room, and the fragrance of flowers filled the hall.

"The palace will be converted to electricity this year," Mr. McBride said. "The king became fascinated with electric light in Paris, on his trip around the world five years ago. He's determined that the palace be a showplace for modern marvels."

"He went around the world?" Laura said.

"He's the very first monarch to do it," Mrs. McBride said. "He was received in the courts of Japan, Siam, India, Egypt, all over Europe — Spain, France, England, he even had an audience with the pope in Rome."

"And he's the first monarch ever to visit the United States," Lucien said.

"All examples of his extravagance," Uncle Stephen added in a low voice.

Could someone Mr. Thurston said was mentally unbalanced and unable to grasp important subjects travel the world and meet with so many different rulers and powerful people?

"How was the king able to communicate?" Laura said.

"He speaks good English," Lucien said. "You'll see when you meet him in a minute. Come this way."

Laura paused to look up at paintings in gilt frames hung around the hall, portraits of regal-looking Hawaiians dressed in plumed hats, epaulettes, stately gowns, and coats tied across with sashes and pinned with medals.

"Those are the former kings and queens of Hawaii," Lucien said.

More guests were arriving in the hall and Lucien beckoned Laura toward the ballroom. A servant opened the doors to let them enter. There were strains of classical music and the murmur of conversation. The elder McBrides went in first, with Lucien behind them. Uncle Stephen offered Laura his arm and they followed the McBrides to stand in the receiving line to meet the king and queen.

The ballroom glittered with the light of incandescent chandeliers that shone and reflected in mirrors on the walls. People already presented to the royal couple filled the hall. They chatted in small groups, or made their way around the room, greeting others until they settled in a cluster. Most of the younger ladies wore white gowns, with natural flowers in their hair. The older ones wore black or colored silk. Laura was happy to see that her neckline was not too low, according to the styles the other women wore. The men dressed in tails, or, if they were associated with the court, in elaborate uniforms with cordon and lace. Had it not been for the variety of tinted faces, it could have been a ball at the mansion of a San Francisco millionaire.

A page passed along the line, giving the ladies engraved dance cards with tiny pencils attached by ribbon. A crowd of officers in full-dress uniform from the American and English warships scrutinized possible partners as more guests arrived.

The king and queen stood at the front, just below the dais, with members of the royal family on their right and guests of honor on their left. On either side, bearers waved *kahilis*, intricate feather standards on long poles, which Lucien said were signs of the highest royal chiefs. He leaned toward Laura and whispered.

"Sometimes, parts of those poles can be the bones of ancestors."

Escutcheons with royal orders hung at intervals on all four walls. The gilded oval frames, lined with velvet and covered with glass, displayed Hawaiian royal orders and orders of foreign governments conferred on King Kalakaua from countries like Sweden, Hungary, Venezuela, and Portugal.

Laura studied the ladies as they curtsied, and mentally rehearsed her turn. Watching Americans bow low before a king, some even kissing his hand, was odd enough. Even stranger was watching white men bow before a colored king, a reversal of the ordinary relations she was used to in San Francisco.

The chamberlain announced a familiar name, and Laura saw Clara and Lorrin Thurston approach the receiving line. They made curtsies and bows to members of the royal family. In front of the king and queen, Clara made a deep curtsy, and Lorrin stepped up and bowed low. They moved swiftly down the line, greeted the American guests of honor, and then blended into the crowd.

Next were Judge and Mrs. Dole. Uncle Stephen had told Laura that the tall, bearded gentleman was the supreme court justice

Mrs. McBride had mentioned the other night at dinner. The Doles proceeded down the receiving line at a slower pace, with greetings and a bit of conversation for each of the royal family. Judge Dole bowed to the king, then straightened up, and they conversed like old friends for a few moments.

Finally the McBrides were called, and performed their protocol. Then it was Laura and Uncle Stephen's turn. As she was introduced, Laura stepped forward to curtsy before the sisters of the king, Princess Likelike and Princess Lili`uokalani, and their husbands, who were both white men. The princesses were stately and beautiful in their elegant gowns. When Laura wobbled a little as she arose from her curtsy, Lili`uokalani gently smiled at her.

Laura stopped in front of King Kalakaua and Queen Kapi`olani, and shyly met their gaze. Kalakaua's eyes were large and luminous. His Windsor-type uniform was resplendent with gold cord, embroidered cuffs, and a collection of royal-order medals pinned to his chest. The queen was dressed in a lace-trimmed gown, crossed by a sash pinned with a jeweled medallion. Her wavy black hair, piled high, was graced with a tortoise-shell comb and a diamond star. Laura steadied herself, then curtsied deeply with head bowed. When she straightened up, the king and queen nodded and smiled.

Laura moved on to the guests of honor, the USS *Alert's* captain and the US minister. She felt odd curtsying in front of Americans, so she dipped slightly and looked around for where to go next. Seeing Lucien approach from the side of the room, she walked toward him.

"I know I promised to introduce you around," he said, "but I'd like to have the first dance."

Laura handed him the dance card, and he signed his name on

the top line. Uncle Stephen joined them.

"Save a dance for your uncle, Laura," Stephen said, almost jovial. "Lucien, don't be filling up that card. You know it's not appropriate to monopolize a lady at a ball."

Lucien gave the card to Stephen. "I only saved the first dance. I promised to introduce Laura around so she can start making acquaintances."

"That'll be fine," Stephen said. "I need to catch up on news with some of my business associates. We can meet again in the garden after the midnight refreshments. You'll have had plenty of dancing by then." He walked off across the floor to where Judge Dole and his wife were talking with the Thurstons and two other couples.

Lucien offered Laura his arm, and they moved from group to group making introductions. He seemed to know almost everyone, and gentlemen from each group signed Laura's dance card until it was nearly filled with the names of young officers and the sons of planters, businessmen, and politicians. Lucien looked toward the dais. The last arriving guests were making their way through the receiving line.

"The king will give the signal to start soon," Lucien said. "Let's go to that group by the door. I see a few more friends." He guided Laura across the ballroom.

A young Hawaiian man addressed Lucien. "Well, Counselor, I wondered when you'd come and introduce your beautiful cousin."

"She's not my cousin, she's my neighbor. Laura, this is David Kahiko, one of our legislators. David, Laura Jennings."

"A pleasure to meet you, Miss Jennings. May I have the honor of a dance?"

Laura looked at her card. "I have two dances left — one after

Mr. Stillman, and one just before the midnight supper."

"Just before supper is perfect," David said. Laura held out the dance card. He took it, signed his name, and handed it back. "Please call me David. We're all family here in Honolulu."

Laura looked up at him. "Yes, of course, but only if you call me Laura."

He had luminous dark eyes like the king. His skin was a shade lighter, but he had similar regal Polynesian features. He smiled at her, and Laura felt a peculiar warm sensation, like she'd just been included in a secret.

"Laura it is," David said. "I'll find you just before midnight."

At a sign from the king, the Royal Band, stationed on the verandah outside the ballroom, struck up a waltz. Lucien held out his hand to Laura. She took it and he circled her waist, drawing her onto the dance floor.

The whole room swirled and turned, rhythmically rising and falling with each step. The royal Hawaiians and guests of honor joined in with enthusiasm. As the number came to a close, Lucien pulled Laura close and whispered, "If it wasn't improper, I would've signed every line on your dance card."

Before Laura had a chance to answer, the waltz ended, and Uncle Stephen stepped up for the next dance. Lucien walked away toward his new partner. Once again, the band played, and couples swept around the room.

"Remember, Laura," Uncle Stephen said, "when you're dancing with young men you don't know, not too much conversation."

"Yes, sir."

"And just because they've met you here doesn't mean they have the right to presume any familiarity when you meet them later."

"Yes, sir."

"Lucien's a different case because, well, he practically grew up at our house. He comes and goes like he's one of the family. You needn't worry about him. He's a perfect gentleman."

The waltz ended, and a young American naval officer approached.

"Remember what I said, Laura."

"Yes, Uncle Stephen."

The music began again, this time a polka. Stephen stepped to the sidelines, and the young officer assumed the starting position, put a gloved hand at Laura's back, and they danced away.

The band played song after song, and Laura danced with a different partner each time. The officers of the USS *Alert* chatted about their tour in Japan and Siam, some admitting they were anxious to get home to San Francisco. The Honolulu residents talked about upcoming parties and picnics, or their latest travels. Laura watched the other dancers glide by, some stiff and methodical, some with grace and rhythm.

She especially noticed Lili`uokalani. Like all the married women, the princess danced with a succession of different partners. To dance with only one man at a ball, even your husband, was considered discourteous. Tall and erect, Lili`uokalani swayed in a fluid motion, like a long-stemmed flower in a gentle breeze. She seemed lit from within, almost as if she were in love with every man she danced with.

Between dances, liveried pages served tea and ices. Ladies opened their fans to cool down. Married ladies fanned themselves slowly, while engaged ladies fanned quickly. Just like in San Francisco, young women used their fans to flirt. Carrying the fan open in the left hand meant "Come and talk to me." Touching the tip of the fan with a finger meant "I must speak to you." Placing the fan's handle to the lips meant "Kiss me," and placing the tip of the closed fan to the lips meant "I love you."

The women wielded these lacy tools in the direction of the intended recipients with such finesse that, if you blinked, you missed the signal. The wide skirts and all the fluttering gave the appearance of butterflies. Laura saw one lady, a waxen doll with yellow curls, say yes to something, resting her fan for a moment on her right cheek and flashing her eyes across the room at one of the English officers. The young man smiled. The whole exchange took two seconds.

Laura sighed and accepted tea from the tray of a passing page. She had learned these signals when her father sent her to Lunt's dancing school on Polk Street in San Francisco, where Professor Lunt, as big as a whale but light on his feet, instructed young society scions in the latest dances. She went to the school to "be finished," as her father said, but it was also a place she might meet the "best people" of the city. Growing up with only her father to guide her, Laura found some of the girls' attitudes strange. She didn't want to spend her life at parties, or making and receiving calls. She wanted to do something that mattered.

The band started another song. Laura had no partner signed up, so she stood at the side to watch. A beak-nosed old gentleman with tanned skin and gray whiskers approached.

"Do you reverse?" he said.

"I beg your pardon?"

"Do you reverse in the waltz?" His eyes twinkled. "The king gives out party favors to the dancers he likes. Would you care to give it a try?"

The couples whirled around the ballroom, all committed to one direction. Laura watched them dance by.

"Yes, definitely," she said.

The old gentleman offered his arm, and they entered the fray.

He guided her along in the same direction as the other dancers, maneuvering toward the center of the floor. When they had an opening, he reversed their direction, guiding Laura through the dancers that came their way like a ship through an obstacle course. They switched left and right, laughing at near misses. They danced past Uncle Stephen whose mouth dropped open, and then past King Kalakaua who was dancing with his queen. The king laughed at their antics, and when the dance stopped, he applauded. The room joined with him. He waved for them to come to the front.

"Once again you chart an unusual course, Premier Gibson," the king said with pleasure. Laura looked at the old man, wide-eyed. She didn't realize she'd been dancing with an important official.

He gave the minister a small box wrapped in satin tied with gold braid. The page offered another box to give to Laura, but Kalakaua shook his head and whispered to the servant. The page went to a table at the rear of the dais and brought back a medallion strung on a gold and red-striped ribbon. It looked like a crusader's cross topped with a gold crown. The king motioned for Laura to turn around. He put the ribbon around her neck and tied it at the back. People in the crowd looked surprised.

"You're quite bold to reverse in the waltz," he said. "Well done."

Laura turned and curtsied. "Thank you, Your Majesty."

The king signaled the band to play. It was the last dance before the midnight supper. David Kahiko walked to the front of the room and stood next to Laura, offering his arm.

"Ah, Akahi," Kalakaua said. "You've found a suitable partner." The king smiled.

"I think so, Your Majesty," David said. He led Laura to the

floor, and put his arm around her as the final waltz began.

Dancing with David was different than with any other man she'd ever danced with, even Andrew. Others had been polished, expert in their movements, holding her properly according to etiquette. Some danced in silence, some conversed, and a few attempted to flirt. There was always a sense of tension.

David moved as if he were music, on his dark face the pure enjoyment of having his arms around her, swaying together. It felt natural, somehow comforting. Yet there was a wistfulness too, as if a spell would break when the music ended.

"You know, it's not common for the king to give a medallion like that at a ball."

"Then why would he give it to me?" Laura asked.

"I think he likes your spirit."

"Why did he call you a different name?"

"Akahi? Hawaiians have a custom of giving nicknames. Some particular thing you remind them of, an animal, a flower, some characteristic."

"What does Akahi mean?"

"All Hawaiian words have more than one meaning, but basically it means 'first, one, or once.' I got the name because I'm an only child." The music was winding down. David smiled. "You know, the last man you dance with before the midnight supper has the obligation to accompany you for refreshments."

Chapter 7 ————

David offered his arm to escort Laura through the ballroom's large double doors. Pages swung them open wide for the guests to walk across the formal entry to the state dining room.

"Will they serve Hawaiian food?" Laura said, remembering the old man in the reading room on the *Mariposa* who'd told her that Hawaiians ate raw fish alive.

"Probably not for this crowd," David said. "You'll have to come to a *luau* to get real Hawaiian food."

"What's a luau?"

"A Hawaiian feast. I'll invite you sometime."

They walked through the sliding koa-wood doors to the dining room where long tables were filled with cold delicacies — roast pheasant and turkey, baked ham, broiled fish, lobster, small pastries filled with meat, plates of asparagus and sliced tomatoes, platters of cheese, and huge bowls of strawberries and iced watermelon. There were coconut, sponge, and fruitcakes on the sideboards, crystal dishes of bonbons, and urns of coffee and tea. Pages circulated offering glasses of champagne from large trays.

The tables were adorned with shining candelabras, flowers in silver vases, French china, Bohemian crystal, and English silver service. The Royal Hawaiian Band had moved to the verandah outside the dining room, and began to play excerpts from classical opera. Portraits of European kings gazed down on guests as they filled their plates and hovered around the table, eating and drinking.

"I don't like 'perpendicular' refreshments," David said. "I like to eat sitting down. Would you mind taking supper in the garden? The pages will come around to serve drinks."

Laura nodded, and they picked up plates and silverware, moving around the table to make their selections. David led the way to the gardens outside. Tables and chairs were set up under broad trees strung with colorful Chinese lanterns, flickering like fairy lamps in the dark. Gardenia centerpieces radiated a bewitching scent that filled the night air. People grouped themselves around tables to eat, or promenaded the grounds to flirt, talk politics, or gossip.

Laura followed David to a table under a tree at the edge of the lighted area, away from the crowd. The moon and stars glowed close to the earth, and music from the verandah drifted in the soft breeze. They set their plates on the table, and he held her chair as she arranged her skirts and sat down. He sat across from her, smiling.

"Why are portraits of European royalty hung in the dining room?" Laura said.

"They were gifts to various Hawaiian kings from the crowned heads of Prussia, France, and Russia. The Europeans were well aware of the value of being able to land in these islands to restock their ships with food and fresh water." David cut up a slice of roast pheasant. "There's an English admiral among them too — Richard Thomas. About forty years ago, he returned the islands to the Hawaiians after a British officer used his warship to seize control of the government."

"The officer took over the country?"

David shrugged his shoulders. "He had big cannons, and we didn't. But then, Admiral Thomas sailed into Honolulu, forced the man to stand down, and restored control to the king."

Laura shook her head, then took a bite of fish.

"Speaking of royalty," David said, putting down his fork, "perhaps I should give you a Hawaiian name now that you've had a royal honor yourself." He thought a moment. "How about *kamali`i.*"

"What's that?"

"It means 'princess.'" David smiled and sat back. "But you need something more distinctive, just for you. Let me see." He took a bite and chewed while he thought, looking at Laura intently.

"Maybe *hikina.* That means 'east' or 'arrival.' You arrived from the east, and your light hair looks like the sun."

A page stopped at their table with a tray of champagne. He set a glass in front of Laura and another in front of David, then moved off toward the tables near the gazebo.

David lifted his glass. "A toast."

"To what?" Laura said, picking up her champagne.

He touched the edge of his glass to hers. "To welcome you to Honolulu."

"Thank you."

Laura smiled and sipped her drink. David was easy to talk to, like she'd known him a long time. He seemed to be at ease too, yet never crossed the line by being too familiar. She watched people stroll the grounds. Some glanced her way and turned their heads to comment to their companions. Most couples were white or Hawaiian, but not mixed. There were a few white men with Hawaiian women, but not the other way around. Laura pushed a piece of lobster to the edge of the plate with her fork.

"How about *pulelehua?*" David said.

Laura looked up. "Pardon me?"

"Pulelehua. It means 'butterfly.'"

"Why butterfly?" The annoying thought of ladies in the ball-room, fluttering their fans, came to mind.

"Your lacy dress reminds me of a butterfly."

"All the women here are wearing lacy dresses."

"You're right," David said. "Too common." He picked up a strawberry, bit off the fruit, and set the stem on his plate. He sat forward in his chair. "I know, this is perfect. You have blue eyes like the sea. And you're wearing aquamarine and pearls from the deep ocean. You are *Malolo*."

"What's malolo?"

"A very special creature." He smiled and started to explain.

Laura watched David's animated face. His eyes shone. But then she was distracted by a couple who passed their table. When they were a few yards ahead, the woman glanced back at Laura, then leaned to whisper to her companion as they walked away. Laura looked down at her still-full plate. She began to feel a sense of unease, like standing at the edge of a precipice where she couldn't see the bottom.

"Laura?"

She looked up. "Yes?"

"I said, you don't seem too hungry. Would you like to walk a little?"

"Oh, sorry." She looked around. "I guess I'd better find my Uncle Stephen. He said to meet him after the midnight supper."

"Sure." David looked puzzled. He rose to pull back Laura's chair.

Laura stood and adjusted her wrap. David offered his arm, and they walked back toward the palace.

"I trust you've enjoyed your evening, Laura."

"I have, I'm just a little tired."

As they rounded the corner to go up the main staircase, Uncle Stephen and the McBrides were coming down.

"There you are," Uncle Stephen said to Laura, ignoring David. "We sent Lucien to look for you."

"Good evening, Mrs. McBride," David said and nodded. "Mr. McBride, Mr. Price." He nodded at each man in turn.

"Mr. Kahiko." Uncle Stephen nodded back. "Thank you for retrieving my niece." He extended his bowed arm, signaling for Laura to step to his side, as if she were a trained bird that should perch there.

"Ah," David said. "Laura's your niece." Laura moved next to Stephen and took his arm. "Lucien said she was a neighbor, but he didn't say which one. We had the last dance, and as etiquette demands, I was obliged to see that she had an escort for the midnight supper."

"I appreciate your thoroughness," Uncle Stephen said.

"My pleasure." There was an awkward silence. "Well, if you'll excuse me, I meant to say goodnight to some old friends." David bowed slightly. "Mr. McBride … ladies." They nodded back and David climbed the palace steps.

"Wait here," Mr. McBride said to Stephen. "I'll go call for the carriage. Keep an eye out for Lucien."

Uncle Stephen turned to Laura, eyes narrowed. "With all the eligible young men here tonight, I don't know why you're wasting your time with that *hapa-haole*."

Laura didn't reply. Mrs. McBride looked away across the grounds as if searching for her son.

"I think I see Lucien with that group by the gazebo, Stephen. Would you go fetch him?"

Stephen walked off abruptly, and Laura's arm dropped to her side. Mrs. McBride moved closer to her.

"Did you have a good time tonight, dear?"

"Yes, thank you. It was lovely," Laura looked down.

"Don't fret about your uncle, my dear. He's got strong opinions, and sometimes he doesn't think before he shares them."

Laura glanced up. "What's hapa-haole?"

"It means 'half-caste' — half Hawaiian and half white."

"Oh."

"Perhaps there's something you should know. How can I put this delicately … ?"

"What, Mrs. McBride?"

"Here in the islands, it's rare that Hawaiian men marry white women. It just isn't done, you know. And white men don't often marry Hawaiian women. They don't have to because, well," she hesitated. "I don't know how else to say this. The Polynesian ideal of morality is below the Caucasian, and Hawaiian women are very free in sharing their charms, if you know what I mean."

"But both the royal princesses are married to white men," Laura said.

"That's another story, my dear. The royal women own property and confer position and status. Prudent young men building their careers and fortunes see those liaisons in a very different light — oh, here's the carriage now."

Laura and Mrs. McBride moved back as the high-stepping horses rounded the curve of the palace driveway and stopped in front of them. Mr. McBride jumped down from beside the driver to help his wife and Laura into the carriage. Uncle Stephen and Lucien came striding across the grounds to join them. When they were all seated, the driver started the team toward the gate.

Laura looked back for a last glance at the palace. She couldn't be sure, but she thought she saw David's face at a lighted window, watching the carriage pass by.

Chapter 8 ———

September 4, 1886

It's been months since I've written in this journal. The summer has just slipped away. Next week Lizzie and Hannah start back to school at Punahou. I'm glad they'll have a chance to get out of this house. They're hardly allowed to be children. And Uncle Stephen doesn't understand how Aunt Katherine's illness affects them. Several times they've come crying to me after some comment of their father's.

When they're at school all day, I don't know what I'll do with myself. Every which way I turn, Uncle Stephen has a complaint. Since he saw me with David Kahiko at the ball, it's like he wants to steer my whole life. I still like to think about David sometimes. The way he danced, his smile. But I doubt I'll ever get to see him again. As Mrs. McBride said, "It just isn't done, you know." Especially when you live in this household. I feel like my mind is in a corset, not just my waist.

Lucien is my accomplice to get out of the house. When I feel like a fluttering bird in a cage, he takes me to picnics or luncheons on visiting naval ships, with Uncle Stephen's blessing, of course. Lucien is devoted to making me feel comfortable here. It's hard not to grow fond of him.

We went to visit one of his family's plantations. I've never been to the Southern states, but life on sugar plantations here, I imagine, must be like plantation life in the South before the Civil War, except in Hawaii the laborers are Chinese coolies, and the overseers are Portuguese.

I've met much of polite Honolulu society now. The men's talk is all business and politics, while the women plan parties and outings. Everyone gossips — who's talking to whose wife at the band concert, who drank too much at the last luau, who was seen at the *hula* dances. It can be tiresome. But I think it comes from a lack of any real news and being so far away from the rest of the world. Still, the people are hospitable.

Last Saturday, Lucien and I went to Judge and Mrs. Dole's for a luncheon. Princess Lili`uokalani was there, and I was seated next to her. When she found out that Hannah is twelve and Lizzie eight, she invited us all to a luau at her beach home today. She said her niece, Ka`iulani, is almost Hannah's age and they'd be good company for each other. The princess told me she loves to entertain her niece's little friends. She and her husband, the governor of Oahu, have no children of their own.

At first, Uncle Stephen said we couldn't go. But when Lucien offered to escort us, he relented. Lucien will be calling for us any minute, and the girls are so excited. This will be my first real Hawaiian luau.

I wonder if they'll have hula. I don't think so, since children will be there. Effie Williams said that hula dancers wear only skirts and anklets, no tops — and do more than just dance. The hula is strongly condemned by the Americans here, though I've heard that American men do go. Effie told me that sometimes, late at night, you know hula is going on because you can hear the drumming of calabash gourds from the direction of Waikiki. She named some married men (I won't say whom) seen returning home in the wee hours of the morning along the Waikiki road.

Well, the Polynesian ideal of morality may be below the Caucasian, as Mrs. McBride said, but as far as I can see, in practice, it's about the same.

Laura heard steps coming down the hall. She blotted her journal with a sheet of paper, wrapped it in a silk scarf, and slid it under stacked linens at the back of the wardrobe.

There was a tap at her door. "Laura?"

"What, Lizzie?"

"When are we going?"

"We'll go when Lucien gets here," Laura said through the closed door.

"Can I come in?"

"I'm still getting dressed. Go downstairs and watch for the carriage."

"Okay."

Soft footfalls receded toward the stairwell and faded down the stairs. Laura placed a straw hat on her head, adjusting it so the flat bow was at the left. How nice it would be to have a flower lei around the brim, like the Hawaiian ladies wore, but she didn't want to see the "I am not amused" look on Uncle Stephen's face. She heard Lizzie pound up the stairs, yelling.

"Lucien's here. It's time to go."

The wide, level Waikiki road ran toward Diamond Head, past comfortable villas, grass huts, and palm-lined white sand beaches. Bicyclists and surreys traveled in both directions. Toward the mountains, the land was planted with rice paddies and taro patches. Near a stream that entered the ocean, fishermen worked on nets next to their canoes. The road came close to shore, and Laura marveled at surf riders astride long wooden planks, riding in front of breaking waves as easily as if they were standing on a street corner. Near Kapiolani Park, a group of women equestrians, dressed in long, flowing skirts and jaunty hats, with garlands of flowers hung about their horses' necks, galloped boldly past.

"Those are *pa'u* riders," Lucien said. "Pa'u is the name of their long skirts."

Before reaching the park, Lucien turned the carriage onto a trail toward the beach. By the water, people were seated on straw mats laid on the sand next to a thatched hut. Small Hawaiian children ran about and played in the surf, unencumbered by any clothing. Farther out, a few men and older children paddled surfboards and outrigger canoes.

"Will we eat at the beach?" Lizzie said.

"No," Lucien said. "There'll just be refreshments. We'll probably spend the morning here and then go up the road for a late lunch at Hamohamo, the princess's country house."

One of the princess's retainers jumped up and came to hold the reins of the horse while Laura, Lucien, and the girls climbed down from the carriage. The retainer led the horse and carriage down to some palm trees, and tied it up in the shade. Another servant approached to adorn them with sweet-smelling leis, nodding and repeating, "Aloha, aloha." She led them to greet Lili`uokalani, who sat with a group of ladies in the shade of the thatched hut. They were all dressed in bright-colored holokus, with flowers around their necks. Laura and the girls curtsied to the princess and her friends, while Lucien made a low bow.

"Welcome, children, welcome," the princess said. "Please, take some refreshments." She motioned to her retainer to make room near her. "Bring all these lovely girls around me like a lei of beautiful flowers."

The other guests made room for them, and passed them green coconuts with straws sticking out of holes bored in the top to drink the coconut milk. Bowls of sliced papaya and mango were also offered, along with a sweet made of taro root.

"Perhaps the girls would like to try canoeing," the princess said. "Ka'iulani is out there with some of the guests now." The princess pointed toward the sea where several canoes floated, waiting to catch a wave. "She's quite an able paddler herself."

Lizzie turned to her cousin. "Oh, may we, Laura?"

"We didn't bring bathing costumes," Laura said.

"Don't worry, my dear," the princess said. "We have holokus of various sizes in the hut here. They serve quite well. Why don't you change so you'll be more comfortable? Lucien, there are some gentlemen's bathing costumes too."

"Thank you, Your Highness," Lucien said. "The girls can go. I've had many chances to canoe." He sat on one of the straw mats. "With the week I've had, I'd just as soon rest in the shade. I might roll up my trousers later and go wading a bit."

The princess smiled and nodded toward a retainer. "Wakeki, help the young ladies with the holokus."

Laura and the girls followed Wakeki into the thatched hut, which was cool and dim inside and smelled strongly of dry grass. The floor was covered with fine woven mats. At one end, on a raised platform covered with layers of broad lauhala leaves, a number of holokus were laid out. Wakeki lifted them one by one, holding them up to size them against the height of the girls. They chose three that seemed the closest fit, and Wake-ki stood guard at the door while the girls changed. They kept on their short pantalettes, and wiggled into the bright Mother Hubbard-style dresses. They laid their cotton smocks on the platform, tucked the rest of their underwear inside, and lined up their buttoned shoes along the wall.

After replacing the leis around their necks, they emerged from the hut. Laura blinked in the bright sun. Lizzie bounced across the sand to the water, where two canoes lay waiting. Hannah ran after her. Laura hesitated, feeling a little indecent, almost as if she were on the beach in her nightgown. Still, the lack of the tight corset was a relief.

"So, Malolo. You've come home to the sea."

Laura turned, still squinting in the glare. David Kahiko stood at the side of the hut, water beading on his bare chest and dripping from his hair. She was taken aback for a moment. Men normally wore bathing costumes that covered their chests and arms. David was dressed in the traditional Hawaiian *malo*, a cloth draped about his loins.

David smiled. "Are you coming canoeing? Your cousins are already going out with Ka`iulani."

Laura looked toward the water. Lizzie, Hannah, and a tan, slender girl with long black wavy hair were in a canoe headed out toward the reef, paddled by two brown men.

"Come on, Laura. Kapena and I will take you out." David jutted his chin toward an older Hawaiian man who waited by the canoe. He turned toward the ladies in the shade to address Lili`uokalani. "Will any of you come with us, Your Highness?"

"No, Akahi. You go along." She glanced around at the ladies, who concurred. "We're quite content here."

Laura looked about for Lucien. She saw his shoes and socks at the edge of the straw mat.

"Lucien walked down the beach with a few people who arrived while you were changing, Laura," the princess said. "They're collecting coconuts to put on ice for the luau this afternoon. Go along, now. You'll enjoy the canoe ride."

"Yes, Your Highness." Though she felt strangely naked with no shoes or stockings, and little underwear beneath her holuku, Laura made a brief curtsy.

Smiling, the princess waved her away. David made a slight bow, then headed toward the canoe. Laura trotted after him. The sand was hot, and she was glad to reach the cool water. A wave rolled in, and the clear sea washed up her legs and wet the bottom of her dress.

David held out his hand to help her into the outrigger. Laura took it, but avoided looking at him or at Kapena, who also wore a malo. She stepped into the dugout and seated herself where David indicated, in the middle. He and Kapena pushed the canoe into the water and jumped in, David at the front, Kapena behind Laura. Plunging the paddles rhythmically into the sea, they headed toward where large swells were forming.

"You just stepped into living history," David called over his shoulder. "This is one of the very canoes used by King Kamehameha, who unified these islands a hundred years ago. Kapena's grandfather was one of his confidants, and this canoe has been passed down in the family."

He turned back to his paddling as the canoe faced the rising swells. One began to crest, and the canoe rose up into it and slapped down on the other side. The whitecap loosed a shower over them, and Laura yelped. David glanced back to make sure she was all right. She smiled, and he faced the front again. Moisture glistened down his back. She watched his muscles tense and relax as he repeatedly drove the paddle into the water. Laura shook her head and droplets scattered. The sea breeze was exhilarating after the stifling atmosphere at Uncle Stephen's.

They finally caught up to the other canoe. Lizzie and Hannah waved as David and Kapena came about and faced their canoe toward shore. Ka`iulani steered her canoe to line up with theirs, and the men began to paddle in front of a rising swell. Ka`iulani called to David.

"We'll race you to shore, Uncle."

"You're on, Princess," David called back. "Let's go, Kapena. Don't miss this one."

The two began to paddle hard as the translucent green swell rose high behind them. Laura felt the outrigger lift up. She glanced back at the wall of water and grabbed the edges of the canoe with both hands. The wave flung it forward, and it sped down the front of the crest faster than a sled down a hill. The wind blew her hair back, the sea spray misted her face. It was like flying. She heard squeals, and looked to the side to see the other canoe moving ahead of them. Their outrigger slowed, so David and Kapena began to paddle to regain momentum. Again, they shot forward, neck and neck with Ka`iulani's canoe. The little girls were yelling, "Go, go, go." David signaled something to Kapena and Laura felt the canoe's pace slacken. He turned his head to Laura.

"We're going to give them a little edge. I want them to win."

Laura nodded encouragement.

Ka`iulani's canoe pulled away, two lengths in front of them, and raced toward shore.

Suddenly, Kapena shouted to David, "Too slow, Akahi. Too slow!"

Before they could paddle to gain speed, the cresting wave caught up to them and poured over the canoe like a waterfall, swamping it. Laura, David, and Kapena were thrown out. The churning wave somersaulted Laura underwater. Breaking the surface with a gasp, she felt a strong arm grab her around the waist and hold her up. David pulled her, coughing and choking, to rest on the hull of the canoe. Kapena bobbed up and swam to join them.

Ka`iulani's canoe reached the shore. The girls got out, and the men, seeing the other canoe in distress, headed back out to help. David saw them coming and grinned, holding Laura firmly around the waist as the overturned canoe undulated in the passing swells.

"Hang on, Malolo. They're coming to take you to shore."

Laura clung to David with her arms around his neck. The hem of the holoku floated up to reveal her pantalettes. Her hair was plastered to the sides of her face, and the salt water stung her eyes. Held against David's bare chest in the rising and falling waves, she found it hard to catch her breath. He hugged her to him with one arm around her waist so she wouldn't slip away, and with the other he clutched the shifting canoe. He smelled of coconut oil, and she was intensely aware of how the thin holoku fabric clung to her skin. In the trough of each swell, she tended to slip down, and he lifted her up and held her tighter.

As the other canoe came alongside, David steadied Laura and guided her to grasp the men's hands. They pulled her in and got her seated. Then one of the Hawaiians jumped in the water.

"Get in the canoe, Akahi. I'll help Kapena bring this one in."

David smiled, hoisted himself into the canoe, and grabbed a paddle.

"This time, Laura, we'll give you a proper ride."

He and the other man steered the canoe clear of the capsized hull and the men in the water. Then they pointed the prow of the canoe toward shore. They looked back, watching for the right swell, letting two go by. As the third rose up, the men began to paddle hard in front of it. The wave towered behind them, beginning to crest. Laura peeked back and closed her eyes. Just then, the canoe shot forward, like an arrow from an invisible bow, and flew toward the shore. She opened her eyes when she heard the crunching beneath the canoe and the hiss of foam on the sandy beach.

The men jumped out and pulled the canoe up on shore. Ka`iulani ran up, Hannah and Lizzie behind her.

"Are you hurt, Auntie?" The little princess's dark eyes were wide with concern.

"No, no, I'm fine," Laura said.

One of the retainers came with a towel for Laura, and inquired on behalf of Lili`uokalani whether she was all right. Laura nodded. She took the towel and dried her hair, then wrapped it around her shoulders for fear the wet holoku might be revealing.

"We go Hamohamo eat lunch soon," the retainer said. "You like change wet clothes?"

"Yes," Laura said. She started to follow the retainer when she saw Lucien hobbling along the shore, leaning on the arm of another young man. Lizzie ran down to meet them, and scurried back with the news.

"Lucien's been stung by a jellyfish and his foot is all swollen."

"That can be really painful," David said. He headed up the beach toward the two men. When he reached them, Lucien placed his arm across David's shoulder. They brought him back to the shade of the hut, and he winced as they helped him down onto the mat. His foot was twice normal size, and his face was feverish, moisture beading on his forehead.

"I'm sorry, but I'm going to have to go home," Lucien said.

Lili`uokalani came to look at him. "You must stay off of that foot and keep it elevated. I'll have one of my retainers drive you."

"We'll go get our things," Laura said. Lizzie looked crestfallen. Hannah was poker-faced.

"No, Laura," Lucien said. "You and the girls don't have to leave."

"Don't be silly. We'll go with you."

"Really, Laura. The girls have looked forward to this luau. Go ahead, I'll be fine."

"If you'd like to stay," the princess said, "my retainer will take you back home in my carriage afterward."

Lucien nodded, his smile strained by the pain.

"Well, I guess so," Laura said, "if Lucien doesn't mind."

&

Compared to the princess's mansion at Washington Place in Honolulu, the beach house at Hamohamo was a simple home. Set under spreading trees, it was one story with a sloping roof and a wide *lanai* on three sides. The retainers had gone on ahead to set out mats for the luau and decorate them with ferns, flowers, and fragrant maile vines. Calabash gourds and polished bowls of koa wood were filled with pink poi or baked taro. When the guests were seated on the mats, the retainers brought out avocado salad, fish steamed in ti leaves, and tender roast pork. Bowls of oysters and seaweed were passed, as well as platters of island fruit, and soft green coconuts to be scooped out with spoons.

Servants stood next to Lili`uokalani and Ka`iulani, gently waving the royal feathered kahilis while the guests ate and talked. Seated next to Laura, David explained the different foods and how they were prepared. He showed her how to eat "two-finger" poi, dipping his index and middle fingers into the large common bowl and, with a quick twist, popping them into his mouth. Laura imitated his motion, but dripped poi on the mat. The sour, pasty taste surprised her after David's expression of pleasure.

After they ate, the guests moved from the lanai out under the trees to sit on benches or mats on the grass. The children entertained themselves exploring the grounds and playing hide-and-seek. Several people brought out ukuleles and guitars and began to sing. The Hawaiians harmonized together as if they'd practiced like a choir, weaving subtle melodies that blended with the swaying of the palms and the fragrance of the ohia blossoms that dropped from the trees.

Laura was glad she'd decided to change into another holoku instead of her fitted summer dress. All the women guests were in holokus. The men had changed to loose-fitting shirts and pants, and most everyone was barefoot. She sat, relaxed, eyes closed, with her legs stretched out and her back against a tree, listening to the languorous melodies.

David borrowed an ukulele, began to strum a song, then stopped. "Come tutus," he called. "Show us your hula."

Laura opened a cautious eye to see whom he was talking to. Three venerable Hawaiian ladies sitting together on a bench laughed, but obligingly stood and walked toward him. One stopped to pluck hibiscus blossoms from a bush. She handed one to each woman and one to David, and they all tucked a flower behind their ears. David started to strum again. The ladies held out their arms to one side and began to dance. Though they were plump as dumplings, their surprising grace conformed to the wind in the trees and the rhythm of the waves. They danced in unison, each fluid movement of hands and hips flowing into the next, evanescent as mist, their ancient, wrinkled smiles like sunshine streaming through clouds to make everyone happy.

The afternoon passed so softly away that Laura only realized the time as the sun was setting. The Hawaiians looked as though they might go on and on into the evening, but she knew she needed to get the girls home soon. She stood up to look for them. Hannah and Ka'iulani were sitting on the lanai, talking, and Lizzie had dozed off in the chair next to them.

Laura began to worry. The position of the sun meant that it was probably past six o'clock. It'd be getting dark soon. Princess Lili'uokalani noticed Laura standing, and beckoned her.

"Are you ready to go?"

"Yes, Your Highness. But we need to change our clothes to give you back the holokus."

"Oh, no, dear. Wear them home and keep them. Those colors look lovely on you."

"Thank you, Your Highness," Laura said, but she wasn't sure about wearing the holokus home.

The princess directed a retainer to bring the carriage. Laura went to get Hannah and wake Lizzie, whose freckled face was sunburned and warm to the touch. She whined a bit when Laura asked her to get up. There was no sense in trying to change them back into their own dresses, it would take too much time. When the carriage pulled up, David lifted Lizzie in his arms and put her on the seat where she promptly curled up and went back to sleep. Laura and Hannah made the rounds saying proper thank-yous and good-byes. Princess Lili'uokalani kissed them on the forehead and told them to come again. Little Ka'iulani embraced Laura and Hannah. She looked forlorn as they got in the carriage.

David swung into the seat across from Laura. "I'm going to ride along to keep the driver company on the way back."

By the time they turned on the Waikiki road toward Honolulu, the sunset had transformed the earth into a different planet, awash in unfamiliar colors with black palms stenciled against a sharp, coral horizon. Above them, gold streaks brushed across aqua skies that darkened into deep space. The crashing whitecaps along the shore threw mist up like stardust, and the sea turned purple beneath a rising moon.

They rode along without speaking, and Hannah fell asleep against Laura's shoulder.

"Good day today," David finally broke the silence.

"Yes," Laura said.

His expression was at once grateful and wistful. That same look she'd seen when they danced at the ball — what seemed to be a supreme happiness in the beauty of the moment, and a realization that in the next it would all be gone. It reminded her of little Ka`iulani's face as they were leaving Hamohamo.

"David..."

"Yes?"

"Why did Ka`iulani call you 'Uncle'? Are you related?"

"No, children here call all adults 'Uncle' or 'Auntie.' It's a sign of respect."

"She looked a little sad when we left."

"Yes, she's an affectionate child. She gets very attached to her friends."

Lizzie turned over in her sleep, and David reached to keep her from falling off the carriage seat. He held his hand at her back until she settled down again. He looked up at Laura.

"She's also sad because her governess is leaving next week to get married. They've been together for several years, so it's like losing a close relative."

"Of course," Laura said.

"Her former governess died suddenly, so the princess is sensitive to loss."

Laura thought of Ka`iulani's small, sweet face and ethereal dark eyes.

"She seems fragile, in a way."

"In a way," David said, "but she can be strong-willed. When her governess told her she was getting married, Ka`iulani sneaked into her bedroom and scratched up the picture of her fiancé. And when he came to call later, the princess said she hated him." David laughed. "Of course he was unnerved, and asked what he'd done to make her say that. And she said, 'You're taking my governess away. She came out to Hawaii for me, not for you!'"

Laura smiled. It was spirited behavior, especially for such a little princess.

When they pulled into the circular drive at the Price home, it was dark. David got out and helped Laura and Hannah down from the carriage. He picked Lizzie up and carried her up the stairs to the front door. Still barefoot, Hannah and Laura followed him.

The gaslight burned in the front-door lamp. As Hannah reached for the knob, the door swung open. Uncle Stephen stood, a cigar in his mouth, the smoke curling up in the light. He looked startled to see them in Hawaiian dresses and Lizzie carried in David's arms.

"Where's Lucien?" Stephen said.

"He got stung by a jellyfish and had to go home early," Hannah said.

"Good evening, Mr. Price," David said.

Stephen took the cigar from his mouth and flung it over the verandah into the bushes. "I'll take Lizzie." He held out his arms.

David transferred the girl to him and stepped back. Stephen looked down at his daughter. "Hannah, go upstairs. You need to let your mother know you girls are all right."

"Yes, Papa." Hannah went inside and up the staircase.

Stephen glared at David. "Thank you for bringing them home."

"Actually, I'm just riding along. Princess Lili`uokalani sent them in her carriage."

"Oh," Stephen said. "Well, thank her for me." He began to close the door. "Laura, come inside."

She turned to David. The porch light flickered, illuminating his face and making his dark eyes shine. She stepped toward the door. "Thank you, perhaps we'll see you next time."

David nodded, glancing at Stephen. "Sure, next time." He made a slight bow and went down the stairs to the waiting carriage.

Laura walked past her uncle into the foyer. She heard the hoof beats of the horse retreat as the carriage moved down the driveway and out onto the street.

"There won't be any 'next time,'" Stephen said, and banged the door closed. His voice was tense, sharp. He called for Kimiko. She appeared at the top of the stairs. "Come and put Lizzie to bed." He walked up a few steps toward Kimiko as she made her way down to meet him. Laura followed behind him. He turned his head. "Laura, wait for me in the library. I want a word with you."

Laura backed down the few stairs she'd climbed, and walked to the library. She pushed the heavy door open, and sat in the chair in front of Uncle Stephen's desk. Whenever he wanted "a word" with her, he saw her in the library. The "word" extended into many words, and was always a dressing down. After her long day, she didn't feel up to it. She hoped it'd be brief. She stared at her bare feet, noticing the granules of sand between her toes.

Stephen entered the library and closed the door behind him. Instead of going to sit behind his desk as he usually did when he gave these lectures, he stopped next to Laura's chair. She looked up at him. His lips were pressed tight and his eyes, slits.

"What were you thinking, Laura?"

"Sir?"

"You bring my girls home after dark," he reached forward and lifted the drooping flower lei around her neck, "dressed like common barefoot kanakas." He yanked the lei. The string that held the flowers broke, and they fell to the floor.

Laura jerked back in the chair. "I'm sorry Uncle Stephen. I didn't realize the time —"

"There's a lot of things you don't realize, Laura. But you'd better start."

"The girls wanted to go in the water and the princess gave us the holokus —"

Stephen raised his voice. His face reddened. "What am I supposed to think when I send you off with a proper escort and you come home in the dark with some questionable half-caste you don't even know?"

"I know David. He was just —"

Laura didn't see the hand until it smacked her cheek and her head snapped sideways. Her mouth dropped open and her eyes teared. She gasped and blinked repeatedly, then raised her hand to the side of her face. It stung, but not as much as the shock that ricocheted through her body like a bullet. She stared, aghast, at her uncle.

"Don't you ever contradict me." Stephen leaned over her. "Get down on that floor and pick up your mess."

Laura slipped out of the chair onto her hands and knees, picking up the fallen blossoms. A tear rolled diagonally down her red cheek. She could feel his eyes on her, but she didn't look up.

Stephen shook his head. "You're just like your father, Laura. No sense. Stand up."

Laura got up and stood with her head down.

"Look at me," Stephen said.

He put his finger under her chin and lifted her head. He gazed at her with an odd smile on his face. He didn't seem angry. He looked as if he were enjoying himself.

"You're in my house now, Laura. My rules. And you'll do what I tell you. I don't want you associating with that boy, understood?"

Laura sniffed and nodded.

"You should be thinking of someone like Lucien." Stephen's voice was low and modulated. "He has a future, and an alliance between our families could make you very secure indeed. Right now, you're destitute. You should use your charms more thoughtfully."

He turned her head to one side to examine the cheek he struck and then turned her face back toward him.

"That hurt me more than it hurt you. I just want what's best for you. Here, give your Uncle Stephen a hug." He put his arms around her.

Laura closed her eyes and stiffened as he pulled her close. She was relieved when a tap came at the door. Stephen released her.

"Yes?" he said.

Kimiko opened the door. "The girls in bed, Mr. Price. Something else you want?"

"No."

Kimiko began to close the door. Then she saw Laura's face and hesitated. "You want something else, Miss Laura?"

"Yes, thank you, Kimiko," Laura said. She sidestepped passed Stephen toward the door. "I'd like you to come upstairs with me. I have some things for the laundry."

"Go ahead," Stephen said. "And get to bed early. We have church in the morning."

Chapter 9 —————

Somewhere between the hymns "O God, Our Help in Ages Past" and "Take My Life and Let It Be," Laura made up her mind. She sat in a pew near the front of the church, with Hannah and Lizzie between her and Uncle Stephen. On the carriage ride that morning, whenever he looked her way, Laura averted her eyes. Only Lizzie spoke, chatting about the Noah's Ark pageant the Sunday school would put on in a few weeks. She was going to be an elephant. When they walked up the aisle at church, people greeted Stephen with smiles, like he was a pillar of the community. But sitting in the pew so close to him made Laura tremble. She had to leave the Price household.

As the Rev. Henry Parker preached, he mixed his religious admonitions with sarcasm toward the king, and thinly veiled endorsements for the annexation of Hawaii to the United States. Laura glanced around at the congregation. The whites seemed to accept it all matter-of-factly. The Hawaiian faces betrayed no emotion. Laura was glad Princess Lili`uokalani, a member of the church, had not been present to hear such a sermon.

On the way out, they ran into Mr. and Mrs. McBride, and Uncle Stephen stopped to talk. Lucien's foot was better, they said, but he probably wouldn't return to work for another day or two.

"May the girls and I call on him this afternoon?" Laura said. Uncle Stephen's look approved.

"That'd be lovely," Mrs. McBride said. "I'm sure he'll appreciate the company. How about after lunch?"

When they returned home, Laura went to her bedroom to change. She opened the wardrobe door and reached to the back of the closet. She brought out a small wooden box, and sat at the vanity table. She opened the top, took out a stack of folded bills, and counted them. Two hundred thirty-two dollars. All that was left from the sale of her father's shop after the creditors were paid off. It wasn't much. She put the bills in the box and placed it back in the wardrobe.

She took off her straw hat, changed out of her church attire, and put on a soft muslin dress — one of her prettiest — one Lucien had remarked on the day they went out to his family's plantation. Then she unclasped the black pearl ring from around her neck and cupped it in her palm. The gold flowers surrounding the pearl glinted in the sunlight. She stared at it a long time, then sighed. She clasped it again at the back of her neck and tucked it inside her dress.

"I can't part with it, Papa."

She brought out Grandmother Jennings's aquamarine with diamonds, then thought better of it, put it back in the bureau, and closed the drawer. She walked down the hall to Aunt Katherine's bedroom. The door was closed, so she rapped lightly.

"Come in."

Laura turned the knob and pushed the door open. Her aunt was in a chair by the open window, watching two mynah birds hop from branch to branch. Laura sat across the small table from her. In the daylight, her aunt looked especially frail.

"Will you have lunch with us, Aunt Katherine?"

She didn't turn her face from the window. "I don't think so, dear."

"The girls and I are visiting the McBrides this afternoon."

"That's good. Give them my regards, won't you?"

"Of course. ... Aunt Katherine?"

Katherine continued to look out the window. "See how those birds chase each other around the tree? They bicker and bicker. They can fly away anytime, but they stay in the tree and squawk."

"Aunt Katherine, may I ask you something?"

She turned. "Certainly, Laura, what is it?"

"Well, Lizzie and Hannah will be going back to school this week, and there won't be much for me to do here ..."

Her aunt was so pale, a watercolor faded by the sun, slightly out of focus, like she might be disappearing. It spurred Laura on.

"I was going to study medicine, Aunt Katherine. When Papa died, I had to give that up."

Her aunt nodded. Laura paused.

"Could you lend me the money to go back to school in San Francisco? I was accepted at Cooper Medical College there. It's not too late for me to get in this year. I'll pay you back when I start a practice, I promise."

Katherine smiled. "That's a wonderful idea, dear."

Laura sat forward in her chair.

"But you'll have to ask your Uncle Stephen. He handles all the money." She looked back out the window. "How lovely it'd be to fly away like a bird, wouldn't it?"

&

*A*fter lunch, Laura, Hannah, and Lizzie walked to the McBrides' home. Though it was just a quarter mile up the road, most ladies would've taken a carriage. They didn't like any exertion that made them perspire. Laura told the girls she needed some air and to stretch her legs. She thought the walk would give her time to think through her approach to Lucien, but her coiled nerves propelled her forward in a quick-time march, and they reached the entrance of the McBride estate within minutes.

As they walked up the tree-lined drive, a bead of moisture meandered down Laura's temple. She stopped in the shade of a banyan to pull a handkerchief and a fan from her bag. She dabbed the sweat around her hairline, and briskly fanned her face, then handed the fan to Lizzie.

"Here, fan my back for minute. I need to cool down."

While Lizzie fanned, Laura looked at the massive banyan, its branches sprawled out in all directions, the large limbs held up by thick columns of contorted feeler roots that grew down from the branches into the earth. The bundles of intertwining roots fed the branches and held them up. They reminded her of a word David told her at the princess's luau. *Ohana. Oha* was a sprig or branch. Ohana meant family or clan. David said Hawaiians felt they shared a universe with the spirits of their ancestors — just like the roots that burrowed deep and unseen under the ground and supported the growth of the tree above. Laura wished she could feel the support of strong roots like that, especially now. She took the fan from Lizzie, and continued to fan her face as they walked up to the house. Mrs. McBride met them at the door.

"You girls look so warm," she said. "Laura, why don't you go see Lucien in the drawing room. He's waiting for you. Hannah, Lizzie, come with me. We'll get Tamiko to make us something cool to drink."

Lucien sat on a sofa, reading a book, his leg resting on an ottoman. He smiled broadly when Laura appeared at the door. She walked across the room and sat in a chair next to him.

"Is it better?" She nodded toward his foot.

"Yes, I should be able to go back to work Tuesday." He lowered his voice. "You look lovely, Laura. I'm so glad you came."

In the past, Laura had brushed aside such comments with a demure response or changed the subject. Now they seemed like a lifeline.

"You're always so kind. It was the least I could do."

"So, how was the luau? Did you like it? Was it too strange?"

"Strange?"

"You know, the food, the customs."

Laura pictured the grandmothers with blossoms in their hair dancing to the ukulele music, and the handing around of food in calabashes. She remembered the freedom of the holoku and the ease of sitting barefoot under the palm tree in the warm afternoon. She heard the children laughing as they played hide-and-seek, saw David's smiling face when he explained Hawaiian words, and felt Lili`uokalani's gracious kiss on her forehead as they were leaving.

"I wouldn't call it strange," Laura said.

Mrs. McBride and the girls entered the drawing room, followed by a Japanese servant carrying a tray of iced tea.

"We brought you something to drink," Mrs. McBride said. The girls are coming to the conservatory to see my canaries. A few of them have laid eggs. We'll be back in a bit."

"Thank you, Mother," Lucien said.

The servant drew up a side table, placed the tray of iced tea on it, bowed, and departed. Laura looked around the drawing room, so similar in its way to the same room in the Price home. It'd seen a lifetime of receiving calls, gallons and gallons of iced tea and lemonade, and endless rounds of polite conversation. It all went with a house like this and whoever inhabited it.

"Laura?"

"Yes?"

"What were you thinking just now? You had the most peculiar look on your face."

"Oh, nothing." She looked down for a moment. "You've been so good to me. I hesitate to ask —"

Lucien leaned forward. "What is it?"

Laura wondered how much she should tell him.

"I need your help with something."

"You know I'll do anything I can."

"Lizzie and Hannah go back to school this week, and I'm going to be at a loss for something to do."

"Yes?"

"So I thought I'd get a job."

Lucien sat back. "What do you mean?"

"Well, isn't there something I could do at your law firm?"

"All the help at our office are men."

"Do you know any shopkeepers? I know a bit about dry goods."

"Ladies of your standing don't work as shop girls in Honolulu."

Laura cocked her head. "Well, what do ladies of my standing do?"

"Nothing, really," Lucien said.

Exasperated, Laura reached for a glass of tea. Then she remembered David telling her Ka'iulani's governess was leaving.

"What about being a governess? That's basically what I do now with Hannah and Lizzie."

Lucien thought at moment. "That might be possible, because you'd be properly protected in a respectable home." Laura pressed her lips together to keep from making a comment. He picked up his tea. "Say, I heard that Princess Ka`iulani's governess is getting married. I see Archie Cleghorn downtown almost every day. I could ask him if they've replaced her."

"Who's Archie Cleghorn?"

"That's Ka`iulani's father. You met him in the receiving line at the ball. Princess Likelike's husband, the tall Scotsman with a full beard."

Laura vividly remembered the receiving line with the king's two sisters, Lili`uokalani and Likelike, radiant in ball gowns and royal jewels. Their husbands, standing at their sides, weren't as clear. They were both tall, full-bearded white men.

"I'd be so grateful if you'd inquire about that position," Laura said.

"You'd have to live at Ainahau, their place at Waikiki. I don't know if your uncle would like you being so far out of town."

"Just find out about it, Lucien, please. We don't need to trouble Uncle Stephen until we know what's possible."

&

*L*orrin Thurston saw Lucien walk past his office door. He leaned out and called down the hall after him.

"Hey Lucien, did you get the Irwin contract finished?"

"Yes, I just took it over to their office for signatures."

"Good. Say, I saw you out the window talking to Archie Cleghorn in the street. What's up?"

"Not much," Lucien said. "I was just asking if they've replaced their governess."

"Why do you care?"

Lucien walked back toward Thurston's office. "Mr. Price's niece is interested in the position."

Thurston turned his head back inside his office. "You didn't tell me that, Stephen."

Lucien blanched. Laura's uncle was in Thurston's office.

"Tell you what?" Stephen said.

"That your niece is going to work as Ka'iulani's governess."

"Where'd you get that idea?"

"Young McBride, here." Thurston waved Lucien inside.

"Hello, Mr. Price," Lucien said as he entered and shook Stephen's hand.

"Who told you that nonsense about Laura working as a governess?" Stephen said.

"Well, she didn't want to trouble you until she knew whether the position was open. Mr. Cleghorn said they'd be glad to interview her, since she comes from such a good family."

"When did she talk to you about this, Lucien?" Stephen said.

"Just a couple days ago. She asked me to inquire about the position, since I see Cleghorn downtown all the time."

Stephen slammed his fist down on the desk, and Lucien jumped. "This is ridiculous! That girl is getting out of hand. I can't believe she went behind my back like this."

"She didn't mean anything by it, Mr. Price," Lucien said. "Don't be mad. She was just looking for something to do, now that the girls have gone back to school."

"Well, there's no way I'm letting her go to work —"

"Wait a minute," Thurston said. He turned to Lucien. "Excuse us for a minute. I want to speak to Stephen alone."

Lucien left the room, walked quickly to his office, and shut the door behind him. He hoped he hadn't caused any problem for Laura, and he hoped Thurston would calm Stephen down.

Thurston turned to Stephen, who was still fuming.

"Take it easy, Stephen. This could work in our favor. It wouldn't hurt to have a pair of eyes and ears inside the royal family."

Stephen shook his head. "I don't know. I don't want her living outside the household. Besides, she'd be useless for that. She's too naive."

"All the better. She can be a source of information and not know it. As a governess, she'll be part of the family and around intimate conversations."

"Well, you can see she's not very forthcoming about what she's doing," Stephen said. "So I don't know how we'd get any information out of her."

"She confided in Lucien," Thurston said. "She seems to trust him and tell him things she doesn't tell anyone else."

"That's true, but will Lucien cooperate?"

Thurston sat on the corner of his desk and thought a moment, stroking his mustache.

"He doesn't have to know he's cooperating, at first. We can just continue to encourage the relationship. Let them get closer. He knows how to keep his ear to the ground. I think we can count on his loyalty when the time comes."

Chapter 10 ———

September 23, 1886

Once more, I go to live with strangers. But at least this time I'm employed. I met with Mr. Cleghorn and Princess Likelike last week. The day before yesterday, a courier arrived with the message that they offered me the position of governess to Ka`iulani. Today, Lucien will drive me out to their home at Ainahau near Waikiki. Kimiko is helping me pack my things.

Aunt Katherine was happy for me — her "little bird who's flown away." Strange, but she had almost a look of relief when I told her. The girls were upset until I said it would give them more chance to come to the beach. Surprisingly, Uncle Stephen accepts all this, but I wouldn't say he's supportive. He told me not to do anything that would reflect badly on him or "his family." He's made sure I never felt part of it.

&

*L*ucien turned the carriage into a long, shaded drive bordered by tall palms, crowned with bushy fronds. He nodded toward a configuration of sticks at the entrance.

"Those are *kapu* sticks."

"What's kapu?" Laura said.

"Sacred, taboo, forbidden, like 'No Trespassing.' They're a symbol of royalty. This is the Cleghorn estate."

Between the palms, Laura caught glimpses of the Aina-hau grounds, planted with an unending variety of trees and flowers.

"Mr. Cleghorn is a horticulture enthusiast," Lucien said. "He's had specimens sent here from all over the world."

They passed acres of flowering shrubs and trees, fragrant cinnamon and sandalwood, mango and guava. Lofty palms were clustered around lily ponds set with Japanese stone lanterns and crossed by rustic wooden footbridges. Turtles dozed on rocks at the water's edge.

In a clearing at the end of the drive, next to an immense banyan tree, was a spacious house surrounded by wide verandahs, its doors and windows open to the cool breeze. The carriage neared the house, and strutting peacocks scattered to stand at the edge of the clearing, screeching their distress at being disturbed. From a path beyond the banyan, Ka`iulani came trotting up on a white pony with flowers braided into its mane and forelock. Lucien's horse whinnied, and the little princess rode up to the carriage to let the animals make acquaintance and sniff noses.

"Mama," she called toward the house. "Miss Laura is here. Tell Kainoa to come get her luggage."

Three Hawaiian servants emerged, two men and a woman. The woman went to Ka`iulani and held the reins of her pony while she jumped down. The men unloaded Laura's luggage and took it into the house. Princess Likelike appeared on the verandah. Her beauty had struck Laura the week before, when she'd interviewed with her and Mr. Cleghorn, but it was a business meeting, everyone formal and proper. In the morning light, the princess was stunning — relaxed, yet still every bit mistress of the household.

"Ka`iulani, bring Laura in to see her room." Likelike beckoned them in. "Lucien, will you stay for coffee?"

"You're most kind, Princess, but I must go on to work."

Laura turned to Lucien. "Thank you for this." If they'd been alone she thought she might have kissed him.

Affected by the intensity of her gratitude, so softly spoken, Lucien swallowed before he could speak. "I'm glad to be of help."

Ka'iulani held her hand up toward Laura, who was still seated in the carriage. "Come on, Miss Laura. Mama wants you to come in."

One of the Hawaiian men helped Laura get down from the carriage. At one side, a peacock spread and rustled his lustrous, jeweled tail, which shone emerald and sapphire in the sunlight.

The little princess laughed. "Look, my peacock is dancing for you." She took Laura's hand to lead her in the house. "After coffee, can we play croquet?"

"All right," Laura said. She looked back toward Lucien.

"I'll visit often," Lucien said. "If it's all right with the Cleghorns, of course."

Ka`iulani looked up. "It's all right to visit, Uncle, but you mustn't take Miss Laura away."

☙

October 7, 1886

I've been at Ainahau two weeks. It's much more relaxed here than at my uncle's house. I never realized how tense I was while I lived there. I had to be on my guard and watch every little thing I did. It got so I hated to leave my room.

Time seems different here. Nobody hurries, but everything gets done. Princess Likelike let me suspend Ka`iulani's lessons so we could get acquainted. She's a dear little girl, every bit as affectionate as David said, but she can be willful. In that, she's not unlike her mother. They come from ancient chiefly lines, and their servants show them extreme deference, but with evident affection. The princesses are more forbearing with me. Since I'm not a native subject, I'm allowed more leeway.

Each morning, Ka`iulani and I go riding. She takes her pony, Fairie. They gave me a bay gelding they call Pua'a, which means "hog," and it suits him. Every time we stop, he pulls his head down to try to eat grass, or chomps at leaves on low branches. I've been so sore. I've never ridden cavalier fashion before, only sidesaddle, and my thighs ache. Whenever we see people as we ride, the princess does what she calls *haawi ke aloha*. I think it means something like "give love and greetings." She makes a gentle bow in recognition of the people she meets, and never fails in this.

Sometimes we gallop along the beach and go for a sea bath. Other times we ride up to Diamond Head, where Lookout Charlie gives us coffee and hardtack. He watches for ships approaching Honolulu.

Mr. Cleghorn is kind and polite to me, a true gentleman. His Scottish accent is quite charming. He came to

Hawaii when he was just sixteen, and became a successful importer with stores on three islands. Princess Likelike is gracious and generous, but I wouldn't want to be on her bad side. Like most men, Mr. Cleghorn may have ideas of being master of his house (or lord of his castle), but the princess is a chiefess and used to being in charge. They do have their rows. Unlike Aunt Katherine, Princess Likelike does not back down.

Today they were arguing about dinner arrangements for the legislators that are coming to Ainahau this evening. Mr. Cleghorn is a member of the Privy Council and a close advisor to King Kalakaua. Princess Likelike told me they often have members of the government here for discussions and entertainment. She said, "Archie says it's wise to know one's enemies," though I'm not sure what she meant by that. Ka`iulani and I are allowed to sit in because she'll rule as queen someday, and her father and mother want her to have a familiarity with matters of state.

The princess already has a sense of her destiny, and has natural poise I've not seen in cultured ladies twice her age. And next week, she'll just be turning eleven.

♧

Ka`iulani lined up her mallet with the painted wooden croquet ball.

"Just one more shot," Laura said. "Then we have to get ready for the guests tonight."

"Oh, Miss Laura, I want to finish the game. Please?"

Laura leaned on her mallet. "It'll take too long. We don't have time." Hearing hoof beats, she turned. A lone rider was coming up the drive. "See? People are arriving already."

"That's just Uncle David," the girl said.

Laura straightened. David rode up the drive to where they were playing under the banyan tree, then dismounted. A servant came up the path from the stable and led his horse away.

"I'm glad you came early, Uncle. Finish the game with us."

"My pleasure, Princess." David smiled at her then looked at Laura. "I heard you were out here. I'm glad." He picked up a mallet. "Where are you in the game?"

"Ka'iulani was going to make one more shot, and then we have to get ready for dinner," Laura said.

Ka'iulani seemed ready to stage a protest.

"Just one more shot would be wise, Princess," David said. "You don't want to keep guests waiting on account of a croquet game."

She sighed, but obediently tapped the ball through the wicket. Her servant, Kainoa, came down from the verandah to put the game away.

David consoled her. "I'll come someday just to play croquet with you … and Miss Laura."

As they walked up to the house, Laura glanced sideways at David. He was looking back at her. She lowered her eyes, and they climbed the steps to the verandah. David sat in a rattan chair.

"I'll wait here until dinner," he said.

Laura and Ka'iulani entered the house. The large main room was already prepared, with two linen-covered tables set with crystal and china, surrounded by bentwood and cane-back chairs. It looked like two dozen guests were expected. The floral chaise longues had been pulled to one side of the room around oriental carpets to make a conversation area. Kainoa came in and took Ka'iulani to her bedroom to dress, and Laura retired to hers.

After she'd changed for dinner, Laura debated whether to join David on the verandah. Her memory of dancing with him at the ball was mixed with the scent of coconut oil and salt water, the feeling of his strong arm around her waist, holding her tight against him; and the vision of his handsome brown face, singing body-swaying melodies at the luau, interrupted by the gazes and whispers of strangers. She was relieved to hear more guests arrive, and the comforting buzz of welcomes and greetings in which she knew she could hide for a while.

At dinner, unlike in the Price household, conversation was not restricted to chitchat. The guests discussed the rebuilding of Chinatown after the devastating fire last spring; the increasing aggression of Germany's policy of colonization in the South Pacific; and the possibility of Hawaii forming an alliance with Samoa and perhaps Tonga, as the few remaining independent islands.

The talk turned to the reciprocity treaty that had expired in 1883. Laura remembered Aunt Katherine talking about it while telling her how the Price family had grown rich so quickly.

"Have you heard about that?" the gentleman next to her asked.

"Not much," Laura said. "Just that the king negotiated it with the United States years ago. My aunt said it's why the planters have done so well."

"That's right," the man said. "It gave Hawaiian sugar special status in the United States, made it less expensive for Americans to buy, and more profitable for the planters."

"What'll happen now that it's expired?"

"It continues on a year-to-year basis by mutual agreement. However, with the activity of Germany and Britain in the South Pacific, America is agitating to renew it. They want the right to use the harbor at the entrance of Pearl River to coal and repair their ships."

"Will Hawaii sign a new treaty?" Laura said.

"Most legislators are against ceding any territory that might threaten our independence," the gentleman said. "But a few that represent islands with large plantations, like Lanai and Maui, think it might be necessary in order to prevent financial ruin in the kingdom."

The guests pushed back their chairs to continue their conversation and take after-dinner liquors on chaise longues grouped to one side of the dining area or on the verandah. Laura noticed Ka`iulani stifling yawns, and asked Kainoa to put her to bed. Princess Likelike and Mr. Cleghorn moved from group to group to make sure their guests were happy, and Laura wandered outside. Kukui-nut torches cast flickering shadows across the lawn, and a gigantic moon was rising above the treetops.

On the verandah, David was sitting with two men. They stood up to leave. He got up with them, saw Laura, and waved for her to come over.

"Laura," David said, "these are my colleagues in the legislature, Curtis Kupaka and Daniel Aeko. Gentlemen, Miss Jennings."

The two men bowed.

"Excuse us, Miss Jennings," Mr. Aeko said. "We're just heading back to Honolulu, and must say goodnight to our hosts."

"Certainly," Laura said. She looked around for the princess and Mr. Cleghorn. "I believe they're still in the house."

The gentlemen nodded, and walked toward the door.

"Would you like to sit down, Laura, or walk a little?" David said.

Laura looked out at the kukui torches burning in the dark. Beyond them, the woods were dense and silent. Muted conversation from the house was interspersed with occasional laughter. She looked back at David, who waited for her answer. He smiled.

"Walk with me a little, Malolo. The moon is up." He pointed toward the dark trees. "Just down that path I can show you a silver sea."

Laura glanced back at the open door where light poured onto the verandah.

"It's not far," David said. "They won't even know we've been gone."

Down the moonlit path, they stopped next to a lily pond. The full moon, reflected in the still water, made the dark trees and pale lily flowers stand out in black-and-white relief. David touched her shoulder, and she looked up at him. He motioned for her to follow a little farther. Past a grove of sandalwood trees, the illumined foliage gave way to a vista of glistening sand, and beyond, the promised sterling sea. A swatch of moonlight rippled on the water, and all around was mystic silver, all colors blended into one.

He pointed to a grassy spot under a tree near the sand. They sat in silence a few minutes, the air still and warm. The moon outshone the nearest stars, bathing the earth and sea in holy light.

"You never told me why you came to Honolulu."

Laura looked at the shimmering ocean, which extended into the oblivion of deep night. Back there somewhere, in some direction, was the life she'd left. Bustling San Francisco with the clanging cable cars, her admittance papers to medical college still in some folder in a file cabinet, waiting to be thrown out. The little dry goods shop on Kearny Street with the upstairs apartment, now inhabited by strangers, and two fresh graves with small headstones among the marble monuments at Laurel Hill Cemetery.

Now all that spilled out. She told David about her last months in the city, about the carriage accident that had killed her father and Andrew and left her with nothing. He listened quietly, watching her face. It was a relief to finally tell someone, and surprisingly, she felt no need to cry. David absorbed it all, held it all, without any comment.

"My father begged me to come here before he died. I wanted to go to medical school, but there was no way I could afford it."

David leaned over and picked up a handful of sand, letting it pour from his fist in a thin stream.

"You know, I'm an orphan too. My mother died when I was born."

"What about your father?"

"He didn't stick around."

"Who took care of you?"

David looked back out to sea. "My grandmother raised me, in a little house up toward the Pali."

The conversation ebbed, each lost in thought. David turned back toward her.

"Your aunt and uncle are so rich. Why did you come out to work for the Cleghorns?"

Laura started to say what she'd told everyone else, that she wanted something to fill her time now that Hannah and Lizzie had gone back to school. Instead, she blurted the truth.

"I had to get out of that house."

"Why?"

Laura hesitated. "My uncle," she finally said. "My uncle—" Her voice wavered. A lump rose in her throat, and she shook her head. "I can't say any more."

David took her hand and kissed it. She looked at his face, illumined by moonlight. He stroked her cheek.

"Don't worry, little Malolo. You're safe here."

He put his arms around her and drew her close. She leaned against him, remembering the strength that had embraced her as they danced, and had lifted her up above the waves in the sea. She felt his heartbeat, and closed her eyes, enfolded in the warmth that felt safe and electric all at the same time. David held her awhile without speaking, then breathed a deep sigh. He drew back and kissed her forehead. Standing up, he offered her his hand, on his face a look of tenderness mingled with something like regret.

"We'd better go back now," he said. "We've been away a long time."

Chapter 11

Ka'iulani sat, pouting, on a bench beneath the banyan tree, and pulling apart pieces of bread to toss to the peacocks gathered at her feet. Laura came down from the verandah to call her in for lunch.

"Why the long face, miss?"

"I wanted a birthday party like last year with all my friends. Only Mama and Papa's friends are coming."

Laura sat at her side. "The king himself is coming, and he hasn't been out here for a long time. The most important legislators and the ambassadors from the foreign legations will be here too. You're a very important young lady." She wiggled a finger into Ka'iulani's ribs to make her laugh. "And they'll be bringing fancy presents, I'll bet." The princess wriggled away, giggling. "Besides, your Aunt Liliu said we can go to Washington Place later in the week to plan a party for all your friends." She stood up. "Come on now, and wash up for lunch."

Laura took Ka'iulani's hand and walked back to the house. She couldn't help thinking about the event tomorrow at Ainahau. The kingdom's most prestigious men and their wives would be there, many loyal Royalists, but also some of the opposition Reform Party, most of them white and many, missionary descendants. It seemed a strange way to celebrate the eleventh birthday of a little girl.

୧

The next day, starting at noon, carriage after carriage arrived at Ainahau for the birthday luau. Princess Likelike and Mr. Cleghorn waited at the door, ushering in guests to be presented to Ka'iulani. Dressed in a pink satin frock and stationed between tall, feathered kahilis to symbolize her royal rank, the little princess greeted each new arrival. So many presents were offered that they filled an adjoining room.

Laura watched the Royalists and Reformers display obeisance to the child by curtsies and bows. She wasn't surprised to see Lorrin Thurston and Judge Dole arrive, along with their wives, as prominent politicians with the Reform Party. After Mr. Thurston's outburst that night at dinner in the Price home, though, Laura thought his deference to King Kalakaua was hollow and insincere.

It did surprise Laura that Lucien came with them. He wasn't in government, and despite his family's wealth, he had no real standing in political circles. Perhaps Mr. Thurston wished him to become more acquainted with government matters. Since most of the attendees were married and much older, Laura was glad to see him. His work kept him in Honolulu, and he hadn't been able to make good his promise to visit.

As soon as Lucien had paid his respects, he made his way to Laura's side.

"Good news," he said. "Thurston has a new client at Waikiki. He said I could do the initial legwork, so I'll be out here more often." He smiled, then added in a low voice, "And then I can stop in to see you."

Laura felt a brief shiver, like something closing in on her. Though she wanted to encourage Lucien to visit, she had a prick of guilt. She was fond of him, like an older brother. He clearly had something else in mind.

Lunch was announced, and the guests helped themselves at tables loaded with steamed fish, *imu*-baked pig, poi, shellfish, seaweed, and other Hawaiian delicacies prepared in the ancient style. Sideboards overflowed with dishes geared to the tastes of the Americans and Europeans.

When the feasting was through, King Kalakaua rose and made a stately bow in the direction of his little niece.

"I arise to propose the health of Her Royal Highness Princess Ka`iulani. On this occasion I'm proud to pay this compliment to my niece as a member of the direct line. I hope that she'll grow up with all the advantages of the period, so that she may fill her future position to the credit of the nation."

The king nodded at one of the members of the House of Nobles who stood to add his acknowledgment.

"May she indeed live to be the 'Hope of the Nation.' May her education be such that when, in the natural events of life, she may rule over this land, may it be a rule of wisdom, always retaining the love of her people. Surely all here will say with me, 'Aloha nui' to the Princess Ka`iulani."

The guests all raised their glasses to cheers of "Hear, hear" and "Aloha nui." The princess, looking small and delicate, bowed in various directions, returning their affection.

After lunch, the guests retired, with cool drinks, to the verandah or to the shade of the banyan. Ka`iulani accompanied her mother and father from group to group to talk with the guests and see to their comfort.

Lucien left a friend on the verandah, and strolled over to where Laura sat on a bench beneath the banyan.

"It looks like Thurston and Judge Dole are settled into a long conversation. How about taking a walk around the grounds?"

Laura nodded.

As they walked the paths, Lucien talked with enthusiasm about his work at the law office. In just the few months Laura had known him, he'd gained confidence. She envied him, in a way. He had a profession, and didn't have to worry about being "protected in a respectable household."

Her thoughts drifted to the calculations she'd made in her journal. She had no expenses to speak of, so if she were frugal and saved her earnings, within four years she'd have enough to go back to San Francisco and put herself through medical school. She'd be only twenty-three, and by then, Ka`iulani would no longer need a governess.

Mr. Cleghorn had opened an account for Laura at Bishop Bank. With the exception of the few dollars she kept for spending money, all her pay went to savings. And it was earning interest. Mr. Cleghorn said that one day, when they were downtown, he'd take her in to sign papers so she'd control her own account. A pleasant thought.

Laura followed Lucien across a footbridge that spanned a pond. Spotted orange-and-black koi lazed in the shallows. A tiny green frog sprang from a lily pad to plop into the water and dart under the broad leaves as they passed. On the other side, they sat to rest on a bench beneath a spreading mango tree.

"You know, Laura, your uncle's not too happy about you being out here."

"What do you mean?"

"I heard him talking with my father when he stopped over the other day. He says this is just temporary, that he'd rather have you under his roof, taking care of Hannah and Lizzie."

"But I like it here, Lucien. I want to stay." Laura stood up, shaken. Her daydream of saving to go back to San Francisco disappeared in a flash of fear that Stephen might still control her.

Lucien jumped up. "I didn't mean to upset you. I just thought you should know how he felt." He took her hands in his. "I'd do anything to help you, you know that."

Laura looked up at him.

"I want to take care of you, Laura."

His voice was soft, his fervent gaze shifting almost imperceptibly from a desire to help, to a desire for her. He pulled her to him. That day in his parlor, when she went to visit him, she'd seen his infatuation as a source of assistance. Now, as he leaned toward her, the thought crossed her mind that this desire could be a shield, and if it were ever necessary, perhaps even a weapon. Lucien put his arms around her, and bent down to kiss her. And Laura let him.

&

On the carriage ride back to Honolulu, Thurston called up to Lucien, who sat beside the driver.

"What are you grinning about, McBride?"

Lucien turned around. "Nothing, I just had a good time at the luau, that's all." Still smiling, he turned back to face the front.

"That's the thing," Thurston said to Judge Dole, seated across from him in the carriage. "Too many people were having a good time. What do you think, Sanford?"

The gray-bearded judge thought a moment. "The princess does seem to inspire a devotion to the monarchy."

"My point exactly," Thurston said.

"What point is that, Lorrin?" Mrs. Dole said.

"That we're going to have to keep an eye on our little princess.

She's definitely an asset to the Crown."

Mrs. Thurston glanced sidelong at her husband. "What do you have in mind, dear?"

"Right now, just to keep an eye out." He looked back at Judge Dole. "Though it might be time for one of us to be in the cabinet to have a better vantage point, wouldn't you say, Sanford?"

§

$\mathcal{P}$rincess Lili`uokalani sat at her desk in the library at Washington Place, writing in her accounts book.

"Went to Goo Kim's and ordered six yards of white figured lace at 5 cents a yard. Then at Waterhouse's No. 10 Store, ten yards pink glacé at 10 cents a yard. Two collars at $1.00. Two tablecloths at $2.50 each."

Her mother-in-law hobbled in, leaning on a cane at each step.

"Lydia, I want my breakfast."

Princess Liliu looked up. "Didn't Wakeki leave it out for you in the kitchen?"

"There's nothing there but poi, evil-smelling fish, and seaweed. I want that filth off my table."

Liliu sighed, and pushed back her chair. "Come on, Mother Dominis. Perhaps I can find you some bread and coffee with milk."

As the princess assisted her to the kitchen, walking step by step at her side, Mother Dominis continued her tirade.

"I want your things out of the garden house, Lydia. How long are you going to take? My Chinese servants should've been in there by now. These Hawaiian retainers have no sense about how to run a respectable household and take care of a proper lady."

Liliu sat her mother-in-law at the kitchen table, and removed the fish and seaweed to the sideboard. It was perfectly fresh and smelled delicious. She picked off a piece of seaweed and put it in her mouth. If only Mother Dominis would eat some *kala*. Hawaiian mothers gave the family seaweed to eat whenever there were arguments. They also used it as a poultice to soothe festering wounds. Kala meant "to forgive," and forgiveness meant healing.

"Wakeki's working on it. She should be finished soon." The princess plucked a cup and saucer from the cupboard, and set water to boil for coffee.

Liliu hated to give up the garden house. It was her very own refuge at Washington Place, ever since she'd married John Dominis and moved into his mother's house. There she could write her songs, play the ukulele or zither without anyone interrupting, and have her friends in for tea. She loved being in the garden among the flowers and greenery. At night, she'd sit there and watch the moon. John didn't stay home evenings anyway. Sometimes he was away for days at a time. He left her alone, and went out with his friends, attending to his own comfort and pleasure. Little Aimoku was proof of that. Dr. Trousseau, a card-playing partner and their family physician, tried to protect her from "John's irregularities," as he called them. But when a child fathered by John with one of her servants was to be born in her own household, Trousseau felt duty-bound to tell her.

Now, she'd begun to like solitude. John could be so provoking. He often criticized her brother, the king, and his cabinet, especially the prime minister. Mr. Gibson had his faults, to be sure, but he loved the people, spoke the language fluently, and encouraged the king's efforts to preserve their dance and music and to increase the diminishing native population.

Funny, how she used to yearn to be with John. When he'd stay away too long, she'd had a servant carry a letter begging him to come see her. She dreaded sending the notes, though. He seemed to delight in pointing out her misuse of English. But then, he spoke so little Hawaiian, she couldn't write in her native tongue.

"Did you hear me, Lydia? I said the coffee is boiling."

"Oh, yes, Mother Dominis. I was just thinking of something."

Liliu cut slices of bread, poured coffee and milk into the cup, and served it to her mother-in-law. She set out silverware, butter, and jam.

"I'm going to cut some flowers for the table, Mother. Ka'iulani and her governess are coming this morning to plan a little party for her friends."

"Didn't that child just have a big party?"

"That was an official lunch. This will be a children's party."

Mother Dominis called after Liliu as she went out the kitchen door. "Don't be cutting my roses. You don't do it properly. Stay away from them."

❧

*W*ashington Place was a lovely house that looked like a stately Southern mansion. Princess Lili'uokalani told Laura that her husband's father had been a ship's captain, and had built the house for Mother Dominis, his Bostonian bride. Still, there was something very lonely about it.

The princess's husband, Governor Dominis, arrived just as Wakeki was setting up for lunch. He greeted Ka'iulani with a stiff bow, shook Laura's hand, and nodded to Lili'uokalani. He was tall and thin, with a dark beard and dark eyes.

"Where's Mother?" he asked.

"She's resting in her room," Liliu said. "Will you eat with us, John?"

"No, just have Wakeki bring two trays upstairs. I'll eat with Mother."

During lunch, two ladies stopped by to discuss the formation of a women's bank by the Lili`uokalani Benevolent Society. They were also helping the princess raise money for a school for girls. She asked them to stay and eat.

Another friend arrived, with two little boys, age three or four, and an eight-year-old girl in tow. Ka`iulani jumped up from the table to greet the children. She brought them over to Princess Liliu who hugged them all.

"These are my *hanai* children, Laura," the princess said. "Hanai is an ancient bond that's made when a child is given to another family to raise as their own." She pointed to each one in turn. "This is Kaipo, Aimoku, and Lydia. Kaipo's mother is one of my retainers, and so is Aimoku's. Lydia's mother died when she was just a week old. I took over their support as their hanai mother."

Kaipo and Lydia were pure Hawaiian, but Aimoku was lighter skinned with light brown hair. He was reserved and shy compared with little Kaipo, who wiggled like a puppy when Ka`iulani picked him up.

"I was a hanai child myself," the princess went on. "When I was just a few days old, I was given to a family descended from King Kamehameha. From then on, I was their child, with all the rights of a natural daughter. It's a custom not well understood among the haoles."

"Perhaps someone would hanai me," Laura said, only half joking, "since I'm on my own now."

125

The princess looked at her a long moment. "Yes, sometimes it's hard to be all on your own."

Governor Dominis appeared at the door of the dining room. Seeing so many ladies eating and talking, and children squirming, he turned to go.

"We're taking the children to town after lunch to see a ventriloquist. Would you like to go, John?" Princess Liliu said.

"Not today, Lydia. By the way, Mother's disturbed that the garden house is still not cleaned out. Perhaps you could see to that this week."

Chapter 12 ———

January 19, 1887

The New Year is here, but Ainahau is somber and still. Even the peacocks are quiet. Just before Christmas, Princess Likelike fell ill, and the doctors can't find what's wrong. She won't eat, and gets weaker and weaker. The servants tiptoe around, whispering that a *kahuna ana ana* is praying her to death. But no one would do that. Everyone loves her. It doesn't help that Mauna Loa, on the island of Hawaii, erupted violently this week. Even the princess says the volcano goddess, Pele, has come for her. What's more alarming to the servants though, are the schools of red fish that have come up from the deep sea. They believe it's a sign of the coming death of an *ali`i* — a high chief.

Ka`iulani is distraught. She can't concentrate on her lessons, and neither can I. Mr. Cleghorn tries to revive his wife's spirits by promising her all sorts of things, even a trip to San Francisco when she's better. Princess Lili`uokalani comes out several times a week to sit with her sister and try to cheer her. And the king visits when he can get away from the pressing affairs of state. Nothing seems to help.

&

Lorrin Thurston walked into Lucien's office. He was bent over his desk, writing.

"What's the news out Waikiki way?"

Lucien straightened up in his chair. "Your client seems happy with the progress of his case."

"That's good. Anything else?"

"Well, I stopped by the Cleghorn place, but I didn't stay long."

"Why not?"

"Princess Likelike is really ill." Lucien swiveled his chair around. "The Hawaiians say a kahuna ana ana is praying her to death."

Thurston smirked. "These kanakas and their witch-doctor superstitions."

"I know," Lucien said. "But they're serious about these things. The whole house out there feels like a morgue."

"Hmm." Thurston sat on the edge of the desk. He pulled at the chin hairs under his lip. "So how's Price's niece?"

Lucien tried to stifle the smile that appeared on his face at Laura's mention.

Thurston shook his head and chuckled. "You're transparent, McBride."

"What?" Lucien protested, but the smile persisted.

"What do you two talk about when you visit? Do I hear wedding bells?"

"No, not yet." Lucien rolled his chair back a little and looked down to pick an imaginary piece of lint off his shirt. "We haven't talked much in the past few weeks, especially since Likelike's illness has gotten worse. I just stop in for a few minutes to pay my respects, and ride on back to Honolulu."

Thurston nodded, then reached for a piece of paper and a pencil. He leaned over the desk and scribbled a brief note, folded the paper, and sealed it in an envelope. He handed it to Lucien.

"Next time you go out, walk this over to Price."

On his way out at noon, Lucien dropped the envelope off with the clerk at Stephen's office. Stephen had already left to go home for lunch. When he returned that afternoon, he found the note on his desk, and slit it open with a letter opener.

Stephen—

Have you heard the news about Likelike's illness? Lucien says the kanakas at Ainahau think a kahuna ana ana is praying her to death, and they're all very disturbed. What do you make of it?

Better yet, what can we make of it? In my opinion, the only "witch doctor" in this kingdom is the king himself. He must be praying for the death of all the planters, the way he refuses to yield on ceding Pearl Harbor to renew the sugar treaty. Something's got to be done to disturb that.

Lorrin

PS: Your plans for the "merger" seem to be going forward. Young McBride is smitten.

Stephen smiled briefly, then furrowed his brow. He sat thinking a few minutes. Finally he took out a clean sheet of paper and a pen and scratched out a few paragraphs. He blotted the paper, folded it, and called for his clerk.

"Put this in an envelope, and take it over to the editor at the *Gazette*. You won't have to wait. I don't need a response."

The clerk left the office, started up the street, then sprinted the last block when a sudden shower came down. He ducked under

the awning of the newspaper office, and smoothed back his hair.
A bell above the door jingled as he opened it. The editor came to
the counter and took the rain-spattered envelope. He unsealed
it with his index finger, and unfolded the sheet of paper.

Sam—

You know the old *kanaka* tradition that when a powerful chief wants to curry favor with the gods, he makes a
human sacrifice; the more powerful the spirit of the person
sacrificed the more powerful the favors the gods bestow.

I've heard from credible sources that the king is traffick-
ing in sorcery in an attempt to rid himself of his political
difficulties, and is behind the sad news that our princess
Likelike is near death's door.

Just thought you'd like the scoop. I suspect it'll run in
the Hawaiian-language papers after you print it. Might
stir up some interesting discussion. Dispose of this note
in your usual manner.

Stephen

ಬ

Kaʻiulani entered the dim room and stood still. Light flowed
through the crack in the door, like a wedge of energy from the
outside world, then stopped, unable to reach the far corner at the
other side of the room. As her eyes became accustomed to the
dark, the little girl moved step by step toward the bed in the corner. Two retainers gently fanned kahilis at the head of the bed.

"Leave us now," Princess Likelike whispered.

The servants moved toward the wedge of light and out the
door. When it closed, the room was silent except for Likelike's
breathing.

"Sit down, Ka`iulani." She drew a raspy breath. "I have something to tell you."

The little girl sat in a chair next to the bed. Likelike shifted a hand toward her, and Ka`iulani reached to grasp it. Minutes seemed to tick by before the princess spoke again.

"Your father would never believe me if I told him, so I must tell you. I've seen your future."

"What do you mean, Mama?"

Likelike struggled to get a breath to form the words.

"I've seen it all clearly. I had to warn you. You'll go away from here for a long time. You'll never marry... and you'll never be queen."

Princess Likelike's breath came in short gasps. They scared the child, who wanted to call her father, but was afraid to move.

The agitated breaths smoothed out, and the princess spoke again, her voice just above a whisper.

"I'll die soon, my darling."

"Mama, please."

"Don't cry, now." She squeezed Ka`iulani's hand. "We'll be together again."

Ka`iulani's tears started. She knelt at the side of the bed, put her face on the blanket, and began to sob. Likelike placed her hand on her daughter's head.

Mr. Cleghorn heard her distress and rushed in, flinging the door open. Light flooded the room, but stopped short of the shadowed bed.

"Take the child out," her father told the retainers who'd followed him in.

They led her away, and Cleghorn sank down in the chair next to the bed. Ka`iulani broke loose from the servants and ran from the house into the yard.

Laura found her down at the stable, her tear-streaked face buried in Fairie's mane. The pony stood still as a statue, his head across her shoulder as if he understood. Laura loosened the child's arms from around his neck, hugged her close, and walked her back to the house. Ka'iulani clung to her waist.

King Kalakaua and Princess Lili'uokalani arrived and joined Mr. Cleghorn in Princess Likelike's room. The family physician was summoned. Laura and Ka'iulani kept vigil in the parlor as hours passed. Around five o'clock, Mr. Cleghorn emerged from the bedroom. He looked drawn and old.

"It's over," he said.

Tears welled up in the little princess's eyes, and Laura fought back her own.

"Laura, if you'd be so kind as to receive callers, I think Ka'iulani and I will retire to our rooms for a while."

"Of course, sir."

Mr. Cleghorn took his daughter's hand, and they walked to the back of the house toward their bedrooms.

Throughout the evening, carriages wheeled down the long drive and people gathered on the grounds around the house. David Kahiko arrived after dark, and helped Laura greet the continuing procession. As the moon rose, barefooted Hawaiians, their soft tears flowing, thronged beneath the banyan to pay their respects and sing mournful chants through the night. The mesmerizing sound wafted up, mixed with the scent of gardenia blossoms piled high in the yard by friends who knew they were the princess's favorite flowers.

It would be a source of wonder that no gardenias bloomed on the island for years after, especially at Waikiki.

Chapter 13

Wakeki opened the massive front door at Washington Place. She squinted into the early morning sun that angled under the trees and onto the wide verandah. A royal courier handed her a note.

"For the Princess Lili`uokalani." He bowed and departed.

"Who was that, Wakeki?" the princess called.

The retainer closed the door. She scuffed back to the kitchen and set the message on the table in front of Liliu.

"From the king," she said, and set about preparing breakfast.

Liliu opened the sealed note, read it, and gasped. Wakeki turned from the stove.

"The king had accepted Queen Victoria's invitation to attend her jubilee, but he says he's decided not to go because it's unwise for him to travel now." Liliu looked up. "He wants me to accompany Queen Kapi`olani to the celebration in London."

"When?"

"We have to sail April twelfth. That's only a week from now."

Liliu read the letter again. Rulers were coming from all corners of the British Empire and other nations to honor the fiftieth anniversary of Queen Victoria's reign. The king wrote that he knew Liliu still grieved for their sister, and he hoped the trip might lighten her heart. She'd be able to visit old friends in San Francisco, meet the Dominis family's relations in Boston, sightsee in New York, and be presented to President Grover Cleveland when she and Queen Kapiʻolani passed through Washington, D.C. After attending the jubilee as official representatives of the kingdom, the king wished for them to visit several European capitals to reinvigorate Hawaii's relationship with other monarchies.

There was so much to do before they sailed. Liliu instructed Wakeki to begin preparations directly after breakfast, then decided to drive out to Ainahau to tell the good news to Kaʻiulani, and stop downtown on the way back to make some purchases.

&

On the verandah at Ainahau, Princess Liliu shared the news of her trip with Kaʻiulani, Laura, and Mr. Cleghorn. David Kahiko arrived while they were talking, and joined them for tea. He'd come out to consult with Mr. Cleghorn on some upcoming legislation. Laura suppressed her delight in seeing him again, but hoped he'd stay for the afternoon.

Kaʻiulani asked question after question about sailing two oceans, riding a train across the wild American continent, and life in the British Isles. Finally, Liliu put down her teacup and rose to leave. She kissed her niece and Laura, told them she'd write from London, and they walked with her to the waiting carriage. David held her hand to assist her up. The driver headed his team down the palm-lined drive, and Mr. Cleghorn turned to go back to work in his library.

"I'm going to read over your draft, David," he said.

Kaʻiulani watched until her aunt disappeared from view. She clutched Laura's waist and looked up.

"Everyone's leaving, Miss Laura. Don't you leave me too."

"I'm not going anywhere, my dear." She stroked the child's hair. "How about a game of croquet?" She smiled at David. "I bet we can beat Mr. Kahiko."

David smiled back. "I'd like to see you two try. I'll set up the game right now." A rider came cantering up the drive. "Well, look who's here," David said. "We can have a foursome."

The horse slowed, trotted up, and Lucien reined him in.

"What are you doing here, David?"

"I could ask you the same question."

"I thought I'd stop in on my way out to Waikiki." Lucien dismounted and handed the reins to a servant who took the horse away. "I passed Princess Lili`uokalani coming out the entrance. She's up here pretty early."

"She came to tell us about her trip," Laura said.

"Her trip?"

"She's going with Queen Kapi`olani to Queen Victoria's jubilee in London. They leave in a few days."

"I didn't know just anyone could show up to that affair," Lucien said.

"Just invited royalty," David said. "Perhaps you're unaware of the long relationship between our two kingdoms. You must know Queen Victoria was godmother to Crown Prince Albert, the son of Kamehameha IV. Or don't they teach Hawaiian history at Punahou?"

Lucien grinned. "I must have been daydreaming the day they covered that. All I remember about Hawaiian-British relations is the time Lord Paulet took over the kingdom."

"And Queen Victoria ordered him to restore it to the rightful monarch." David turned away. "Come on, McBride. We're going to play a game of croquet with Ka`iulani. Help me set up the wickets."

Ka`iulani cheered up as the game progressed. For such a leisurely pastime as croquet, Lucien and David whacked the balls with unusual force. When Laura stepped back to take a turn, she stumbled on a wicket and fell sideways. David caught her in his arms.

"Did you twist your foot?"

Laura wiggled her ankle. "No, it seems all right."

"Step on it gently to make sure," he said.

He supported her against his chest as she tested her weight. She smiled up at him. "It's okay," she said. "Thank you, David."

Lucien leaned against the banyan, arms crossed, watching the interchange. He looked down, digging a hole in the dirt with the toe of his boot. He'd always liked Kahiko, thought he was an upstanding fellow, but he didn't want him holding Laura like that, not even by accident. He looked at the two of them again. Laura was taking an awfully long time to stand back up. She shouldn't be smiling at David that way. She should be smiling that way at him. He was the one who'd kissed her, right here in the woods at Ainahau; the one who wanted to take care of her; the one who wanted to propose to her. She was his.

❧

In the packed hall, Lorrin Thurston called the gathering to order.

"Gentlemen, I welcome you to this meeting of the Hawaiian League. For those of you who've just taken the oath and are joining us for the first time, I remind you that you're sworn to keep this organization and its proceedings secret. For everyone's safety, we keep no written minutes. Our intent is to secure efficient, decent, and honest government in Hawaii." He turned to a gentleman in a military uniform with a wide, flamboyant mustache.

"Now we'll hear from Colonel Volney Ashford on the current development of the Honolulu Rifles."

Ashford rose to speak. "As you know, the Honolulu Rifles are a voluntary militia and the only organized military force serving the Hawaiian Kingdom. We started with one company and now we have three, one composed of Portuguese. A hundred Germans have joined up as well. Our arms shipments are coming in as scheduled through Castle & Cooke and Lack's sewing shop downtown, so in a matter of a few weeks, we'll be ready to be at the service of the League."

A murmur of approval rumbled through the room. Ashford took his seat. Thurston opened the floor for discussion on how to deal with King Kalakaua. Someone proposed letting him remain as a figurehead in a constitutional monarchy. Another called for his abdication in favor of a republic. That raised other questions — whether they wanted Hawaii to stay independent or be annexed to the United States.

Ashford sprang to his feet. "No more waiting around. When we're ready, I say we kill the king, and fill the government offices with members of the League. Then we can do whatever we want."

There was boisterous response, some in favor, some opposed. Judge Sanford Dole stood, and the room became quiet.

"I'm no more a fan of Kalakaua than you are, Colonel Ashford. But I think that, as far as possible, we should use legislative means for our ends. Perhaps we should give the king an opportunity to accede to our demands."

Thurston interrupted him. "The time is ripe now to bring about a crisis." He pointed toward Lucien standing against the back wall. "My young colleague here found out that Lili'uokalani is leaving this week for Europe. She'll be gone several months.

With the heir apparent out of the country and Likelike deceased, the only other person in line for the throne is a little girl." He turned to Dole. "I'd say, Judge, this is the opportunity we've been waiting for."

❧

*P*rincess Liliu supervised her servants as they packed the steamer trunks for her trip to London. She didn't notice Mother Dominis standing at the door, hunched over her cane, watching.

"Bring my husband's suits that are lying on the bed in the other room," the princess said.

"Why are you taking John's suits?" the old lady demanded.

Liliu looked up. "Mother, I already told you. The king agreed that John could accompany us to Queen Victoria's jubilee. It's a great honor for him. You should be happy."

"Well, who's going to take care of me while you're gone?"

"Your nurse will take care of you, just as always. You'll be fine."

Mother Dominis turned away and slowly limped down the hall, emitting occasional groans loud enough to be heard in the bedroom. Liliu shook her head, then returned to the packing. When they were finally finished, she asked one of the servants to call for the carriage driver to deliver the trunks to the wharf for loading on the *Australia*.

❧

*T*he next morning, when John went out to the carriage and Liliu was on her way downstairs, Mother Dominis's nurse rushed out on the landing of the stairwell.

"Princess, please come back up here. Mrs. Dominis has fallen!"

Liliu returned upstairs and entered her mother-in-law's room. Two Chinese servants were lifting her into bed. She had an anguished look.

"Mother, are you in pain?"

"Yes, I think I broke something."

"Let me see," Liliu said. "Where does it hurt?"

"My left leg. Oh, oh, oh," the old lady said as Liliu felt down her leg. "It hurts all over."

"I can't find anything wrong." Liliu turned to the nurse. "Miss Davis, send for Dr. Trousseau. We've got to get on to the wharf."

Mother Dominis glared. "Surely you're not going to leave me in this condition?"

"I don't see anything wrong, Mother. The doctor will be here shortly to make sure."

Mother Dominis raised her voice. "Lydia, I want you to send John to me this minute!"

Liliu sighed. She headed down the stairs and out the front door where John waited in the carriage.

"What kept you?" he said.

She looked at him, deliberating. Then she climbed into the carriage.

"I was just saying goodbye to Mother."

&

The horses slowed as they neared the wharf. A multitude of well-wishers was on the pier to see the royal party off. Liliu got down from the carriage, and Ka`iulani and Laura came up to adorn her with leis. Mr. Cleghorn was with them.

"I had to come to say goodbye, Auntie," Ka`iulani hugged

her. "I already said goodbye to Mama Mo`i. Papa Mo`i is on the ship with her now."

Liliu turned to John. "We'd better board. The king and queen are already here."

"They won't sail until the king leaves the ship," John said.

"He's coming off now," Cleghorn said, pointing toward the gangplank. The king descended, followed by royal attendants. He spied Liliu and proceeded their way. Laura and Ka`iulani curtsied as he approached, and the men bowed. The king hugged his sister.

"Kapi`olani is waiting for you. Have a wonderful trip." He kissed her on each cheek. "Now, you better get up there; the queen's a bit anxious. She's never been on such a big ship before."

He saw Laura and smiled broadly.

"Well, here's our bold dancer. I hear good things about you from Mr. Cleghorn." He winked at Ka`iulani. "Is our little princess well behaved at all times?"

"Oh, yes, Your Majesty," Laura said.

He smiled. "That's good." The king turned back to Liliu. "I wish I could go with you, sister, but my duty is here."

§

Ka`iulani wanted to stay until the ship was out of sight past Diamond Head. Liliu and Kapi`olani had become mother figures to her, now that Likelike was gone. When they could no longer see the ship, Mr. Cleghorn took his daughter's hand and started for the carriage.

"I need to stop at my office before we head back to Ainahau."

"I don't want stay at your office all afternoon, Papa."

Laura could see that Mr. Cleghorn was intent on his purpose, and a confrontation was brewing. "How about we go up to visit Hannah and Lizzie while your father takes care of his work? It's not that far, and they should be home from school by now."

"Oh, may we, Papa?"

"Yes, I'll have the driver take you up there. But be back at five o'clock to pick me up."

Laura was sure that Stephen was still at work too, so there was little chance of running into him. She didn't want to give him any opportunity to even think about her moving back under his roof. But she did miss the girls and Aunt Katherine.

Kimiko heard the carriage pull in, and opened the door just as Laura and Ka`iulani climbed the steps to the verandah. When she saw the royal visitor, her normal reserve was lit by surprise. For just a moment, her eyes got wide, then she caught herself, and made the lowest, most graceful bow Laura had ever seen. Still bowing, she opened the door wide and backed into the foyer.

Lizzie was upstairs hanging over the banister to see who was there. When she caught sight of Laura and Ka`iulani, she shrieked, and bounded down the stairs. She pulled up in front of the princess, made an awkward curtsy, then turned, and called her sister.

"Hannah! Come quick!"

Laughing, Ka`iulani hugged Lizzie. Then Lizzie hugged Laura. Hannah came out of her bedroom.

"Lizzie, quiet. You're going to wake Mother — oh!" She saw who was there, and hurried down the stairs. She curtsied properly to Ka`iulani, and then they hugged each other.

Laura smiled. "Where's my hug?" She embraced Hannah.

Kimiko stood in the corner, head still bowed. Laura looked over.

"Girls, take Ka`iulani to your room to play so Kimiko can get back to her work. I want to see your mother."

The girls clambered upstairs, Laura trailing after them. The smell of the house and the familiar creak of the landing made her uneasy. She turned down the hall toward Aunt Katherine's room. The door was open a crack, and she peeked through. Katherine was lying propped up in bed. She appeared to be asleep. Near her face, hazy afternoon sunbeams splayed on the pillow. She was so pale, almost transparent, like a wandering spirit come to rest. Laura thought to back away, but something drew her in.

She edged the door open. It squeaked, but Katherine didn't wake. Laura walked to the side of the bed, relieved to see the slight rise and fall of the coverlet from her aunt's shallow breaths. She said a silent prayer for Katherine — for her cousins, really, because she saw how Ka`iulani suffered from the loss of her mother. Then she heard a carriage pull into the driveway. What if Uncle Stephen were home early?

She walked quickly from the room, down the hall to the stairwell, and stood stiff against the wall. Looking around the corner, she could just see a man's boots as Kimiko opened the front door to admit him. Laura's heart skipped a beat, and she tried to think of some plan of escape. Then she heard Lucien's voice.

"I was passing by and saw the Cleghorn's carriage."

"Yes," Kimiko said. "Miss Laura and the royal princess stopped to visit."

Laura came downstairs. Lucien was surprised at how glad she looked to see him, but it made him happy. They went to sit on the verandah, in the same place where he'd told her, months ago, that he'd be honored to be counted among her friends.

Laura's anxiety eased as Lucien talked about his clients, his work, and the news about town. But then he leaned in and told her something in a confidential tone that made the hair rise up on the back of her neck, though she didn't know why.

"It won't be long," he said, "before we see some changes around here. I can't say what it is right now, but there are big doings afoot in Honolulu."

Chapter 14 ————

I went to an exhibition drill of the Honolulu Rifles last week. In the evening, they sponsored a dance. It was a grand affair attended by all the best of Honolulu society. Uncle Stephen was there, but every time my dance partner moved near him, David cut in and waltzed me away in the other direction. He even did it to Lucien, twice. What a look on Lucien's face, especially the second time.

The Rifles are expert marksmen and look very smart in their military uniforms. Funny, though, how there are no Hawaiians. They're all Portuguese, German, and American. After the drill, King Kalakaua presented a Hawaiian flag to Colonel Ashford, the drillmaster. The colonel made a touching acceptance speech. He called the flag a beautiful emblem of the unity of many peoples in the Hawaiian Kingdom, blended together in political and racial harmony, under the king, its honored sovereign. King Kalakaua thanked him for his kind words, and said he appreciated the patriotism of the Rifles.

We haven't heard anything from Princess Lili`uokalani since she sailed for England. I hope we do soon. It's been over a month, and Ka`iulani is dying for a letter.

Gaellen Quinn

&

July 6, 1887

Alexandra Hotel, London

My dear Ka'iulani and Laura,

Please forgive the long delay in sending you news. Since we left Honolulu we've had such full days. It's a luxury to sit and write a leisurely letter. This afternoon we attend the last event of the jubilee — a garden party for the royalty from around the world gathered at this historic event. We're staying at the same hotel as princes from Japan, Siam, India, and Persia.

When we left San Francisco on the train, we passed through Sacramento, Salt Lake City, and Denver. At one point we stopped in the mountains. Some of our party got off to play in the snow, rolling it in balls and pelting each other — a novel experience for those who come from a land of perpetual summer. Perhaps Laura has seen this before, but Ka'iulani, you'd have found it amusing, I'm sure.

The vastness of America amazed me. Surely those who agitate politically in Honolulu can't imagine this great country would ever have an interest in our little islands so far away.

In Washington, D.C., we were formally presented to President Grover Cleveland and his lovely young wife. They gave the queen a lock of George Washington's hair as a gift! One day we took a steamer to visit Mount Vernon and the resting-place of the first president. May is a beautiful time of year in those parts, wildflowers and trees blooming everywhere. I was reminded of home and your lovely place at Ainahau.

In Boston, I met your Uncle John's relatives for the first time. Many are educators. They were enthusiastic about my efforts to establish a women's college in Honolulu. In New York, we went sightseeing. The most interesting thing was the Metropolitan Museum. We saw a mummy wrapped in lengths of linen. When they unwrapped yards and yards of cloth to expose a small, dark hand, I had to turn away. It spoke too clearly of death.

We set sail for England on *The City of Rome*, the largest steamship I've ever seen, with perhaps a thousand souls aboard. It was fun to watch the strange mixture of humanity — musicians, health seekers, tourists intent on seeing the world, and a few like ourselves, bound for the jubilee. To pass the time, I composed songs or read in the ship's library. It was a pleasant crossing, except for one thing: for days, the mist was so thick that the ship's foghorn never ceased, night or day.

When we reached the wharf at Liverpool, there were thousands of heads as far as the eye could see. I asked someone why, and they said the populace had heard that the "Queen of the Sandwich Isles" was aboard, and they'd come out to meet her and her suite. The moment we touched British soil, we were the official guests of Her Majesty Queen Victoria, and my dears, for the first time in my life I understand what it means to be royalty in the rest of the world. No wonder, after his trip around the world, the king made efforts to solidify the status of Hawaiian royalty in ways his subjects of foreign birth could understand, like having a coronation and building a proper palace. The Hawaiian people have always honored their chiefs, but others may need tangible evidence in order to give them their due.

In London, we met with Queen Victoria. She thanked us for coming so far to see her, and spoke enthusiastically about meeting King Kalakaua when he was in England six years ago. She said she's never forgotten his visit. She asked me about the schools in Hawaii. When we left, she kissed Kapi`olani on both cheeks, and me on the forehead.

Before I met her I was told that Her Majesty is short, stout, and not at all graceful. I disagree. She's a queenly woman with a kind face, evidence of a gentle spirit within. How often are people so misrepresented! You wonder sometimes at the motives.

The jubilee celebration at historic Westminster Abbey, and the banquet afterward, were all you might imagine. I won't go into detail, since you'll likely read accounts in the Honolulu papers. Among the special honors we were given, Her Majesty put one of her own carriages at our disposal, and sent an escort of her Life Guards to accompany us from the hotel.

At the banquet, Queen Kap`iolani and I sat with the European kings and queens. Kap`iolani was escorted by the Prince of Wales, heir to the British throne. Prince Alfred, the Duke of Edinburgh, escorted me. All in all, it was a splendid affair, and we were shown such kind hospitality. The pageantry is beautiful, but I must admit, I sometimes tire of all the pomp.

We're looking forward to visiting various foreign capitals in Europe. I'll write more news from there. For now, I send you both my aloha.

Your Aunt Liliu

Liliu blotted her letter and set it aside to dry. Then she opened her letter, dipped her pen in the ink well and wrote a note:

"John has been sad today and so am I. Is there trouble at home?"

૭

The chamberlain tapped at the door of the library and opened it a crack. The king was seated at the end of a long table in the center of the room. Books stacked in front of him hid his head, which was bent over a large tome.

"What is it?" Kalakaua said, without looking up.

"Prime Minister Gibson to see you, Your Majesty."

"Show him in."

The tall, white-haired old man entered, and the chamberlain closed the door. Gibson bowed and sat in a high-backed chair next to a bookshelf. The king straightened up and, with a weary look, pushed his chair back to face him.

"I've ordered the customhouse to report on any unusually large shipments of arms and ammunition," Gibson said. "The Royal Guard has been doubled, the palace barricaded, the cannon emplacements have been dug, and the electric lights installed to light the grounds."

The king nodded slowly. "I appreciate your efforts, Walter, but I think our preparations are inadequate. I've had a visit from the US minister. The Hawaiian League is going to hold a public meeting to announce their demands."

Gibson sat forward in his chair. "We should appeal to the US minister to land marines to support us, Your Majesty."

"He wouldn't offer support, said he won't interfere in our domestic affairs. He recommends I make my peace with the League."

"Then we'll go to the foreign legations."

"I've spoken with them," the king said. "They won't intervene either." He glanced away, then back at Gibson. "The League wants you out, Walter. They want me to name a new cabinet. My back is against the wall."

Gibson sat back in his chair. Kalakaua continued.

"I'll call out the Honolulu Rifles for protection the day of the meeting, but we can't predict what'll happen. For your own safety, you may want to leave the kingdom."

"What about the assassination threats against you, Your Majesty?"

The king shook his head. "There have been threats against the royal family for years. I don't think they'll try anything so rash. What worries me is assassination by the pen. These lawyers are adept at legal machinations invisible to my people."

Gibson hung his head. "You've done so much to enrich those men. I can't stand their ingratitude." He looked up. "Perhaps we made mistakes, Your Highness. Perhaps our aim of 'Hawaii for the Hawaiians,' stirred up resistance. But you never excluded them or any race in your efforts. Everyone benefited, even noncitizens. Just because you tried to revive the customs of your people and rule as a true ali`i — "

"It's all right, Walter," the king said. "It's all right. This is just one more battle in a war that started decades ago, and I'll continue to do the best I can for all my subjects." He pushed his chair back and stood up. Gibson stood with him, and the king embraced him. "I'm sorry, my friend. You've been a loyal advocate for my people. They won't forget you."

✍

Inside the armory, dressed in his Honolulu Rifles uniform, Lorrin Thurston stood to address members of the Hawaiian League. Outside, all available members of the militia not on duty elsewhere in town were lined up in formation.

"We've drafted the demands we'll present to the king this afternoon," Thurston said. "Gibson must be dismissed, a new cabinet must be formed, and the king must promise to reign, but not rule."

The banker, Charles Bishop, rose and was recognized.

"We've been notified that the king has already dismissed Gibson and the cabinet. One of our members, William Green, has been asked to form a new ministry."

There were shouts of approval, and Thurston, smiling, raised his hands for silence.

"That reminds me of an old story I heard somewhere about a man going out to shoot a coon. The coon said, 'Don't shoot, I'll come down.' The king is the coon, and this meeting is the gun." Then he added, "The king called out the Rifles this morning to patrol the streets and keep the peace while this meeting is going on, but we know whose orders they follow."

There was thunderous applause, and various members got up to add their comments. Then a motion was made and passed that a new constitution should be framed at once to make the changes in the government permanent. Thurston accepted responsibility for drafting it.

&

On Laura's afternoon off, she left Ka'iulani with her servant, Kainoa, and then, with Mr. Cleghorn's permission, was driven into Honolulu to do some personal shopping. When the carriage reached downtown, she wondered why the lei makers, usually stationed on corners of the shopping streets, laughing and calling out friendly greetings or playing ukuleles, were absent. The town was quiet. Shops were closed, and just a few Chinese walked warily down the side streets.

She asked the driver to go up to Beretania Street to stop in at the McBrides'. Perhaps they knew what was going on. The carriage passed a hall where her friend, Isobel Strong, gave dancing lessons. It should've been full of prancing children this time of the afternoon, but it was locked up tight. The place belonged to Prime Minister Gibson, who rented it out for events. He'd let her friend use it for nothing, because her husband was away, being treated at a sanatorium. Across the street, in the garden of Mr. Gibson's home, were two members of the Honolulu Rifles. Despite their stiff stance and uniforms, Laura recognized them as the pleasant salesmen who'd often waited on her in shops on Fort Street. She raised a hand in greeting, but they stared straight ahead as the carriage passed, and she lowered her hand.

In front of the McBride mansion, Laura got down from the carriage, ran up the stairs to the front door, and rang the bell. Tamiko came, and told her that Mr. McBride and Lucien were out, and Mrs. McBride was napping. Laura left her card to let them know she'd called, and walked back to the carriage.

They pulled out of the drive onto the street. A jeering mob had gathered at the front of the Gibson home. Two men led Mr. Gibson and his son-in-law out of the house at gunpoint.

As they passed through the crowd, someone slapped Mr. Gibson and knocked off his hat.

Laura stood in the carriage to try to see what was going on. The stately old gentleman was pushed along in the crowd toward the wharf, his son-in-law stumbling behind him. Laura sat down, and told her nervous driver to follow at a safe distance.

Where Fort Street met the waterfront, a unit of the Honolulu Rifles waited as the drillmaster, mounted on his horse, directed some men to fit nooses to the yardarm of a ship in the harbor. The crowd pressed in to watch. Laura's driver stopped about a block away, and she sat for a moment, not knowing what to do. Weren't the Rifles supposed to disburse mobs and keep the peace? Then she saw Lorrin Thurston come out from a side street and head toward the wharf. She got down from the carriage and ran after him.

Thurston stopped at the perimeter of the crowd, looking left and right. Several men toward the front had begun to chant, "Hang them, hang them." Thurston felt a hand at his back, jumped, and then turned. He looked startled to see Laura.

"Mr. Thurston, please, do something! They're going to hang Mr. Gibson."

Thurston's face reddened, as if he were angry or embarrassed. He looked past Laura up Fort Street and saw the British commissioner hurrying toward the crowd. Then he looked at the wharf where Colonel Ashford, still astride his horse, gave an order to take Gibson and his son-in-law on the deck of the ship, where the nooses swayed in the breeze. Glancing at Laura's pleading face, Thurston hesitated a moment, then pushed through the mob to the colonel.

"What are you doing, Ashford?"

"I'm going to make an example of old Gibsy, here. Strike some terror into this community. Then they'll know we're a force to be reckoned with."

Thurston jerked his arm in a circle like he was calling someone over. "Get them off the ship. They're being charged with …" He had to think a moment. "High crimes and misdemeanors. We're taking them into custody for trial."

Colonel Ashford frowned. His voluminous mustache twitched, and he told his men to bring the prisoners down and hand them over to Thurston, who ordered members of the Rifles to escort them to the jail and lock them in for the night with an armed guard. Then he accompanied Laura to her carriage, and told the driver to take her straight back to Ainahau.

A few days later, Mr. Cleghorn found out that Mr. Gibson and his son-in-law had been arraigned on charges of embezzlement, but since no substantiating evidence was found, they were freed. They left for San Francisco the next day, traveling, Mr. Gibson remarked, "for my health."

&

*W*illiam Green laid a document on the table in front of King Kalakaua.

"As you requested, I've taken steps to form the new ministry, Your Majesty."

Kalakaua read the list of names appointed to the cabinet: Green established himself as premier and minister of finance; Godfrey Brown, minister of foreign affairs; Lorrin Thurston, minister of the interior; and Clarence Ashford, the drillmaster's brother, attorney general.

"Premier William Green, minister of finance." The king looked up. "Quite a step up for a Honolulu merchant. You're all members of the Hawaiian League?"

"Coincidentally, Your Majesty." Green smiled.

The king nodded. "Yes, coincidentally."

Green handed him a pen to sign off on the cabinet. "And we'll have a new constitution for your signature by July sixth."

The king signed, and pushed the paper back toward Green. "What's going on with Gibson and his son-in-law?"

Green's smile crooked at an odd angle. "Since we saved them from the lynch mob, they've left town."

"Saved them from Colonel Ashford, you mean."

"He can get worked up if he's not reined in," Green said.

&

*O*n July 6, the new cabinet arrived to meet with the king in the Blue Room of the palace. Kalakaua kept them waiting. When he finally entered, it was as if a thundercloud had swept into the room. He listened, sullen and silent, as William Green read the new constitution. It stripped the king's powers, and gave them to the cabinet. Kalakaua's scowl darkened as the list of qualifications for voters was read. All voters must satisfy property or income requirements. Most native Hawaiians wouldn't qualify. Finished, Green laid the constitution on the table before the king. The room was deadly quiet.

"Will Your Majesty approve and sign the document?" Green finally asked.

Kalakaua glowered at the four self-appointed ministers. "Without the ratification of the people or their representatives?" He shook his head. "You're asking me to abrogate the constitution established by King Kamehameha III. It's been the law of the land for the last twenty-three years."

The ministers sat silent.

Kalakaua fingered the document on the table in front of him. "And it discriminates against voters based on race."

"Not on race," Thurston said. "Only on condition." He smiled. "If people don't have the income or property to qualify as voters right now, this constitution offers them an incentive to improve their condition so they can vote."

"But," Kalakaua said, "it says white men can vote after a short residency in the islands, without even becoming citizens. Oriental immigrants, even those who've been naturalized, are permanently barred."

Again, the ministers sat silent.

Kalakaua continued with questions and comments, interspersed with periods of silence when he'd gaze into space. Then he'd resume his argument, only to be rebuffed by the four ministers. They grew more irritated as the day wore on. The sun was going down when Clarence Ashford, the attorney general, abruptly stood up and looked down at the king.

"Must I remind you that we are now the legal cabinet, and in charge of the only organized military force in the kingdom?"

Green nodded, then placed a pen in front of the king, looking him straight in the eye.

"Even Judge Dole, who you know is fair-minded and moderate, has said if you don't sign this new constitution, you'll be attacked, and a republic will be declared."

Kalakaua stopped his protest, and stared at them in silence. Finally, he reached for the pen. "You've made your point, gentlemen," he said, "as clear as the point of a bayonet."

$\mathcal{P}$rincess Lili`uokalani and Queen Kapi`olani returned from the garden party at Buckingham Palace, talking happily about their upcoming tour of Europe. A page stopped them as they crossed the lobby of the Alexandra Hotel.

"There's a message for you from the United States."

Liliu went to the concierge's desk, and he handed her the cablegram. A friend who'd sailed from Honolulu on June 30 had sent a telegraph to New York when he reached San Francisco, and it was then sent by undersea cable to London.

The princess read the message and stood motionless, remembering the one-line note jotted in her journal that morning before they left for Queen Victoria's party: "Is there trouble at home?" The cable stated simply, "A revolutionary movement has been inaugurated in the Hawaiian Islands by those of foreign blood or American birth."

Liliu translated the cable for Queen Kapi`olani. The trip back would take almost a month. They determined to leave for Honolulu at once.

Chapter 15 ————

July 24, 1887

$\mathcal{M}$r. Cleghorn deposited my monthly pay in the bank today. He showed me the account book when he returned to Ainahau. It made me happy to see how after only ten months my savings are growing.

He went to the bank early because the news in town is that Queen Kapiʻolani and Princess Liliʻuokalani are due back from England any day. When their ship arrives, there'll be such crowds that the shops and bank might close. Kaʻiulani was so excited that we rode straight up to see Diamond Head Charlie at the lookout. He promised to send word the moment he spies any large steamship headed for the harbor.

It's hard to believe we'll soon be celebrating Kaʻiulani's twelfth birthday. When I first came, she was just a little girl. She's grown taller, and is filling out her dresses. I try not to smile when she asks her father delicate questions. Mr. Cleghorn's Scottish reserve gets the better of him and he says, "You must speak to Miss Laura about that."

Life has been good here. Kaʻiulani and I are more like friends now than governess and charge. She still does her lessons dutifully, but we have an unusual bond, perhaps because we each lost a parent so recently.

I'm glad the queen and princess will be back soon. There have been such strange changes in the government. Imagine Mr. Thurston in the cabinet, the one who couldn't tolerate the king's policies, now one of his closest advisors. And Mr. Ashford, the brother of Colonel Ashford, who nearly hanged Premier Gibson. He's there as well. I don't know the others, but they're men of foreign ancestry. The last cabinet had three native Hawaiians. This one has none. I wish I knew what was going on.

Out here at Waikiki, I don't always hear the town news, and Mr. Cleghorn has been unusually quiet of late. The British commissioner, Mr. Wodehouse, has been here several times to confer with him. They go off walking the grounds where no one can hear them. David and Lucien haven't come lately either. They're busy, Mr. Cleghorn says, with political matters and work. Maybe it's just as well. There's some new tension between them. Ka'iulani thinks it's because they both like me. She folds her arms and, with a stern face, says that I'd better not go away with either of them. But I remember Lucien saying it wouldn't be long before we'd see big changes. How did he know? It feels like something's shifted and starting to spin. I hope the return of the royal ladies will put it all to rest.

&

(W)ell-wishers thronged the wharf, waiting to welcome Queen Kapi'olani and Princess Lili'uokalani home to Honolulu. All the ships in the harbor were decked with celebration bunting, but the mood of the crowd was subdued. Mr. Cleghorn, Ka`iulani, and Laura boarded a small tugboat that chugged out to the steamship *Australia* to bring the royal party ashore. They stood at the prow, straining for a glimpse of the queen and princess. When Ka`iulani caught sight of them, she waved so hard that Mr. Cleghorn leaned over to remind her that people were watching, and she should comport herself in a manner befitting a princess. She held back, but only until her royal aunts alighted on the deck of the tugboat. Then she leapt forward to embrace them and adorn them with leis of flowers and maile vines.

When the tug reached the wharf, the crowd pressed forward. Thousands of tear-streaked brown faces lifted toward the ali`i in welcome, sharing the royal women's grief without a word being spoken. Their joy and sadness rose and fell like the crests and troughs of great waves that broke again and again in gentle, rolling cries of "Aloha, aloha."

The men of the new cabinet met the party when they stepped onto the wharf, shook their hands, and escorted them to a royal carriage. The king's staff accompanied them to `Iolani Palace where Kalakaua waited to greet them.

Mr. Cleghorn stopped his carriage behind the royal party as the king walked down the steps to meet his wife and sister. He looked glad to see them, but his face was marred with the mark of some great strain, like someone who hid a deep, bleeding wound beneath his coat. Laura remembered the lynch mob that had almost murdered Mr. Gibson, and wondered.

ᐫ

"*D*amn the king!" Thurston paced across Judge Dole's office and spun on his heel. "He's supposed to comply with the advice of his ministers, but he won't even see us." He started back across the floor. "Then he vetoes everything we send him."

"I reviewed the law," Dole said. "It's within his right."

"You should've taken away the veto power when you drafted the new constitution, Lorrin," Stephen Price said. "There's going to be hell to pay if we don't get that sugar treaty renewed. The planters are frantic. If we don't have favored status with the United States for our exports, there are only one or two plantations that can survive."

"Sit down, Lorrin." Dole nodded toward a chair. "Let's think this through."

Thurston slumped in the chair at the front of Dole's desk.

"To sign the treaty, the United States is pushing for exclusive use of the Pearl River as a harbor," Dole said.

"And Kalakaua said he'd veto that," Stephen said. "All the natives oppose it."

"Maybe it doesn't matter, though," Dole said. "You can override his veto with a two-thirds vote in the legislature. Just remind him, and perhaps he'll come around. He really doesn't have much choice."

Thurston perked up. "You're right. I think we can pull in a few favors and get two thirds. But the king has gotten very chummy lately with the British commissioner and Archie Cleghorn. I don't like the looks of that."

"Wodehouse would like the British to have closer ties with these islands," Dole said. "They'd be an important link in a chain from Canada right on down to Australia."

"And Cleghorn, being Scottish, wouldn't mind that a bit," Stephen said. "He may see it as protection of his daughter's claim to the throne. The king's health hasn't been so good. I wouldn't put it past Cleghorn and Wodehouse to propose a regency, with them in charge, to reign on Ka`iulani's behalf until she reaches the age of majority."

Thurston drummed the desk with his fingers. "Kalakaua might agree to something like that, just to spite us." He put his fingertips on a bronze paperweight on Dole's desk, and slid it back and forth. "We need to make some new moves on this chessboard." He sat up straight. "Say, what about approaching Lili`uokalani? She's educated by Americans, a loyal church member, and even on the Board of Missions. Plus, she's a woman." He grinned. "And in a crisis, women tend to obey the closest man."

Stephen laughed, and nodded approval. Thurston stood, and picked up his straw hat from atop the old iron safe. "We need to hogtie the king, remove every bit of influence he has in running this kingdom." He put his hat on his head and turned to Stephen. "Next time you're playing cards with John Dominis, let me know. I'm up for a game."

Stephen rose to go. "I'll do that, Lorrin. What kind of game did you have in mind?"

Thurston threw his arm around Stephen's shoulder. "A game where the jacks are wild and the queen is the high card." He laughed and looked at Dole. "See you later, Sanford."

When they were gone, Dole sat thinking about his trip with Princess Lili`uokalani to Niihau to see about the preservation of a species of bird. He remembered how the natives flocked to greet and honor her, carrying gifts of food wrapped in ti leaves.

When they toured the island, she'd commented that she'd like to introduce o'o birds on the island of Kauai, where Dole grew up. On its wings, the o'o has a choice yellow feather from which the royal cloaks of the ancient Hawaiian chiefs were made. Since there were just a few tiny yellow feathers on each bird, hunters captured them, plucked the coveted feathers, and let the birds go. It could take generations to make just one cloak.

"There's a flower on Kauai similar to the lehua blossom," the princess had said then. "The o'o drinks its nectar. So you see, Judge, how they are true Hawaiians?" He was struck by the lilt in her voice. "Flowers are necessary for their very life."

Her radiant expression was so like his Hawaiian *kahu* growing up. His mother had died when he was just a few days old, and he wouldn't have survived, except that his missionary father put him in the care of a Hawaiian woman who nursed him, loved him, sang him *meles*, and taught him Hawaiian lore. As he grew, other children teased that he was of American blood, but of Hawaiian milk.

Dole felt in his vest pocket, took out a worn, folded note, opened it, and looked at the paper a long time. It was a faded, penciled scrap of a Rudyard Kipling ballad:

Oh, East is East and West is West and never the twain shall meet,
Till Earth and Sky stand presently at God's great Judgment Seat....

☙

"It should not have been done, Kunane," Princess Lili'uokalani glared across the breakfast table at the king.

The king looked back, his face solemn. "I didn't see any other way to hang on to the monarchy and keep the kingdom independent."

"Ceding Pearl Harbor to the United States is like making a

nest for the fox in the hen house. You know the history. These people are never satisfied. You give and they take more."

"If I vetoed it, the cabinet would override me with a vote in the legislature. It'd be another humiliation for the monarchy, more evidence of our powerlessness. Anyway, it's not permanent." A retainer came to the table to offer the king a platter of sliced pineapple. He waved her away and looked back at his sister. "If the treaty ends, the navy leaves."

Liliu shook her head and set down her teacup.

"My dear sister," Kalakaua went on. "Our prosperity depends on this sugar treaty. You know I'm looking for ways to change that, but changing an economy takes time. This is the best option we have right now."

"So you cheerfully go to work in the cause of those who abuse you."

Kalakaua wiped his mouth with his linen napkin. "Is that not what we were taught by our missionary teachers?"

"Don't mock, Kunane. You know how I feel about that. Just because the Missionary Party is so unchristian doesn't mean there's no value in the religion."

Kalakaua sighed. "You're right. I'm sorry." He lowered his voice. "There's something I want to share with you, Liliu, that I've never told anyone. It weighs on me."

Concerned at his somber tone, she leaned in.

"When I was a boy, maybe only five years old, our grandfather told me a prophecy of our ancestor Liliha. She said that the Kamehameha dynasty would die out, and that our family would come to reign, but would lose the kingdom to foreigners. I never told you because I didn't want to worry you with what may be just an old superstition." His smile was sad. "But so far, two parts of that prophecy have come true. And my health is failing."

Liliu was shaken, but maintained a calm demeanor. Kalakaua continued, pronouncing her birth name.

"Liliu Loloku Walania Kamakaeha. Even your name means 'tearful eyes and burning pain.' I fear what you'll see in the future. If I've erred, please forgive me."

Liliu straightened up. "You're not making it easy, Kunane. You ask me to forgive something I think is totally wrong, that leads down a path from which we may never recover. If we're to lose the country, you took a giant step toward it by signing this treaty." She rose to go.

"Don't go away *huhu*," the king said. "It's not time to be mad at each other. I need your support."

Liliu looked down at him. Compassion and indignation warred in her heart. She knew he always did his best for the country, thinking that if the wealthy haoles were satisfied with their material gain, they'd remain loyal to the crown. He'd believed the wealth of the sugar trade would spread throughout the kingdom, not enrich one class only. He'd never foreseen that material greed would beget political greed, and turn childhood friends into traitors. She was angry that he'd given in to their pressure, but most angered by what the Missionary Party had done. She was just too peeved to admit it.

"You are the king. But what you've done is unforgivable."

"Dear Liliu, don't you turn against me too. What was that old prayer? 'It's in pardoning that we are pardoned.'"

Liliu suppressed a shudder. The next line was, "And in dying that we are born to eternal life." He was only in his fifties, but he looked so old and tired.

The king stood, came round the table, and took Liliu's hands in his. "When you forgive me, raise our flag over Washington Place. I'll be able to see it from my bedroom window at the palace." He leaned forward and kissed his sister's forehead. "I'll look for it every day."

&

October 12, 1887

I've never seen Ka`iulani so excited. Princess Liliu invited us to spend a whole week at Washington Place. She's arranged a dance to celebrate her birthday. Privately, she told Mr. Cleghorn that she's concerned the princess might be missing her mother. But she told Ka`iulani, now that she's growing up she needs a more grown-up party. All her friends are invited. Hannah and Lizzie will be there. It'll be fun to see them and spend a week in Honolulu. It seems impossible it's already been a year since I came to work for the Cleghorns.

&

*P*rincess Liliu heard the carriage drive to the side of the house next to the kitchen window where she and Wakeki were mixing up a cake for Ka`iulani's party.

"That should be John," she said, wiping her hands on her apron.

John opened the screen door and walked into the kitchen.

"Did you bring the fish for the luau?" Liliu asked.

"I was busy taking some boxes to the wharf for the Aldriches."

Wakeki, who faced the counter, measuring flour and milk into a bowl, turned to look over her shoulder at John. Her eyes narrowed. He ignored her.

"Send Joe for it," John said. "I've got things to do today."

"Won't you be here for the party?" Liliu said.

"No, I'm playing cards this evening. Besides, I can't stand the noise with all those children around."

"Come in the parlor for a minute," Liliu said. "I need to speak with you about Mother."

John walked out of the kitchen, with Liliu behind him. He went into the parlor and turned.

"Well, what is it?"

"She's getting weaker, John. She won't get out of bed. She misses you when you're gone so much."

"I'll go talk to her."

"I think she slides down on purpose to get your attention." Liliu paused. "We never know how much time we'll have with loved ones. Remember how fast my sister declined. One day she was full of life, and a few weeks later —"

"What's your point, Lydia?"

"Your mother regrets not having grandchildren. Wouldn't it lift her spirits to know she has a grandson? Aimoku looks so much like you. She must suspect —"

"It's out of the question. I don't know why you even bring it up." John walked past her and up the stairs.

&

Ka'iulani's dance was like a miniature ball. The young guests, dressed in gowns and suits, were announced by one of Liliu's servants as they entered, and were presented to the little princess and her aunt, just as the chamberlain would do at the palace.

Lucien brought Laura's cousins. Lizzie bounced along as usual, unable to hide her excitement, but Hannah surprised Laura. Her quiet demeanor mixed well with formal dress and she appeared quite grown-up.

While the young people danced to the music of the Royal Hawaiian Band, practicing the steps they'd learned at Mrs. Strong's dance school, Lucien walked with Laura around the grounds at Washington Place. She wore a simple silk gown, and instead of doing up her hair in a French knot, let it hang unrestrained. Lucien caught a trace of Chinese jasmine, but she wasn't wearing flowers. He thought it might be perfume. He didn't know she'd learned from Ka'iulani how to hide pikake blossoms in her hair.

"I'm glad you're in town," Lucien said. "We finished work for Thurston's client at Waikiki, so I won't have a chance to go out to Ainahau as much anymore."

Laura nodded. "I'm glad I'm here too. It'll be nice to spend a week."

Lucien turned to her and took her hands. He longed to kiss her, to touch those soft lips again, but kukui-nut torches lit up the grounds, and too many people were around.

"I want to see you more."

"You can come every day I'm here."

"No," Lucien said. "I want to be with you for more than just a week."

Laura tilted her head and looked up at him. He felt disoriented, intoxicated. He leaned toward her, unable to resist. As he drew closer, she turned aside. Her hair brushed his cheek, and the scent of jasmine set him on fire.

"Why, Mr. McBride," she said, lowering her eyes. "That sounds serious. Perhaps you'd better explain your intentions."

Laura walked ahead, smiling to herself. Lucien waited a moment as if dazed, and then caught up to her.

"I'm sorry, Laura. That was too forward of me."

She glanced up. "I accept your apology."

Flirting was such guilty fun. She lowered her eyes again. But he was getting so intense. And at the same time she flirted with him, she really wished David were there.

&

*L*ucien did come every day that week after work, sometimes bringing Hannah and Lizzie to play. He was confused about how happy he was every moment in Laura's presence, and how he couldn't concentrate much at work when he was away. Something else disturbed him — how she stayed free, just beyond his grasp. He wanted her. He wanted to have her. She let him get close, sometimes almost let him kiss her again, and then just moved away. It was like trying to catch a rainbow.

There was something more too. She no longer wore her proper muslin dresses. She always had on bright holokus, like the Hawaiians. She was tan now, her light hair vivid against her skin, and her blue eyes the color of cornflowers in wheat. She walked about Washington Place barefoot, her long hair flowing, adorned with flowers behind her ear and garlands around her neck. Her speech was woven with Hawaiian words, and she and Ka`iulani giggled together like sisters.

The very worst was the last day when she was getting ready to go back to Ainahau. He was in agony. Then David Kahiko arrived, just back from a trip to the big island of Hawaii with the king. They'd gone, he said, to look into developing new forms of agriculture that could diversify the economy in the islands. The very worst was how Laura lit up when she saw David.

168

ଉ

Stephen Price shuffled the cards and dealt them to the men at the table. Dr. Trousseau looked at his hand and folded. John Dominis fanned out his cards, moved one from the edge to the middle, and remained quiet. Mr. McBride seemed content, and Thurston fidgeted in his chair. In turn, the men drew from the deck and discarded until they were ready to play their hands.

"So, Governor," Thurston said to John, "you may be one of the most important men in the kingdom soon."

"How's that?" John said.

"We're tired of Kalakaua's vetoes. He's nothing but a hindrance, and we mean to get rid of him. We're going to ask your lady to take the throne."

John raised his eyebrows.

"As long as she's cooperative," Thurston said, "you'll no longer be just the husband of a princess. You'll be a queen's consort. Head of the royal household and master of ʻIolani Palace."

John sipped his whiskey, but said nothing. The men played their hands, and John raked in the pot.

"Looks like luck is with you, Governor," Thurston said, nodding. "A good sign."

ଉ

After breakfast, Princess Liliu sat on the verandah at Washington Place, making notes in her journal. She looked out at the golden shower trees as a flock of white doves flew over. Up toward Nuuanu, soft clouds edged in rainbows fell like leis around the mountain greenery. She wrote a few more lines.

I dreamt that I stood on a lava bank. A white *tapa* cloth was spread on the next bank, and with some trouble I climbed up. They say good fortune is coming to me.

For the first time in a year, John has been attentive. I mention it because it's so unusual, and I'm happy to have him so. We returned from the races at 5:00 p.m. and had supper out on the grass. He was rather in a faultfinding mood. However, he became good-natured and slept up here last night. John is … lovesick(?) What a change.

Chapter 16 ———

January 27, 1888

Mr. Gibson died in San Francisco. His son brought his body back to Honolulu, honoring his last wishes to be buried in the islands. Now that he's dead and can cause no trouble for the Missionary Party, their editorials about him are actually charitable. But their personal comments are not.

When I was downtown, I joined the line of mourners filing past his bier to pay their last respects. The Hawaiians came by the thousands, many in tears. Mr. Gibson was loyal to their king, and had done his best for them. I cried when I remembered how he asked me if I "reversed in the waltz" at my first ball. The kingdom seemed much happier then.

When I reached the open coffin, I was shocked to see that through some process of the embalming, Mr. Gibson's skin had turned quite black. The contrast of the dark skin with his white hair and beard was startling.

Out in the street, I happened to see Judge Dole and Mr. Thurston. Lucien was with them. They'd been ahead of me in the line moving past Mr. Gibson's coffin. I nodded toward them, and when Lucien saw me, he immediately took his leave to greet me. He was amused by some joke they'd shared. He said one of their friends remarked that Mr. Gibson's complexion was approximating the color of his soul.

I told him an old Hawaiian man in line in front of me thought differently. When he viewed Mr. Gibson's body, he took off his hat in respect, held it to his breast, and said, "Now he's one of us."

&

*L*ucien drove his carriage up to the front of Washington Place. A retainer came to take the reins of his horse. Wakeki met him at the door.

"The princess will see you in her library." She pointed to the salon at the left of the entry.

Bits of conversation he'd had the day before with Stephen Price and Lorrin Thurston ran through his mind as he walked toward the salon.

"The princess will be receptive to you, Lucien. You know her better than we do," Thurston said. "And she distrusts me, given how I became a cabinet minister."

"That's right," Stephen said. "She may suspect an ulterior motive in what is just a simple suggestion."

Since when is changing monarchs a simple suggestion? Lucien didn't really want to be here. The princess could be direct and forceful when she had a mind to. And he didn't know whether what Thurston and Price were asking was the best idea anyway. He liked Kalakaua, with all his faults. He'd done some good things for the country, hadn't he? Just because he vetoed their bills — wasn't that his right as king?

Liliu turned from her desk as Lucien walked in.

"Your Highness," he said, and bowed low.

"So formal, Lucien," the princess said. "Please, sit down. Is this an official visit?"

Lucien sat in a chair next to her desk. Too agitated to think of pleasantries, he jumped right in. "I've come with a request from the Hawaiian League."

Liliu's face grew serious. She straightened and sat back. "What is it?"

"Well, they're frustrated that the king vetoes every bill. They want to know if you'd be willing to reign if he were dethroned."

Liliu stared at him. "What do they mean by 'dethroned,' Lucien? What do they propose to do to him?"

"I...well —"

"How is he to be dethroned? Murder?"

"No, Your Highness! They didn't say anything like that."

"What did they say?"

"Just that they want the king to retire, and that if you'd take the throne, they'd back you."

Liliu turned away and looked out the window. "Just because I support these missionaries in their good works, they think I'll cast in my lot with them on anything, even my own brother's overthrow."

She thought of all the times they'd come to her for donations or help, and had never gone away empty-handed. She turned back to Lucien. He shrank under the heat of her steady gaze.

"The king may do some things that I don't agree with, Lucien, like ceding the use of the Pearl River to the United States. But I'm appalled that these people, many of whom I've entertained in my own home, now expect me to cooperate in a conspiracy against the lawful authority of the king." Her eyes flashed. "You can tell them no. That's final."

Lucien stood to go, and bowed. "Please don't be offended with me, Your Highness. I'm just the messenger."

Liliu softened. He looked so young. She nodded and waved him away. He left, and she turned back to her desk to lift her cup. Her hand trembled, and coffee spilled into the saucer. Later that evening, she went and told the king.

❧

*O*n Stephen Price's verandah, Thurston sat sipping a cold plantation tea. He swished his glass to mix in the pineapple juice that had settled to the bottom.

"Maybe Lili`uokalani wouldn't refuse to take the throne if there were a native revolt to unseat the king."

"A native revolt? How could that happen?" Stephen said.

"There are a few malcontents around town. They're not happy that Kalakaua ceded Pearl Harbor to the U.S. They must know, like Lucien said, the princess doesn't like it either. Maybe we can fan their discontent to petition the king to abdicate and make her queen."

"I don't know," Stephen said. "What if it gets out of hand? They might throw the cabinet out too."

"There's not much chance of that." Thurston smiled. "With the new US minister in town and American warships always in the harbor, I'm confident that American lives and property will be protected."

"And their positions in the government?" Stephen said.

Thurston raised his glass in a toast. "That too." His smile widened. "I've heard tell that Stevens, our new minister, is an ardent annexationist from way back. And he's not too happy about any British leanings in our little kingdom either." He sat back in the wicker chair and finished off his tea. "By the way, I think your 'merger' may be falling through."

"What are you talking about, Thurston?"

"I can't get an honest day's work out of young McBride lately. He's so moony over your niece." He picked a spearmint leaf out of his glass and chewed it. "He won't concentrate, and he forgets things. He's falling behind in his paperwork."

"I'm sorry for your trouble," Stephen said, smiling. "But that sounds like the merger is progressing."

"It takes two for a merger."

"What do you mean?"

"From what Lucien let slip, I'd say your niece has set her sights on other horizons."

Stephen set his ice tea on the table. "What other horizons?"

"Well," Thurston said, "to hear Lucien tell it, she's gone native; wears holokus all the time, goes barefoot, flowers in her hair, speaking Hawaiian with the young princess … and making eyes at David Kahiko."

"Damn!" Stephen said. "I told her to stay away from him."

"Well, Lucien would like some help with that. I suspect he's ready to propose, but she's distracted with that half-caste."

"I've got to get her back from the Cleghorns," Stephen said. "Maybe if I told her Katherine needs her."

"I don't know," Thurston said. "She knows you have plenty of help here. I think the only way you can get her back is for her job to end."

"But Cleghorn's happy with her work. He's mentioned it several times. Do you think we can pressure him to fire her?"

Thurston pushed his chair back from the table and stretched his legs. "He wouldn't have to fire her. If Ka`iulani no longer needed a governess, the job would just disappear."

Stephen sat back. "What are you thinking?"

"I'm thinking," Thurston put his chin in his hand, tapping his cheek with his finger, "we could kill a whole flock of birds with a couple of well-placed stones."

❧

March 25, 1888

*T*wo days ago, I went with Ka`iulani and Princess Liliu to attend a ceremony to throw the switch that would light Honolulu for the first time. Mr. Thurston, in his capacity as minister of the interior, escorted us.

It was dark when we reached the light station above the city. Mr. Thurston said a few words about progress in Hawaii, and then a chair was brought for Ka`iulani to stand on so she could reach the switch. The superintendent of the light station helped her up, and we all looked toward town. She threw the switch, and almost instantly, all Honolulu was ablaze in electric light. It was thrilling and shocking at the same time — like something beautiful yet unnatural.

Mr. Thurston was gracious to the princesses, but something in his manner makes me very uneasy. I just can't put my finger on it.

As we went through town on the drive home, the horses shied away or tried to leap over the unfamiliar bands of light and shadow that striped the streets, cast by the gleaming lampposts along our route.

❧

As the carriage pulled up in front of the quarantine hospital, Laura felt her heart beat faster than usual. Don't worry, she told herself. The hospital, built by the king to provide medical exams for lepers before they were sent to their permanent home at Molokai, hadn't opened yet. She and Ka`iulani were to join Princess Lili`uokalani and other invited guests to welcome seven Catholic nursing sisters just arrived from Syracuse, New York.

After Father Damien died of the dreaded disease, there was an acute need for nurses at the leper colony on Molokai. The king sent inquiries to many countries and to people of many religions, asking if there were any, men or women, who would volunteer. There was no response for a long time. Anyone who went to Molokai would have to live there the rest of their lives, in isolation with the lepers — and chances were slim they'd escape Father Damien's fate.

The king invited all the religious denominations in Honolulu to greet the sisters and honor the service they'd come to offer. Laura thought that for such a noble act, even those whose tenets differed from the Catholics' would come to welcome the nuns. When she and Ka`iulani entered the hospital, however, aside from Princess Liliu and the king and queen, only seven other women had gathered to receive the sisters. Among them was her friend, Isobel Strong, who ran the dance school.

Laura and Ka`iulani made their curtsies before the king and queen and Princess Liliu. Then Laura sidled up to her friend.

"Isobel," she whispered, "where is everybody?"

"It's an embarrassment, isn't it?" Isobel whispered back. "Everyone I talked to had some kind of excuse — too busy, headaches, or other engagements. But I think they're afraid, or else they're bigoted, and don't like Catholics."

When the sisters arrived, the royal family greeted them. Then everyone had a tour of the hospital, which had been decorated with fresh flowers. It was simple, but neatly arranged, furnished with cots, linens, and white-painted furniture. The nuns seemed pleased.

The king's speech thanking the sisters was so sincere that Laura blinked to keep back tears. It looked like it was all Ka`iulani and Isobel could do to keep from crying too. There were no chairs in the room, so the women stood listening, their lacy dresses and flowered hats in sharp contrast to the pale, black-robed figures next to them.

The sisters were shown their quarters, where they'd stay a few days before leaving for Molokai. They were tired from their long trip, overland from New York and then by steamship to Honolulu, so the ladies took their leave to let them rest.

At the front of the hospital, the king and queen prepared to depart in their carriage. Ka`iulani talked with Liliu. Seeing Isobel and Laura walking together, the king beckoned to them.

"I was pleased with your husband's painting of the new Japanese laborers at work in the cane fields," he said to Isobel. "We've been able to improve conditions for the workers, and they've sent good reports back to Japan about their treatment. The emperor may be willing to let more come. These people are important to the continuing prosperity of Hawaii, so I'd like to send you and your husband to paint at another plantation. I want to give the picture as a gift to the mikado."

Isobel dipped in a curtsy. "I'm sure my husband would be honored. Unfortunately, I can't join him. I'm expecting my mother and stepfather for a visit."

A few other ladies came out of the hospital and walked toward the king's carriage to say goodbye.

"They're sailing up from Tahiti," Isobel continued, "where they've been living in hopes of improving Mr. Stevenson's health. He suffers respiratory problems."

"Who's Mr. Stevenson?" said one of the ladies who'd overheard the conversation.

Isobel turned to answer. "My stepfather, Robert Louis Stevenson. He's written several books."

"I've never heard of him," the woman said. "What's he written?"

Isobel was surprised the woman didn't know, but even more surprised when the king replied, "*Treasure Island,* and *Dr. Jekyll and Mr. Hyde.*"

&

*L*aura and Ka`iulani were doing lessons under the banyan at the front of the house when they noticed a tall, thin figure ambling up the shaded drive. Ka`iulani grabbed Laura's arm, her dark eyes wide.

"I think it's Mr. Stevenson," she said in a low voice. "Papa said he met him at the Thistle Club last week and invited him to call." She looked back up the drive. "What do we do? Papa won't be home till dinnertime."

"Well, we'll just offer him tea, I guess," Laura said, standing as the gentleman made his way toward the banyan.

Ka`iulani stood and brushed out the folds of her holoku. Laura tried to think of something to say as the famous writer approached. He was willowy, with long dark hair, and wore an odd costume — not quite slovenly, but careless — loose flannel pants and a velveteen jacket over a flowing shirt and tie. His gait was light and graceful, and as he neared, his large eyes seemed to glow warmly, like embers, in his slender face.

"Good afternoon," he said. "Mr. Cleghorn did me the honor of suggesting I call." His Scots accent left no doubt.

"You're Mr. Stevenson," Ka'iulani said.

He nodded.

"My papa won't be home for a while, but would you care to stay for tea?"

Mr. Stevenson smiled. Laura invited him to sit on the bench with Ka'iulani, and went to call Kainoa to bring tea.

When she came back, Mr. Stevenson was already regaling the princess with tales of his family's harrowing adventures sailing up to Hawaii from the southern seas. His talk bristled with black squalls astern to port, waterspouts ahead to starboard, and lashing rains, all animated by seafaring slang and soothed by romantic names of strange island ports like Nuka Hiva, Anaho, and Taaka Uku.

The girls sat spellbound as he continued with stories of shipwrecks, cannibals, pirates, and Polynesian legends. The Pacific, he said, was a stirabout of epics and races, virtues and crimes. His words played like light and color to illumine images he created in the air before them, in which their time lay alongside something ancient and beautiful. They glanced up only when Kainoa brought a tray with tea and biscuits, for a moment not certain if she were one of his vivid apparitions.

"I never knew the world was so amusing," Mr. Stevenson said. "All our visits to the islands have been more like dreams than realities. I've had more fun and pleasure these past months than ever before, and more health than any time in ten long years." He accepted a cup from Kainoa and thanked her, then took a sip. "Though the sea is a deathful place, I like to be there. Fine, clean emotions. Air better than wine. And I like squalls — when they're over." Laura and Ka`iulani laughed. He gently shook his head and smiled. "And to draw near to a new island, I cannot say how much I like."

The afternoon passed in genial conversation, Mr. Stevenson asking many questions, and listening intently to the girls as they talked. He commented with bits of poetry or affectionate laughter. Not until Mr. Cleghorn's carriage came up the drive did they raise their heads to see it was dusk. Mr. Stevenson rose to greet his fellow countryman, then asked if they might come to meet his family later in the week at their rented house down the way at Waikiki.

☙

After the Cleghorns and Laura had visited Mr. Stevenson's family, he often stopped at Ainahau in the afternoons when he took daily walks for his health. He said sometimes his house swarmed with curiosity-seeking haoles from Honolulu, and he needed to escape. And Mrs. Stevenson told Laura that he preferred the company of Polynesians, whom he called, she said, "God's sweetest works."

He'd entertain Ka`iulani and Laura with stories of Scotland, or sweep them up in discussions of literature and poetry, treating them as equals in the conversation, then make them laugh by telling them he wrote his own "paper people" to please himself and God Almighty, with no ulterior purpose. Sometimes he seemed a wise man, other times a boy who loved pickles and adventures. He'd play croquet as any number of fictitious characters he'd invent on the spot and bring to life in high drama. Sometimes he'd bring his flageolet, and weave tunes like a master spirit, attracting the peacocks to scrutinize this new, rare bird.

One afternoon, when Ka`iulani had gone with her father to Honolulu, Mr. Stevenson stopped by and sat awhile under the banyan to talk with Laura.

"I've been spending time with the king," Stevenson said, his eyes bright. "And what a king he is, like you'd find in a fairy tale." He laughed. "We've been going over the book he wrote on the legends and myths of Hawaii. It's a fine piece of work."

His enthusiasm for Kalakaua stood in sharp contrast to the mumblings Laura had heard from some of the people in Honolulu. Her own experience of the king as kindly and intelligent was undermined by their backbiting, like a subtle poison that colored her thoughts and feelings with misgivings she couldn't shake.

"You know, Mr. Stevenson, you hear so many...things said about the king."

"Oh, and especially from the religious set, wouldn't you say?" He regarded her knowingly. "You're a mature young lady, Laura, so I won't mince words with you. I can tell you things perhaps I wouldn't say in the presence of our little royal maid." Stevenson's face grew serious. "Their cloak of religion is hard to penetrate, mixed up as it is with enduring truths. But I'll tell you one thing, lassie. I do not call by the name of religion that which fills a man with bile."

"Well, they say he's a drunkard, but I've never seen him drink."

"Oh," Stevenson said, "it's true the king can drink any sailor under the table. He'll take a whole bottle of fizz like it was a small glass of sherry. One day I calculated five bottles of champagne in one afternoon, and at the end, the king was quite presentable, even perceptibly more dignified." Stevenson's smile returned, and he leaned in and lowered his voice. "I hear his

secret is to drink a glass of milk mixed with poi before he enter-
tains visiting ships' officers. The concoction saves his stomach
and keeps his head clear."

He leaned back against the banyan. "And yet I wish perhaps
he wouldn't drink so much. There's a lingering sadness he strives
to cover up with the title of 'Merry Monarch,' the dark sadness
of being blotted out." He sighed. "I see it all over the Pacific. The
French in the Marquesas and Tahiti, the Germans in Samoa, the
missionaries here. My own people in India, for that matter. It's
the damned plague of superiority."

"What can be done?" Laura said.

He sat forward, and shook his head. "If I knew that, my dear,
I could change the course of history. The richest part of the joke
is that the missionaries are fine, talented fellows. But this civilization of ours is a dingy, ungentlemanly business. It drops too
much out of a man."

"But they call the king 'uncivilized,'" Laura said, "for trying to
revive the hula. And they say he's not capable of grasping important subjects, and that he brings all kinds of bad influence into
the kingdom."

"Ah, my dear," Stevenson said. "You know, I never meet the
king but that he has a book in his hand. I applaud his efforts to
lift up the people and reinvigorate their spirits with music, art,
and dance. If anything would lift a people, it's that. It springs
out of the deepest parts of us. And I understand his political
efforts too. He wants to introduce any element that will erode the
Missionary Party's dominance, so he looks for ways to diversify
the economy away from sugar. And he's interested in bringing
diverse peoples who will add to the prosperity of the kingdom,
and whose ways are more like the Polynesian than those of
New England. He told me that, on his trip around world, he

was impressed with Buddhism, and even thought to encourage it here as a counterpoint. Anything to dilute the Puritan poison that's killing the people."

Stevenson looked up into the canopy of the banyan, quiet for a moment. Laura watched his eyes follow a bird from branch to branch.

He looked back at Laura. "One thing the king told me about his trip impressed me the most: that in all the countries he's visited, the rulers are segregated from their people and dare not walk among them without armed guards. Yet, Kalakaua said, he moves freely anywhere in his kingdom unaccompanied. Though Hawaii's a small country, and not wealthy compared to some empires, the aloha of his people is greater to him than all their jewels and territory."

Stevenson folded his arms across his chest. "And now, the 'undiscussables.' I suppose you've also heard stories of hula orgies at the palace and the king's boathouse?"

Laura felt a red heat rising up her neck toward her face. She looked down.

"You needn't be embarrassed. I've been to both places for evening entertainment. Do you know what we do?"

She glanced up and shook her head.

"We're served sandwiches, and then we tell stories, recite poetry, and sing songs. Sometimes Isobel's husband draws caricatures of the guests. But I've heard the same gossip you have, that the king chooses a companion for the night by rolling a ball of twine into a group of ladies and selecting the one it reaches, or that half-naked hula dancers entertain." He paused. "Let's suppose that's a fact."

The blush reached her cheeks. She wanted to look away, but Stevenson's eyes held her gaze.

"Let's suppose the king has a weakness for women. Then, perhaps, that wouldn't serve to elevate him, it's true. But does it lower him beneath other men of prestige and position in this society? I daresay, from what I know in the short time I've been in Honolulu, such behavior would only prove that he's their equal." He shrugged his shoulders. "And what conversation for the parlors of missionaries. It draws more a picture of their own hearts than that of the king's." Stevenson crossed his legs, and put his elbow on his knee and his chin in his hand.

"He's a good man, Laura. Full of the joy of life and of laughter. He strives to do the best for the people, whatever his faults. I wonder if these missionaries ever thought how Christ was so continually substituting affirmations for the 'Thou shalt nots' of the Old Testament.' To love one's neighbor as oneself' is certainly harder, but states life so much more actively, gladly, and kindly, that you can begin to see some pleasure in it."

Laura was on the edge of tears. He made so much sense.

"I see it more important to do right than not to do wrong. And further, the one is possible; to do the other has always been and will ever be impossible."

Laura wiped away a teardrop that slid down her cheek.

"Now then." Stevenson leaned toward her. "I didn't mean to make you cry. Perhaps I've spoken too frankly." He pulled a handkerchief from his pocket and handed it to her. She dabbed her eyes.

"No. I like what you're saying; it's a great relief."

"And so, milady." Stevenson strove to cheer her up, "What of your bright future?"

She told him how she'd come to Hawaii, and alluded to her discomfort in the Price household. She confided her happiness in her companionship with Ka`iulani, and her growing savings toward a medical degree. He grasped her thought with heart and sympathy. Waving his long, slender hands like a magician, he unfolded her imaginary career in brilliant detail before her. When she asked him how he knew, he said it was his specialty to eavesdrop at the doors of hearts.

"Well," Laura said, "to be honest, I sometimes despair of it, sir. It seems a long way off."

"Let me tell you a story," the writer said. "One night when we were on the *Casco*, sailing up from the southern seas, I lay on deck under a wide and starry sky, the night as warm as milk. All of sudden I had a vision. It came on like a flash of lightning. I simply returned back into the past, back to Edinburgh. I remembered all that I'd hoped and feared knocking about on Drummond Street in the rain and the east wind; how I feared I would make a shipwreck, and yet timidly hoped not. How I feared I should never have a friend, far less a wife, and yet passionately hoped I might; how I hoped, if I did not take to drink, I should possibly write one little book. And now, what a change!"

They sat in silence looking at the cool greenery surrounding the clearing. The breeze rippled the topmost leaves of the banyan. Bird song echoed from the palms that spiked above the pandanus trees. Stevenson smiled, picked up his flageolet, and warbled a riff in response. The birds became quiet, as if listening. He lowered the flute from his lips, set it in his lap, and smiled at Laura.

"I feel somehow," he said, "as if I should like that incident set upon a brass plate at the corner of that dreary thoroughfare, for all young people to read, poor devils, when their hearts are down."

Chapter 17 ————

*T*hurston tucked a loaded six-shooter in his coat pocket and looked up at Stephen Price.

"The king doesn't like me. Last time I went to visit him in the bungalow on the palace grounds, I heard footsteps outside the door and a lot of whispering. So this," he patted his pocket, "is just a little insurance."

"Damned shame a cabinet minister has to carry a gun to see the king," Stephen said.

Thurston nodded. "But you know, in the past the sovereigns were held above the law. This way, I'm prepared to respond to an attack without waiting for an official indictment."

The two men walked down the stairs to the street, and Thurston climbed into a waiting surrey.

"I'll let you know how our meeting goes." He grinned down at Stephen. "Here's to slinging the first stone."

&

*A*t the palace, the chamberlain showed Thurston to the library. The king was reading at his table when his guest was announced.

"Come in," Kalakaua said.

Thurston glanced behind him, then walked in, and bowed.

The king looked up and motioned to a chair at the table. "Please, take a seat."

Thurston pulled it out to one side, so his back wasn't to the door, and sat down.

"What is it you wanted to see me about?" the king said.

"Well, Your Majesty, as minister of the interior, I'm concerned with all those things that will improve the kingdom into the future."

The king remained expressionless.

"And after thinking through some of the cabinet's actions since we took office —"

"Took the office," the king said.

"Ah … yes, took office, I think that one of those actions may have been ill-advised."

The king raised a skeptical eyebrow. "Which one?"

"When we called back the young Hawaiians who were studying abroad."

The king regarded him for a long moment. "What do you have in mind, Mr. Thurston?"

"Among other things, Your Majesty, a well-rounded education for those destined to take the throne, including seeing some of the rest of the world and how it's governed."

"Are you proposing to send my wife's nephews back to school?"

"Well, perhaps, but I'm most concerned about the direct line. About the Princess Ka'iulani. In the normal course of events, she's the one most likely to ascend the throne. She should have our support in furthering her education to prepare her to reign."

Kalakaua studied Thurston. "What do you mean by 'our support?'"

"Simply that the cabinet should agree to financial support for the princess to continue her education abroad, and petition the legislature to approve the expenditure."

"She's still a child, really," the king said. "Just thirteen this year."

"That's the best time, while her young mind is still growing. Besides, she's quite mature for her age."

Thurston thought of Ka`iulani's dignity at the city lighting ceremony, and the crowds that had pressed to see her. She was more popular than ever.

Kalakaua tried to read his intentions. This cabinet had done its utmost to bind him hand and foot. Why were they now holding out an olive branch of sorts? They knew his views on the importance of education for young Hawaiians. And he did want Ka`iulani to have the best advantages to prepare her for the future.

Thurston shifted in his chair. "Your Majesty has often referred to how much you enjoyed your own world travels."

The king nodded. Perhaps, whatever their agenda, he should grab this opportunity to get financial backing for the princess's education.

"When would you petition the legislature for funds?"

Thurston smiled for the first time since entering the library.

"I think we could put a resolution in front of them next week. It might be best if the princess could leave just before summer, get settled in, and then start school somewhere in the fall."

"Did you have a place in mind?"

Thurston thought a moment. "No," he said. "That would be up to Your Majesty."

The Last Aloha

&

April 15, 1889

*M*y world has ended. Ka`iulani will leave for England on May 10th to attend boarding school. She's devastated, and has been pleading with her father not to make her go since we received the notice from the king three weeks ago. I'm to pack up my things by the end of the month.

When Mr. Cleghorn showed me the king's proclamation, my first concern was for Ka`iulani. It's so far away, and she's still so young. And then I thought about my savings. Did I have enough to support myself while I looked for new employment? I knew there wasn't enough to go back to San Francisco. When I asked Mr. Cleghorn about going to the bank to put the account under my signature, he said he'd made it easy for me. Since he was downtown every day, he asked Uncle Stephen to go with him to the bank, and transferred the account to him! He said when I move back, I can change it over to my name. He just assumed I'd go there because, of course, a "respectable" young woman doesn't live by herself or work for a living. Now I'm trapped.

Ka`iulani spends her days riding Fairie along the beach. One afternoon I found her down at the stable, brushing her pony and crying. She confided her mother's dying words — that she'd be sent away for a long time, that she'd never marry, and that she'd never be queen. The king's proclamation says she's to return in one year, but she's terrified her mother's prophecy will come true.

Mr. Stevenson has tried to cheer us both up. He tells

Ka`iulani lovely stories of England to ease her fears. And he wrote a touching poem for her about going from her island to his island. One day he jokingly lectured us in a headmaster's tone that "to preserve a proper equanimity is not merely the first part of submission to God, but the chief of possible kindnesses to those about us." I think he sees how Ka`iulani's sadness affects her father. Then he smiled and added, "A little decent resignation is not only becoming, but is likely to be excellent for the health." Perhaps that's how he's made his own peace with the blood on his handkerchief and his medicine bottles.

I had to immediately practice "a little decent resignation," myself because he told us his family is leaving Hawaii as well — headed back to the islands of the southern seas. I can't believe I'll lose them both so soon. It's too much to bear.

⁎

*L*aura put the bright, folded holokus in her trunk. Then she wiggled into her corset, pulling the drawstrings at the back. She heard Kainoa go by her room, and stuck her head out the door to ask her to come and tie the corset tight.

"Why you no wear holoku?" Kainoa said. "Mo' betta."

"My Uncle doesn't allow me to wear them at his house."

Kainoa tied the corset, shaking her head, but said no more. When she left, Laura put on the corset cover, then pulled on a muslin dress. She tied her hair into a French knot and put on her white straw hat. She noticed the light dress and hat made her face look more bronzed. She was glad about that, though the tan would probably fade within a week or so. Then everything would be back to the way it was before she had come to Ainahau.

David came out to play a last round of croquet. It wasn't quite fair, because the corset was a disadvantage. She couldn't lean over to take the shots like she could in her holoku. Still, it was one more game for old-time's sake.

David offered to drive her back to the Prices', but she didn't want to risk her uncle's anger. She told him Lucien had arranged to pick her up around noon. After the game, when Ka`iulani went in the house to ask Kainoa to serve tea, David turned to Laura.

"If you need anything, Malolo, send one of your uncle's servants to the legislature with a note. I'm there almost every day." He took her hand and kissed it. "Don't be sad. I'll keep my eyes open for another opportunity for you. Something will turn up."

Laura looked back toward the house. "Ka`iulani's heartbroken about leaving."

"She is a little young to be leaving home for such a long time. I was surprised when Thurston proposed it to the legislature."

"Thurston proposed it?"

"Yes, as support for the continuance of a strong monarchy. He met with the king, and basically apologized for the cabinet recalling the young Hawaiians who were studying abroad. Then he suggested sending Ka`iulani, since she's in line for the throne. It's a strange request from someone who's always trying to limit the monarchy, but the king accepted it, so I supported the proposal."

"But it's so hard for her," Laura said. "I was eighteen when I left home, and even then it was hard to leave behind everything I knew."

Kainoa was on the verandah, waving at them to come for tea. Just as they sat down, Lucien's carriage came up the drive.

Ka`iulani tried to be brave, but Laura could see the tears begin. Lucien joined them on the verandah, and Laura felt the quiver of tension when David stood to shake his hand.

They sipped tea while the Hawaiian retainers loaded Laura's luggage at the back of Lucien's carriage. No one ate except Lucien, who helped himself to fruit and bread with jam while he carried on the bulk of the conversation. Finally, there was no more delaying the departure. They walked to the carriage, and Laura embraced Ka`iulani.

"I'll be at the wharf next week when your ship sails." Laura's eyes teared. "Look for me."

Ka`iulani nodded, her cheeks wet. She clung to Laura. "I'll look for you until I can't see the islands anymore."

The peacocks screeched as Lucien's carriage moved down the drive. He tried to carry on a light conversation, sharing the latest gossip on the road back to Honolulu. Laura's heart wasn't in it. She felt like she was slipping back into a world that was much too small. But the real dread hit her when she climbed the verandah steps of the Price home and saw Uncle Stephen's triumphant smile as he opened the front door.

§

The next two months, Laura concentrated on lessons with Hannah and Lizzie, now home again for summer vacation, and avoided being alone at any time with her uncle. When the girls were occupied, she'd go upstairs to sit with Aunt Katherine, who had worn away to a whisper. She rarely talked, ate little, and stared with vacuous eyes out the window for hours. After breakfast one morning, while the girls were reading, Laura went upstairs with a tray of tea. Aunt Katherine was gone. Her hollowed out body lay under the coverlet like an abandoned shell, her face still turned to the window. Laura set the tea tray on the table, sat down next to the bed, and sobbed aloud.

&

At the funeral, Laura did what she could to comfort Hannah and Lizzie. She overheard Uncle Stephen make what she thought was a callous remark to one of his business associates who offered condolences — that Katherine had died to him a long time ago. Then he said he was glad Laura was "back home" to take care of him and the girls, and he glanced at her with a strange expression. When the casket was lowered into the grave, Laura saw him staring at her across the open pit. It was an invasive gaze that reminded her of how she'd felt when he embraced her the night he slapped her face and made her get down on the floor to pick up the fallen flowers.

A week later, when the rounds of home visits and people bringing food were finally over, Laura helped Kimiko dispose of her aunt's clothes. She set aside a few things she thought the girls might want: her tortoise-shell comb and mirror, a volume of poetry illustrated with violets, and a tiny book called *Daisies from the Psalms*, which had been open on the nightstand to the page that read, "Unto the upright there ariseth light in the darkness." Kimiko told her there was a trunk up in the attic where Aunt Katherine put all her keepsakes. She went with Laura to unlock the door to the attic stairs.

Laura squeezed around musty old steamer trunks that looked like they'd come around Cape Horn. She moved a few boxes and a wicker baby carriage with porthole windows to reach the humpbacked wooden case with roses painted on the top. It was at the north end of the attic where Kimiko had said it would be. She pulled up a three-legged stool, sat next to the case, and opened the brass latch. Dusty sunlight from the small windows high in the eaves was enough to see by. She was going to just put her aunt's things on top of the other items in the trunk, but when she opened it, she saw a baby's christening gown, so delicately hand-embroidered that she had to take it out to look at it. At first she thought it might be Hannah's or Lizzie's, but the style was older. Underneath it were other little dresses that looked like they might be from the 1850s. There was a tarnished silver baby cup and spoon, and frail needlework samplers wrapped in tissue.

Beneath the samplers was a yellowed envelope with a San Francisco postmark. Laura held it up in the light. It was addressed to her aunt, and the ink had faded brown. She started in recognition. There was no return address, but the handwriting looked like her father's. She opened the flap and took out the letter. It was twenty years old, dated two months and two days after her birth.

Dear Katherine,

Forgive me for not writing sooner. I always felt I owed you an explanation, but there are so many things I can't explain. Like why I fell in love with Malia, or why a family turns against you because of whom you love. Or why you choose to leave your whole life behind.

Stephen said if I wanted a kanaka for a wife, the least I could do was to marry one with property. Malia came from a chiefly line, but her family lost their property in the Great Mahele land division.

I was furious with him. He asked why I would marry

Malia when I could have her as a mistress. Have her! Like so many other haole men do with Hawaiian women. I don't mean to embarrass you, but I must speak frankly. I want you to know the truth.

Malia gave me a beautiful black pearl. I pulled apart our mother's necklace, took the largest pearl, and had it set in gold for her. I had the black one set for me. With these two rings we were wed.

She got pregnant right away. That's why I crawled back to Stephen to ask for a job. I never thanked you for insisting that he give me stock in the enterprise. It was a great help.

When our baby was about to be born, Malia went to her family in the country. She didn't want to have the baby in the city. She wanted it to be born in the old Hawaiian way. She said she'd send for me, and when her mother showed up at my door about a week later, I was overjoyed that we'd soon be together again. But one look at her face and I knew something was wrong.

She said, "Aue, your Malia, baby boy; e make them two." And she started to cry.

After that, I didn't see the point of staying. I was ostracized by my family for what I loved, and what I loved had died. I couldn't keep my mind on business. It seemed meaningless, and I couldn't stand Stephen's condescending remarks as my life fell apart. He agreed to buy out my stock, and that's how I came to San Francisco to start over.

I'm sorry I left you nothing but Mother's unstrung pearls, but I know Stephen will provide all your material needs. Just take good care of yourself, Katherine.

I started a dry goods store and I'm doing all right. One

day, a young woman with sea-blue eyes and hair like the sun came into the shop, and my heart started beating again. We were married last year, and two months ago, our little Laura was born. My life is here now and always will be.

Your brother,

Thomas

&

*L*aura couldn't sleep that night. She kept thinking about her father's letter and the two pearl rings. He'd been married before. A Hawaiian wife and child. Her heart ached when she thought about the time she'd asked him if he'd remarry. Now, his comment, "Two is enough," made sense. The way she calculated it, he'd lost two wives and two babies in less than seven years. If only she'd known, she could have been kinder, done something. But she was only a small child then.

She heard footsteps coming down the hall. It had to be after midnight. Kimiko and the others would be back at the servants' quarters. Besides, the footfalls were heavier than any sound Kimiko would make, or Chun, or Sing. Whoever was coming was trying to tread softly, but failing. Laura lay still, scarcely breathing.

Uncle Stephen had been staying up late and drinking more lately, alone in the library. Maybe he was going to bed. The footsteps stopped at her bedroom door. She heard the knob twist slowly, first left, then right. Laura swallowed. The knob turned back and forth again. She thought she'd flipped the key in the lock before she went to bed, but she couldn't remember. The knob stopped turning. Footfalls retreated back up the hall toward the front of the house, toward Uncle Stephen's bedroom.

The next morning, when Kimiko tapped on Laura's door to

announce breakfast, Laura told her she had a sore throat and would stay in bed and just take tea. When Uncle Stephen left for the office, she got dressed, wrote out a note at her vanity table, and went downstairs to find Sing. He was in the kitchen cleaning up the breakfast dishes.

"Please take this to David Kahiko at the legislature. You know the building where the government offices are, don't you?"

Sing nodded. He wiped his hands on a dishtowel and took the letter. About an hour later, he was back with a note.

Dear Laura,

Get a few things together. I'll come for you this afternoon. You can stay awhile with my grandmother. You'll be safe there. In the meantime, please be careful.

David

&

*F*lushed and excited, Lucien leapt up the stairs of the Price verandah and rang the bell. Kimiko opened the door. Laura was just behind her, with an expectant look that waned when she saw who was there.

"Don't go downtown today," Lucien said, out of breath. "Revolutionaries have taken control of the palace grounds and the government office buildings."

Laura came out on the verandah. She told Kimiko to go back inside and close the door.

"I don't want to alarm the girls, Lucien," she said. "Let's sit over here." She pointed to the wicker chairs near the railing. "What's going on?"

"From what we can tell, it's mostly natives. They're trying to overthrow the constitution. They want the king to sign a new one. But if he does, it's treason. And if he doesn't, it appears they want Lili`uokalani to take the throne."

"Why would the Hawaiians try to force the king's hand like that?" Laura said. "They love him."

"I don't know. But the cabinet called out the Hawaiian League to fight them, and they may ask the captain of the USS *Adams* to land troops tonight to patrol the streets. They can't find the king. He's not at the palace. Some say he went to his boathouse at the harbor. Wherever he is, he's not communicating."

"Well, he's damned if he does and damned if he doesn't," Laura said. "He'll lose either way, it seems to me."

Lucien sat back, surprised at her angry tone. "I just wanted to warn you and the girls." He stood. "I should go tell my folks what's happening."

"Lucien, wait. I didn't mean to snap at you. You look warm. Have something to drink before you go."

Laura stood and walked toward the front door. As she went inside, a slip of paper dropped from her dress pocket. She closed the door behind her, and Lucien saw the note blow across the verandah. He went to retrieve it. When he picked it up, he saw David's name signed at the bottom. He read the note, crumpled it, and stuck it in his pocket. Laura held the front door open as Kimiko walked out with a tray of iced tea, which she set on the table.

"Come sit down, Lucien," Laura said.

"No, I'd better get going."

"You can stay a minute. Have something to drink. Your face has turned red, you need to cool off."

Lucien grabbed a glass of tea and took a few gulps. "I don't know if my parents have heard the news. I need to get over there."

He set the glass on the tray and headed down the steps. Laura looked confused. He swung up in the saddle. "Don't worry, everything will be all right."

He turned his horse and trotted to the street. When he was out of sight of the Price home, he pulled the note out of his pocket. Why did David tell Laura to be careful? Did he know about the revolution? And why was he coming to take her away?

Up the block, Lucien passed Colonel Ashford with a unit of the Hawaiian League, armed and headed downtown. He tipped his hat and continued up the avenue. Then, suddenly, he wheeled his horse around and galloped back to pull up alongside the colonel.

"Colonel Ashford," Lucien said.

"McBride." The colonel nodded.

"I heard they identified one of the instigators. They said he could be headed to this side of town."

The colonel raised his eyebrows. "Who is it?"

"David Kahiko. You know him?"

"Sure," the colonel said. "We'll pick him up. This little revolution will be wrapped up today."

Chapter 18 ———

*L*aura waited all afternoon, sitting on the verandah in the wicker loveseat. Her packed bag was upstairs under the bed. She told the girls to stay inside. Twice, armed troops marched by the house. She worried about David because he worked downtown in the government offices across from the palace. And she worried that Stephen would get home before David got there. Around half past four, Lucien rode up the drive. Laura stood.

"I have news," he said. He dismounted and tied the horse's reins around the hitching post. "The League has secured Honolulu and rounded up the revolutionaries. Seven of them were killed and a dozen wounded. They took about seventy prisoners, and tonight, marines from the USS *Adams* will patrol to keep the peace." He stopped talking. The look on his face darkened. "I'm sorry to have to be the one to tell you...."

"What happened?"

"David Kahiko was arrested."

Laura took a step back. "Why? He'd never do anything against the government."

"They said he was one of the instigators."

"Who said?"

"Just the word around town."

"What will happen to him?" Laura sank onto the sofa.

Lucien walked up the steps and sat next to her. "I went by the jailhouse to find out. I thought he might need an attorney."

Laura put her hand on Lucien's. "What did they say?"

"That the prisoners will be charged with treason." He paused. "If they're convicted, the punishment is death by hanging."

Laura gasped and covered her mouth. "Oh, my God, Lucien."

He put his arms around her, and she leaned against him. He had wanted to hold her like this for so long, to have her depend on him. She looked up.

"What can we do?"

"I'll go down tomorrow to see what's possible."

She smiled at him, a grateful, vulnerable smile. He thought he'd walk through hell itself to have her look at him that way — always.

&

*W*hen Uncle Stephen came home that night, he was in a rare mood, almost gleeful, as if none of the tragic events of the day had happened and his life was moving forward according to plan. He called Kimiko to bring him a brandy, then kissed Lizzie and Hannah on the cheek in quick succession. He stopped in front of Laura and glanced back at his daughters.

"I must give a kiss to all my girls."

He turned back to Laura, put his hands on her shoulders, leaned in, and kissed her on the cheek close to the side of her mouth. She held very still, but flinched when his trim mustache grazed her face. Taking the brandy that Kimiko offered on a tray, Stephen instructed her to bring him another in the library. Then he walked off, whistling.

At dinner, he was already tipsy. He held the chair for Laura, brushing up against her. When he pushed the chair in, he leaned so close that Laura could feel his warm breath at the back of her neck.

"What a day," he said, as Kimiko served dinner. "It was a comic opera." He chuckled. "The Imperial Order of the Coconut, with Emperor Skyhigh hiding out while a bunch of ragtag kanakas played soldier. Our Rifles had them whipped before they started." He picked up his wineglass. "A toast to the success of our new government."

Laura and the girls sat silent. Laura wondered what he meant by "our new government," but didn't dare ask. The king was still in power, wasn't he? Maybe the new government was the all-white cabinet composed of men from the Hawaiian League. She remembered her conversation with Mr. Stevenson, and how graciously he had described the king's intelligence and efforts on behalf of the kingdom. Her uncle's mocking made her lose her appetite.

Stephen waited for the girls to lift their glasses. "Oh," he said, "you only have water." He called for Kimiko. "We need to have a proper toast. Kimiko, give the girls a glass of wine."

Kimiko brought wineglasses, and set one in front of each of the girls. She poured a taste into Lizzie's and then tipped the decanter toward Hannah's.

Stephen glanced at Laura. "Fill them up, Kimiko. I'm feeling good, and I mean to have a proper celebration."

Kimiko made a slight bow, turned back to Lizzie's glass, and filled it. Then she filled Hannah's and Laura's.

"Raise those glasses, my ladies," Stephen said.

Hannah and Lizzie lifted their glasses tentatively, apprehensive of their father's strange mood. Stephen pushed back his chair and stood to give a toast.

"I'm waiting, Laura." She still hadn't touched her glass.

"I don't think the girls should be drinking, Uncle Stephen."

"They'll drink when I say drink, miss. Now raise your glass."

"I'll raise my glass if you let the girls alone."

They stared at each other. Then Stephen smiled.

"My house, my rules, remember? But I'm a reasonable man. I'll compromise. They can each have just a sip after my toast — if you finish off your glass and theirs."

Lizzie began to tear up. Hannah looked down at her plate of beef and potatoes. Both of them still held their glasses aloft.

"They can sit there holding those glasses up all night, Laura," Stephen said. "It's your choice."

Laura lifted her glass.

"Good." Stephen raised his glass, nodding to each of the girls. "Here's to a new era for Hawaii, for moral and decent rule, free from incompetence and corruption. And here's to the good men of the Hawaiian League and the Honolulu Rifles that are making it all possible."

He tipped the glass to his lips, then watched as the girls did the same. Lizzie made a face and turned her head. Hannah was stoic.

"Kimiko, put the girls' wine at Laura's place."

Kimiko picked up the glasses and moved them in front of Laura.

"It's time for your part of the bargain. Drink up."

Laura glared at him, and drank down her glass. The wine was an expensive import, but to her it tasted like spoiled grapes, the alcohol an irritant in her mouth. She picked up the next glass and drank it down, not realizing the effect it would have before dinner was through. Then she finished off the third. Stephen's mustache curled above his tight-lipped smile.

Laura kept her eyes on her plate and just picked at dinner. Afterward, she felt warm and relaxed. What had upset her before just made her sad now, and she found it hard to focus. She didn't notice Stephen signal Kimiko to take the girls to bed. It seemed she just looked up and everyone was gone except her and Stephen. He was gazing at her with an odd expression.

"I want to talk to you about a serious matter, Laura." He got up and came around, steadying himself on the table. He pulled out the chair next to hers and sat down. She pushed back to face him. She wanted to get farther away, but felt dizzy just moving the chair.

He took her hands in his and started to speak. She tried to tune in and make sense of what he was saying.

"...and you probably think of me as much older. But since Katherine died, I've grown fond of you, in a different way, not like an uncle." He leaned in close. "I did advise you to marry someone like Lucien, but I've been thinking. We're not related by blood. When wives die, men often marry their sisters. I can have the preacher up here next week and it'll all be taken care of." He paused. "This is good for you. You have nothing. I have everything you could possibly want and need...and you have something I've needed for a long time."

He put his hands under her arms and stood, lifting her up. He pulled her to him. She drooped like a rag doll. She couldn't make her legs hold her up, and she went limp as he pressed his mouth against her lips. They sank onto the carpet, prone, and she could feel his hand slipping down her waist and lifting up the hem of her dress, sliding back up her thigh. She tried to push him away, but he was cumbrous and insistent. She could barely breathe between the pressure of his kisses and her corset pinching her side.

She felt the room begin to whirl and grow dark. Just before she blacked out she remembered saying, "Uncle Stephen … I think I'm going to be sick."

※

*L*aura woke the next morning with no memory of how she'd gotten into her nightdress and into bed. Her mouth was dry and sour. She pushed back the coverlet and raised herself up on her elbows, but the throbbing in her head made her lie back down. There was a tap at the door.

Kimiko came in with a tray of tea and toast. She set it down on the night table next to Laura's bed.

"You better, Miss Laura?"

"My head hurts."

Kimiko turned her face at a slight angle with a look of concern. "Last night, I put girls to bed. Then your uncle, he call me. Say you fall down, get sick all over."

"How did I get up here?"

"You no wake up, so Chun and Sing, they carry you. I undress you, wash your face."

"Thank you, Kimiko."

"You go rest now. I send girls Williams house. Mr. Price, he already go."

Kimiko bowed and retreated. Laura tried to go back to sleep, but each time she closed her eyes the throbbing in her head seemed more intense, and it mixed with queasy memories of unwanted touches and hot breath smelling of wine. She got up slowly and padded to the bathroom to wash her face. She looked in the mirror at her puffy eyes, wondering if Lucien would have any news about David today.

&

*W*hen Lucien rode up the drive around two o'clock, Laura was waiting on the verandah. She stood up as he dismounted and came up the steps. He told her he'd learned that David would stand trial for treason. What he didn't tell her was what the jailer had said — that he didn't see how any of the captives would be convicted. No Hawaiian jury would convict a fellow Hawaiian they thought was trying to help the king.

"We may be able to save his life," Lucien said. "But even if he's not hanged, the minimum punishment for treason is life imprisonment."

He sat beside her and took her hand. He wasn't lying, exactly — life imprisonment was the minimum punishment. But she looked so distraught it made him feel anxious. Perhaps he should tell her the truth.

He couldn't know her feeling of hopelessness after the experience last night with her uncle, and no chance that David would come for her. And poor David. What could she do for him? Uncle Stephen had said something about getting a preacher. What if he got it in his head to force her to marry him? It wouldn't be hard to do. With his power and influence, he could probably get even a preacher to do what he wanted, and then he'd own her.

"Laura, you're trembling." Lucien thought about telling her what the jailer had told him, that the captives could be out within a few months. But he just said, "Don't worry, we'll do the best we can for David."

He lifted her hands and kissed them. She looked in his eyes and remembered that long-ago kiss in the woods at Ainahau.

"It's an awkward time, I know," Lucien said. "Everything feels crazy. But it's times like these that make you decide what's important."

She saw where he was going. She had a sinking feeling, but didn't interrupt him. Where he was going could stop Uncle Stephen in his tracks, take away his power over her, and keep him from getting what he wanted.

Lucien pulled her to him, closing his eyes. She watched his face until their lips touched, then closed her eyes to see what she felt. What was it? Something under the surface, a small perturbation, dissonant like a humming negative charge, with a metallic taste. Then she identified it, but attributed it to herself — deceit. She wondered if he sensed it too. But when he pulled back, his eyes were glowing.

"I want you, Laura. I want you to be my wife. Will you marry me?"

A flash of memory kept her from answering right away. She saw herself with David at the ball, sitting in the moonlight in the fairy-lantern garden. He was saying, "Malolo, you're Malolo." Then, in an instant, she was on the *Mariposa*, watching flying fish leap from unseen predators in the vast deep. They flew from their watery element to an atmosphere where they couldn't breathe. What strange things to think of at a time like this.

Laura looked down. Lucien still held her hands. Though the afternoon was warm, she felt cold. She thought of her plans for medical school. She thought of David in prison for life, or worse. Then she thought of her uncle who'd be home soon. She looked up.

"Yes."

"Yes?" Lucien seemed startled that his long-held wish was suddenly granted.

"Yes. Will you stay until Uncle Stephen comes home so we can tell him?"

He lit up. "Of course," he said, and hugged her.

Laura pulled away. "Lucien?"

"What?"

"How would you translate malolo?

"It means 'flying fish.' Why?"

When the carriage came up the drive, Lucien jumped up. He'd planned to ask Stephen to see him in the library, but couldn't contain himself. Chun stopped in front of the house, and Stephen got out. He climbed the verandah steps, and Lucien came forward to shake his hand. Laura stood behind him.

"Lucien?" Stephen sensed something was up.

Lucien beamed. "Laura has agreed to marry me. I want to ask you for her hand."

Stephen glanced at Laura. Looks passed between them like high-voltage darts.

Chapter 19 ————

Lili`uokalani sat at the grand piano in the drawing room of the palace, waiting for the king. She tinkered with the keys, composing a melody. Her fingers paused on the keyboard as her thoughts drifted to her sister, Likelike, now gone, and her niece, Ka`iulani, so far away in England.

She remembered the day she'd composed her song, *Aloha Oe*, so many years before, having seen her sister say goodbye to a loved one when they left the Big Island. Now the Royal Hawaiian Band played the song at the wharf for all the departing steamship passengers. Yet "Aloha Oe" had so many meanings — a spirit of love, affection, greeting, and tender farewell. No English words alone or in combination could really express it. That was the way with so many Hawaiian words. She played a few bars, and the king walked into the parlor.

"I'm not leaving yet," he said, smiling. He sat on the divan across from the piano.

Liliu turned on the piano bench. "I know, and I'm begging you not to go, Kunane. The weather in the United States will be getting cold now. You're not used to it, and you're not in the best of health lately."

"I think colder weather would do my health good," the king said.

"Then think of my health. I've had a recurring fever for three weeks. When you go, I must assume all the affairs of state as your regent."

The king smiled. "My dear sister, you look fine. You've never protested my trips before. Usually it's the queen. What's really bothering you?"

Liliu looked down at the black and ivory keys. "I don't know. It's a lot of things … a feeling."

"What kinds of things?"

She looked back at the king.

"Well, for one, I went to the annual picnic at Punahou last week. You know, the big one where all the Congregational Sunday schools meet?"

The king nodded.

"The leading families and clergy weren't as cordial to me as they were last year."

"That's what bothering you? Oh, my dear, those people —"

"It's not just that. It's the recent violence, the uncertainty in the business community.…"

"That uncertainty is exactly why I must go," the king said. "The reason your friends in the Congregational societies are a little cool these days is because the annexationists are stirring them up."

"What do you mean?"

"Now that the McKinley Act will end Hawaii's favored status for sugar, they're saying the only way to avoid economic disaster is to annex Hawaii to the United States. We gave the U.S. rights to use Pearl Harbor, and I think I can get them to give us back favored status, just like I did in '75 with President Grant. That way, the Missionary Party will have nothing to agitate about."

Liliu shook her head. "It's always that same clique. They're never satisfied. They want to rule, or ruin us. And now you go to work again on their behalf."

"I go to work on behalf of my country. I want to preserve our independence and the throne. If I benefit the agitators in the process, that's all right with me." The king coughed.

Liliu's voice edged up. "You gave away Pearl Harbor for favored status, and now that status has disappeared with a stroke of a pen. They do whatever they want. What makes you think it'll be different this time?"

The king gave her a melancholy smile, shaking his head. "It doesn't look like I'll see our flag raised for me anytime soon."

Liliu sighed and turned back to the piano. She played a few notes, then stopped.

"I had a dream, Kunane. A dead man was trying to strangle me." She looked up at her brother.

He was quiet a long moment. "I won't be gone that long, sister. It's a necessary trip." He leaned over and folded his hands in front of him. "Perhaps when you assume the regency, you should just work here during the day, and always have a lady in waiting with you. Go home to Washington Place to sleep. We only have twenty-five royal soldiers to guard the palace."

&

September 20, 1890

It's been months since the revolt. The trials are finally progressing through the courts. No one knows what will happen. I've longed to see David, but Lucien checked several times and told me no one is allowed to talk to the prisoners.

Living with Uncle Stephen has been strained to say the least. But he's never touched me again since Lucien asked to marry me. Lucien pushed for an early wedding. I've managed to put it off with one excuse or another, knowing that once it's done, my life will be like my aunt's or Mrs. McBride's — confined to tiresome social visits, painted fans, and cups of tea.

Mr. Thurston was over the other day. He said if anyone wanted to know what it's like to be in hell without waiting for eternity, they should be in a divided cabinet. They're all frustrated, but it seems that however they try to control the king, he's quite skillful in fending them off.

We'll celebrate the holidays with the McBrides, and I know I'll be expected to give them a wedding date so it can be announced. But I don't want to give up my dreams. I remember how Mr. Stevenson wove such a vision of it all with his beautiful words. Now the Stevensons live in far-off Samoa, and my friend, Isobel, went with them. Little by little I lose everyone dear to me, and my life closes tight like a clamshell.

ॐ

Three days before Thanksgiving, David Kahiko trotted his horse up Beretania Street and turned into the driveway of the Price mansion. The horses near the carriage house pricked up their ears and pranced along the paddock fence, tossing their heads as he passed.

When Kimiko opened the front door, he handed her his calling card. She took it with both hands and bowed low.

"Are Mr. Price and his daughters in?"

"No, sir."

He smiled. He'd hoped they weren't. "And Miss Laura?"

Kimiko nodded, and with a graceful sweep of her kimono sleeve invited him in. He followed her to the drawing room, and sat down to wait. A stack of engraved cards and envelopes were spread on the table at the side of the sofa. He picked one up.

MR. & MRS. JAMES D. MCBRIDE
and
MR. STEPHEN J. PRICE

Request the honor of your presence
To celebrate the marriage of

LUCIEN CHARLES MCBRIDE
and
LAURA MARIE JENNINGS

Saturday, March 3, 1891
10:00 am

KAWAIAHAO CHURCH, HONOLULU

RECEPTION TO FOLLOW AT THE MCBRIDE HOME
212 BERETANIA STREET

RSVP

David stared at the card in his hands, not comprehending at first. Then he thought he should get up and leave quietly. Laura appeared at the door, her eyes bright.

"Oh, David!"

He smiled to see her, forgetting the card for the moment. She rushed to him, arms out. He hesitated, then embraced her, kissing both cheeks. She smiled up at him, radiant.

"But how did you get here? How are you?"

Feeling awkward, he let her go, then stepped back.

"They let us out to go home before the holidays."

"But the trials —"

"It was all a sham. They did it to harass us. They knew they'd never get any convictions. They just kept dragging it on for some reason. Finally, one of the leaders of the revolt threatened to tell all he knew about some haoles' behind-the-scenes involvement, and we were released the next day."

"They said you were one of the leaders."

"Who said?"

"Lucien said it was the word on the street."

"That's ridiculous."

Laura saw the wedding announcement in David's hand.

"Please, sit down. I asked Kimiko to bring some refreshments. She'll be in any minute."

"Maybe I should go, Malolo." His voice got soft. "That's another meaning of the word, you know. The flying fish that jumps from mate to mate. I wondered why you never came to see me at the prison, but I guess this explains it." He held up the card.

Laura looked confused. "But Lucien said the prisoners couldn't have visitors."

"How did he know? Did he ever check?"

"He said he went several times and the answer was always no. He said he went to offer you his services as an attorney."

"I never heard from him. But I had a lot of other visitors."

"Oh, my God." Laura remembered the day on the verandah when Lucien asked her to marry him and they'd shared a kiss, when she thought it was her charade that made her feel uneasy, and all the time ... She shook her head. "He told me they'd probably hang you, that maybe he could save your life, but no matter what, the least you'd get would be life in prison." Tears stung her eyes and rolled down her cheeks. "I thought I'd never see you again." She yanked the invitation from his hand and shook it at his face. "You never came. That's why I agreed to this. That, and my uncle and ... oh, my God." She covered her face with her hands and started to sob. David pulled her close and sat her down on the couch, his arms still around her.

"Laura, listen." He stroked her hair. "I worried about you the whole time I was in prison. I was on my way up here to get you when Colonel Ashford and a unit of the Rifles stopped me on the street and arrested me. I tried to talk my way out of it, but it started to get ugly. I thought maybe I could appeal to the Hawaiian guards at the prison, but when I got there, they'd all been replaced with haoles. It wasn't until the following week the regular guards came back, but by then all the charges and legal paperwork were in place, so there was no way out except to go through the process."

She stared at her lap. Her voice still trembled. "Lucien lied to me. He proposed after he told me you'd never be coming back. I had to stop Uncle Stephen. I was afraid he'd force me to marry him. I didn't see any other way."

"Are you saying —"

"I'm saying I don't want to marry Lucien."

David lifted her chin. "Then come with me now."

"To your grandmother's?"

He smiled. "That's a possibility, but you can't earn any money there."

"What do you mean?"

"I thought you were saving to go to medical school. Wouldn't you'd rather be somewhere you can make money?"

"Where?"

"Princess Liliu is acting as regent while the king is on his trip to the United States. She's looking for another personal attendant to work as a live-in secretary. I stopped by to see her when I got out. She asked about you, and I said you'd be perfect. She's waiting to hear from you."

&

January 17, 1891

With all the changes, I haven't had a moment to write in my journal. I'm so happy in Princess Liliu's household. She pays me a generous sum, I think, considering I also get room and board. And I've started my own bank account, in my own name this time. Someday I'll ask Uncle Stephen for the money in my other account. Right now, it would be a bit indelicate, considering how abruptly I left.

I know they were all shocked. Fortunately, the wedding invitations hadn't been sent out. I felt worst about Lucien's parents. They've never done me any harm, and I didn't want to hurt them. I didn't say anything about Lucien's deceit. I just told them that instead of getting married just now, I wanted to follow my dream of going to medical school, and that I had an offer to work as Princess Lili`uokalani's attendant.

The princess's carriage came to get me the day before Thanksgiving, and David was sitting next to the driver. Lucien knew I was leaving that day, and he stopped by, supposedly to see Uncle Stephen on a legal matter. Perhaps he thought he'd dissuade me. When he saw David, I could see him put two and two together. I think it dawned on him that I must know he lied. He seemed embarrassed, and then I think he got angry.

Uncle Stephen was most definitely angry. He'd been angry since the first day I told him. He said I was ungrateful. I should think about Hannah and Lizzie, and not so much about myself. Well, Hannah's now seventeen, and Lizzie, thirteen, and both are quite capable of caring for themselves. Hannah's almost the same age I was when I first came here and was expected to help manage the house and the servants.

The girls didn't say much. I never told them my feelings about being engaged, but I think they suspected the truth. Some things transmit between women without any words, especially when they live in the same household.

But I've put all that behind me. Life at Washington Place feels more relaxed than it used to. I wonder if that's because old Mother Dominis died, and the princess feels free to do what she likes instead of adhering to her mother-in-law's Puritan ways. The house is always full of flowers and visitors, mostly Hawaiians. There's so much music — they sing and play instruments at the drop of a hat. Every morning, a chanter softly wakes the princess. We rise early for personal meditation, then the princess calls her retainers together to read Scripture and have devotions. Every day after breakfast, women arrive with fresh flowers as a tribute. Then the princess and I walk to the palace to attend to the work of the kingdom.

Mr. Dominis rarely comes into the house. He sleeps in the bungalow on the grounds, supposedly because his arthritis makes it difficult for him to climb stairs. The princess tries to draw him into the life of the household. She's a warm, affectionate person, but he's so cool to her. She's considerate of his wishes and values his advice. I think she'd like to have more support from him, with all her state responsibilities, but he holds himself apart. I don't know why. All I know is, whenever he's around, it's like watching a shadow fall across the sun.

I see David a little more often now, but not as much as I'd like. We're all so busy with work. He's always sweet and gentle toward me, but a bit reserved too. Perhaps it's because he's in the royal household. The Hawaiians have so much respect for their ali`i. The word "respect" isn't even strong enough — it's more like reverence.

There's news from travelers arriving from San Francisco that King Kalakaua is planning to return to the islands soon. He's been gone two months, and I know Princess Liliu will be happy to have him back. Every week, while she's been regent, there's been some new rumor of secret meetings to overthrow the monarchy, or a telephone message saying someone plans to attack the palace. I never knew how beleaguered the royal family was, despite the kingdom apparently prosperous, and the king at work, even now, to make it more so.

Wakeki says the princess wants me in the garden, so I'll continue this later.

&

*L*aura noticed that Wakeki had a bundle under her arm, held tight against the gusts of wind that lifted their skirts when they stepped off the verandah. Princess Liliu stood beside the tall white flagpole near the driveway. The attached ropes flapped in the strong breeze and clanged against the pole.

"That no regular wind," Wakeki said, turning back to Laura. "That wind calling somebody."

The princess smiled as they walked up. "Help me get hold of these ropes, Laura. Wakeki, you attach the flag."

Laura grabbed the flapping lines and held them taut while Wakeki clipped the Hawaiian flag to the rope. The princess pulled it steadily until the striped banner reached the top of the flagpole, snapping in the breeze.

Liliu looked up, smiling. "When the king returns, he'll be able to see our flag flying for him." She turned to Laura. "Before he left, I was unhappy with him. He told me that when I was ready, I should raise the flag so he could see it from his window at the palace. Then he'd know all was forgiven."

She motioned for them to follow her to the verandah, out of the wind. Smoothing back her tousled hair, Liliu climbed the stairs, Laura and Wakeki behind her.

"Forgiveness is one of the hardest things, I think," Liliu said. "Especially when you feel what's been done is truly wrong. But there seems to be something reciprocal in it." She nodded for them to sit down.

"You mean like, 'Forgive us our debts as we forgive our debtors?'" Laura asked.

"Yes," Liliu said. "Our Christian teachers taught us that, and we accepted it because we understood it. There's a cleansing effect. Like our *ho'o pono pono*."

"What's that?" Laura said.

"*Ho`o* means 'to call forth.' *Pono* means 'justice, goodness, harmony, peace.' In our language, when a word's repeated, it's emphasized. So pono pono means 'the most great justice, the most great peace.'"

Wakeki nodded her head.

"Living on small islands in the middle of the Pacific," the princess said, "our ancestors had to develop ways to maintain peace and restore harmony quickly. The life of the community depended on it." She smiled. "Way out here, it wasn't so easy to just pick up stakes and leave if they were unhappy with each other."

"How does it work?" Laura said.

"First, the people come together and pray. Then they talk, unraveling layer after layer of the situation, all expressing their views frankly, but with courtesy. Finally, the group asks for forgiveness for everyone — all forgiven together. We don't pinpoint blame on just one party, because we're all connected."

The princess looked up at the flag. "You've heard how Hawaiians believe in the power of utterance? How when something is said, its existence has begun?"

Laura nodded.

"It's the same way when forgiveness is deep and sincere. It has the power to call forth great goodness, the spirit of aloha." The princess looked at Laura, who was held for a moment in her deep gaze. "We don't create this goodness. It arises when we allow the conditions for it to arise."

"Well," Laura said finally, "it's sure to lift the king's heart when he returns."

The princess nodded. "The whole of Honolulu is being decorated with flags and bunting to welcome him, and near the wharf even a special arch that he'll ride under on the way to the palace. I had a white banner made to hang at Merchant and Fort Streets. It says, 'Aloha Oe,' to mean, 'Love Forever.'" She looked up again at the waving flag. "But this is the banner he'll be looking for."

&

$\mathcal{F}$rom his lookout, Diamond Head Charlie spied the USS *Charleston* steaming toward Honolulu. As it sailed closer he could see the royal standard in full display standing out from the mast against the hard wind. King Kalakaua was onboard!

Charlie had to alert the town to get ready to ring the fire bells and prepare the royal salutes from the battery at Punchbowl and from ships anchored in the harbor. He got up to get a better view before he started down the hill and stood staring. Except for the royal standard, all the *Charleston*'s flags were at half-mast, and the yards were cockbilled in token of mourning. Charlie thought about the visitor from Kona the week before who'd said the red fish had come up from the sea. He'd just wondered at it then, since none of the ali`i were ill.

He hurried outside, untied his horse, and swung up into the saddle. He turned back once to take a last look at the *Charleston*, then dug his heels in the horse's flanks and galloped down toward Honolulu.

As the *Charleston* put into port, the bright banners and festive garlands that decorated Honolulu for the king's return were taken down or hastily covered with black drapes. The rumor spread from mouth to mouth, happy smiles replaced with dread or disbelief, until it was finally confirmed: Kalakaua was dead. Wailing dirges arose spontaneously, and a small boat headed for the *Charleston* to bring ashore the king's remains.

Heralds began to roam the streets, proclaiming Lili`uokalani as queen.

Chapter 20 ⎯⎯⎯⎯⎯

*L*ucien raced up Fort Street from the wharf, skidded into the doorway of the Bishop Bank Building, and climbed the stairs to Thurston's office two at a time. He stopped on the second-story landing to catch his breath, then opened the door.

"Mr. Thurston!"

Down the hall, Thurston stuck his head out his office door.

"The king is dead!" Lucien said. "They're bringing his body off the *Charleston* now."

Thurston walked out of his office. "Are you sure?"

Lucien, still gasping for breath, nodded.

They faced each other in silence. From the direction of the wharf they heard an eerie wail rise and fall, soon joined by other voices in a crescendo of grief. The Hawaiians chanted meles for their king.

Thurston stood uncharacteristically still, his hands in his pockets. Finally he spoke.

"This is what we used to call missionary luck. Our plan to unseat Kalakaua and put Lili`uokalani on the throne is accomplished. Telephone Price and Dole and get them over here. We have to make sure the new queen is sworn in immediately — and especially that she takes the oath to uphold our constitution and reconfirms the appointment of our cabinet." He smiled. "She's a woman with no experience, she'll be easily led. We ought to make good progress now."

&

*W*hen John Dominis walked through the door of the palace, Liliu went to meet him. Laura walked just behind her.

"Thank you for coming so quickly, John."

Laura wished Liliu's husband could show a little affection at such a time, but he just nodded.

"Why did the ministers call a meeting now?" Liliu asked. "The king's body is being transported here to the palace. I haven't had a moment to collect my thoughts since the ship docked."

"They want you to take the oath of office."

"I don't want to do this now. Can't it wait until after the funeral?"

Laura's heart went out to the queen. Her normally radiant face, dazed with sorrow, looked to her husband for some support and comfort.

John shook his head. "No, you must do it. They've decided."

He led the way to the throne room where the cabinet ministers, members of the Privy Council, and the justices of the supreme court waited. As they entered, Laura couldn't shake the feeling that they looked more like a gallows jury than like ministers of state. The chief justice rose to administer the oath, and then the minister of the interior proclaimed Lili`uokalani Queen of the Hawaiian Islands. He also read a statement lauding the era of King Kalakaua as one of remarkable and increasing prosperity.

Laura looked from official to official, scarcely believing her ears. These were the carved and wooden faces who'd opposed the king at every pass. Now they were praising his reign.

They all adjourned to the Blue Room. Laura felt a slight chill as she walked through the door, enough to make her shiver. She didn't know this was the place Liliu had met with her brother for the last time before his trip and told him of her dream of being strangled by a dead man.

The chief justice approached Liliu to extend his condolences on the king's passing, as well as congratulations on ascending the throne. He leaned in to offer advice in a low voice. "If any of the cabinet proposes something to you, say yes."

Liliu seemed confused, then tried her best to receive each official and listen with attention as they filed past. Finally, all the officials except the cabinet had gone.

The minister of foreign affairs rose and began a stumbling speech, saying that the cabinet would have to continue in office. It sounded like an apology. The minister of finance came to his aid, interjecting that no changes could be made in the cabinet except by action of the legislature.

"Gentlemen, if you please," Liliu said, her voice frail and pleading. "I don't see the necessity of mentioning such a matter right now. At any moment, the remains of my dear brother will arrive here. I'm already overcome, and I ask your consideration."

The attorney general pushed the point. "Madam, you'd best understand the situation and accept it now."

Liliu turned to look at him. Then she seemed to awaken as if from a trance. She took a breath, lifted her chin, and sat up straight, regarding the men as though the mantle of office wrapped around her like a royal cloak and she remembered she was now the queen. Her words were firm.

"I have no intention of discussing this or any other political matters until after the king's funeral. I bid you good day, gentlemen." She didn't wish them aloha, but simply nodded her head in a gesture of finality.

Laura's eyes grew wide at Liliu's strong dismissal. The cabinet ministers were taken aback, but obediently left the room.

&

February 25, 1891

It was dull and gloomy the day they brought the king's remains up from the USS *Charleston*. Crowds followed the wagon all the way from the wharf, but when the casket passed through the gate, the clouds parted, and a triple rainbow crested over the palace grounds, like a last welcome home. The haoles seemed surprised, but the Hawaiians agreed it was the sign of a true ali`i.

Admiral Brown accompanied the casket from the ship. He met with the queen and told us about the king's last days in San Francisco. He'd been received with festivity everywhere he traveled in California, but he was feeling ill and prepared to sail for home. He must have known he was dying, because he talked into one of the new Edison recording machines to leave a message: "Tell my people I did my best." The admiral said thirty thousand turned out to pay their respects at the funeral in San Francisco. King Kalakaua was the first monarch to die on American soil.

When Admiral Brown went back to the *Charleston*, the natives were so touched by his kindness to the king that hundreds went aboard with tokens of their aloha — old-fashioned spears, calabashes, fruit, shell necklaces, and flowers. They wanted to give the admiral mementos to remember Hawaii wherever in the world he might sail.

Here in Honolulu, thousands came in from all the islands

to attend the ceremonies. There were Anglican services, prayers offered by the minister of Kawaiahao Church, Masonic rites, and a ceremony of the Hale Naua Society, the fraternal organization the king himself had founded to interweave ancient Hawaiian wisdom with scientific practices. Descendants of the chiefs stood watch, bearing the royal kahili standards, and meles were chanted. Later, some newspapers reported that the events were pagan and idolatrous. The writers couldn't have attended the same ceremonies I did.

I saw an interview in the *San Francisco Chronicle* with the wife of a Honolulu doctor who was visiting there. She told them the queen was unpopular, hadn't gotten along well with her brother, and had had kahunas pray him to death. Then she said that, before the king's death, she'd been personally invited by the princess to his welcome-home ball and had truly looked forward to it! This is how she repays favors from the royal family? Fortunately, the Honolulu papers and some American papers are supporting the queen. The articles describe her as beautiful, well educated, tactful, and a woman of statecraft. Of course, she's all that and more in my eyes.

She got a strange letter from Charles Bishop, who owns the bank and was married to her hanai sister. He said he regarded the moral influence she could exert as more important than anything else she could do. Then he wrote something very odd — that she'd live longer and be more popular by not trying to do too much. What did he mean? It reminded me of the comment of the chief justice the day she took the oath of office — that she should say yes to whatever her cabinet proposed!

For as long as these haoles have lived in the islands, it seems they still don't understand the minds of the royal family, especially a chiefess. They think they should just be able to tell her what to do and she'll accommodate them, like their own wives do at home.

I had the sad duty of attending Lili`uokalani as she lowered the flag she'd raised just days before, the signal to her brother that all was forgiven. He never got to see it. She let it fly at half-mast, and on the day of the funeral, had it laid across the king's coffin before he was interred at Nuuanu. Now the flagpole at Washington Place stands bare, its ropes tied tight.

The queen told me she'll officially nominate Ka`iulani as the heir apparent to the throne. Finally, we'll have some happy news to send to our dear princess. Perhaps her fear of her mother's prophecy that she'd never be queen will be put to rest at last.

&

At ten o'clock on the day following the final ceremonies of the king's funeral, the cabinet gathered to meet with the queen. The four men seated themselves, and waited for her to open the meeting.

"Gentlemen," Liliu said, "what is the business of the day?"

The minister of the interior spoke first. "It's necessary, Your Majesty, that you sign our commissions, reconfirming our appointments, so that we may proceed to the discharge of our duties."

Liliu paused for a moment. "I would expect you to submit your resignations before I can act."

The ministers looked at each other and back at the queen.

"Gentlemen," Liliu continued with a straight face, "if you're already my cabinet ministers, why do you need to appeal to me to confirm your appointments to places you already fill?"

The four sat without responding.

"You were the king's cabinet," Liliu said. "If you do not resign, I don't see how I can issue you new commissions."

"But, Your Majesty," the attorney general said, "the constitution distinctly states that no change of ministry should take place except by a vote of 'lack of confidence' passed by a majority in the legislature."

The others nodded their assent.

"That's true," Liliu said. "But I've reread the document, and there's no provision for the continuance of a cabinet after the death of the sovereign." She regarded their looks of hesitation and confusion. "I cannot simply issue you new commissions over my royal signature. If you have doubts, I suggest this matter be referred to the supreme court for their decision."

&

*L*orrin Thurston paced the floor of his office, fists clenched. "That pigheaded, stubborn, stupid, tricky —"

"Wait a minute, Lorrin," Judge Dole said. "Going off like a rocket isn't going to solve anything. Since the supreme court found in favor of the queen, we're just going to have to live with it."

"But she just eliminated all our men from the cabinet." Thurston stopped pacing, and turned to John Stevens, the US minister, who sat opposite Stephen Price and Lucien. "I'm sorry, John. It looks like this will slow down our plans."

The US minister nodded. "She's surrounded herself with some of the worst elements of the country, natives and persons of foreign birth. Now she's got a cabinet composed of her tools."

Lucien wondered at that comment. The queen's new cabinet was composed of moderate men of good standing in the community and not unfriendly to America, though none had any missionary connections. And most of the Privy Council was re-appointed.

"Never mind," Stephen said. "It's just a matter of time until she'll have to yield and place herself in the hands of the respectable men of the country as the only way to retain her throne."

The US minister took a letter from his pocket and unfolded it. "I don't want you to lose heart, gentlemen. Here's a message I received from Admiral Brown of the USS *Charleston* last week from San Francisco. He wrote, 'It looks to me as if Her Majesty should be taught a lesson, which will do her good.'" Minister Stevens re-folded the paper and put it in his vest pocket. "He's assured me that a properly informed commander will have his ship in Honolulu Harbor."

Dole looked uncomfortable. "Maybe, John, you can just go talk to her ... officially. She's traveled through the United States. She's seen the power of the country, and holds it in high regard. Let her know we expect her to reign, but not rule."

"I can give it a try," Stevens said. "But I agree with Thurston. She's more stubborn than her brother, so I don't hold out any great hope she'll see the light."

Dole pulled out his watch and pressed the top to release the engraved gold cover. He rose from his chair. The others got up with him.

"Let us know how it goes," Dole said. Minister Stevens nodded. The men shook hands all around and left Thurston and Lucien to their afternoon's work.

Thurston sat back down at his desk and looked off into space, shaking his head and rubbing his beard.

"You okay, Mr. Thurston?"

He looked up. "You don't know how easy you've had it all your life. I've had to fight for everything I ever got." He ran his hand through his hair. "With my father dead and my mother always working, people pitied me, looked down on me. It made me mad." His voice changed. "Even the damn kanakas thought they were better than me. Can you believe that?" He looked away, staring out the window.

Lucien stood still. He'd never heard that tone in Thurston's voice before.

"One time," Thurston said, "when I was just a little boy, I wanted some sand for something I was building near the summer home of Princess Ruth. God, she was a big old thing — six feet tall and nearly four hundred pounds." He sniffed. "No friend of the missionaries, that's for sure. She was heathen till she died." Thurston pursed his lips, a faraway look in his eyes. "She saw me taking sand off her beach, stomped across the street, and stopped where I was digging, just towered over me, glowering. I sat frozen in her shadow. She looked down and said, 'Go home, haole boy.'"

He turned to Lucien. "I was just a kid. What would it have hurt for me to take a little sand off her beach?" His voice grew cold. "After that, whenever kanaka kids gave me grief, I'd fight 'em. I wasn't going to let them or anyone make me feel small again." He locked on Lucien's gaze. "I decided way back then that, one day, I'd take care of it once and for all. And I did. I married myself a rich woman, I got myself through a prestigious law school, and I've built myself into a leader in this community. I'll be damned if I'm going to let some sooty 'queen' get the better of me."

಄

"US Minister John Stevens is here, Your Majesty," the chamberlain announced.

"Show him in," the queen said.

Laura walked over to stand behind the queen's chair as John Stevens strode into the room, made a cursory bow, and looked around for a chair. He was a tall, angular man with craggy features and white hair and beard. Before the queen invited him to be seated, he pulled up a chair, sat down, and swung his left leg over the arm, his crotch facing toward them. Laura tried to hide her dismay. No gentleman would sit that way in front of a lady, and certainly not a queen. Liliu, however, remained calm.

Without so much as a "by your leave," he began to read a document that seemed to Laura more a scolding than an official communication. He reiterated the supreme authority of the constitution, and his hope that the queen would maintain the right of her cabinet to administer the laws so that she might avoid — he paused, then puffed out each word of the phrase with added emphasis — "the embarrassments and perplexities of sovereigns not blessed with free and enlightened constitutions." He leaned back and forth as he read the rest, his tone arrogant and overbearing.

When he finished, Lili`uokalani stood and, in a dignified voice, thanked him for coming. He sat looking up at her, waiting for a response to his points. She said nothing. Finally, he got up, made a halfhearted bow, and departed.

Liliu walked to the window. Her formerly erect shoulders slumped a little. Her face was strained. Finally, she turned back to Laura.

"It was their so-called 'free and enlightened' constitution that

232

they forced my brother to sign under threat of being dethroned or killed. It broke his heart and led to his death, and took the vote away from my people."

Chapter 21 ———

August 30, 1891

Mr. Dominis died this week. No one expected it. A tragedy, in its way, because the last six months he'd at last made some small effort to be helpful to the queen. Before he died, she set out to tour all the inhabited islands — even the leper colony on Molokai — to be among the people and see to their needs. Mr. Dominis couldn't go because his rheumatism was bad, but he did surprise the queen by building her a large wooden lanai on the north shore of Oahu to receive guests during her visit there. It held about one hundred fifty people, who came to the receptions and dances to honor her. She was so touched at his thoughtfulness that she hurried back to Honolulu to be with him.

He was confined to bed, attended by Dr. Trousseau, who didn't think the situation was critical. The queen watched at his bedside for days. In spite of the doctor's reassurance, she became agitated one afternoon. Then she did the most remarkable thing: She sent for his little son, Aimoku, and Aimoku's mother. Before they arrived, Mr. Dominis died, the queen at his bedside. Later there were vicious rumors that it had been his mistress at his bedside, sobbing, while the queen merely looked on.

I don't know how to feel about his death. It seems like he's abandoned her again, just when she needed him most to advise her how to deal with all the Western men around her. But she says only kind things about him.

The tour to the other islands was extraordinary. It's impossible to know the real Hawaii when you only stay in Honolulu. That woman interviewed in the *San Francisco Chronicle* who said the queen was unpopular didn't know what she was talking about. No matter where we went, thousands of natives thronged to meet the queen, bearing gifts tied up in ti leaves, and singing meles. On Molokai, the lepers constructed an arch of ferns at the foot of the landing, and hung a banner that read, ALOHA IKA MOI WAHINE, which means "Love to Our Queen." After the leper band played the Hawaiian National Anthem, we visited the sick, then had lunch with the nursing sisters the king recruited years before. They've done miracles, and the queen has promised even more support.

Everywhere, there were exuberant expressions of love and devotion. On every island, they decorated the landings with vines and flowers, and held huge luaus. Even all the haole and missionary families did their utmost to shower her with attentions, hosting dances and luaus at their fine homes.

I was happy that David came with us, though his official duties left little time for us to talk. He told me the queen's new policy to reduce the kingdom's expenses (including her own salary) has been well received, and business is good despite the sugar situation.

There was a strange moment. We took a commercial ferry to Mahukona on the Big Island, and the queen sat to talk with passengers. I was sure I'd soon be below in a bunk, seasick, but the day was calm, so I strolled the deck to look for David. Then I saw Judge Dole and Lucien come around the corner. I didn't know they were aboard. Lucien had already spotted me, but Judge Dole kept coming in my direction so he followed. The judge greeted me and asked about the queen. I pointed to where she was sitting, and he went on. Then I was face to face with Lucien.

He said hello, but from the red in his cheeks it was apparent he was more embarrassed than I was. He seemed to be searching for words. The look in his eyes was like a child who knows he's done wrong and expects wrath, yet hopes for forgiveness. I asked why he and Judge Dole were traveling. "For business," he said. Then a cloud came over his face. He looked past me at someone else. I heard David's voice behind me, and Lucien muttered that he needed to catch up to Judge Dole. He tipped his hat, turned, and headed off in the opposite direction. I assume he walked around the other side of the ship. I didn't see him again until we docked. He and Judge Dole disappeared in the large crowd that had gathered at the landing to welcome the queen with a noisy salute of Chinese firecrackers.

&

Laura hurried into the queen's study with a stack of mail and newspaper articles. She'd placed the letter postmarked from England on top, hoping the queen would open it first.

Liliu looked up from her desk. "How's the news this morning, Laura?"

"Good, Your Highness. The newspapers are praising your

trip around the islands as a sign of your 'democratic attitude' and attention to what the people want."

"It's a Hawaiian tradition that the voice of the people is the voice of God. What they've told me is that they want a strong monarchy and a stronger voice for themselves in the government." She smiled. "But I don't know if that's what the newspaper editors had in mind."

"And there's a note from Minister Parker," Laura said. "He says your minister in Washington wrote that the United States has declared they won't interfere in Hawaiian affairs, except at the desire of the queen. Basically, you have the United States' help for the asking."

"That's an important letter. Make a note to remind me to ask Minister Parker to show me the original."

Laura nodded, then set down the stack of mail. Spying the letter with British stamps, Liliu smiled at Laura, then slit the envelope, and scanned its contents.

"It seems our little Ka`iulani is becoming a woman of the world. She's doing well in French, German, and English, and takes painting and singing lessons." The queen stopped and looked down, her eyes moist. She always tried to hide how much she missed her niece, but her tone turned soft and sorrowful. "She has such a sweet soprano voice." She cleared her throat and handed Laura the letter. "Evidently, she's taken her appointment as heir apparent very seriously, and is applying herself to learn all she can about government and history."

Laura listened with one ear as she read the letter. Ka`iulani described a visit to the Isle of Jersey that had reminded her so much of home, and she felt her young friend's deep longing to return.

"She's asked me to appoint her father governor of Oahu," the queen said. "I had someone else in mind, but I want to encourage her. I'll grant her request."

"When can she come home, Your Majesty?"

"If it were just a personal matter, I'd have her back today. She's all I have left now. But if anything were to happen to me, she'd take the throne, or a regency would be formed to rule on her behalf until she reaches the age of majority. It's more important than ever that she finish her education."

The queen picked up the envelope and a smaller envelope slipped out.

"Well, here's a little postscript with your name on it."

She passed the note to Laura, who stood awaiting further instructions. Liliu smiled and inclined her head toward the door. "Go ahead, read your letter. Come back in half an hour to see if any of this correspondence requires a reply." She pointed to a document at the edge of her desk. "And then I want you to take this to Willie Kaae to copy for me."

Laura curtsied and left the room. She went out to the verandah, and sat in a chair at the side of the house. Holding the small envelope in her hands, she thought about the last time she'd seen the princess, whose letters sent in the intervening two years indicated a growing maturity and a new sense of independence. Ka`iulani wasn't a little girl anymore. Laura wiggled her thumbnail under the edge of the envelope and lifted it open. The letter was dated before news of Mr. Dominis's death could have reached her, and the tone of her sixteen-year-old chatter reminded Laura of herself, just before the tragedies that had brought her to Hawaii.

Dear Laura,
England is "jolly good" and all that, but I'm aching to get

out of this cold and damp and back home. I want to bury myself under sweet-smelling leis and go riding with you on the beach at Waikiki and up Diamond Head to see Lookout Charlie.

I'm so happy you're working with my aunt. She has no one to look after her, really. I worry when I get the political news from Honolulu. I feel like I should be there with her, but when I mention it in letters, she tells me to finish my education and then hurry home.

I'm getting quite an education here — the usual subjects, of course, including etiquette and how to comport myself. Did I tell you I wear reading glasses now? Too much studying. But as I told my aunt, I feel the weight of the future coming on, and I want to do a good job for my people.

In the meantime, I must tell you (keep it a secret) that the young men here are most attentive. I spent a weekend at my guardian's home in London, and we simply went the pace while we were up there. Don't be shocked. I have a bit of a flirtation going on *pour le moment*. I can't wait to see you again. I have piles to tell you!

Love,
Vike
(What they call me here — for Victoria, my middle name)

&

Thurston threw down a month-old copy of the *London Daily Telegraph* on Sanford Dole's desk.

"What do you make of this?"

There was a glowing account of publisher Sir Edwin Arnold's

visit to Honolulu and his regard for Lili`uokalani.

"Hmm." Dole read the article. "Says, 'every inch a queen... noble grace... lofty gentleness.'"

"Yeah," Thurston said, "and some of the Honolulu papers reprinted it this week. With Ka`iulani being trained in England, the Brits are getting entirely too cozy with our monarchy, if you ask me. The US minister's not happy about it. He thinks they have definite designs here. We need to shake things up."

Dole raised his eyebrows. "You're the one who suggested sending Ka`iulani away to school."

"I didn't know the king would send her to England. I thought maybe San Francisco."

Dole sat back. "Well, what concerns me is the growing immigration of Chinese and Japanese. They're more likely to take us over than the British — just by sheer numbers."

"Either way, we can't sit by and do nothing."

"The trouble is," Dole said, "things are going pretty well in the country now. The queen's more popular than ever. I could see that by her reception in the outer islands. Her economy program has stimulated business. People are content. Maybe we should just give her a chance and see how it goes."

"And wait for some other power to grab us? Come on, Sanford. It's only three generations ago that our great-grandfathers threw off the British yoke. I don't want it put back on us now. And that's what we'll have, if things keep on the way they're going. You have the American revolutionary blood in your veins. I can't see you being content under a monarch."

Dole thought of the taunt of his childhood friends: *American blood and Hawaiian milk.*

"There are some dissatisfied types around," Thurston said. "Maybe a little local agitation is in order."

"It wasn't all that effective last time," Dole said. "When the native 'agitators' were jailed, they almost spilled the beans, and threatened to tell who was really behind the effort to get the king to abdicate."

Thurston jumped up. "All I know is that annexation is the only way to save the country, and I'm willing to risk almost anything to see that happen. If we have to create a sense of danger so the United States will sit up and take notice of their own interests in the Pacific, then I'm all for it."

"What are you proposing, Thurston?"

"We have to destabilize the queen. Create an environment like a kaleidoscope, so that every time she turns around, things have changed. We can make her appear incompetent to the American government so they'll be concerned about losing Pearl Harbor to some other power that might threaten US security. Minister Stevens understands what I'm after, and he supports me. We have to move before he's replaced and we're back to square one."

"Lorrin ..." Dole stopped him. "We've been friends since we were kids. I know you want the best for Hawaii, and you're entitled to your opinions, but what you're talking about now is treason."

Thurston crossed the floor and stood for a moment with his back to Dole. Then he turned around.

"It's no more than what the patriots of 1776 committed against King George. We're Americans, Sanford. And I want Hawaii to have all the privileges and freedoms of America. It's safer for us and better for the economy. If we don't achieve annexation soon, we'll have to live in fear of being grabbed by England, Germany, Japan, or maybe even Russia. Where will Hawaii be then?"

Dole leaned forward. He knew all those powers had imperial intentions in the Pacific.

"What do you have in mind, Lorrin?"

"I say we let the rumors fly that the queen is becoming pro-British. Try to get the US to keep a warship in Hawaiian waters permanently to protect American interests here. We can encourage the malcontents of mixed blood to voice their opposition. I've known some of them since I was a kid, and they're only happy when they're on their way to a fight. They've always been the odd men out, so they hardly care which side they're on, as long as they think there's something in it for them. We need to get our men back in the cabinet, and I want to drum up support in the community, like we did with the Hawaiian League. But this time, I want an Annexation Club."

&

*L*aura reluctantly stacked the morning's letters and newspapers to take to the queen. The San Francisco Examiner was the worst. The writer reported that the kingdom was rocked by riots and plagued by the sorcery of a "black pagan who wanted nothing short of absolute monarchy." He went on to stress the extreme danger to the white citizens from such a savage queen.

How was she supposed to show Liliu such articles? That same reporter had called on the queen and was surprised she spoke good English. He thought he'd have to communicate through an interpreter. And at the very moment he'd written that dangerous riots were supposed to be happening, he'd been enjoying Hawaiian hospitality at a peaceful picnic.

Perhaps she could overlook the ignorance of American correspondents, who were never the type to let truth get in the way of a sensationalized story, but the Hawaiian clergy who wrote such lies to the American papers were unforgivable. On the occasion of the queen's ascension to the throne, Reverend Serano Bishop had written that Lili`uokalani had a gentle and gracious demeanor, good sense, fine culture, the affection of her people, and the high regard of the foreign community. Now, for some unknown reason, he'd submitted a column to the *New York Independent* claiming she was the debauched queen of a heathenish monarchy peopled by kahuna sorcerers and idolators. Laura put that paper at the bottom of the pile, hoping the queen wouldn't read it.

She shook her head as she lifted the stack of correspondence and headed for the queen's office. And if that weren't enough, there were rumors running around of insurrection, supposedly spread by the more radical element in the legislature. They even attacked the queen as a woman, saying they didn't want to be ruled by a doll, and that no woman ought to reign because they're weak and have no brains; that she filled a position ordained only for men since the beginning of creation.

Thank goodness the queen had the assurance of help from the United States whenever she needed it.

Chapter 22

*L*orrin Thurston descended the stairs from his office and walked out on the wooden sidewalk just as Willie Kaae swung open the door from inside Bishop Bank.

"Whoa, Willie!" Thurston put out his hands and halted to avoid slamming into the door.

Startled, Willie looked up. "Oh, Mr. Thurston. I didn't see you." He let the door swing shut.

"You should watch where you're going."

Willie hung his head. "Yeah, I'm sorry."

Thurston regarded his downcast stance. "Why so glum?"

"I tried to get a loan to pay my debts, but it was refused."

"Aren't you still working for the queen as a copyist?"

"Yeah, she pays me good, but I've been playing cards too much, I guess."

Thurston smiled. "It's not the playing that's the trouble, boy. It's the losing."

Willie stared at his feet. "I've been doing my share of that. My girl is mad, and she won't see me till I pay off my creditors."

Thurston thought a moment. "How much are you behind?"

Willie glanced up and named a moderate figure. Thurston studied his face, then nodded back toward his office.

"Come on upstairs with me, Willie. I've got a proposition that could help you get back on your feet."

❧

In the hallway, Laura met Wakeki carrying a tray of tea to the queen's study.

"I'm on my way there," Laura said. "I can take it in."

She entered the study and set the tray down on a side table. The queen was just finishing her German lesson.

"Stay and have tea with us, Laura. Fräulein Wolf said she'll tell our fortunes."

The queen was always entertained by Fräulein Wolf's "sixth sense," rare among haoles, though common among Hawaiians. Laura was glad for some diversion. The news lately had worsened. The queen's first cabinet had been dismissed a few months back by a legislative vote of no confidence. Every cabinet she'd named since was voted out, sometimes within just a few weeks, and once within two hours. The opposition never gave them a fair chance. The legislature wouldn't let any other business be done until they had a cabinet they approved, and the result was a stalemate. Government employees went unpaid, bills were postponed or ignored, and the legislature met only to adjourn.

As a result of the chaos, which the newspapers blamed on the queen, business investment waned and the economy plunged into recession. In consultation with British Foreign Minister Wodehouse, the queen had finally named a cabinet acceptable to the legislature. Laura hoped things would settle down at last.

"Good afternoon, Fräulein Wolf," Laura said. She poured tea, served the queen and her guest, and took a seat. Many of her haole friends consulted Fräulein and had her in to entertain with mind reading and astrology at their lanai parties. But Laura didn't give her powers much credence. "I hope you'll have good news."

Fräulein sipped her tea, then replaced the cup in the saucer. "We'll see what the spirits have in store." She smiled, sat back in her chair, and closed her eyes. Little by little her head sagged toward her chest. Laura thought she'd fallen asleep. Then, all at once, she sat up straight and her eyes flashed open. She told them she saw a tall, bold Hawaiian warrior clothed in a feathered cape and helmet, accompanied by attendants carrying magnificent kahilis.

"He is Kamehameha the Great. He's come to advise the queen."

Fräulein Wolf described him in detail, and Liliu nodded to Laura that her rendering was correct.

"He says a man will come to you with an opportunity for great wealth that will pull the country out of depression. Watch for him."

Laura hoped it was true. The country needed new income, the sooner the better.

"And he's warning you to beware of certain individuals. Their initials are L. T, C. B., and — well, it's not clear — either S. D. or S. P."

Laura tried to connect the initials to people. L. T. could be Lorrin Thurston. He was no friend of the monarchy, that was clear. What worried her was that if 'L. T.' meant Lorrin Thurston, he'd just gotten money from the legislature for a trip to the United States, supposedly to see about having a Hawaii exhibit to promote the kingdom's products at the World's Columbian Exhibition next year. What was he really up to?

C. B. Could that be Charles Bishop, the banker? But the queen had lived with him and his wife, Pauahi, her hanai sister, when she was younger. Why would he want to do her harm? Yet there was that letter he'd sent when she ascended the throne, telling her she would be happier and live longer if she didn't try to do too much. What did he mean by that?

And S. D. or S. P. That couldn't be Sanford Dole. He was well regarded in the community and a long-time friend of the queen. She'd just been to his home last week to attend an evening lecture, though the subject, the French Revolution, was a bit queer. Had that been put together as an object lesson about what could happen to monarchs? A little too close to home, considering the current chaotic conditions. Fortunately, after a full day of state affairs, the queen was tired and had drifted off to sleep. She was embarrassed later, but Laura was glad she hadn't had to endure the whole talk. No, Sanford Dole didn't really make sense. The queen had appointed him to the Privy Council as one of her closest advisors.

Maybe it was S. P. then … S. P.? Her uncle, Stephen Price? He was close with Thurston and Bishop. And he'd raised a toast to a new government.

Fräulein Wolf closed her eyes. "King Kamehameha is fading, but another spirit is appearing to me now. No, two — no, wait — it's three. A white man with two beautiful women. One is white, with hair like the sun, and the other, dark like the night … she's Hawaiian." Fräulein opened her eyes. "They're all smiling at you, Laura."

Laura sat back in surprise, and clutched a hand to her chest where she felt the black pearl ring under her blouse.

"They say you'll be joined forever with the one you love, but in a surprising way." Fräulein Wolf closed her eyes again. "Oh, wait. They're growing faint. Both women are holding out bundles for you to see, but I can't make out — "

"They're babies," Laura said.

The queen turned to look at her.

"I see something else," Fräulein Wolf said, her eyes still closed. Her face grew serious and she was quiet. Then, slowly, her eyes opened, looking darker than before. She spoke softly. "No, I'm sorry, I didn't catch the details. It faded too quickly."

"Can't you tell us anything?" the queen said.

Fräulein leaned forward to pick up her teacup. "Only that great love and great loss can be intertwined."

&

*L*aura was glad to get out of the tension in Honolulu and spend a few days with the queen, entertaining friends at Waikiki. She thought if she saw another article like the one on Friday, she'd march down to the newspaper and smash the presses herself. Ever since she'd come to Honolulu she'd heard criticism of the king's expenditures for state occasions. Now, the same people blasted Lili`uokalani because her entertainments lacked the lavishness of Kalakaua's! Would the monarchy's critics never be satisfied?

The luau preparations were complete and a few guests had already arrived. Laura wondered if it would have that same sense of ease and contentment she remembered from her first luau at Hamohamo. Kalakaua had been under attack even then, but if Liliu had been affected, she hadn't let it show. Now she was the storm center, but here she was greeting guests with that same grace she'd shown all those years ago.

David would arrive soon. It was a luxury to think about a few hours with him. But Liliu had invited other close friends in the government, so perhaps it wouldn't be just an afternoon of relaxation. Riding out in the carriage, Liliu looked as though she had something else in mind.

When David rode up and dismounted, Laura felt the same strong connection. She thought of Fräulein Wolf's message from the spirits saying she'd find great love. She did love him, and she felt love from him, but always with a question behind his eyes. He never relinquished a certain reserve. If anything, it had grown since he'd been in prison. He'd embrace her in greeting, or kiss her cheek, but that was all. Did he doubt her sincerity since she'd once agreed to marry Lucien?

No proper lady would approach a man on such a matter. One must wait to be pursued. But she had a very unladylike urge to confront him directly. Unfortunately, the day's venue didn't allow the privacy for such an encounter. More people were arriving, and soon lunch would be announced. As she walked toward the mats where people were sitting, David came up to her — again, a friendly embrace and a kiss on the cheek.

During lunch they sat next to each other. David put delicacies on her plate, urging her to eat. He shared news from work and mutual friends. Every time he looked at her, his glance was warm and caring. She felt his desire to be close to her. But when she began to flirt, she sensed him draw away, and again saw that doubt in his eyes.

When lunch was almost through, the queen divulged her intention for the afternoon.

"I've been thinking about some changes I want to introduce, and I'd like you all to be my sounding board."

The guests put down their bowls and cups.

"A man came to me two weeks ago with a proposal to create income for the kingdom."

Laura sat up a little straighter. Fräulein Wolf's prophecy.

"He represents a company from Louisiana that sets up lotteries. He showed me how it could generate money for much-needed public works. It's been used in the United States to fund things like roads and universities."

David leaned toward Laura. "It'd be good to have some alternative income the Crown controls."

The queen looked around at her guests. "I've inquired of various members of the community, and there seems to be general support, especially from shopkeepers and manufacturers. What are your opinions?"

"If public works were funded, it would create jobs, and the money would go into the hands of more people instead of just a few," David said. "I know better roads and a railroad on the Big Island would be most welcome. Small farmers could get their produce to other markets, and it would help diversify the economy away from sugar."

Mr. Kupaka, one of the legislators Laura had met at Ainahau, spoke up.

"The opposition is trying to force bankruptcy on the country to forward their scheme of annexation. We have to find ways to counter them. I'm all for it."

The others nodded their assent.

"Well, another measure I'm considering," the queen said, "is to license the importation of opium. With the large population coming in from Asia, illegal importation is threatening to get out of control. This way we can begin to regulate it, if not entirely suppress it."

Little alarms went off in Laura's head. Drugs and gambling — what would the Missionary Party make of it? The British minister spoke.

"I think that's well advised, Your Majesty. The British government adopted licensing instead of prohibition. It's gone a long way toward regulating the importation and sale of the drug in our colonies."

Mr. Aeko, another legislator, voiced Laura's concern.

"The opposition may try to make political hay out of these measures. They'll scream 'morality,' as they usually do, but it's their own pocketbooks they're concerned about. They're not going to like any big moneymaking enterprise they don't control, like a lottery. And it's not such a well-kept secret that some of our fine upstanding missionary boys have made some tidy profits in the opium trade. That's why they'll oppose licensing. They don't want to have to identify their involvement publicly."

The queen nodded. "Nevertheless, would you favor licensing?"

"Yes."

There was a murmur of agreement.

"There's an even more pressing matter," the queen said. "There are rumors our newly appointed cabinet may be dismissed soon by another vote of no confidence. The constitution forced on my brother made the monarch inferior to the cabinet, and the opposition has used that power to make the cabinet a perpetual football. All my official acts require the cabinet's advice and consent, but they've made sure no cabinet lasts long enough to get any work done. They've brought the business of the kingdom to a standstill.

"My people, including some of you here," she nodded at several present, "have repeatedly petitioned me to revise the constitution to give the monarch more power and regain the vote for Hawaiians. My efforts to call a constitutional convention have been blocked at every turn."

Color rose in her cheeks. "Where, I ask you, in any other sovereign nation on earth, are men allowed to vote, seek office, and hold positions of responsibility without being citizens — and at the same time, to prevent the citizens from voting? That will have to change!

"I do not intend to deprive any foreigners of their rights, and all are welcome to apply for citizenship, but I must respond to the wishes of my people." She looked around at their faces, expectant and apprehensive about what was coming next. "I have determined that the only way to save the country is to make the monarchy stronger and promulgate a new constitution."

Laura watched the reaction of the queen's friends. Some looked thoughtful and hopeful, but others seemed alarmed. The last time people tried to overturn the Bayonet Constitution that had been forced on the king, men were shot and imprisoned. Had Kalakaua signed a new constitution, his opponents would have called it treason.

Lili`uokalani sat erect and resolute. Laura's misgivings turned to pride. The queen was standing up for justice. And Laura decided then, no matter who arose to oppose her, or what the consequences, she'd stand with her.

Chapter 23 ———

*L*ucien waited in the carriage, watching for Lorrin Thurston to come down the steamship's gangplank. He spotted him, stood up, and waved. Thurston waved back and then disappeared into the crowd on the wharf. Within minutes, Lucien saw him outpacing a slight Chinese man who pushed his luggage in a wheelbarrow. Thurston headed toward the carriage, his gait bouncier than usual.

"Good news," he said and climbed up next to Lucien. The Chinese man loaded his luggage in the back and Thurston tossed him a few coins. "Bishop and I had a great trip."

"Yeah?" Lucien started the horse up the street.

"I think we made headway in persuading the president that the entire Hawaiian population is in favor of annexation." Thurston grinned. "And folks in Washington told us that if conditions in Hawaii compel us to act and we go to them with a proposal, the administration would be exceedingly sympathetic."

"You talked to the president?"

"Not directly, no. But I did talk to a senator on the foreign relations committee, the secretary of state, and the secretary of the navy. The naval secretary was the one who delivered me the encouraging message."

"I didn't know the secretary of the navy had the power to set

US policy," Lucien said.

Thurston looked at him, annoyed. "He's not setting policy, he was just communicating the sentiment of the administration."

Lucien nodded toward a folded newspaper on the carriage seat. "The lottery bill is up for a vote this week."

Thurston picked up the paper and unfolded it. The article reported that many of the "respectable and responsible" citizens of Honolulu opposed the bill and had petitioned the queen to stop it. The queen had responded that if the legislature passed the bill, she wouldn't veto it.

"How's the vote look?" Thurston said.

"We can defeat it."

He looked back at the paper, reading and musing.

"Do you want to stop at the office before going home?" Lucien said.

"For a minute."

Lucien turned the horse right at the next street.

Thurston folded the paper over twice, then smacked his palm with it. It popped like a gunshot. The horse bolted. Lucien yanked the reins, and the horse fell back to a trot, nervously flicking its ears.

"Sorry," Thurston said. "I was just thinking. So many of our people seem outraged by this lottery bill. You know, maybe we should let it pass."

"Let it pass?" Lucien shook his head. "Why let it pass if so many people are against it?"

"That's just it," Thurston shifted in his seat to look at Lucien. "If it passes, the outrage against the throne grows, which puts the queen in a bad light. If we work it right, that outrage can become an uproar that'll support our plans. Let's call on a few legislators today to make sure they don't show up for that vote."

&

January 10, 1893

The lottery bill passed this week. David came to tell the queen about the strange absence of its most vocal opponents on the day of the vote. He thinks they're up to something. The attacks on the queen have intensified again. Now the papers say she's controlled by a spiritual medium who dictates all her decisions. I suppose they've seen Fräulein Wolf come to the house to give her German lessons. It's so unfair. Since the merry-go-round of cabinet changes, the queen has almost no one near her she can really trust.

And then there's the anonymous note she got this week. It scared me. It said that the American minister, along with some residents, intend to perfect a scheme of annexation with the help of some of her advisors. There's danger ahead, it said, and the enemy already in the house.

The queen has decided she must act now to promulgate a new constitution. That's the only way she'll ever get control of the cabinet again, and be able to choose people who will support her efforts. Besides, petitions have poured in from all the islands for a new constitution. Several of the queen's advisors have shown her drafts they've written. After considering all views, she wrote a draft of her own, and asked me to hand it to Willie Kaae to make several copies and then distribute them to her cabinet. They've promised to support her, and everything's ready to announce the new constitution in the next few days.

*L*ucien walked into Thurston's office with a stack of papers and set it on his desk. "Here are copies of the palace correspondence made by Willie Kaae." He pulled a document from the pile. "This is a new constitution."

Thurston thrust out his hand. "Let me see that."

He skimmed through the text and stopped at a passage on page three.

"Damn it! She's trying to reverse control of the cabinet." He tossed the document on the desk. "There's no end to it. If she gets her way, we're back to where we were before Kalakaua." He rubbed a vein that had popped out on his forehead. "How many people know about this?"

"Willie said it's been in the works for a few weeks. There's going to be a ceremony at the palace after the close of the legislature on January fourteenth."

"Well, she'll have to get the signatures of the cabinet to make it law. You get a message to them today that, if they don't want blood on their hands, they'd better not act without letting us know in advance." Thurston stood up. "Is the *Boston* back in port?"

Lucien nodded.

"Well, get going then. And notify Dole and Price too. I'm going to see Commander Wiltse and the US minister."

*J*ust before the queen left to give her speech, she called her four cabinet members together in the palace drawing room.

"Gentlemen." She acknowledged each one with a pleased look. "When the ceremony to close the legislature is ended today, I'll

have my chamberlain announce to the officials and foreign representatives that they're invited to the palace this afternoon for a
special meeting. I wish to see you all back here in the Blue Room
at noon to sign the new constitution."

The queen rose to go, and the cabinet ministers stood, glanced
at each other, and bowed. As soon as she had left, John Colburn,
the minister of the interior, turned to the others.

"What do we do now?"

"I say we go downtown to talk to Thurston, and fast," Attorney General Peterson said.

The other two said nothing, but didn't object. Peterson headed for the door.

"We'll meet you back here before noon," Colburn said, and
followed him.

&

*D*owntown, in the law office above Bishop Bank, the ministers told Thurston the queen's intentions. He listened, his jaw
set and his eyes fixed on the two men.

"You did the right thing by coming here, gentlemen."

"What should we do?" Colburn asked. "Resign?"

"Absolutely not," Thurston said. "If you resign, she'll just appoint
someone in your place to sign the new constitution. You've got
to go back and stall her. I'll send someone to let Captain Wiltse
on the USS *Boston* know that the situation could get violent and
that he should stand by with troops ready to come ashore to
protect American lives and property." Thurston stood to shake
the ministers' hands. "You're good men. You may have prevented
bloodshed by your action today. Go back and stand firm."

&

𝒲hen Colburn and Peterson arrived back at the palace, they were surprised at the crowd of Hawaiians gathered on the grounds, dressed in their Sunday best, and the palace guards lined up at attention. The queen had just returned, and the official guests from the legislature were congregating in the throne room.

The two hurried to the Blue Room where the other two ministers waited. Before they could speak, they heard the queen's chamberlain announce her arrival. As the queen entered the room, all four of the ministers stood and bowed.

"Be seated, gentlemen," the queen said. She was resplendent in a lavender gown, with a coronet of diamonds on her head. The retainer who held her train arranged it at her feet as she sat down. Laura followed, and stood at the queen's side.

Outside, the Royal Hawaiian Band struck up a tune, while a procession of Hawaiian men in formal attire and top hats entered the palace, one carrying the text of the new constitution on a blue satin pillow.

The queen smiled at her ministers. "This is an historic occasion, gentlemen. Today we strengthen the independence of the Hawaiian Kingdom and secure the rights of its people by signing this new constitution." She signaled the chamberlain to have the document brought in and placed on the table before them.

"Your Highness," Colburn said. He glanced around at the other ministers. "We haven't had a chance to read and study this in depth."

The queen stared at him. "You've had it for days now. You agreed three days ago to hold this ceremony at the close of the legislative session."

Laura watched Colburn to see what he'd say next, but Peterson spoke.

"Yes, Your Highness. Maybe this is premature. We aren't familiar with all the provisions of the new constitution. We didn't realize you wanted to go forward with it today. And certainly you wouldn't want us to sign something we haven't read."

The queen took a long, slow breath to control herself. Then she beckoned the chamberlain to approach.

"We have guests in the throne room, and my people are waiting on the grounds for the announcement that they have a new constitution, but for your benefit, I'll have my chamberlain read the document aloud now."

The chamberlain stepped forward and began to read the constitution, page by page, pronouncing each word crisply, occasionally casting a look of disdain toward the ministers. As soon as he finished, the ministers launched into a debate about signing the document, protesting that they needed more time to confirm the legality of its proclamation.

The queen held up her hand for silence, then spoke in a low, clear voice. "You all encouraged me in this enterprise. You led me to this precipice, and have now left me to leap alone." She looked at them one by one. "I have no more desire to listen to your advice. I've decided to promulgate this constitution — and I'll do it now."

Peterson leaned forward. "Please, Your Majesty. Wait just two weeks. I assure you, a new constitution can be signed by then." The other ministers nodded their assent.

The queen looked at them a long time in silence. Laura looked at them too. They were probably all fine fellows, like Mr. Stevenson said to her so long ago beneath the banyan tree at Ainahau. Fine, talented fellows, he'd said. That was the richest part of the joke. Fine, talented, spineless fellows.

Without betraying any emotion, the queen stood. The ministers jumped up.

"Based on your assurances that the new constitution will be promulgated within two weeks, I'll wait. I must attend now to our guests."

She adjourned to the throne room, with Laura just behind her. The guests all rose as the queen entered, walked calmly to the dais, stepped up onto it, and turned to face them. She began to speak evenly, without any flutter in her voice. But her face reminded Laura of King Kalakaua's sad countenance as he walked down the steps to greet his wife and sister when they returned from England, after the Bayonet Constitution had been forcibly imposed.

The queen told the assembled guests that she'd been prepared to respond to the voice of her people and proclaim a new constitution, but that she'd met with obstacles that prevented it.

"I am obliged to postpone the granting of a constitution for a few days. Return to your homes peaceably, and continue to look toward me, as I will look toward you. Keep me ever in your love. You have my love, and with sorrow, I dismiss you."

She stepped down from the dais and walked toward the door. Heads turned to follow as she left. She entered the great hall and walked slowly up the wide koa-wood staircase to the second-floor verandah. When a few in the crowd below saw her, whispered voices passed the word, "The queen, the queen." All raised their eyes and the crowd fell silent. She addressed them in Hawaiian, saying what she'd said in the throne room, and then dismissed them.

"Go with good hope, and do not be troubled in your minds, because within these next few days, I will proclaim the new constitution. Retire to your homes and maintain the peace."

&

Thurston smiled as the twelve men he'd called to serve with him on the Committee of Safety filed into his office. Three of them, like himself, had been born in Hawaii of American parents. There was one American, a German, and an Australian who were naturalized Hawaiian citizens, two Scotsmen, and four other Americans. All fine, talented fellows.

"Gentlemen," Thurston said after they took their seats, "I appreciate your participation on this committee. The intelligent part of the community has got to take matters into their own hands and establish law and order. We are hereby declaring that the queen's action to overthrow the constitution is revolutionary, and that she's likely to persist in this manner. I move that we take steps at once to form and declare a provisional government with a view toward annexation to the United States."

Stephen Price seconded the motion.

"Any discussion?" Thurston asked.

The men shook their heads, and Thurston called for a show of hands. It was unanimous.

"Price," Thurston said, "report on our visit to US Minister Stevens with Cabinet Ministers Colburn and Peterson."

Stephen stood. "The US minister agreed that the queen's actions can be considered revolutionary. Although his government promised previously to support her, he said he'd recognize the cabinet as the government, and give them the same assistance that has always been afforded Hawaii by US representatives."

There was a murmur of approval. Stephen continued.

"And he said he'd recognize a de facto government if we held the government building, the palace, and the police station."

Ҩ

The queen's marshal pushed past the servant at the door and stormed into her study. Laura, taking dictation, jerked her head up and dropped her pencil on the floor.

"Your Majesty," the marshal said, "I just got word that Thurston and his cronies intend to announce that you're in revolution against the government and declare the throne vacant."

Laura, who'd bent to retrieve her pencil, sat up. "How?" Then she glanced at the queen. "I'm sorry, Your Majesty."

The queen shook her head. "Never mind, Laura." She turned to her marshal. "Mr. Wilson, what's this all about?"

"They say you illegally moved to sign a new constitution, but your cabinet prevented it, and that you told your people you'd sign another one within a few days. They're going to use that to try to dethrone you. I want permission to swear out warrants and arrest them."

"I'll need the cabinet's approval." The queen addressed her servant. "Ask the chamberlain to call the members immediately." Then she nodded at Mr. Wilson. "Please, be seated. They should be across the street at the government building."

Laura got up. "I'll call Wakeki to bring tea."

When the ministers had assembled in the queen's study, Marshall Wilson told them that Thurston had formed a committee to overthrow the throne. Two ministers supported his desire to swear out warrants, but to Laura's surprise, Peterson and Colburn spoke against it, saying it might precipitate a conflict.

Laura watched the cabinet argue back and forth. Precipitate a conflict? What would they call a threat from the so-called Committee of Safety to dethrone the queen? Wasn't that already a conflict?

"Let's ask the advice of some conservative businessmen," Colburn said finally. "They'd know how these committee members think and how to defuse the situation."

With the queen's consent, six men were called to meet with her and the cabinet that same afternoon. They reviewed the problem, and advised her that the whole issue was the constitution.

"If you do not back off of this, Your Majesty," one of the businessmen said, "you could very well lose the throne."

Laura looked at the men sitting around the Blue Room — such a small group. She thought of the large crowd of Hawaiian subjects the queen had asked to go home peaceably the other day. And how her cabinet had assured her she'd be able to grant their wishes in two weeks. Now they were asking her to permanently surrender her efforts to strengthen the independence of her kingdom through restoring the monarchy's power and the vote to her people. And if she didn't, she might lose the kingdom forever.

The queen reluctantly agreed to sign a proclamation to assure the community that the matter of a new constitution was at an end. But the only community that wanted such assurance, Laura knew, was the one composed of men like those before her.

&

Marshall Wilson went downtown to call on Thurston at his office and let him know the queen would do nothing further about a constitution.

"I know what you fellows are up to, Thurston," he said, "and I want you to stop."

Thurston set his pen down and looked up with a smug smile. "We're not going to stop, Charlie. It's gone too far, and we intend to take care of this once and for all."

Wilson left in a huff and Thurston returned to finish his letter to US Minister Stevens.

The queen, with the aid of armed force and accompanied by threats of violence and bloodshed from those with whom she was acting, attempted to proclaim a new constitution. This conduct and action have created general terror and alarm. We are unable to protect ourselves without aid, and therefore pray for the protection of United States forces.

Chapter 24 ———

*W*hen the queen's marshal heard that American troops had landed, the blood drained from his face. They'd taken up positions alongside the government building across from the palace, and he had only a handful of poorly equipped royal guards. There were city police, but they weren't a fighting force. He hoped the marines were onshore to do practice drills. He went to tell the queen, and found her and Laura having an early supper. They had the verandah door open to hear the Royal Hawaiian Band, which was playing its regular evening concert just up the street at the Hawaiian Hotel.

The queen assured Wilson that she hadn't asked for any troops. She called immediately for Governor Cleghorn and the two cabinet ministers who had agreed to sign out warrants, and sent them to meet with the US minister and ask his intentions. With them she sent a note, restating that she'd uphold the present constitution.

When they arrived at Stevens's residence, his Oriental serving man showed them to the drawing room. After about fifteen minutes, Stevens still hadn't appeared. Cleghorn sat, legs crossed, foot bobbing, growing angry that the US minister was keeping him and two of the queen's highest officials waiting. And he worried that his daughter's rights as future queen might be imperiled.

When Stevens finally joined them, Cleghorn tried to restrain his irritation. The three men rose, and the US minister shook hands all around, affecting an easy, unconcerned manner.

"What can I do for you, gentlemen?"

A cabinet minister handed him the note from the queen. Stevens opened it, then looked up, shrugging his shoulders.

"I've already been informed of the queen's decision." He folded the note and handed it back.

Governor Cleghorn, his Scottish "Rs" trilling, got right to the point.

"Her Majesty wishes to know your intention for landing the *Boston's* troops."

Stevens didn't answer.

The Scotsman started to turn red. "Is it annexation?"

"No."

"Then," Cleghorn made an effort to keep his voice steady, "by the queen's request, we ask that the troops be withdrawn."

Stevens leveled his gaze at Cleghorn.

"Kindly put her request in writing," a smile played about his lips, "and if it's in a friendly spirit, I'll reply in kind." He extended his arm toward the door. "Now, if you'll excuse me, gentlemen, I must get back to work."

Cleghorn jammed his hat on his head and aimed for the exit, the two ministers behind him. He said nothing until they were seated in the carriage.

He gazed up toward the mountains above the Nuuanu Valley, as if stunned, then back at the men sitting across from him. He shook his head and lowered his eyes.

"Gentlemen, our independence is gone."

ℚ

In the dark, Lucien made his way around the spiky palm bushes and up onto the trellised front porch of the Dole home. He knocked, and Mrs. Dole came to the door.

"Good evening, ma'am. Is Judge Dole in?"

"Why, Lucien, what are you doing out so late?"

"I'd like to speak to the judge."

She held the door open wider, and Lucien stepped inside.

"He's in the parlor. Go on in."

By lamplight, Judge Dole sat reading a book on the birds of North America. Seeing Lucien, he placed an envelope to mark his page and shut the cover.

"Lucien." He nodded.

"I'm sorry to disturb you, Judge Dole, but they want you to come over to the office to head this affair."

Dole shook his head. "No. Why won't Thurston take it?"

"He's sick in bed from working day and night since this whole thing started. Mr. Price has fallen sick, and some others too. They need your help."

Dole looked down at the book in his lap. A few moments passed before he set it on the table next to his chair and stood up.

"All right," he said. "Let's go."

When they reached the Bishop Bank Building, there was no one around. The electric lampposts cast more shadow than illumination, mottling the dark sidewalk. Muted, plaintive ukulele music came from the direction of Cunha's Saloon. Down toward Chinatown where most nights, sailors stumbled along with their arms around half-caste women, the streets were oddly quiet. As they trudged up to the second-story landing, their footfalls sounded hollow on the wooden stairs, and Dole thought revolution seemed a terrible, lonely business.

In Thurston's waiting room, only eight of the thirteen members of the Committee of Safety were present. In the dim light, two men smoked cigars, the tips glowing, smoke curling up as they puffed. The rest sat silent. They perked up when Dole entered. He acknowledged the men with a "good evening," and pulled up a chair.

"We want you to head the new government, Sanford," one man said.

"So I heard," Dole said. "Before we take this thing too far, gentlemen, and people get hurt, I'd like you to consider something."

Lucien sat down in a chair against the wall, and one man put out his cigar in a sand-filled spittoon next to him.

"The queen issued a proclamation that she's done with the matter of a new constitution. Can't we let this thing rest?"

A heavyset, balding man with a long goatee spoke first. "We don't believe she'll let it rest. If we don't dethrone her, there's plenty in Honolulu that will. You hear the threats on her life all the time."

Dole knew of those threats, and thought, *perhaps the queen should be dethroned, if only for her own safety.*

"Well, you men know the Hawaiians love their monarchs as much as we love our republics. Wouldn't it make sense for the peace and security of the kingdom to name Princess Ka`iulani to succeed the queen, and have a regency?"

Lucien felt the stir of indignation in the room. Exclamations erupted: "That won't work; we're tired of the monarchy — we don't want anything more to do with it." A clean-shaven man with glasses and a slick part in his hair made the plea once more.

"We need you to head this thing, Judge. It's got to be you or Thurston."

Dole looked around at the men, now sitting up, agitated, tense. He knew there was no going back.

"Let me sleep on it, gentlemen. I'll let you know in the morning."

He rose to leave, and Lucien jumped up.

"I'll go with you, sir."

On the way back, they walked a few blocks in silence. Finally Lucien spoke.

"Will you take the leadership, Judge?"

"I said I'd sleep on it."

Lucien hesitated, his brow furrowed. "Do you mind if I tell you something?"

Dole glanced sideways at him. "What is it?"

"I don't like the changes I'm seeing in Mr. Thurston."

Dole kept walking, looking ahead. "What do you mean?"

"I know he's fed up with the monarchy," Lucien said. "But lately he's revealed some things to me that make me think when he says he wants to 'take care of it once and for all,' he's not just talking about dethroning the queen. Judge…"

Lucien stopped and pulled at his arm. Dole turned to face him.

"…I think he's trying to create a sense that the situation is violent so he can justify violence. If you don't take the lead, sir, I fear what'll happen to the queen and those around her. I fear there'll be a bloodletting if Thurston gets hold of this."

Dole stood, his arms hanging heavy at his sides. Not just his arms, but his whole body felt heavy with the weight of change, the weight of tumbling history, colliding cultures, the weight of lies and deceit. Every time he read those articles in the newspaper describing Lili`uokalani as a bloodthirsty, black pagan savage, his mind flashed back to the forests of Niihau. How she told him, her voice like a song, that the o'o birds were true Hawaiians because they needed flowers for their very life. He saw her sitting in his own parlor, discussing literature and music. He saw her speaking with grace and eloquence before the legislature. He wanted to tell Lucien how the beauty of Hawaiian women made him burn, and their gentleness made him ache. How the sweetness of the native men's attitude of "hail fellow well met" broke his heart. But there in the soft, tropical night scented with ginger blossoms, his taciturn New England blood prevailed.

"I said I'd sleep on it."

Dole went home, but his sleep was fitful. He dreamed of volcanic eruptions — red, burning, churning lava flowing to the sea, turning to blood and hissing steam as it dropped over cliffs to meet the cold ocean. He awoke frightened and soaked with sweat.

જી

Thurston's voice echoed down the stairwell as Dole slowly climbed the steps to his office.

"Last week the sun rose on a peaceful city. Now it's in turmoil, and whose fault is it? Queen Lili'uokalani's. She wants us to sleep on a slumbering volcano that will one day spew out blood and destroy us all."

Dole stalled on the stairs, remembering his dream of volcanoes. As he'd passed through town, he'd noted a crowd of Hawaiians gathered on the opera house steps.

"The man who has no spirit to challenge the menaces to our liberties has no right to keep them. Has the tropic sun thinned our blood? Or do we have the warm, rich blood that loves liberty and dies for it?"

Dole heard mumbles of response. When Henry Baldwin asked if they might not use constitutional means to achieve their ends, he was howled down. Dole resumed his climb up the stairs.

Thurston's timbre intensified. "The responsible members of the community must protect it from revolutionary uprisings like this royal aggression. Unless we take radical measures, the queen's actions will damage our credit abroad and decrease our guarantees of life, liberty, and property."

Dole appeared at the doorway of the office, and Stephen Price stepped forward to shake his hand.

"Good to see you, Sanford."

Dole nodded at the thirteen men of the Committee of Safety gathered in the room. He crossed the floor to stand by the window. All faces turned toward him, awaiting his decision.

"Gentlemen, after much consideration on how I might be of assistance in this endeavor, I've decided to accept your request to head the provisional government. This morning I wrote out my resignation as judge and sent it to the queen's secretary."

There was a burst of backslapping and jubilant grins.

Thurston stepped forward. "There's no time to lose. The US minister told us he'd recognize us if we held the government building, the police station, and the palace. His troops are stationed to protect American lives and property, and the Honolulu Rifles are assembling at the armory to back us up."

Dole thought of the crowd of Hawaiians at the opera house, and glanced out the window. Five big Hawaiian policemen stood on the opposite sidewalk, looking up toward Thurston's office.

"There are people gathering, and some Hawaiian police just across the street," Dole said. "How do you propose we get to those buildings?"

Stephen Price smiled. "I've arranged a little diversion. John

Good is downtown filling his buckboard with arms and ammunition. We think that'll keep the eyes of the police directed away from where we're headed."

Just then a shot rang out from the direction of King Street. The men looked at each other.

"That wasn't part of my plan," Stephen said.

Thurston moved to the window to see the police run toward downtown, the townspeople following them. He turned back to the committee.

"The street has cleared, I say we go now."

The men looked to Dole. He nodded and they got up, filed down the stairs, and headed uptown toward the government building. When they got there, it was almost deserted. A clerk told them everyone had gone downtown to see about the ruckus and the cabinet had gone over to the police station to write to the US minister to ask for his help.

Thurston smiled broadly. He pulled out a proclamation he'd prepared, and read it to the few bewildered clerks who were still there. He stated that responsible government was impossible under the monarchy; that the queen was deposed, her ministers and marshal ousted, and a provisional government was established to remain in force until union with the United States was achieved.

Members of the Honolulu Rifles arrived, and surrounded the government building. The new provisional government declared martial law, and sent messengers to demand the surrender of the police station.

By five o'clock that afternoon, before the queen had surrendered, US Minister Stevens recognized the provisional government as the legitimate government of the Hawaiian Islands.

&

The cabinet ministers waited for the queen in the Blue Room of the palace. When she and Laura walked in, the men still made the same formal bows, but the way they lowered their eyes when the queen looked at them directly made Laura nervous.

"What have you come to tell me, gentlemen?" the queen said, motioning for them to be seated.

One spoke."A messenger came to the police station to say the Missionary Party has taken the government building. Sentinels from the Honolulu Rifles have surrounded it. They've declared a provisional government until they can annex the islands to the United States, and they're demanding surrender of the police station and the palace."

Laura glanced at the queen. She stiffened.

"There are nearly three hundred men under arms at the police station. Couldn't you put up any resistance?"

"Marshal Wilson wanted to fight, but with the marines still in place, we didn't want to risk it."

"Where's Marshall Wilson now?" the queen said.

"He's holding the police station."

Liliu showed no emotion, but was secretly glad one of her officials had stood up to them. But of course it was no use against the superior force of the United States. Stevens said he had landed the marines to protect American lives and property, but there was never any threat from the Hawaiians. If there had been, he would've stationed troops around American homes and the US legation, not across the street from the palace.

It was just like the time of Kamehameha III when Lord Paulet illegally used his warship to grab the islands in 1843. The king surrendered under protest then, and Queen Victoria restored the monarchy a few months later.

"Your Majesty," Peterson said, "we don't see any way to avoid bloodshed unless you surrender to the provisional government."

"And if I decide to do this," the queen said, "to whom do I send this surrender?"

"Well," Peterson said, "Thurston's over there…"

Laura shook her head. That was no surprise.

"…but Sanford Dole is the president, so I guess we'd deliver it to him."

A shudder crossed Liliu's face, and her eyes blinked rapidly. She caught herself and sat up straight, her voice tense.

"You may leave now, gentlemen. I'll call for you when I've made my decision."

The men got up, bowed, and left the room. Liliu nodded to the chamberlain to leave and close the door. She turned back to Laura, her face stricken.

"I could imagine this of Thurston, but it never entered my mind that one I had reason to believe was my friend…"

Her voice trailed off and she hung her head. They sat in silence as the sun went down and the room darkened.

&

That evening, the queen sent a letter to Marshall Wilson instructing him to surrender the police station to the provisional government. She also sent a sealed envelope to Sanford Dole at the government building, still waiting with Thurston and the others for her reply to their demands.

The cabinet minister handed the envelope to Dole who accepted it and endorsed its receipt.

"Received this day by the hands of the late cabinet, 17th day of January, AD 1893."

The ex-cabinet minister took the receipt and left the building.

Thurston reached for the envelope. "It's done, Sanford. It's done! All we have to do now is go to Washington and present our treaty for annexation. They've already said it'll be favorably received."

Thurston was practically hopping in place. Dole handed him the envelope. He slit it open and stood still, reading.

"My God!" he said. "This is no surrender!"

"What?" Dole said.

The other men gathered around.

"You signed off and accepted her protest, Sanford. She claims we were assisted by the US minister." His voice edged up. "She hasn't surrendered to the provisional government at all." He rattled the paper at them. "She surrendered to the United States, and has petitioned them to undo the illegal actions of the US minister and reinstate her as the rightful and constitutional monarch of Hawaii."

Chapter 25 ———

February 1, 1893

It's outrageous. The provisional government (everyone calls them the PGs now) chartered a ship with Crown funds they'd seized, and sent an envoy to Washington to petition for annexation. The queen asked that her representatives be allowed to sail with them so the facts of both sides could be heard, and the PGs refused! She had to wait two weeks for the next ship, which leaves tomorrow. Thurston's party will arrive in Washington this week. I've heard President Harrison is favorable to annexation, and Thurston will try to push it through before Harrison leaves office.

We have one ace up our sleeve: Grover Cleveland was reelected, and will take office on March 4th. He received the queen at the White House on her trip to England a few years back. She says he's fair-minded and knows she's not the "pagan savage" they make her out to be in the press.

Yesterday, the PGs raised the American flag over the government building, and the US minister is keeping marines there — supposedly as protection during the "negotiations" with Washington. On our way downtown, we drove by the building. The queen turned her face away and said, "May heaven look down on these missionaries and punish them for their deeds."

She doesn't go to church anymore. The last time we went, Reverend Parker's sermon was nothing but bald-faced abuse against her — with her sitting right there! Can that be godly? We still do devotions in the morning with her retainers at Washington Place, and sometimes she goes out to spend the day in a little thatched hut near Waikiki, where she can be alone with her thoughts.

She'd love to have her hanai children come to Washington Place now that all her family's gone, but she won't do it — too many threats.

&

Sanford Dole handed Thurston's letter across the desk to Stephen Price.

"It's not going to be as easy as he hoped."

Stephen read Thurston's account of his progress in Washington. President Harrison was favorable, and the annexation treaty had been submitted to Congress. But when President Cleveland took office, he'd withdrawn the treaty from the Senate for reexamination.

"Look at the end of the letter," Dole said. "Cleveland appointed James Blount of Georgia as a special commissioner to investigate what happened in Hawaii. He'll arrive here by the end of the month. Blount was the one who brushed Thurston off when he went to Washington last time. He's the former chairman of the House Committee on Foreign Affairs."

"Says here, his word will be paramount in all matters concerning the United States and the islands," Stephen said. "What's that supposed to mean?"

"I suppose that Cleveland will rely on his report to decide whether to resubmit the annexation treaty to the Senate." Dole shook his head. "Paramount Blount. Our whole future rides on that man."

"Well, from what Thurston says here, Blount's close-mouthed about what he's going to do." Stephen turned to the next page of the letter. "There's one bright spot."

"What's that?" Dole hadn't seen any bright spots in Thurston's message.

"Princess Ka`iulani's visit to Washington. Thurston says he's been able to angle that to increase the legislators' fears that the British have their eye on annexing Hawaii. After all, the princess is being made over in the image of an English-style sovereign. That could work in our favor." Stephen looked up. "He says anything we can do on this side now to discredit Lili`uokalani will be helpful. You got any ideas?"

"I don't." Dole stood up. "I'd better get on to the office. We're moving the executive headquarters over to the palace. It's got better barricades, and we can put a permanent garrison in the basement."

Stephen handed the letter back. "Okay, I can noodle on this awhile."

&

Laura stacked the mail and newspapers to take into the queen's study. She placed the *San Francisco Examiner* at the bottom of the pile. Criticism against the queen had increased since it was announced that President Cleveland was sending a special commissioner to investigate the overthrow. There was a debate on in the United States about Hawaii and annexation, and the queen wanted to know the public thinking. But how could Laura show her articles that said she was "immoral, heathenish, incapable of ruling a civilized nation, dangerous, bloodthirsty" — and the most heart-wrenching epithet of all — "a dirty squaw."

There were rumors that clergymen were sending these reports to the papers. If Reverend Parker's tirades from the pulpit were any example, it wasn't hard to believe. Mr. Stevenson was right: What a picture they painted of their own hearts.

Laura sighed. Better to think ahead to the future and Blount's visit. She put the *Examiner* aside. Tomorrow would be plenty of time for the queen to see that. How much could one person stand in a day anyway? Almost daily, petitioners came — some to suggest she take money from the PGs to abdicate, and others to urge resistance. For now, Laura wanted Liliu to concentrate on the letter postmarked from Washington, D.C., addressed in Ka`iulani's handwriting.

"The morning mail, Your Highness," Laura said, setting the stack of correspondence and papers on the queen's desk.

Liliu spotted the envelope. "Ka`iulani — I was hoping for news from her." She picked up the letter. "She's still so young, just seventeen. I worry people may try to use her to push their own advantage."

"She may not be experienced in politics," Laura said, "but I can tell you one thing: that girl has a mind of her own."

"Yes, and that may be her saving grace." The queen opened the letter and began to read.

My dear Aunt,
It's been so hard to be away and hear the dreadful news from home. When my guardian saw reports in the newspapers coming from America that said Hawaiians are

uneducated savages, incapable of governing themselves, he said I should go to the United States to plead our cause to end that argument forever. I was afraid at first. My time in England is spent studying and learning how to walk into a room gracefully. How could I stand up to these men?

But then I thought of you and how you said that the ali`i must do all in their power to protect the people. I thought someday the Hawaiians might say, "Ka`iulani could've helped us, but she didn't even try." So I determined to go and speak out on our behalf.

I hope you'll be pleased. Crowds in New York, Boston, and Washington thought they'd see a "barbarian princess." But the reporters have made much over my "dignity, beauty, and intelligence." There were always many of them waiting to discuss "the Hawaiian question." I've enclosed some clippings of their articles.

I spoke at Wellesley College and the Massachusetts Institute of Technology. You'll laugh. A friend from England studying there brought a number of young men to my talk. They stayed after, and one of them told me he'd been born in Hawaii. So I looked at him directly and said, "Why then, you belong to me." You never saw such a blush on a man!

When we reached Washington, I saw the Hawaiian flag flying over Wormley's Hotel where the provisional government's delegation is staying. Yet I'm told they raised the American flag over the government building in Honolulu. A curious state of affairs.

I received an invitation to visit President and Mrs. Cleveland at the White House. I was simply infatuated with Mrs. Cleveland. She's very beautiful, but all beautiful women are not sweet, as you know. Mrs. Cleveland is both. President Cleveland was quite kind. Since it was a personal visit and not a state visit, we didn't discuss politics, but he made it clear he intends to see justice done.

Before I left Washington, the National Geographic Society threw a gala ball in my honor, and the Women's Suffrage Association had me as the guest at a huge benefit. So many people wanted to get in, they had to bring police to help control the crowd.

I've clasped so many hands, seen so many smiles. I spoke to the American people, and I believe they've heard me. We're back in New York now and sailing for England tomorrow. How I wish I were sailing for Honolulu instead! I'd hoped '93 would be the end of my "exile" after four years away, though I know I must be patient until this situation clears. I try to be cheerful, but I'm so homesick. I'm longing to see you all.

Love,

Ka`iulani

Liliu finished reading as the chamberlain appeared at the study door.

"There's a group of kahuna women to see you, Your Majesty."

"Who are they?"

"One is Kaika, Cecil Brown's kahuna. I don't know the others."

"Show them in."

The chamberlain left, and Liliu turned to Laura.

"I wish they hadn't come. Most of these people are sincere, but with all the talk of me being pagan, I have to be careful. Remember Aimoku's birthday, when we killed a pig for the luau? The pig happened to be black. The next thing I hear, I'm a sorceress, making animal sacrifices, just because I like to observe Hawaiian customs from time to time."

She straightened the papers on her desk into neat piles. "The missionaries decorate their Christmas trees every year, but I've never called them Druids." She folded Ka`iulani's letter, put it in a drawer and lowered her voice. "I don't know who might be sending these kahunas."

A moment later, the chamberlain returned and ushered in three old Hawaiian women dressed in white, with yellow handkerchiefs around their necks and red bands on their hats. They bowed low to the queen and kissed her hand. One gray-haired crone stepped forward and began to speak in Hawaiian. Laura understood enough to catch her drift.

They'd come from a great gathering of kahunas who'd met to devise a method to restore the queen to the throne. The god of the missionaries now seemed partial only to the haoles. They wanted to return to the old ways. The queen could have the throne if she followed the instruction of Hiiaka, from the family of Pele, the volcano goddess.

The kahunas proposed to lead the queen in a procession to the palace, past the guards, and seat her on the throne. They'd be in front to stop the mouth of the gun. Once the queen was on the throne, they'd die. Perhaps death would not come at once, but in a few days. Then they'd know the gods had accepted their sacrifice.

Laura was touched by the women's willingness to die for their queen. But she knew that, even if they were sincere, the soldiers at the palace would no longer hesitate to fire on old ladies. And if they'd been sent by enemies, the queen's every word and act were being scrutinized to be used against her. She had to be careful.

Liliu heard them out, then stood to thank them, saying she was honored by the offer of their sacrifice. "But the Bible is my guide," she told them in Hawaiian. "I'll take my instructions from there."

&

*W*hen Special Commissioner James Blount arrived at the wharf in Honolulu, representatives of the provisional government were out in force to meet him. They offered housing, transportation, and every convenience he and his wife might need for their stay in Honolulu. He thanked them, but refused all offers.

The queen sent a carriage as well, which he also declined, but graciously accepted the leis that were placed around his and his wife's shoulders.

Once they were settled in their cottage on the grounds of the Hawaiian Hotel, Blount's first request was that the American flag flying over the government building be taken down and the marines returned to their ship.

The queen was hopeful, but sent word immediately that the Hawaiians should not make a scene as the haoles had done when the American flag was raised. Many Hawaiians gathered to watch, and kept silent, but some couldn't keep back tears. The men removed their hats, and the women shaded their eyes as they watched the Hawaiian flag rise up the pole once again.

Afterward, Stephen Price hurried across the street to Dole's office.

"Damn that Georgian," he told Dole. "He and his Confederate cronies tried for four years to haul down our flag in the Civil War and never did it. Why is he allowed to do it here in Honolulu?"

"Be patient," Dole said. "So far he's been cordial and neutral. Let him do what he came to do."

Stephen smiled. "Sure, but he may uncover a few surprises while he's here."

"What are you talking about, Stephen?"

Stephen shook his head. "If I told you, it wouldn't be a surprise."

Dole's eyes narrowed. "Look, too much of this can backfire. Thurston's still in Washington, working for annexation. He's our official minister now. Official positions require some decorum. I wrote him that he's to stop making the Hawaiians out to be dangerous and worthless. Why would America want to annex a territory full of shiftless barbarians?" He stood up. "Whatever you've got planned, I want you to stop it."

"Okay," Stephen said. "Take it easy, I'll take care of it."

&

November 1, 1893

*F*inally, progress. US Minister John Stevens was recalled. No one in the queen's household was sad to see him go, me least of all. The nerve of him, ordering marines to back up the PGs with no official sanction.

Commissioner Blount completed his investigation in early August. When he left Honolulu, a large crowd gathered at the wharf to see him off. The Hawaiians covered him and his wife with leis. The provisional government band sent him off with a rousing rendition of "Marching Through Georgia" — which I thought was small and petty.

A new US minister is supposed to arrive any day now.

This waiting is agony, and business is down because no one knows which government will be in power.

Before Blount left, a large cache of explosives was found buried next to the PG barracks. The queen was blamed, of course, until a PG policeman admitted he'd been ordered to plant the explosives to throw suspicion on the queen so the PGs could deport her. He never said why he hadn't set them off, but thank goodness he didn't. Many people could have been hurt or killed.

David came by last week. I was so happy to see him and have a chance to talk. He's frustrated with how the queen is portrayed in the newspapers and how the provisional government tries to crush all opposing opinions. One reporter from the *New York Herald* wrote that the queen was "well-read, intelligent, and answered questions worthy of a lawyer." When that issue of the *Herald* showed up in Honolulu, the writer was still here, and he was threatened with being tarred and feathered.

Still, the queen continues to ask her people to be patient and keep the peace. And it's her voice, more than any law the PGs can invoke, that has kept order in this community.

&

The new US minister, Albert Willis, arrived at the wharf on November 4. Without talking to anyone, he immediately secluded himself in the cottage that Commissioner Blount had occupied on the grounds of the Honolulu Hotel. A member of the American Board of Missions who sailed on the same ship had fed Willis stories of angry PG revolutionists and bloodthirsty natives. Willis hoped by laying low for a while that tensions would subside, but his seclusion only served to raise anxiety and increase rumors, while the whole city awaited news of Blount's report to President Cleveland.

Willis finally sent a messenger to invite the queen to meet with him at the cottage. Laura was angry that the US minister would ask the queen to come to him. Men were riding around town with guns, and there had been more than a few threats against her life. Spies were stationed at the Congregational Church across from Washington Place, and one night, one of Liliu's retainers surprised a man sneaking around the lower verandah, but he leapt over the wall and fled.

"It's so wrong for him to ask you to come here," Laura said as she and the queen descended the carriage in front of the Honolulu Hotel. "He should be calling on you."

"Never mind, Laura," Liliu said. "What I do now, I do for my people."

They walked to Snow Cottage, where Mr. Willis's secretary met them at the door and ushered them into a parlor divided by a Japanese screen. The secretary gestured toward a sofa, inviting Laura and the queen to sit, then left the room. A few minutes later, Mr. Willis entered, made a slight bow, and pulled up an armchair in front of them. He was bald, with a full beard and white, crusty eyebrows that hung forward in front of his eyes. He cleared his throat and began to speak.

"I bear the kindest greetings to you from President Cleveland." He cleared his throat again, seeming uneasy. "He sends regrets for the unauthorized intervention of our minister. He hopes to do all in his power, with your cooperation, to right the wrong which has been done to you."

Laura wanted to jump up and shout. The queen nodded her acknowledgment but said nothing. Then Laura heard a stirring behind the screen. She glanced at the queen who seemed to hear it too.

"I was told, Minister Willis," the queen said, "that this interview would be alone and in confidence."

"It is," he said. "My wife is in the next room, but she won't disturb us." He paused. "And my secretary is somewhere in the house."

Minister Willis cleared his throat again. "Now, Your Majesty, I must ask if you'll consent to sign a proclamation of general amnesty and grant complete protection and pardon to those who've overthrown your government."

The queen hesitated, a glimmer of surprise on her face. "I'll abide by the laws of my country, in consultation with my cabinet."

"But in the matter of your own opinion," the minister went on, "how do you feel?"

Laura began to dislike Minister Willis. The queen had answered. Why did he press her? Did it have something to do with that noise behind the screen?

"I assure you," the minister said, "this is merely a confidential conversation for my own information."

The queen waited a moment and then responded.

"Our laws say those guilty of treason shall suffer the death penalty, and their property will be confiscated by the government."

"Would you carry out those laws?" the minister said.

"It's not within my constitutional power to grant amnesty. But if it were to be granted, it'd be on the condition that they leave the country."

"That they be banished?" the minister said.

The queen sat up a little straighter. "I'm sure, Minister Willis, you know that this is not the first time these men have moved against our government. If they're permitted to remain, they'd continue to agitate, and I fear their next offense would be even more serious for our country and our people."

"So your decision would be, as head —"

She interrupted him. "I said I'd consult my cabinet, but that would be my inclination."

"I thank you, Your Majesty," Willis said. "I'll be sending your response back to my government. Please do not mention this matter to anyone. When I hear back, I'll be in touch with you again."

&

"Lucien," Sanford Dole said, "did you see this communication from Willis?"

Lucien nodded. "It doesn't say anything." The letter was several flowery paragraphs from the US minister, extolling hearty goodwill between governments.

"We have to get him to spell out his position. We need to know if he intends to restore the queen." Dole wrote out a note, folded it, and handed it to Lucien. "Take this over to him and wait for a response. I don't like that he's met with her and not with us."

Lucien walked the few blocks from the palace to Snow Cottage — well, not the palace; the PGs had forbidden anyone to call it the palace. It was now the "Executive Building." All the trappings of monarchy had been removed and the rooms made over as offices.

When Lucien got to Willis's cottage, the secretary showed him into the parlor. He handed him the note, and the secretary left to take it to the minister. As Lucien stood waiting, he noticed the Japanese screen that divided the room was partly folded back. There was a desk behind it, on which piles of papers were stacked up. He looked back toward the door. No one was coming yet.

He moved toward the screen, curious as to what the paperwork of a US minister might look like. At the corner of the desk his eye caught sight of the name "Laura Jennings" on a set of notes. He bent closer and saw it was a transcript of a conversation between the queen and Minister Willis, regarding what should happen to the people responsible for the overthrow if she were restored. Laura was listed as the queen's lady in waiting. He skimmed the notes and stopped short at a single line.

"So, your decision is behead...." There were two question marks in the margin, made by the secretary, with a note to ask the minister to confirm the statement.

Lucien heard steps down the hall, and jumped to sit on the sofa facing the door. The secretary entered, and Lucien stood up.

"Minister Willis says you can tell Mr. Dole in regards to his note that pending a response from our government, he's scheduling a second meeting with the queen. After that, he'll be in touch with him."

Lucien thanked him, and the secretary showed him to the door. When he got back to Dole's office, Stephen Price was there.

"What did you find out?" Dole said.

"They're waiting for some information from the United States. Then they're going to schedule another meeting with the queen."

"I don't like the sound of that," Stephen said.

"Did they say what the first meeting was about?" Dole said.

"No, but—"

"But what?" Stephen said.

"I happened to see a transcript of some notes on the secretary's desk."

"And?" Stephen said.

"Minister Willis asked her what she'd do to the people responsible for the overthrow."

The room was still. Lucien looked down, avoiding their eyes.

"What did it say, Lucien?" Dole said.

"Whatever it said," Stephen said, "this proves they intend to put her back on the throne."

Dole looked at Lucien's face.

"Wait a minute, Stephen. I want to hear from Lucien."

"I saw the word 'banished...'" Lucien looked up. "...and then it said, 'behead.'"

Stephen's mouth dropped open. "She means to chop off our heads?"

"It doesn't make sense," Lucien said. "Beheading was never used by the Hawaiians, even in ancient times. There were question marks in the margin —"

"Well, as long as I have something to say about it, there's not going to be any 'banishing' or 'beheading,'" Stephen said. "No more waiting around."

&

The day American newspapers arrived in Honolulu announcing, "savage black queen intends to behead all whites," Minister Willis showed up at Washington Place. Wakeki took him to the parlor and went to fetch the queen. When Blount had told him he feared for the queen's life if she were restored to the throne, Willis hadn't paid much attention. But since those newspapers had spread around town, he'd heard more than a few threats that the queen would be shot on sight.

When she came into the parlor, Willis stood and abruptly asked her if she'd be willing to rescind the death penalty. Liliu protested that she'd never said she'd invoke the death penalty, only that she'd consult her cabinet.

Willis interrupted, saying the American public was outraged, and unless she was willing to extend a full pardon, the United States would not recognize her sovereignty. He told her she had one day to make up her mind, and that if she persisted in her views, her life might be in danger. He made for the door, brushing by Laura with a brief tip of his hat brim as she passed him in the entryway. Laura found the queen still sitting on the parlor sofa, staring into space, shaking her head.

David came later that day to warn the queen that there were men on the roof of the church across the street with rifles aimed at Washington Place. He urged her to leave the house for her own safety. After the sun went down, she and Laura, dressed in nuns' habits, walked through the gate to the Episcopal Church next door. A carriage took them to a hotel downtown, where they were guarded throughout the night.

 &

December 19, 1893

The night at the hotel was sheer terror. We didn't know whom to trust or who might try to assassinate the queen. David had men patrol around the hotel, and two retainers guarded the door, but at any minute they could've been overpowered.

We sat up all night. Liliu prayed and read the Bible almost till dawn. Once she asked me, "How can I forgive these people? Why should they go unpunished?" I didn't know what to say. Of course I feel the same. She went back to her reading. In the low lamplight, I could see tears.

I don't know who spread rumors that she said she'd behead the opposition, but it was a black-hearted thing to do. That was never her intention. Certainly she'd like them out of the country — they've been making trouble for years.

I had dozed off in my chair and just before dawn, Liliu shook my arm to wake me. She said she'd made her decision. She was composed, but sad. We turned up the lamp, and she dictated a message to Minister Willis. In it she said she must not feel vengeful to any of her people. She'd forgive and forget the past, trusting that all would work hereafter for the future good of the country. Minister Willis will be presenting her decision to the PGs this week. And finally, all this will be at an end.

&

Minister Willis walked up the steps of the Executive Building to deliver his message to Sanford Dole. He wondered what the country must have been like under the monarchy to have such a palace as this. It was stately, but not extravagant, as it had been described to him. He could imagine carriages arriving in the palm-lined drive, elegant men and women in fancy dress, and an orchestra playing. A few Honolulu residents had told him stories of Kalakaua's time. He remarked that it sounded quite picturesque. Someone replied that they didn't want a picturesque kingdom, but a place where they could make money.

His vision of a Hawaiian Kingdom ended when he reached the top step. The front door was sandbagged. On the verandah, a cannon manned by soldiers was pointed toward King Street. He went inside where black-suited clerks sat at desks lined up around the great hall. One of them approached and took him to Dole.

The two men shook hands but remained standing.

"The queen has accepted all the conditions of the United States government, and has extended full pardon and complete amnesty," Willis said. "Is the provisional government willing to do the same and restore the queen?"

Dole was brief. "We'll take the matter under consideration and get back to you." He had the clerk escort Willis to the door.

Four days later, Dole delivered the provisional government's statement to Willis:

> We have done your government no wrong; no charge of discourtesy is or can be brought against us. We have stood ready to add to our country a new star, to its glory and to consummate a union which we believed would be as much to the benefit of your country as ours. If this is an offense, we plead guilty to it.
>
> We do not recognize your right to interfere in our domestic affairs. The provisional government respectfully and unhesitatingly declines to entertain the proposition of the President of the United States that it should surrender its authority to the ex-queen.

Chapter 26 ⎯⎯⎯

"Now what do we do?" Stephen Price crossed his arms and leaned back against the wall of Thurston's office. "Cleveland supports the queen, and annexation's going nowhere."

"I don't think the US will force the issue," Dole said. "They'd have to use arms against us. No politician wants to use American arms against Americans."

Thurston sniffed. "I say let's restore the queen."

Dole's eyebrows arched.

Thurston smiled. "Yeah, restore her for forty-eight hours. Then overthrow her again, accepting no protest."

Stephen ran a hand through his hair, and let out a puff of air. "Well, what about money? A pension for her and Ka`iulani for life, if she abdicates."

Dole shook his head. "We've put out feelers about that. She flat-out refused."

"Before I left Washington," Thurston said, "some people told me we ought to form a republic. The very idea of a young republic is attractive to Americans. They won't care how it's formed."

"A republic would mean giving the vote to all citizens," Dole said. "We didn't hold a vote for the annexation treaty you took to Washington because the majority of Hawaiians wouldn't support it. If we formed a republic, we'd just be voted out." He pulled out a handkerchief and wiped his moist brow, then his nose.

"You okay, Sanford?" Stephen asked. "You look white as a ghost."

"Yeah, I'm okay. Just caught something I can't shake." He put his handkerchief back in his pocket. "Anyway, I've had some correspondence on this with Professor Burgess at Columbia. I thought we'd get an expert opinion. He sees Teutonic political genius as the driving force of civilization in Europe, America, and even here in the islands where we've introduced a written language, civilized institutions, and Christianity."

Thurston nodded. "We've always done the best thing for Hawaii."

"Burgess thinks only a Teutonic populace is capable of self-government, and that even southern Europeans are dangerous to individual liberty."

"Well, we'd control the vote," Thurston said. "We'll just have voters swear allegiance to the republic. That'll keep away the Royalists. And we can use high property qualifications so only the best element of the country will be eligible."

"If we limit the vote to people who were born here or who become naturalized," Stephen said, "that'd keep the Chinese and Japanese out. We don't have naturalization treaties with their countries."

They sat in silence a moment.

"We should require voters to speak, read, and write English," Thurston said. "And explain the constitution in English too. That'd eliminate most Portuguese."

"You're not describing a republic," Dole said. "You're describing an oligarchy."

"Well, it won't exactly have all the elements of a republic," Thurston said.

Stephen jumped in. "But we can put together a convention to write a new constitution. Make it look enough like a republic to establish our legitimacy to go back and petition the US for annexation."

Dole stood up, his voice tired. "You may as well get started on it. I don't see another way anymore. If you'll excuse me, gentlemen, I'm going home to lie down. I don't feel well."

&

July 5, 1894

Yesterday, Sanford Dole proclaimed Hawaii a republic with himself as president. There was no election, no voting. And the PGs proclaimed a new constitution!

I can't believe it. The queen lost her throne to these men because she wanted a new constitution to restore the vote to her people. Now, the PGs have a new constitution to keep the vote away from the people. And they do it in the name of "liberty!"

David was here this morning. He was so disturbed. The United States will do nothing, and it's rumored that Willis will officially recognize the Republic. President Cleveland's hands are tied because the United States Congress refuses to intervene. They want to maintain relations with the islands because of their strategic position.

Since US troops are back on their ships, David says the Republic has been recruiting beach bums and other drifters as military guards and outfitting them with weapons. He heard that a bunch of them, stationed in the palace basement, got drunk and ransacked the place, making off with jewels, art, furniture, and rare feathered cloaks before the Republic's officers could stop them.

David had a private conference with the queen. When they came out of her study, Liliu looked uneasy, and David's face scared me. I've never seen him like that. After he left, I asked the queen if anything was wrong. She just said, "No, don't worry. As long as the islands haven't been annexed, there's still hope."

She went out to her thatched hut at Waikiki this afternoon to be alone.

&

David Kahiko tied the reins of his horse to a scrubby tree and headed cautiously the last hundred feet toward Diamond Head Charlie's lookout. The new moon shed little light on the dark, steep path. His boots loosed a few rocks that slid backward and bounced down the hill. He could just make out a silhouette as Charlie got up and stood at the door of the bungalow.

"David?"

"Yeah, it's me."

"Come on in."

"Any sign of the *Waimanalo*, Charlie?"

"She's out there. Come have a look."

David entered the bungalow, and crossed to the front window, which faced the sea. He waited a few minutes, then saw three flashes of light in succession.

"That's the second time," Charlie said.

"Then they'll offload the guns tomorrow," David said. "We were going to do it at the entrance to the harbor, but there are too many soldiers running around downtown, even after midnight. They'll land them just below Diamond Head tomorrow night."

In the dark, Charlie froze. "Shh." There was a rustling outside the door. He reached for his rifle, which leaned against the wall.

"Who's out there?" Charlie said.

No one answered.

"I have a gun," Charlie said. "You better say who you are."

A faint voice answered, "It's just Willie."

"Willie who?"

"Willie Kaae."

"Damn it, Willie," David said. "What the hell are you doing sneaking around like that? Get over here."

Willie came to the door.

"I'm not sneaking. I was going to meet my girl. There's a place back down that gulch we go. Her parents don't like me coming round their house, so she meets me up here sometimes."

"So why aren't you waiting for her at the gulch?" David said.

"She didn't come. Maybe she couldn't get away. I saw you coming up the path and I thought you were going to have coffee with Charlie, so I followed you over here." He tried a smile. "You got any biscuits, Charlie?"

☙

*L*aura left Goo Kim's with her arms full of packages. She'd picked up the cloth the queen wanted for curtains, along with extra spools of thread, and yards of assorted bright-colored cotton to make holokus for the household retainers.

Pushing the shop door open with her back, she turned toward the street, her packages in front of her. The bag with the spools slipped out of her hand and fell on the boardwalk. Balancing the other bundles, she stooped to pick it up. A hand reached out to retrieve the bag. She raised her head. It was Lucien. He helped her up.

"Hello, Laura."

"Lucien."

They stood for a moment without talking.

"Let me help you with those," he said. "Where's your carriage?"

"The driver's waiting around the corner."

He took her bundles, and they walked down the sidewalk.

"How've you been?" Lucien said.

"Good."

They turned on Merchant Street. A Hawaiian boy was holding the reins of Laura's carriage. The driver was gone.

"Where's Joe?" Laura asked.

"He go Fort Street see one friend down there," the boy said. "Say he run back here *wiki wiki.*"

Lucien loaded the packages in the carriage. "I'll wait with you, Laura. Let's sit on that bench in the shade."

He pointed across the street and offered his arm. She hesitated, then took it. They waited for a buckboard to pass, and walked across the street to sit in silence beneath the flowering tree. Laura stared straight ahead. Lucien glanced at her, started to say something, and stopped.

"Whatever you're trying to say, Lucien, just say it." She continued to stare across the street.

"I was going to say," he started, his voice low, "that I thought you and David would be married by now."

Laura turned to look at him. "What makes you think that?"

"Isn't that why you broke our engagement?"

Laura turned back to look across the street. "Not exactly."

"Well, he asked you, didn't he?"

"That's none of your concern, but —"

"But what?"

"It's complicated, Lucien. I don't know how much I can say."

"Laura." The tone in Lucien's voice made her turn back. "I know you don't want me anymore." He paused. "But I'd still like to be counted among your friends."

She looked in his eyes. "You lied to me."

"I'm sorry. I wish I could make it up to you somehow."

His eyes dropped, and Laura felt her heart drop with them. Deceit had brought them together, but it hadn't been only from his side. Her voice softened.

"Lucien, look at me."

He looked up.

"I'm sorry too."

The question in his eyes made her search for a way to tell him the truth.

"After my aunt died…"

"Yes?"

"My uncle pressed me to marry him."

"Marry him?"

"I thought he might try to force me."

Lucien looked at her a long time. "So you agreed to marry me."

She nodded and put her hand on his arm. "We were good friends, and, well, at the time, I didn't see any other choice. Please forgive me, Lucien. People like my uncle take whatever they want and think no one can stop them."

Lucien looked away. Laura put her hands in her lap. They watched a few carriages pass by.

"Like this whole political situation," Laura said. "I know my uncle had something to do with the queen's overthrow. How does he look at himself in the mirror?" She turned to Lucien. "You work with Thurston — he's another one. How do they justify it?"

The driver was walking up Merchant Street.

"There's Joe," Lucien said, and stood up. He looked down at Laura, not knowing how to answer her question. "I guess they just wanted a permanent relationship with the United States. They say it's the best thing for the Hawaiians. Isn't it?"

Laura looked up at him. "I don't know, Lucien. Did they ever ask them?"

❧

*L*ucien took long strides to keep up with Stephen Price as they hurried to Sanford Dole's office at the Executive Building. They jogged up the stairs and dodged the sandbags. The soldiers guarding the front door saluted. They found Dole reading behind a mountain of paperwork stacked on his desk. He looked up as they entered the room.

Dole waved his hand at the piles of documents and newspapers. "You see what I have to deal with here. Everyone and his brother wants a government position, claiming they're supporters of the Republic. I've got to keep track of our commission in Washington working on annexation, and keep tabs on all the reporters to make sure their articles don't do any damage —"

"Sanford," Stephen said, out of breath.

Dole stopped.

"Willie Kaae was just by Thurston's office. He said he saw David Kahiko up at Lookout Charlie's last night, talking about unloading guns off a ship down at the foot of Diamond Head."

"When?" Dole said.

"Last night," Stephen said.

"No, when are they supposed to unload them?"

"Willie said tonight."

"Then you better have David Kahiko picked up." He pulled a blank piece of paper toward him and wrote a quick note. He blotted it, stamped it with a seal, and held it out to Stephen. "Take this to the officer in charge of the garrison, in the basement. I'm requesting him to send out some men to find Kahiko now. Then we'd better get troops down to Diamond Head before it gets dark."

Stephen took the note, and headed for the basement, Lucien behind him. When they got downstairs, the officer wasn't there. He waved the note in front of the men so they could see the presidential seal. Lucien saw one man slide a whiskey bottle behind a column with his left foot.

"I need ten men to ride out to Diamond Head." Stephen picked them out. "You, you, and you, step forward. Okay, and you two ... and you five over there."

The men gathered around.

"There's some suspicious activity out there. Kanakas may be unloading guns near Diamond Head. Go check the area. And I want you to get one, in particular — David Kahiko. Do you know who he is?"

A couple men grinned. One nodded. "Sure, we know him."

"Well, get going. You need to be out there before dark."

"Come on, boys," the soldier who'd hidden the whiskey said. "Let's go have a little fun."

Stephen and Lucien climbed the stairs behind the soldiers. When they were out of earshot, Lucien turned to Stephen.

"You were supposed to tell them to pick David up. You said, 'Get him.'"

"What's the difference?"

"They might think you want him killed."

Stephen shrugged his shoulders. "If they cut off the head, the body will die. Might be the best thing after all."

ॐ

*L*ucien spurred his horse toward Waikiki. The sun was going down and it was hard to see the road. The horse hit a puddle and stumbled. Muddy water splattered up on Lucien's pants and jacket. He pulled back on the reins to lift the horse's head, and slapped its flank with his riding crop. The horse leapt forward to regain its stride.

When they were leaving the palace grounds, Stephen had invited Lucien back to his house for dinner. He kept encouraging him to spend time with Hannah. Lucien declined, saying he had something to attend to that evening. He excused himself and went directly downtown where his horse was stabled. The soldiers at the palace had a rough reputation. He'd never forgive himself if David were shot.

He'd passed the soldiers on their mounts trotting along King Street to the Waikiki Road. Busy nodding to women along the way, they didn't notice him slip by. As soon as Lucien was past town, he dug his heels into his horse's side and galloped at top speed.

Near Diamond Head, Lucien came upon a group of about twenty Hawaiians on the road. He reined in his horse. The animal danced, its nostrils flaring, the sweat on its neck turned to foam.

"I want David Kahiko," Lucien said. "Where is he?"

The men seemed nervous. One of them at the back called out.

"No let no PG traitor pass by here."

"I have to see him," Lucien said. "Let me through."

He urged the horse forward. The Hawaiians pressed together to block the road. Lucien kicked the animal again to try to break through. A Hawaiian waved his arms and the horse reared up, startled. When it came down, its hooves grazed two Hawaiians at the front and they fell on the road. A shot rang out. Lucien slumped forward, then fell off the horse, hit the ground, and lay still. The horse wheeled on its hind legs and bolted toward town.

The soldiers coming up the road heard the shot and saw the riderless horse run past, stirrups flapping. They kicked their horses' sides to start them running.

A voice cried out, "Soldiers coming!"

The Hawaiians scattered for the gulches as the soldiers cantered up and stopped where Lucien lay on the ground. One jumped down from his horse to kneel next to him.

"Those kanakas were armed," the lead soldier said. He turned in the saddle to two men behind him. "Ride back for reinforcements. It's a revolt."

Chapter 27 ———

$f$or a week, David Kahiko evaded the soldiers and blood-hounds that scoured Diamond Head and the gulches and val-leys in the mountains behind it. Cannon shelled the slopes, and sharpshooters set up cross-fires to trap the rebels who'd fled up Manoa Valley. Surprised by the government soldiers, most reb-els were without guns or food. They weren't soldiers. They were blacksmiths, house painters, stevedores from the harbor, tram drivers, and clerks. Little by little, they surrendered, wounded, exhausted, and hungry.

David lost a boot when he crossed a tumbling stream, dis-carded the other one, and climbed up steep crevices barefoot to hide deeper in the mountains. He ate wild bananas where he could find them, and got soaked in torrential rains. Finally, the shelling stopped. The echo of bullets ricocheting in the canyons stopped. The baying of hounds stopped. Unshaven, his feet cut and bleeding, David limped down the mountain and headed back toward Honolulu.

In town, he crept along side streets and alleys, keeping alert for soldiers until he reached Beretania Street. He saw a carriage with two policemen turn into the drive at Washington Place, and ducked behind the wall of the Episcopal Church to watch. A crowd of Hawaiians gathered outside the fence.

In a few minutes, the queen appeared on the verandah, flanked by policemen. Laura followed just behind her. The police escorted the queen to the carriage, and the crowd of Hawaiians moved closer to the garden gate. Their faces were somber, questioning. The queen looked toward them, bowed her head briefly, and lifted one black-gloved hand. The policemen helped her into the carriage, then drove out through the crowd. The eyes of the Hawaiians followed their queen, and old-time heart-rending wails burst forth, trailing the carriage down the street.

David moved through the wooden gate between the queen's garden and the Episcopal Church, then jumped up on the side verandah. He crouched down and inched toward the front of the house.

"Laura," he whispered. "Laura."

She turned, saw him at the corner, and hurried over. He took her hand, and led her back through the wooden gate to the churchyard.

"Oh, David, I was so worried about you. You're limping. Are you all right?"

"Yeah, I'll be fine. What happened here?"

"They've arrested the queen. They said they had a warrant, but they wouldn't let her see it. What do we do? Hundreds of people are being locked up. Their names are in the paper every day."

"The rebels?"

"Not just rebels. Anyone who's sympathetic to the queen — the publishers of the Hawaiian newspaper, foreigners, businessmen. We heard even the Sisters here at the church are going to be arrested. The PGs declared martial law, and anyone on the streets after nine-thirty at night has to have a pass."

Guards arrived to disperse the crowd. An official with a detail of soldiers climbed the steps of the verandah and entered the house. David pulled Laura down next to the wall.

"It's not safe here," he said. "You've got to come with me now."

☙

*B*y late afternoon, David and Laura had stolen their way past the stately homes at the lower end of Nuuanu Street and past the Royal Mausoleum to the upper Pali Road, where the city ended and taro patches began. The few people they saw in the street were hurrying to get somewhere before dark and didn't look at them twice. The road became rocky, and the valley narrowed. Cliffs jutting up from the cool, green hills gleamed red in the setting sun. A thousand feet below, the twinkling city lights stretched in the dusk toward the sea where slender masts marked the location of ships in the bay.

Next to the road, a stream cascaded down the mountain. When they came to a place where they could cross, David took Laura's hand and helped her step from one mossy rock to the next. Then he led her through the trees on a faint path until they came to a small frame house under a large shade tree, with flowered vines on the lanai and an herb garden at the front.

"E Tutu," David called softly.

The door cracked open.

"Akahi?"

"Yes, it's me."

A small woman with white hair swept up in a bun, her brown face shining, opened the door. She was dressed in a striped holoku with a small lace collar; a knitted, fringed shawl covered her shoulders.

"Come in, come in," she said in Hawaiian.

David let Laura walk in front of him up the stairs to the lanai.

"Tutu, this is Laura. Laura, this is my grandmother, Iwalani."

The old woman reached out her arms to hug Laura, and kissed her on both cheeks. "You call me Tutu," she said.

She started to embrace David, but stopped, looking at his whiskered face, tattered clothes, and bare feet. "You were in the revolt, Akahi?"

"I'm okay, Tutu. I had to stay in the mountains for a few days."

She hugged him, then turned to go in the house. David and Laura followed. Flames flickered in small calabashes filled with kukui-nut oil, and soft woven mats covered the floor. There was a simple rattan sofa with bright cushions, and a few rattan chairs at a table covered with oilcloth. Through a doorway, Laura could see a four-poster koa-wood bed in the next room. On the wall were portraits of King Kalakaua, Queen Lili`uokalani, and Princess Ka`iulani. A kahili with black feathers stood in one corner.

Tutu nodded for them to sit, then took a shallow pan to the back lanai to get water from a barrel. She brought the pan, set it at David's feet, and gave him a small towel, then went into the kitchen. She returned with powdered herbs and stirred some in the water. She spoke to him in Hawaiian.

"You soak while I get supper."

David eased his swollen feet into the water. Tutu went toward the kitchen.

Laura got up. "May I help you?"

The old woman smiled and beckoned for her to come. She handed her a large bowl of poi to put on the table, along with roasted taro root, dried salted fish, and seaweed.

"Sorry," Tutu said in English. "So simple food."

"Don't worry, Tutu. Laura's been living with the queen. She's used to Hawaiian food."

"With the queen?" Tutu said, looking at Laura.

"She's her secretary and lady in waiting." David swished his feet gently in the pan. "I have some bad news, Tutu."

The old woman leaned on the back of a chair, looking at David, then back to Laura, putting two and two together.

"What happen to the queen?"

"They arrested her this afternoon."

The tiny flames in the calabash gourds wavered in the darkening room. Finally, Tutu spoke in Hawaiian.

"I'll close the shutters. The mosquitoes will be out soon."

She walked to each window, drew the wooden shutters in, and bolted them. Laura rubbed her arms to keep warm.

"I bring you *kihei*," Tutu said.

She went to the bedroom, returned with a shawl, and draped it around Laura.

"Sit," she said. "Eat now."

David dried his feet, limped to the table, and sat down. Tutu passed him a plate. He dug into his first real meal in a week.

"Feet better?"

He nodded, his mouth full.

"Tomorrow I go up the road, see Hiku," she said. "Get shoes and clothes for you."

During dinner, David told them how his men, surprised by soldiers, had had to flee to the mountains. When he found out what had happened, he tried to join them, but the artillery shelling prevented him from reaching them.

"Somehow the PGs discovered our plan before we could execute it. Without arms or food, and no one to direct them, the only thing my men could do was surrender." He turned to his grandmother. "I don't think it's safe for me to stay here. They may still be looking for me." He glanced at Laura. "But I want Laura to stay a few days, until I find out what's happening in town."

The old woman nodded.

"I'd like to go to the queen, David," Laura said.

"Wait a day or two. I'll come back if it's all right, or I'll send someone."

He pushed back from the table. Laura stood to clear the dishes.

"I have an herb salve for those cuts, Akahi," Tutu said. She carried the leftover poi to the kitchen, and returned with a small wooden bowl filled with a greasy substance. She handed it to David, and he spread it on his feet. It smelled spicy, like sage.

"You tired?" Tutu said to Laura.

She nodded.

"You okay sleep with me in big bed over there?"

Laura nodded again.

"Then come with me one time. I show you place wash up."

Tutu spoke in Hawaiian to David. "Akahi, you take the sofa, and I'll bring you blankets." She smiled. "It'll be like when you were a little boy."

Laura went with Tutu out through the kitchen and down the stairs of the back lanai. David lay down on the sofa. Minutes later, the women were back. He was already asleep. Tutu went to the bedroom and brought out a blanket. Laura helped her unfold it. They raised it over David, and let it settle on top of him. He didn't stir.

They went to the bedroom. Tutu carried a kukui-nut lamp and set it on the dresser. She swung the door almost closed. Laura took off her dress and shoes, leaving her chemise and pantalettes on. She folded the dress, laid it on the dresser, and set her shoes at the end of the bed.

"I sit awhile, think," Tutu said. "Sleep later."

She turned down the covers, and patted the sheet. Laura crawled up on the high bed and turned, her back against the pillow. Tutu smiled and raised the covers up. Then her eyes fell on the black pearl around Laura's neck. Staring, she reached out and lifted the ring.

"Where you get this?"

"It was my father's."

"Who your father? He live here?"

Laura shook her head. "No, he used to live here, but he moved to San Francisco."

"What his name?"

"Thomas Jennings."

Tutu dropped the ring and covered her mouth with her hands. Then she lowered them to ask another question.

"He in San Francisco now?"

Laura began to wonder about Tutu's continued questions.

"No, he died a few years ago. Why?"

Tutu said nothing for a moment. Then she went to the dresser and opened the bottom drawer. She took out a bundle, slid the drawer closed, and straightened up. She turned toward Laura and held the bundle out to her with both hands. It was a small appliquéd quilt wrapped up as if it held a baby. Laura got a chill. It reminded her of Fräulein Wolf's vision of the two women holding out bundles — her mother, and her father's Hawaiian wife.

"Open," Tutu said.

Laura put the bundle in her lap, and opened the folds of the quilt. It was a pattern of squares with turtle and fish designs, just big enough for a baby bassinet. Inside was a white handkerchief with the initials "TJ" embroidered on one corner. It was tied like a small sack with a piece of cord. Laura looked up at Tutu. She nodded encouragement.

"Open."

Laura untied the handkerchief. From the soft folds of cloth, she picked up a white pearl ring set in gold plumeria blossoms. Her eyes got wide. It was the ring her father had given his Hawaiian bride to match his own.

"Where did this come from?"

"Your father give to Malia."

That was the name in her father's letter that she'd found in the attic.

"How do you know Malia?"

"She my daughter."

Laura's eyes began to tear. She swallowed hard, glancing toward the sitting room.

"And David?"

"Malia's son."

Laura shook her head, her voice a hoarse whisper.

"But you told my father the baby died."

Tutu hung her head. She sat on a small chair next to the dresser.

"When Malia die, and baby live, I afraid they take him. I never see him no more. That why I say that." She sighed deeply. "Couple months go by, I feeling bad. I go look for father, tell him truth. I go where he stay before. People round there say he sail away someplace … maybe San Francisco. Say he no come back no more."

Laura's tears spilled over. For her father's grief when he left the islands, for how she loved David before she knew, for how she loved David now.

"Tutu?"

The old woman looked up.

"Does David know who his father is?"

She shook her head. "I tell him father is haole — *mikanele* man."

"Missionary?"

Tutu nodded. "Say he go back his country when Malia die. That time, many of them go back. I talk all my friends, say keep secret. I no want someday Akahi go way, look for father. But now look like father come back for him."

Chapter 28 ———

Birdcalls woke Laura early the next morning. She lay for a while, eyes closed, listening to the sounds of the mountain forest. No wagons rumbling by. No carriage hooves clopping along the avenue. No soft chanting to wake the queen.

Tutu was already up, but there was no one stirring in the house. Perhaps she'd gone up the road to get shoes and clothes for David. Laura slipped out of bed and dressed. The two rings lay on top of the dresser. She looked through the crack in the door. David was still asleep on the sofa, exhausted after his ordeal in the mountains. Laura stood a long time watching him breathe, her feelings still jumbled. How many times had she thought they'd be together someday? She'd never imagined it like this — with David as her brother.

David moved beneath the blanket. Laura closed the crack in the door to a sliver. He settled down again and soon was breathing deeply. She picked up a towel Tutu had left on the dresser, and tiptoed to the kitchen.

When she came back from washing, David was sitting up, rubbing his eyes.

"Well, Malolo, did you sleep okay?"

"Pretty well. How about you?"

"Like a stone." He grinned, stretched, and got up. "I'm going to go wash." He walked a few paces and looked down. "Tutu's herbs are magic. My feet are almost like new. I'll be back in a minute." He went out through the kitchen.

Laura went to the bedroom, picked up the two rings, put them in the handkerchief, and went to sit at the table. When David came in she asked him to sit down.

"I want to show you something."

She took the white pearl ring from the handkerchief and laid it on the oilcloth.

David smiled. "Tutu showed you my mother's ring."

Laura laid the black pearl next to the white one.

"How about that." He picked up a ring in each hand to look more closely. "They're identical except for the color. Where'd you get the black one?"

"It was my father's."

David looked up with that question in his eyes Laura had seen so many times before, only this time, there was a glint of surprise.

"My father had two rings made, one with the black pearl and one with the white. He gave the white one to Malia when they married." She showed him the initials on the handkerchief. "T J, for Thomas Jennings."

David set the rings down and stared at her. "Then, you're my ... you're my ..."

Laura nodded, blinking to keep back tears.

"Oh, my God." He looked away, shaking his head. "I was so attracted to you when I met you at the ball." He glanced back at her. "But something stopped me; I didn't know what it was. At first, I thought it was because of your uncle. He thinks he's so superior, and I wondered if maybe you'd be that way. But then, when I got to know you ..." David stared at the rings on the table. He drew a long breath and let it out. His voice got soft. "There were so many times I wanted to kiss you." He looked up. "And I just couldn't do it; I felt you were different." He reached to run his fingers over the embroidered initials. "I never knew what that 'T J' stood for. All Tutu said was that my father was a missionary who'd left for San Francisco when my mother died, and that he didn't want me. When I got older, I made some inquiries, but it had happened so many years before, nobody could tell me anything. When I found out you were from San Francisco…" He shook his head again. "My God, Laura, I don't know — maybe something in the back of my mind was trying to put it all together."

"He didn't know about you."

"What do you mean?"

"My father, he thought you had died."

"How do you know that?"

"I found an old letter in my uncle's attic. My father wrote to my aunt from San Francisco saying your grandmother told him Malia died at your birth and that you died too."

"But why?"

Tutu told me last night she did it because she was afraid they'd take you away from her. My father — I mean, our father — felt he didn't have a reason to stay in Honolulu anymore." She reached across the table and put her hand on his. "He wore this black pearl around his neck for the rest of his life, David. He loved Malia, and he would've loved you."

David stood up, pulled her to him, and wrapped her in his arms. She clung to him. "Fräulein Wolf saw a vision. She said our father was with your mother and my mother, and my baby brother who died. They were happy together." Laura looked up at him. "My aunt was your aunt too. My cousins are your cousins. Haole and Hawaiian … we're all the same family.

316

&

When his grandmother returned with clothes and shoes, David dressed to leave for town. Tutu gave him a broad-brimmed hat to hide his face. He hugged his grandmother, then turned to Laura, and touched her cheek with a tender look.

"I'll try to be back tomorrow, or I'll send someone to let you know if you can see the queen."

"Be careful," she said, and embraced him.

&

When David got down near the Royal Mausoleum, he saw a long funeral procession turning into Nuuanu Cemetery, and wondered who was being buried. There'd been so many deaths. Following behind the wagon carrying the casket, he recognized the McBrides, the Thurstons, and the Doles. Stephen Price passed by in his carriage with his daughters. David thought about what Laura had told him, that Hannah and Lizzie were his cousins. How strange he had to hide from them now. He stayed on the far side of the street, and pulled the brim of the hat down over his eyes. When the last carriage pulled into the cemetery, he walked across the road to talk to the Chinese watchman.

"Whose funeral?" David said.

"One McBride boy."

There was only one McBride boy. A lump rose in David's throat, and for a minute he couldn't speak. It was Lucien.

"Do you know how it happened?"

"I hear he get shot last week down Waikiki way."

David thanked the guard and walked on. Lucien, his sometime rival — and his friend — dead. How did he get mixed up in all this? And for what? For nothing. David wiped his eyes with the back of his hand. His men had died for nothing. Lucien died for nothing. Hawaiian history was dying for nothing. He ran down the road in the direction of the prison. He wanted to see his men, see the ones who were still living.

At Beretania Street, he found Wakeki, who was headed downtown. She told him the queen was a prisoner at the palace, but the guards let her cook the queen's meals and bring them in. She was going to the market for fresh fish.

"Can the queen have visitors? David asked.

"No visitors. Just one or two servants see her."

"Can Laura get in as a lady in waiting?"

Wakeki nodded.

"Send someone to my grandmother's place on the Pali Road. Laura is there, but she wants to be with the queen."

"I send Joe up there, get her tomorrow. Where you go?"

"I'm going to see my men at the prison."

"No!" She grabbed his arm. "They keep you."

"I've got to, Wakeki." He squeezed her hand and ran on.

When he reached the prison, he rushed inside. The guard stood up, pointing his rifle, finger on the trigger. Beyond him, David could see the men crowded in the cells, unwashed, thin, fatigued. There were Hawaiians, half-castes and haoles — workers, businessmen, and officials of the queen's government whom he'd worked with all his life.

"Back off, traitor," the guard said. "Or I'll shoot."

"I'm not the traitor," David said, staring him down. "You are."

"We need food, David," a man called out. "All we've had to eat is hardtack and coffee."

Three other guards appeared, rifles at the ready. David whirled around. "What's wrong with you? You know these men. We all grew up together, for God's sake. Get some meat and poi in here and give them a decent meal."

The guards lowered their rifles. The one with his finger on the trigger nodded and they walked out.

"We'll get them the meals, Kahiko. But we're going to have to lock you up."

*J*oe drove the queen's carriage, with Laura in the back, down Nuuanu Road. She wished she knew where David was. Joe didn't know. He said only that David had met Wakeki in the street and had asked her to send him to pick her up. They passed the cemetery, and Laura saw the fresh, mounded dirt on new graves inside the wrought-iron fence. Such new graves, all close together like that. Martial law was in force, and habeas corpus suspended. God, had they been executed? The PGs could do anything they wanted now, without a trial by jury. She wished Joe would hurry. She wanted to get back to see the queen.

Joe pulled into the drive at Washington Place, and let Laura off at the front door. She ran up the steps. The door was ajar. She pushed it open. Books and newspapers were strewn everywhere, curtains ripped down, furniture overturned. In the library, the queen's desk and files were emptied out. She ran upstairs to the queen's bedroom. Covers were thrown back, garments scattered on the floor, drawers open, and lamps knocked over. She hurried to her room to find it in the same condition. And her jewelry was gone, including Grandmother Jennings's necklace, the one she'd worn to Kalakaua's ball.

She went to the closet and felt along the cedar lining until she found the loose board. She wiggled it off and, with a sigh of relief, pulled out her journal and the medal Kalakaua had given her. *At least they didn't get that.* She heard someone coming up the stairs, so she put the journal and medallion back in the wall, covered them up, and made herself look busy picking up clothes.

Wakeki appeared at the door. "You back, Miss Laura?"

Laura was relieved to see her. "What happened here?"

"Them PG soldiers come in here, make big *pilikia.* Take all the queen's papers, steal her jewelry, dig in the garden. Like *he`e…* octopus. Grab everything."

"Where's the queen?"

Wakeki frowned. "They jail her upstairs at the palace. No let nobody in there."

"I've got to see her, Wakeki."

"It's okay. Tonight, you take dinner over there. They let you in. Then I come later with fresh clothes for her." She pressed her lips together. "We get in there, you'll see."

&

*L*aura followed the guard through the grand entry of the palace, now crowded with office desks. She carried a tray with the queen's dinner and flowers wrapped in newsprint. All the clerks had gone home for the day, so the place was empty. They went up the staircase, and turned down a long hall. At the far end, two guards sat on chairs next to a door. When they saw Laura coming, they stood up.

"Where's the one who usually brings dinner?" one of the soldiers asked.

The soldier guiding Laura answered, "She says the other one's preparing some fresh clothes, but they weren't ready. They didn't want to keep the prisoner waiting for her dinner."

"Hey, don't complain," a third soldier said. "This one's a lot better looking. She can come up here anytime."

Laura ignored him, and waited for him to unlock the door.

He pulled up a large iron ring attached to his belt, and rattled the keys around to select one. He stuck it in the keyhole, turned it twice, and swung the door inward to let Laura pass. He stood close, leaving little room so she'd brush against him as she went by. She pretended not to notice.

Laura put the tray on a table against the wall, and turned to make a deep curtsy. The queen looked up from her writing desk, surprised, but suppressed her joy until the soldier closed the door. Then the two women fell into each other's arms.

The queen's room was sparsely furnished, with a bed in one corner, a small sofa, and a cupboard made of wood with wire screen on the front. There was an adjoining bathroom, and a dressing room at one side, with large windows that opened on the verandah.

Laura told her about the state of her house.

"I know," the queen said. "Wakeki said they've taken everything, even my sheet music. They think I might have written secret messages to my people in my songs. I suppose they thought they'd find some evidence to use against me. They intend to try me for treason."

Laura tried not to appear alarmed. "But no Hawaiian jury would ever convict you."

"It may not be a Hawaiian jury. Under martial law, they can use a military court."

Laura put silverware and a cloth napkin on the little table. She poured a cup of tea. Her hands shook, and she almost spilled it as she set it down.

"Try not to worry, Laura. I've been allowed to see my attorney. Let's not think about it right now. It'll ruin dinner." The queen sat down. "You won't believe this." She placed the napkin on her lap. "I asked them to return a few pieces of jewelry that have sentimental value for me. They said I can buy them back if I want."

"Buy them back? But they're yours."

Liliu shrugged her shoulders, lifted her fork, and started to eat. Laura unwrapped the flowers and put them in a vase on the table.

"We used the paper around the flowers to get you some news. I'm sorry, it's yesterday's." She stacked the sheets of newsprint and set them next to the queen's plate.

"You're so clever," Liliu said. "They won't let me have the paper in here."

She scanned the columns, turned a few pages, and stopped. "Oh, no. Laura?"

"Yes?"

"You didn't tell me about Lucien."

"Tell you what?"

Liliu looked at her and realized she didn't know.

"Tell you what, Your Majesty?"

"Sit down, dear."

Laura pulled up a chair at the table. The queen turned the newspaper sideways so she could see the obituary page. She pointed to the notice of Lucien's funeral.

Laura bent over the paper, reading and rereading. Surely there was some mistake. She'd just seen Lucien a few days ago. He was fine. They'd sat under the golden shower tree on Merchant Street. He helped her with her packages. They both said they were sorry. It seemed like a new beginning. She saw Lucien in his white suit getting her luggage the first day she'd arrived at the wharf in Honolulu. Introducing her to everyone at the king's ball. Red-faced, giving her flowers. Limping down the beach, leaning on David's arm. Full of joy at the prospect of marrying her. Embarrassed on the inter-island ferry. I wish I could make it up to you, he'd said. Still count me among your friends. Shot in the revolt, the newspaper said, defending the Republic. Buried at Nuuanu Cemetery. The new graves, he was one of the new graves.

Tears blurred her vision. She blinked. Drops fell and seeped into the paper.

"He was too young," the queen said. She stroked Laura's head. "Like all of them."

Laura put a hand to her mouth to stifle her sobs.

The queen embraced her, and Laura cried awhile in her arms.

"I don't think I can stand it, Your Majesty."

"I know, I know." Liliu softly patted her back.

"First David, and now this."

The queen stopped patting. "What about David?"

Laura leaned back. "He— he's my father's son."

"What do you mean?"

Laura showed the queen the black pearl ring, and told her of her father's marriage to Malia and how Tutu had revealed the white pearl.

"What a shock." The queen put her hand under Laura's chin and gently lifted her head. "Yet, I'm happy for you." She dabbed Laura's eyes with her napkin and brushed wayward strands of hair back from her face. "You thought of him differently, I know, but now you have a brother. 'Loss, love, all intertwined,' — isn't that what Fräulein said?"

Laura sniffed and nodded.

Liliu sighed. "Yes, and now I'm trying to find the love in all this loss." She stood up and went to the sideboard to pour a cup of tea. She set it in front of Laura. Then she pulled a paper from a stack on her writing table, with musical notes penciled on a hand-drawn staff. It was her song, *Aloha Oe*.

"I'm rewriting this, Laura. Remember how I raised the flag at Washington Place to let the king know I forgave him, and hung a banner across Fort Street to welcome him home?"

"Yes."

"The banner said, 'Aloha Oe.' Back then it meant 'Love Forever.' This time it means, 'Goodbye Forever.' And I hope they'll forgive me."

"Who'll forgive you?"

"My people."

"For what?"

"For losing the kingdom."

Laura sat back. "But you did nothing wrong."

"I don't know, but I couldn't ask my people to fight without proper arms or training. They would've been slaughtered, and there are so few of us left. I've played it over in my head a thousand times, what I could have done differently. For the life of me, I don't know … I just don't know.

"Please, Your Majesty, you can't think —"

The queen put a forefinger to her lips, glancing at the door. She continued in a low voice. "I have a new challenge now, Laura." She drew another of her songs from the pile. It was titled *He aloha o ka Haku* — "the aloha of the Lord" — and dedicated to Princess Victoria Ka`iulani. Laura read the verses. Look not on their failings, forgive with loving kindness, that we might be made pure.

"Aloha is so hard with these people," Liliu said. "How do you love those who take everything you have, and it's still not enough for them? They're not happy unless they crush your spirit. And what's worse, they have no sense they're doing anything wrong at all. There's no awareness, no remorse, no apology, just arrogance." She shook her head, her brow wrinkled. "Do you know how hard that is? To forgive them when they're so self-righteous?"

Laura set the sheet music down and took the queen's hand.

"I'm struggling with this, Laura. But no matter what happens to me, I want Ka`iulani to know. And I want my people to know. They should continue to work for justice, but with aloha. It's our essence, like fragrance is to a flower. Aloha is our spirit. It's who we are. If we don't have that, we're lost, and there is no more Hawaii."

There was a knock and the sound of a key turning in the lock. A soldier swung the door open. Wakeki was coming down the hall with several outfits for the queen. Laura jumped up to help her.

At the door, the soldiers stopped her to search the clothing. Laura stood by while they patted and felt along the seams of each piece. Scowling, Wakeki handed over the garments one by one. The guard who'd opened the door took the queen's corset, feeling it up one side and down the other, then slowly stroked the inside of the bodice in a lewd way, taunting Wakeki. She drew herself up, leaned forward, and spat at him, the spittle landing on his beard near his mouth. Surprised, he dropped the garment, and wiped his mouth with the back of his hand. He glared at Wakeki, then swung his arm around and struck her in the face. The old woman took a few steps back and fell. Laura cried out, and the queen rushed to the door. When she saw Wakeki on the floor, she couldn't contain herself.

"You snakes!" she shouted. "She's just an old woman."

Wakeki cursed the soldiers in Hawaiian. Laura knelt to help her up and pick up the clothes that were dropped. The soldiers barred the open door and ordered Liliu back into the room. She backed up, but stayed where she could see what was happening in the hall.

"Give me the clothes," a soldier said.

Laura held them out, her eyes burning. The soldier snatched them and tossed them in the room, aiming for the table. Most of them fell on the floor. He pointed at Wakeki.

"Stop your jabbering, you old hag. I don't want to see you here anymore." He turned to Laura. "You make sure she doesn't come back. Now, both of you get out of here. No more visiting tonight." He started to close the door on the queen.

Laura could see Liliu's face, red and furious at the treatment of her retainer. She took Wakeki's arm and led her down the hallway to the stairs.

The soldier shut the door and turned the lock with a deft click. Liliu stood staring at the closed door, fists clenched and trembling. Then she swung around, knocked down a chair, and whacked the dinner tray. It went flying, and dishes clattered to the floor. She kicked the fallen clothes to the wall, then fell on her bed, crying.

"I can't forgive them, I can't forgive them! Oh, God, how can I ever forgive them?"

Chapter 29 ———

January 16, 1895

I'm so afraid. So far, every prisoner who's been in court has been found guilty, and the queen's trial comes up in two weeks. Her attorney found out she and six others are to be shot for treason. How that can be, when they haven't even been tried yet! David's been locked up and could be on that list. The news has nearly paralyzed me. The queen says she's prepared to die, but she's so sick at what's happening to her supporters that she's been confined to bed. I can't let my feelings immobilize me. I have to keep going.

Mr. Dole put a blackout on government news. Even the *San Francisco Chronicle* stated that freedom of the press in Honolulu is a myth. Foreigners found guilty are allowed to leave the islands. The PGs don't dare execute them, because they're still pushing for annexation. But the Americans aren't interested.

I finally got permission for the queen's own physician to see her. He said she'd get better if she had fresh air and got the guards to allow her to go out in the carriage. But she refuses to go in public under the PG's guard. I've convinced her to walk with me on the verandah every afternoon.

Yesterday, I ran into Mrs. Dole. It was awkward to say the least. I'd been to her house many times, and the queen often had her in for lunch at the palace. She chatted with me as if she and her husband were still numbered among the queen's dear friends — those dear friends who'd caused her overthrow!

She must have noticed my discomfort because she made an effort to be warm by confiding some things "woman to woman." She said she hoped all this would be over soon, since Mr. Dole had been ill so much. At a meeting at their home, she said he'd acted like he was demented — couldn't put two sentences together that made sense. After that, he left for Kauai for a few weeks, and seemed better when he got back. But now she's worried that his personality has changed. He's become "all lawyer," she said. Then she leaned in, shielding our faces from public view with her parasol, and whispered that the Republic was on its way to ruin, and only annexation would save it from complete destruction.

Well, I already knew that lots of people were disgusted with the PGs, and it's not just the Hawaiians. When I told the queen, she turned to look out the window and didn't say anything for several minutes. Finally, she said Mr. Dole wasn't ill, he was suffering an attack of conscience.

&

Before the overthrow, Sanford Dole used to enjoy his morning walks from his house to his law office. The flower vendors at the corner offered him a bloom as he passed by. Boys with ukuleles and guitars sat on street corners strumming and harmonizing — not for coins — just for the joy of it. *Pa'u* riders in bright skirts, laden with garlands, galloped by in tight clusters, waving. All colors of people promenaded the streets, and in the afternoon, when he walked home, he'd hear the Royal Band at the Hawaiian Hotel playing their latest compositions.

Now the streets were quiet. Commerce was slow. The natives stayed away from downtown. All the Royal Hawaiian Band members had quit after the queen was overthrown. Someone asked how they would live without their jobs. "We'll eat stones," they said.

At night, when he tried to go to sleep, Dole was plagued with a memory of visiting New England as a child. After dinner, he'd gone outside with his cousins, who showed him how to catch fireflies in a jar to light up his room at night. It was a novelty he'd never seen. There were no fireflies in Kauai where he grew up.

Elated, he caught the bugs and closed them in the jar. He punched holes in the lid so they could breathe, and put in leaves and twigs to make them feel at home. In his room that night, he was fascinated, watching them glimmer and blink, over and over, but after a while, their light faded. Worried, he opened the lid to give them more air, but they'd stopped glowing. He grabbed the jar and hurried downstairs and into the yard. He turned the jar over to let them go free, but they dropped to the earth, lifeless.

He was shocked, then embarrassed, so he stamped them into the ground with his foot to erase the evidence that he'd let them die.

As Dole turned the corner on King Street, he passed two Hawaiian women dressed in striped holokus. He tipped his hat, but they looked away. They wore the stripes, he knew, as a silent protest in support of their husbands and brothers in convict's stripes at the prison.

He trudged up the stairs of the Executive Building. Thurston and Price would probably be waiting for him. One more meeting to figure out how to get the US to agree to annexation. Thurston was mad because he'd heard secondhand that Dole's wife had told some people the Republic was failing. Well, maybe it was. Dole had done all he could do to make it work — written the constitution and bylaws, tried to keep the country orderly, taken the brunt of everybody's discontent. But there was one ingredient they didn't have that a Republic required — the consent of the governed.

The trials and convictions worried him. Thurston said, and he was right, that Hawaiian juries would never bring in convictions. But now, the military court was bringing in nothing but convictions, with the most ominous punishments — hard labor and the death penalty. Some haoles were just a little too anxious for executions. Dole had given up praying, but his wife said he wouldn't get sick so much if he'd go to the Lord once in a while. So he sent up a silent prayer as he opened his office door. He didn't want this blood on his hands.

Thurston leapt up from his chair when he saw Dole.

"Price said we should get going with the executions. With the queen and the instigators out of the way, it'll settle things once and for all."

Dole removed his hat and hung it on the hat rack. He looked across the room at Stephen, who was seated on the edge of his desk, one leg hanging off the side.

"That's right," Stephen said. "With them gone, everyone will know we're fully in charge and there's no going back to the monarchy. No one will dare start another revolt. And it'll end the debate in the US about whether it's right or not to annex Hawaii."

Dole crossed his arms over his chest.

"Very tidy solution, gentlemen. And did it ever occur to you that executions based on the scanty evidence being presented in court might alarm Americans? They still hold dear trials by a jury of their peers, and they could look on military courts as the method of dictators."

Thurston threw his hands up. "Well, we've got to get rid of the queen somehow, Sanford. As long as she's around, people will think there's still hope she'll be restored."

In the silence, Dole remembered the autumn at Williams College when he wrote his parents that he'd decided on law instead of the ministry. He thought it might be a steppingstone to influence and power in the government, where a good man could do more for morality and justice than preach to the natives. He remembered the week he graduated — the oratory, the shaking of hands, the sad farewells, the high hopes. This wasn't what he'd had in mind.

"What about abdication?" Stephen said.

Maybe, Dole thought, he had just heard a prayer being answered.

"This whole mess started when she yielded under protest to the United States," Stephen continued. "If she formally abdicates, there's no more protest. It's over. The US will have no reason not to annex us."

"But if we ask her to abdicate, that's like saying we recognize she's still queen," Thurston said. "If she refuses, it could get messier."

"What if we offer her something she wants?" Dole said.

"Like what?" Thurston said.

"Pardon all the prisoners."

"And let all those traitors back on the street to cause more trouble?"

"What do you suggest, Lorrin?"

"Not that."

"You know the treasury's low," Dole said. "And people are getting more riled up. Business is suffering. Trying to pull all these things together is more than we bargained for. We do have to settle this, Lorrin, but the US won't look kindly on the executions of the queen and her supporters. I was never for annexation, but if they don't take us soon, we'll be up for grabs by Japan or somebody else. You don't think the warship *Naniwa* is in port just by coincidence, do you?"

"Okay, okay," Thurston said. "But not full pardon. It'd be a mockery."

"What, then?"

"I don't know. Whatever you have to tell her to get her to abdicate."

"Let's tell her," Stephen said, "that unless she signs the abdication, blood will flow. We can decide on the sentences later."

Ɓ

*O*n the morning of the queen's trial, Laura waited for her in the grand entry of the palace. The government clerks, busy at their desks, looked up each time the heavy front door opened, as military judges, lawyers, reporters, and observers entered the hall to go into the throne room. Portraits of the former kings and queens of Hawaii still hung on the walls above the hall, looking down on them as they passed. Any minute, guards would escort the queen from the upstairs room where she was held prisoner, to the throne room, which had been converted to a court.

The day before, while Laura was serving the queen's lunch, her attorney came by. He'd questioned whether she should appear in court, whether it might not be undignified and a humiliation for her.

"Humiliation?" the queen had said. "What have I left? Anyway, it's their shame."

Laura moved nearer to the throne-room door. The guard stationed there reached to open it for her, but she shook her head, indicating she was waiting for someone. She noticed how the morning sun lit up the dancing Hawaiian maidens etched in the crystal panels of the front door. They were pushed aside as Thurston, Dole, and Stephen Price swung the doors open, walked in, and headed toward where she was standing. Laura wished she was somewhere else, but there was nowhere else to go.

The guard opened the throne-room door. Dole and Thurston, all business, tipped their hats to Laura and went inside. Stephen stopped.

"So what do you think of your precious natives now?"

Laura just looked at him.

"They've caused all this trouble. Got all these people killed. How come you never went to see the McBrides? After all their kindness to you, and you practically married to that boy."

"The Hawaiians didn't kill Lucien."

"What do you mean? The soldiers saw them do it out on —"

"You did it, Uncle Stephen. You and all your scheming."

"That's ridiculous!"

Laura turned away. The government employees in the grand hall lifted their heads from their work, their eyes on Laura and Stephen. The guard reached to open the door to encourage Stephen to move on. He hesitated, as if he wanted to say something else, but then walked ahead. The guard shut the door behind him.

Just then, the clerks' heads turned to look up the wide koa-wood staircase. The queen was at the top of the stairs, a guard at each elbow. Laura saw her shrink from the gaze of all the strangers and take a breath to steel herself. She descended the staircase, not as a prisoner, but as the queen.

Laura made a deep, formal curtsy. When she raised her head, their eyes met, and the queen acknowledged her with a brief, tender smile. As the guards escorted the queen toward the throne room, Laura walked a few steps behind. At the door, the guard stationed there almost involuntarily snapped to attention, clicked his heels, and swung the door open wide.

All eyes turned to Lili'uokalani. She entered the room head up, carriage erect, as if she were attending a royal function. A few people in the crowd stood to curtsy or bow as she passed up the aisle. Memories flooded back to Laura. She saw the glittering throne room at her first ball. Many in this audience had been there then, diplomats, ministers of the Gospel, commissioners, dressed in formal suits or royal uniforms, the ladies in satin gowns and lace, fluttering feathered fans.

She could hear the strains of classical music from the shaded verandah, played by the Royal Hawaiian Band, see couples laughing and talking, and the specters of Kalakaua and Likelike smiling graciously from the dais as the dancers whirled by. Pages served tea and ices to naval officers just in from the Far East, happy to be back on the island, with beautiful women on their arms. She heard the band strike up another song, and saw Lucien extend his hand to her for the first dance, Premier Gibson with the twinkle in his eye, asking if she reversed in the waltz. She felt the touch of the beribboned medallion as Kalakaua tied the prize around her neck, danced the last dance with David, his wistful smile delighting in the moment that would soon be gone.

"The prisoner will be seated."

The judge advocate pointed toward a single chair at the front of the room. Liliu went forward and sat down. The guards positioned themselves behind her on either side. Laura took an open seat in the second row. The throne room had been stripped of its regal splendor. The rug had been removed, the gold and crimson chairs, the royal escutcheons and portraits, the tall feathered kahilis, all gone. Everything was bare, stark, utilitarian, Puritan. At the front of the room, behind a long table, sat a row of white men in uniforms — the military commission.

First, the tribunal required the queen to confirm the statement of abdication she'd signed the week before. That she asserted Hawaii was lawfully in the hands of the Republic; that she relinquished all rights to the throne for herself and her heirs; that she pleaded for clemency for the rebels; that she'd signed of her own volition and without undue influence by the government.

Laura had been in the queen's room when an aide-de-camp from Dole's office presented the proposition. He'd told her if she abdicated she could stay the flow of blood and free all the prisoners. Liliu said if it were only for herself, she'd choose death. But to free her supporters, she'd sign. He came back a few days later with the document, and when she signed it, he told her the prisoners would not be freed, but he thought it might save their lives.

The queen's attorney arose to protest the right of the military commission to try the case, saying that martial law had not been declared when the queen was arrested. He was overruled and instructed, "In these proceedings, you will please refer to the prisoner as 'Mrs. Dominis.'"

The queen was asked to step down. The judge advocate called the first witness to the stand, a policeman who had searched

Washington Place after the queen was arrested.

"Captain Parker," the prosecutor said, "were you in charge of the search at Mrs. Dominis's home after she was taken into custody?"

"I was."

"Will you tell the court what you found there?"

"We found rifles, pistols, bombs, and ammunition."

"Where were these things discovered?" the prosecutor said.

"We found the bulk of them in the garden house on the grounds and buried in the flower beds near the main house. And we found a bomb fragment in Mrs. Dominis's desk."

"Thank you, Captain."

As the prosecutor sat down, the queen leaned and whispered something to her attorney. He rose and walked up next to the witness.

"Captain Parker, did you say you found the bulk of the weapons in the garden house?"

"That's correct. There and buried in the flower beds."

"I understand you were a card-playing partner of the queen's late husband, John Dominis. Is that true?"

"We did play cards from time to time, yes."

"Did you ever play cards in the garden house on the grounds at Washington Place?"

"Yes."

"Do you recall a particular antique collection that Mr. Dominis had decorating the walls of the garden house?"

The policeman's face turned red.

"Yes."

"And could you tell the court what that antique collection consisted of?"

"It was antique pistols, revolvers, muskets, and old Polynesian spears."

A few people in the audience snickered.

"And were these among the weapons your men confiscated that you say implicate Mrs. Dominis in this so-called revolt?"

"But they weren't the only things," the policeman said.

"Oh, yes," the queen's attorney said. "You said there were bombs."

"That's right."

"Can you tell us what the bombs were made of?"

"Coconut shells, mostly."

Some in the audience snickered again.

"You do investigative work in your job, Captain Parker?"

"Yes, I do."

"From your knowledge of procedure as an investigator, is there any way beyond a shadow of a doubt that you can connect the weapons found on the queen's property with her personal involvement in the disturbance?"

"We found part of a bomb in her desk."

"Part of a coconut shell, you mean?"

"Well, sure, it was a coconut shell, but —"

"I'm asking you, Captain Parker, if as a professional police investigator there's any way to connect the weapons you found with the queen."

"Not directly, no, but she must have known —"

"And anyone could have sneaked into her garden and buried those weapons, isn't that true, Captain Parker?"

"Yes, I suppose so."

"Thank you. No further questions."

Captain Parker got up from the stand and sat back down in the audience, his face still flushed.

The judge advocate called his second witness. Willie Kaae shuffled to the front of the room and took the stand, averting his eyes to avoid looking at the queen. Laura wondered why the prosecutor would call the queen's copyist. He was just a clerk. What could he know? She saw Willie's gaze shift past her, looking for someone at the back of the room. She took a quick look behind her and saw Thurston nodding encouragement at him. After Captain Parker's embarrassment on the stand, Laura thought the queen's case had gained some ground. Now, she felt a dark chill.

Willie stammered along, telling the court that he'd copied drafts of constitutions for the queen between 1893 and 1895, after she'd been dethroned, suggesting she planned to use them when she was restored. He also claimed that he'd copied eleven commissions for political offices that Liliu later signed in anticipation of appointing a new cabinet and other officers.

Chief Justice Judd, whom Laura and David had seen enter Washington Place the day Liliu was arrested, was called to the stand. He produced a diary he said he'd found, and read an entry in Liliu's handwriting confirming the date she'd signed the commissions.

The queen's attorney stood to protest.

"What's the date of the diary entry, Mr. Judd?"

"December 28th, 1894. She wrote, 'Signed eleven commissions.'"

"That's before the revolt began," the queen's attorney said. "That can't be submitted as evidence that Mrs. Dominis was participating in a rebellion."

The commission considered the attorney's objection and overruled it. He sat down with a frustrated look on his face.

Next, Charles Clark, who had often eaten at the queen's table, took the stand. He testified to a conversation with the queen —

"Ex-queen," the presiding officer corrected him.

— in which she'd told him the time had come and she hoped it would be a success.

When Clark stepped down, the queen's attorney called several witnesses who swore that Clark's testimony could not be believed, even under oath.

When the last of them left the stand, Liliu went forward. Her attorney questioned her just a few minutes. The testimony was composed and direct, and the judge advocate's cross-examination was fruitless.

Then the queen spoke in Hawaiian. She reviewed the history of her overthrow, how she'd acceded to the request of her people to restore their rights by proclaiming a new constitution, and how a small minority of the foreign population made that the pretext for dethroning her. She said she owed no allegiance to a provisional government established contrary to the will of a people who hadn't been allowed to vote. She had yielded to the superior forces brought against her and to the arbitration of the United States government only to prevent bloodshed. When the provisional government refused the recommendation of the United States to restore her to the throne and declared themselves "a Republic," a few of her people could stand it no more and took the matter into their own hands.

"It would not have received my sanction," Liliu said. "I have always pursued a path of peace and diplomacy." She sat erect. "But I will add that, had I known, their secrets would have been mine and preserved inviolate."

Then she spoke in English, appealing once more for clemency for her supporters, saying that she prayed that Almighty God might deal with the members of the court in their hours of trial as the court dealt with the rebels. She turned to look at the military commission and then back to the audience, her gaze resting on Dole, Thurston, and Stephen Price.

"I ask you to consider that your government is on trial before the whole world. You're commencing a new era in our history. May Divine Providence grant you the wisdom to lead the nation into the paths of forbearance, forgiveness, and peace, and to create and consolidate a united people ever anxious to advance in the way of civilization."

After Liliu stepped down, there was a short recess while the court deliberated on the translation of her statement. Laura went forward and curtsied to the queen, eyes shining. Liliu took her hand and smiled.

"It's so clear what happened, Your Majesty. No one could mistake it."

The gavel sounded, and the court was again called to order. Laura took her seat. One of the officers of the military commission rose to speak.

"It is the decision of this court that the following portions of the prisoner's statement be stricken from the record:

Stricken: That a minority of the foreign population overthrew the monarchy.

Stricken: That they were aided by United States naval forces."

Laura listened in disbelief. How could they strike that from the record? What the queen had said was true. President Cleveland's own special commissioner wrote a two-thousand-page report saying it was true.

"Stricken: That the defendant owed no allegiance to the provisional government.

Stricken: That she pursued the path of peace and diplomatic discussion."

They were striking out every point she'd made. Laura wished she could see Liliu's face, but the queen looked straight ahead without moving.

"Stricken:

That the provisional government prevented a vote.

That the prisoner received no information regarding the insurrection.

That she did not plan to take part in establishing a new government.

That she did not have to recognize the legitimacy of the Republic."

The queen's attorney jumped to his feet. He argued that none of the passages should be stricken from the record. It was the defendant's own view and thus should stand. He denied that the rebellion had been a "war." It was only a riot, so there was no justification for martial law, a military court, or a charge of treason. He reminded the court that most of the state's witnesses had been in prison under the threat of death, and that they were frightened men without knowledge of what the truth was. His final appeal was for the court to judge the queen on evidence only, not on any predetermination of their "moral conviction" or on hatred. He referred to the campaign of slander against the queen's character.

"If you convict her," he said, "it will be an indelible shame, because you try her after she's relinquished all the rights she possessed, and relinquished them for what? For the peace of the country, for the benefit of the people, and for leniency for those imprisoned on her behalf."

The judge advocate of the military commission arose to make his final remarks. He dismissed what he called "the lady's will-o'-the-wisp innocence," and said the men who'd planned and carried out this revolution were her close friends and advisors. So she'd known about the rebellion and had signed commissions preparing to return to the throne. The uprising was on her behalf, while all the while she supposedly pursued a path of peace and diplomatic discussion. She was not so spotless and immaculate, he said, as she held herself out to be, but he denied that any members of the court or the Republic had ever called her or the Hawaiians "bloodthirsty savages." He sniffed, admitting, "Oh, the lady's statement had a good deal of the heroic — she waived all right to any immunity or consideration for herself. But she knew," he said, "if she knew anything, that with the men she dealt with here, she could file emotional appeals of that stripe all day long" — he turned and smiled pointedly at the commission members behind the long table — "and they'd be considered for what they're worth."

There was a murmur in the courtroom as people leaned toward each other with their comments. Something made Laura glance behind her. Sanford Dole sat stoic, expressionless. Thurston was on the edge of his chair, in rapt attention as if listening to a sermon of salvation. Stephen Price returned Laura's gaze with a leer.

Laura turned to the front as the judge advocate closed his remarks:

"The accused has reminded us that she's a woman, and much that is in her statement may well be passed by. I submit to the commission that by all the rules of evidence she is guilty of the charges against her and that she should be so found."

Chapter 30 ————

October 16, 1897

It's been two years since I last wrote in this journal. My
heart wasn't in it since the queen's conviction. I was so
relieved her sentence was only for knowing about the revolt
in advance and not reporting it —"misprision of treason"
they called it — instead of the original charge of treason.
But it hasn't made the last couple of years any easier.

Fortunately, Mr. Dole's "attack of conscience," as the queen
called it, worked to lessen the sentences of all those who
were in prison. No one was executed, though most spent
time in jail, except those who turned state's evidence.

The queen was sick the whole time she was locked up,
and was the last one to be released. Whenever I'd go to see
her, she was quiet, crocheting, playing the zither, or attending to her potted plants and canaries, but underneath there
was some sort of strife going on, though she never shared
it with me. The battle may be over as far as the PGs are
concerned, but it isn't over for the queen.

When they finally freed her a few months ago, she was followed by spies and under threat of assassination. Her nerves
were worn thin. She petitioned Mr. Dole for a passport to

visit San Francisco and her husband's relatives in Boston. She asked David to accompany her, along with a Hawaiian woman who'd been imprisoned. She said she wanted to give them a change of scenery and a respite from the confined atmosphere of Honolulu, where people are still afraid to speak their minds in this so-called Republic.

It wasn't until she was aboard the steamship and half-way across the Pacific that she wrote me a letter saying that, after she visited her relatives, she was going to Washington to continue the fight against annexation. She sent the letter back from San Francisco, carried by a trusted friend heading for the islands. She thought there might still be a chance to save the country for her people. The American secretary of state was so irritated by Mr. Thurston (who'd been in Washington working for annexation during the queen's imprisonment), that he asked for him to be recalled as "persona non grata."

I'm taking care of Washington Place for her while she's away. I worry about her expenses. The PGs confiscated all the Crown lands that gave her most of her income.

There's one thing at least that's cheered my heart. Next month Ka`iulani is coming home! It's been eight years since she left. She's twenty-two today. I can hardly believe it.

Her last letter was a little melancholy, despite the good news that she's returning. She said she often cries for the islands in these sad times, and swears she can hear something calling back to her. She wondered if it was normal that she feels the islands are living things, as real as relatives. One night, she dreamt she heard her peacocks crying in the dark, like they were lost. She woke up aching, because she couldn't let her feelings out.

ଜ୍ଲ

$\mathcal{A}$ light rain fell on the crowd waiting for the steamship Australia to dock. Many had armfuls of maile vines and pikake leis. They talked in hushed tones, some clinging to each other, as they strained for a glimpse of Ka`iulani.

With Liliu still away in Washington, Laura had arranged for a carriage to meet Ka`iulani's ship. She left the driver and retainers who'd come to carry the princess's luggage, and made her way with an umbrella through the throng to the foot of the gangplank. Ka`iulani appeared and began to descend, her father behind her. An awed silence fell over the crowd. She hesitated for a moment. Then, as if remembering her station, she began to make slight bows in each direction in the haawi ke aloha Laura had seen her practice as a child. That movement was the only familiar thing about her. She was slender and graceful in a fitted Parisian traveling suit, with her wavy black hair tied up in a knot under a smart feathered hat.

She was almost on the wharf before she saw Laura. She stopped. Her large, dark eyes expressed a look of anticipation at being home again, with an apprehension that it would not be the home she remembered. She looked like she wanted to hug Laura, and Laura longed to hug her too, but curtsied low instead. When she raised her eyes, they met Ka`iulani's. The princess reached out to grasp her hand.

"Dear Laura, it's so good to see you." Her accent was British.

Laura remembered that she had an umbrella and went to put it up.

"Let me escort you and your father to the carriage, Your Highness."

"No umbrella, please. I want to feel the rain on my face."

As they walked toward the carriage, the crowd gave way. Hawaiian men in frayed coats and hats, women in faded dresses, many children in tattered shirts and frocks, most barefoot, stood silent as the princess passed, smiling gently and inclining her head to one side and the other. At the periphery, haole men and women gathered under umbrellas eyed the scene with uneasy curiosity.

When they were seated in the carriage, well-wishers handed up leis of vines and fragrant flowers until the landau was almost full. As the driver started the horse up Fort Street, Ka`iulani grasped Laura's hand again, her brow furrowed, looking at her father sitting across from them.

"They all look so poor, Papa. I don't remember them looking so poor in the old days."

They crossed King Street, and Ka`iulani asked her father to tell the driver to go up Nuuanu Road.

"I want to see my mother's grave."

The carriage passed through the tall wrought-iron gate at the entrance to the mausoleum. The rain had stopped, and plumeria blossoms drifted down from the trees. They left the carriage and walked into the small chapel to Princess Likelike's resting place. Laura and Mr. Cleghorn hung back as Ka`iulani stepped forward to place her hand on the cold marble of the tomb. She bowed her head, her voice just above a whisper.

"I'm home, Mama. I'm home."

&

*O*n the drive along the Waikiki Road, Ka`iulani let formality go and sat close to Laura on the carriage seat, holding her hand. Laura told her that she'd arranged a reception the following day so the Hawaiians could greet her. The day after, there would be a reception for the haoles.

"But tonight," Laura said, "it's just us." She smiled. "With fish and poi for dinner."

"Yes, my dear," Mr. Cleghorn said. "Dinner in your new house."

When they got to Ainahau, Ka`iulani said she didn't remember the trees being so tall. Pulling into the clearing near the old banyan, she caught sight of the home her father had built while she was away at school. The large two-story gabled house had fluted white columns and a wide lanai across the front.

"Oh, it's beautiful, Papa."

"I had it built fit for a queen," Mr. Cleghorn said.

Laura wished he hadn't said that. For a moment, a shadow crossed Ka`iulani's face, and Laura wondered if she was remembering her mother's prophecy. Then her peacocks came strutting, looking for handouts. She smiled.

"Come on, Laura. I want to see Fairie."

She removed the pins from her feathered hat, took it off, and handed it to her father. She got down from the carriage and disappeared through the trees, calling to the pony. There was a throaty whinny in reply. When Laura caught up to Ka`iulani, she was inside the paddock, her arms around Fairie's neck, her face against his mane.

&.

January 23, 1898

Since Ka'iulani returned, she's tried to live quietly at Ain-ahau, simply as "Miss Cleghorn," but people can't seem to get enough of her — she's invited to so many affairs.

Mr. Cleghorn confided to me that the Republic is in such dire straits that the PGs despair they'll ever achieve annexation. President McKinley reintroduced the bill in Congress, but I guess the queen's efforts in Washington are bearing fruit. There aren't enough votes to pass it. Mr. Cleghorn said he's heard rumors that if annexation doesn't pass soon, the PGs will approach Ka`iulani to take the throne! Thus all the invitations, I suppose. President and Mrs. Dole even had Ka`iulani and her father in their private box at the theater last week. It's all so crazy.

When I asked Ka`iulani how she felt about it, she showed me a letter she got from the queen. Even in Washington, the queen had heard the rumors. She told the princess that she trusted her judgment to make a good decision were the throne offered to her. But she also told her to beware of the PGs. They were liars, deceitful in all their undertakings, and she feared Ka`iulani's heart might be too pure to see their designs. They could offer her the throne, but only as a figurehead, with nothing to say about managing the country. Then Ka`iulani would be in Mr. Dole's present position, despised and in fear of his life.

She wrote that if Ka`iulani refused their offer to be a figurehead it would increase her popularity and weaken the Republic — perhaps to the point of collapse. If there were open elections, and the people called for Ka`iulani to take the throne, the queen urged her to accept, because it would be through the love of the people.

This week the government auctioned off the official belongings of King Kalakaua — wineglasses, dinner service, candelabra. There was an overflow crowd, and bidding was lively, I heard. It's so sad, especially since Queen Kapi`olani is still living, and the royalty so poor now that they couldn't afford to save the items.

There's always another insult. Ka`iulani and I attended a New Year's ball hosted by US Consul General Sewall. He's made it no secret that he supports annexation. At midnight, instead of playing the national anthem, *Hawaii Ponoi*, (one of the few things the Republic kept from the monarchy), the band struck up *The Star-spangled Banner*, and all the haoles smiled, exchanging New Year's greetings as if nothing were amiss! Ka`iulani smiled whenever any of them turned her way, but I was mortified by their insensitivity. On the way home she was so subdued that I worried she'd be ill.

Mr. Dole, I hear, will travel back to Washington soon in one more attempt to win votes for annexation. How long can this state of affairs continue?

&

"Remember the *Maine*," Stephen Price said with a laugh. "How appropriate the ship was the *Maine*, since your folks hail from Maine, Sanford."

Dole, his face dour, looked across the desk at him.

"I don't know that we should feel jubilation at the tragedy of others."

"But when you came back from Washington, it looked like annexation was dead," Thurston said. "Since the *Maine* was sunk at Havana harbor, and the US declared war on Spain, our fortunes have changed."

"One man's tragedy can be another man's fortune," Stephen said. "It happens all the time."

"When the soldiers start to pour through here on their way to fight the Spanish in the Philippines, Congress will finally see what we've been telling them all along," Thurston said. "Hawaii has strategic importance. We're America's first line of defense in the Pacific."

"Well, the thing now," Dole said, "is to make their troops welcome and our port available to refuel their ships. That'll mean more to Congress than anything we can say."

"The whole town's come out in force," Stephen said. "Honolulu's decorated in American flags and red-white-and-blue bunting."

"How are the plans for the picnic coming?" Dole said.

"We're setting up to host twenty-five hundred troops on the lawn of the Executive Building," Stephen said. "We've got thousands of ham sandwiches and a ton of potato salad on the way, and the Honolulu ladies are making hundreds of pies."

"And what about accommodations?"

"We've opened Kapiolani Park, and they're putting up a tent city out there as we speak," Thurston said. "Don't worry. They're going to see that Hawaii is American at heart."

Chapter 31 ————

August 10, 1898

$\mathcal{A}$ month ago, when the SS *Coptic* rounded Diamond Head with its signal flags spelling out the message, Honolulu erupted in screaming whistles and fireworks. Special editions of the newspapers were rushed out with the headline: ANNEXATION!, and guns on the palace grounds boomed out the news.

It was different when the queen arrived home on the *Gaelic* two weeks later. Thousands of Hawaiians greeted her at the wharf in solemn silence, and hundreds followed her back to Washington Place where she stayed up all night receiving those who came to see her.

David sat with Ka`iulani and me on the verandah, to tell us about their efforts in Washington and how they were finally defeated when the Spanish-American War started and Congress determined they needed Hawaii as a base in the Pacific. Once that was decided, they speedily passed a joint resolution in both houses, and sent word to their minister in Honolulu.

Last week, when the naval officer came to the front door with an invitation for "Mrs. Dominis" to attend the official annexation ceremony on August twelfth, I couldn't believe it. How could the American consul be so insensitive? Then I found out Ka`iulani had received an invitation too. The royal women said nothing, just sent their regrets.

&

Rain beat down on the verandah, and a loose shutter banged against the window. Laura woke. Wind shrieked around the house, and the shutter banged again and again. She got up, lit a candle, and crossed the floor in bare feet to bolt it. Then she climbed back into bed. In the candle's glow she could see the clock. It was 4:24 a.m. In a few hours, many of the queen's friends would arrive at Washington Place to sit with her, while just two blocks away, in a ceremony at the old palace, the Hawaiian flag would be lowered for the last time, and the American flag raised.

At dawn, the wind still groaned, and sheets of rain lashed down from the mountains. The old Hawaiian retainers were up early, preparing to receive the queen's guests. When they scuffed along the wood hallway past her room, Laura heard them whispering about kahunas cursing the weather.

She lay in bed until the room grew light, then blew out the candle. She rose, went to the wardrobe, and ruffled through her dresses. Since living at Washington Place, she always wore bright holokus, but the happy colors didn't seem appropriate today. At one end of the wardrobe hung the black suit she'd worn to Aunt Katherine's funeral. She took it out, laid it on the bed, and went to wash up.

Around ten o'clock, guests began to arrive. Laura took them to the parlor to join the queen. They walked across the foyer in quiet, measured steps, speaking in hushed tones, as if arriving for a wake.

Ka`iulani arrived dressed in a black gown, her hair pulled back with tortoise-shell combs. Around her neck she wore a lei of woven o'o feathers. She embraced Laura. Her eyes were dry, but her face was strained.

"I'm all cried out," she said.

David came up the steps. The front door was ajar and he walked in. He bowed to Ka`iulani, kissed her cheek, and then embraced Laura. He noticed the princess's feathered lei.

"Why don't you wear the medallion King Kalakaua gave you, Laura?" David said. "It'll make the queen happy."

Laura nodded, and escorted them to the parlor. The queen, dressed in a black holoku, sat on a divan at one end the room. Ka`iulani went to her and curtsied. David bowed, then they greeted the other guests seated around the room.

Laura returned to the foyer. She opened the front door to see if anyone else was coming, but the street outside was deserted. The queen had requested that Washington Place remain closed up. The house was dim. The rain had stopped, but the air was still and damp. Wakeki came from the kitchen with a tray of tea.

"When you come back from the parlor, will you watch the door for me?" Laura said. "I need to get something from the bedroom."

Wakeki nodded and went on. Laura began to close the front door. She hesitated, then slipped outside. She walked to the edge of the verandah and breathed in the moist air, scented by blossoms that had fallen in the storm. The sound of band music drifted from the direction of the palace, where a crowd was gathering for the ceremony. She went down the stairs and walked up the street to look around. All the Hawaiian homes were shuttered and dark. She kept walking toward the music until she was at King Street.

Nearing the palace, she saw the upper and lower verandahs crowded with spectators looking down on a large platform decorated with starred-and-striped bunting and American flags. The Hawaiian flag still hung from the flagpole in front. Marines from the *Mohican* paraded past the platform down the broad drive toward the street. When the music stopped, Laura was struck by how quiet the crowd was. There was little conversation, and when anyone spoke, it was in subdued tones and whispers.

On the palace grounds, chairs were set up under the trees, facing the platform. People milled around to find seats — Chinese families, Japanese women in kimonos, babies on their backs, their husbands in Western suits. Portuguese grandmothers, bandannas on their heads, herding children. American women in muslin dresses and ribboned hats, carrying parasols, walked with men in suits and straw hats — some with buttons on their lapels that read, TODAY IS OUR WEDDING DAY, showing Uncle Sam taking a blushing Hawaiian bride. There was neither cheering nor shouts and whistles. The atmosphere was more like an execution than a celebration.

Laura looked around. There were almost no Hawaiians, just a few politicians' wives, performing their official duty to be present with their husbands as they made their way to be seated on the platform. And the Hawaiian Band, which the Republic had coaxed back into government service, was lined up ready to play. Then Laura saw President and Mrs. Dole arrive with the men of his cabinet. They were dressed in formal suits and tall silk hats, but the hats were from every epoch since the missionaries had arrived in the islands. They gave an odd, antique appearance. Then the US minister and his staff stepped up on the platform to be seated. Rain started falling again, and the proceedings opened with a prayer.

The US minister made a short speech, then gave President Dole a blue envelope containing a copy of the resolution of annexation. Dole said a few words, and handed the minister documents that transferred the sovereignty of the Hawaiian Islands to the United States. The Hawaiian Band started *Hawaii Ponoi*, the national anthem. The volume dropped after the first few bars, and the notes wavered like a sob. Before the anthem finished, the band members, tears flowing down their cheeks, threw down their instruments and fled around the corner out of sight of the crowd.

President Dole motioned to a man on the platform to wave a white handkerchief. At the signal, the troops presented arms and from the direction of the harbor came the retort of a twenty-one-gun salute from the *Philadelphia*'s cannon, a last tribute to the Hawaiian flag. The bugle corps played *taps*, and the striped banner was lowered for the last time.

Everyone on the platform and on the grounds stood. Men removed their hats. Ladies pulled out handkerchiefs and held them to their faces. A young Hawaiian boy stopped next to Laura to watch the flag come down. His black curls, dampened by the rain, fell wet on his forehead. His large, dark eyes never left the banner until it drooped to the ground and was folded up. Then he bowed his head and walked away.

All was still. The crowd remained standing. The only sounds were stifled sobs of haole men and women who'd been born under this flag and couldn't control their tears. Then the order "Colors roll off!" was given and the Marine Band started *The Star-spangled Banner* as the American flag was raised. Laura heard someone say it was the same American flag that Commissioner Blount had lowered when he came to Hawaii to investigate the queen's overthrow. One of the naval officers on the *Boston*, the ship that had landed the troops, had given it to Lorrin Thurston who donated it for the ceremony. It reached the top of the pole, but hung lifeless until a sudden gust unfurled it. The band played *Columbia the Gem of the Ocean*, signaling the end of the program.

As the crowd began to thin out, Laura turned to walk back toward Washington Place. She passed the gazebo on the palace grounds and heard a voice call to her.

"Laura. Laura, come up here."

It was Effie Williams and some of the ladies Laura had met at luncheons and parties around town. They were posing in front of a young man with a box camera.

"Come on, Laura," Effie said. "We're going to have our picture taken with all our friends."

Laura shook her head. "I can't Effie, I'm in a hurry right now."

"But Laura, it's historic."

Laura walked faster and faster until her walk became a trot. She ran the few blocks to Washington Place, opened the front door, and kept going straight up to her bedroom. She went to the wardrobe, pulled open a drawer, and pushed aside the chemises at the front. Reaching to the back, she took the royal medallion and hurried back downstairs, tying it behind her neck.

In the parlor, a guest had set up his camera on a tripod, and was just slipping under the black cloth to take a shot. In front of him, the queen sat on the divan while the others clustered around her for the photograph. Ka`iulani and David stood at one side, somber, facing the camera. Laura slipped around the back of the divan to stand behind the queen. She grasped Ka`iulani's hand, and the photographer's flash went off in a burst of light.

છ

*L*aura sat at the dining table with the queen, sewing new curtains for the kitchen windows. Wakeki came in, a frown on her face. She addressed the queen in Hawaiian.

"Your Majesty, there are American soldiers in the garden picking flowers and fruit. Some have even come up on the lanai and are peering into the rooms. Shall I send them away?"

Liliu tugged a stitch taut and lay down her needle. For a moment, Laura thought she saw a flicker of exasperation in her eyes. "Laura, go with Wakeki, pick some flowers, and give them to the young men." She regarded Laura's surprise. "They're far from home and on their way to the Philippines. Many of them may never see their country again." She picked up her sewing. "Go on, now."

Laura went with Wakeki to the garden. The soldiers looked embarrassed to see them. The ones on the verandah came down with sheepish grins. Laura picked flowers, gave them bouquets, and sent them on their way. She was about to go back to sewing when she saw Ka`iulani's carriage coming up the street. The driver turned the horses into the queen's driveway. Laura and Wakeki waited at the front of the house to meet her.

Ka`iulani's face was pale. She looked thin and tired.

"Are you all right?" Laura asked.

She shook her head. "I don't know how I'm going to stand much more of this. I just had to come and be with friends."

"What happened?"

"Some Americans came to Ainahau this morning, pounding on the front door. They wanted to know if they could have their picture taken with the 'ex-princess!' Oh, Laura, will they ever leave us alone?"

"Come inside," Laura said. "The queen and I are sewing. Just sit with us awhile. Wakeki will make us some tea."

She took Ka'iulani's arm to walk her to the dining room. The queen looked up and smiled, but her brow furrowed when she saw Ka'iulani's face.

"Oh Auntie, I can't tolerate any more." She sat at the table and told Liliu what she'd told Laura. "We're pushed out of the way like we don't exist, and then they want us on display like some kind of curiosity. I'm trying to appear happy so as not to grieve my father, but I can't keep it up." She rubbed her brow. "I came into town to get my headache pills, but when the carriage got down to Merchant Street, there were so many soldiers staring, I didn't want to go into the store. I told the driver to come up here."

Wakeki came in, set cups in front of the ladies, and poured tea from a porcelain pot.

The queen gave Ka`iulani an encouraging look. "You know, last Sunday I went to St. Andrew's Church. They had a guest minister from the United States. I sat in my usual place in the front row." She picked up her teacup and took a sip. "His talk was about being thankful." She set the cup down, and Laura thought she might advise them about counting their blessings.

"You can imagine my surprise when, in the middle of the sermon, he looked out at the congregation and said, 'You ought to be thankful that you're free from the tyranny under which you've lived, and to be a part of the great United States of America.'"

Ka`iulani's eyes widened. Laura shook her head. If that minister had seen the way the PGs ran the country, he might have had a little more understanding of the tyranny under which they'd lived.

"When I was in Washington," the queen went on, "I attended

services at St. Andrew's there. They had a very fine clergyman who never mentioned politics." She sipped her tea again. "You see, it's not all of them, just a few. When you left for school, Ka'iulani, you were still a child, so you never really knew how we were treated here. It's been going on a long time.

"When the missionaries first came, they called us heathen. Later they changed the word to 'natives,' and finally, 'our children.' They've never quite arrived at the point of calling us 'brother and sister,' but I hold out hope. "*Onipaa,* my dear Ka'iulani. Be steadfast. Don't despair. You're an ali'i, and you can still be an example to your people."

☖

January 6, 1899

The queen went back to Washington. The PGs refused to return her private property that they confiscated along with the Crown lands when they took over. She's going to petition the US government for help to get it back.

Before she left, she asked me to accompany Ka'iulani to a friend's wedding at Parker Ranch on the Big Island. Though the princess still takes her headache remedies, I must say the change of scenery has improved her outlook. Unlike Honolulu, there are no swaggering soldiers or staring haoles. And I continue to tease her about having 'a little decent resignation,' as Mr. Stevenson used to tell us. (Though I find it hard to do myself. I heard from friends that Mr. Dole said he regretted the whole affair and how the queen was overthrown! I only wish he'd regretted it sooner.)

David joined us for the holidays. We've had such fun at the ranch going to dances and picnics that Ka`iulani decided to extend her visit. It's been raining, but we managed to get in some rides. Yesterday we rode to Waipio to stay the night. The local people came out to serenade us in the evening. This morning we rode around the valley, but when it started to rain, we had to hurry back because the path on the cliff gets slippery. Going up the hill, we were hanging on by our teeth, but we had fun on the way home jumping the horses over logs and pig holes.

On the last leg home, the rain cut our faces. It was blowing like cats and dogs. We didn't get in until past sundown, and were soaked to the bone, but thanks to a warm bath, warm drink, and dinner, we're none the worse for it. Everyone wants to go back out tomorrow to ride up the mountain, and perhaps later this week, up to the volcano.

&

"The sun's up, sleepyhead. Let's go."

Laura shook Ka`iulani. She turned over, groaning.

"It's too early, Laura. I'm still tired."

"It's almost nine. We've had breakfast already. Come on, we don't want to start without you."

"Okay." She sat up, stretched, and yawned.

"I'll go tell the cook to put your breakfast on the table," Laura said. "Be out there in ten minutes, okay?"

Ka`iulani waved her away. When Laura was gone, she reached for her headache remedy on the dresser next to the pitcher of water. She opened the small box and spooned some white powder into a glass. Then she poured water on the powder, stirred it, and drank it down.

When Ka`iulani came out for breakfast, Laura and David were already outside, saddling their horses. She ate a bite of scrambled egg and walked out the door.

"There you are," David said. "I've got your horse ready."

He gave her a boost up. She swung her leg over the horse's back and settled in the saddle. Laura kicked her horse to come alongside.

"We'll have sunshine for a little while, but one of the *paniolos* said those clouds over there mean more rain this afternoon."

Ka`iulani looked over at two men standing against the fence. They tipped their cowboy hats, and she nodded acknowledgment.

They started across the pasture toward the mountain, the sun warm on their backs. Ka`iulani's horse pushed forward to lead, so Laura let hers fall in behind her, and David brought up the rear. For an hour or more, they followed a path that meandered along a stream into the forest. The air grew cool and still as the horses climbed higher, and the clouds the cowboys had pointed out that morning descended like a fog in the trees.

The path grew steeper, and Ka`iulani's horse snorted as it strained up the hill. When she came to a level spot, she stopped and turned in the saddle to look back. She thought she could hear Laura and David down the path behind her, but she couldn't see them anymore through the mist. Facing forward again, she patted her horse's neck, waiting for them to catch up.

She heard a stirring in the bushes at the side of the trail, and was startled by an old Hawaiian man who seemed to step out of nowhere onto the path in front of her. He was dressed in a long-sleeved white shirt that reached to his thighs, and he was barefoot. His wispy hair and beard were white, and his brown skin was wrinkled like tanned leather. Leaning on a wooden staff, he looked up at the princess.

"*Maka'ala, e ke ali`i*," he said. "Be careful." He glanced up. "Rain clouds are gathering."

"Yes, grandfather," Ka`iulani said, nodding. "Thank you. My friends are just behind me. We'll be starting back soon." She thought he might be a local man who lived in the mountains. All the local people knew their princess was visiting Waimea. Perhaps he'd seen her from his forest home and had come to pay respects.

The old man jutted the staff toward her with both hands. The horse shied and tossed its head, the whites of its eyes showing. Ka`iulani tightened the reins to hold him in.

"*Maka'ala, e ke ali`i*," he repeated. "Be careful." He waved the staff in the air. "These clouds took your mother."

Ka`iulani gasped.

"Child of Likelike, prepare yourself."

With his eyes half closed, he tipped his head back and started to wail a chant.

Over the mountains silence reigns,
The silence of night that has moved away,
And the silence of night that comes,
The silence of night filled with people,
And the silence of night of dispersing....

The wind came up and the trees began to sway. The kahuna continued his eerie song. The old chant echoed deep in Ka`iulani's heart. She began to tremble. There was a flash of lightning, then a crack of thunder directly overhead. The horse jumped, and Ka`iulani grabbed its mane to steady herself. Big raindrops spattered the leaves and the ground.

'Tis fearful the steps and the narrow trails,
'Tis fearful the amount eaten and left,
'Tis fearful the night past and gone,

The awful stillness of the night that came....

The ancient words reminded her of all that had been lost, and of the pain she wanted so desperately to forget. She yanked the reins to turn the horse's head, kicking its sides.

"Go away, old man," she screamed. "Your Hawaii is gone. It's gone!"

There was another thunderclap. The animal started to gallop down the hill, then slid on the muddy path, nearly colliding with David's and Laura's horses as it passed them. They shouted her name, but she didn't stop. The sky opened in an icy downpour, and they spurred their horses down the mountain trail after her.

When Laura and David caught up to Ka`iulani at the ranch house, she was blue from the cold. They wrapped her in blankets, and the retainers brought hot drinks and soup, but she couldn't stop shivering. Her teeth chattered between sips of tea as she told the story of the old kahuna on the mountaintop.

Laura tried to comfort her, saying the country people around Waimea still hung onto their ways and practiced their old traditions — she shouldn't take what he said literally. But Laura couldn't explain away the alarm she saw in David's eyes when Ka`iulani repeated what she remembered of the old man's chant.

&

When the princess didn't get better after a few days at the ranch, the retainers carried her on a litter down the hill to the inter-island steamer. At the wharf in Honolulu, her father met them with the carriage. They'd taken her home and put her to bed where she'd been for nearly seven weeks.

Laura sat by her bed in the second-story room at Ainahau.

One candle burned on the bedside table. It was after midnight. After sending Mr. Cleghorn to bed, the doctor had gone to take a nap in the parlor. Ka'iulani was pale, and her breathing shallow, but at least she was sleeping.

The long days had passed by with visitors coming and going. Nights of silence with people keeping vigils, retainers laying out food, people leaving, retainers clearing away leftovers, people climbing the steps to her bedroom, whispering in the anteroom, leaving again, silence.

Laura couldn't shake the memories and feelings that came back to her of sitting with Likelike in her darkened room in the old house at Ainahau. When the candle flickered, she looked around, half expecting to see someone passing by. Then there was stillness again, the only sound the tick-tick-tick of the clock.

Laura's head bobbed, her eyelids heavy. When she saw the princess open her eyes, she sat forward. Ka'iulani smiled faintly, then looked past her. Her eyes widened, and she uttered one word, but it was muffled and Laura couldn't be sure. She thought she heard her say, "Mama." And then Ka'iulani stopped breathing.

At that moment a peacock in the yard below let out a piercing cry. Then another joined in, and another — a cacophony of lament rising in the night like an ancient Hawaiian mele. They chorused on and on, waking everyone in the house, and the neighbors down the road, until at last it all died down in an awful stillness.

Chapter 32 ———

Laura walked back home from Queen's Hospital. She crossed the street, hurrying to dodge a motorcar rattling by. They outnumbered the horses and carriages now. She missed the old rhythmic clip-clop of hooves on the street.

As she pushed her front door open, pots and pans clanged in the kitchen, so she slipped inside and down the hallway to the library. She closed the door behind her and sat at her desk, dropping her briefcase at the side of the chair. She nudged her shoes off, rubbing one foot against the other, stretched out her legs, and closed her eyes. After a few minutes, she sat up and looked at the clock on the wall. It was almost dinnertime, but Will wasn't home yet. They always waited for him so she took her journal out of the desk drawer.

April 20, 1917

What a day. Aside from our regular work, the doctors now have to train the staff and volunteers in triage and special emergency procedures. There's been a real frenzy in Honolulu since the United States declared war on Germany, though I don't see how the conflict in Europe could ever reach here.

When I finished teaching, I looked for Will, but he was still doing his class, so I came home without him. Thank goodness when I got here the girls were already fixing dinner. They've become such good helpers. It's hard to believe they're nearly the same age I was when I came to Honolulu.

Laura moved the journal to the left to continue writing on the next page. Some papers shifted, revealing an envelope postmarked "Washington, D.C." The girls always put her mail on the desk for her. It must be news from David. He'd been elected a territorial representative from Hawaii, and had gone to live in Washington with his wife and children. She hadn't heard anything from him since the United States entered the war. She reached for a letter opener and slit the envelope, not noticing the black-rimmed edge on the flap.

She read rapidly down the page. Her eyes stopped at the name of her nephew, Tommy Kahiko, David's eldest son. It was only then that Laura realized the handwriting was shaky. David wrote that Tommy had been lost at sea in a campaign against German submarines off the coast of Europe.

She sat back in her chair and set the letter down. Tommy was like her own. David's family had lived just up the street, and Tommy was at her house as often as he was at home. When David and his family left for Washington, Tommy stayed with Laura and Will to finish school.

When war was declared, Tommy got caught up in the fervor, and before anyone knew what he'd done, went with a bunch of school buddies to enlist. Then he came home, bragging about it to his cousins. Laura overheard them in the kitchen and barged through the door. She told him he was too young, but Tommy just smiled. He said the navy didn't think so, and he wanted to get over there and do his part before it was all over.

There was nothing she could do once he'd signed up. Tommy wrote to his father to let him know. David wrote back saying he wished Tommy had stayed in school, but he knew he'd do a good job at whatever he set his mind to, and told him to be safe.

Be safe. How could a nineteen-year-old boy be safe against German submarines? Tears welled up as Laura remembered the day she'd gone to see him before he shipped out. He was flushed with the excitement of the adventure, not a shred of a sense of danger in his handsome Hawaiian face. Laura thought she could even see a bit of her father in him, in the set of his jaw and his mouth. He was spit-and-polish in his uniform, feeling invincible, like the other young men there, whose families gathered to see them off.

The girls and Will brought at least two dozen leis and heaped them around Tommy's neck. Laura stepped forward and held up the black pearl ring on its gold chain. Tommy knew its story and what it meant to Laura. He bent down, and she clasped it around his neck and tucked it under his shirt. She'd patted his chest where the ring now lay hidden, and told him to keep it close to his heart until he came home again.

In that second, Laura thought she saw something behind the bravado in his eyes — that he understood where he might be headed. He hugged her, and her face pressed against the sweet-scented, dewy ginger blossoms and plumeria.

The library door opened. She quickly wiped the tears from her cheeks.

"Mother?"

Laura thought it would be better to tell the girls when Will was there.

"Yes, dear?"

"Dinner's ready whenever Father gets home." Her daughter stepped forward. "And this was just delivered for you." She handed Laura an envelope.

Laura recognized the distinctive curves of the queen's handwriting. It was an invitation to visit her at Washington Place.

&

*L*aura walked along Beretania Street toward the queen's home. Every house and fence post and climbing vine evoked memories. She stopped for a moment in front of the old McBride mansion. Mrs. McBride had sold it some years before after her husband passed away. With Lucien gone and no other family in the islands, she'd gone back to Boston to live with relatives. The ancient banyan that Laura had stood under so many years before, wishing she could feel the support of her ancestors like the Hawaiians did, was just as massive as it had always been, shading the lawn and the house.

She paused in front of the Price home. Hannah and Lizzie had married years before, and Uncle Stephen had lived there alone until he died. Then her cousins sold the place. They had homes of their own. Laura was surprised when she received an inheritance after the sale. Her cousins admitted that nothing was left to her in the will, but they wanted her to have a home of her own, so when their father's estate passed to them, they gave a share to Laura. It helped a lot because Laura was still doing her residency at Queen's Hospital, struggling on a stipend.

When she reached the front of Washington Place, where she'd lived so many years as the queen's secretary, she stood a long time, overcome with memories. After Ka`iulani's death, when

Laura thought her heart would break, the queen paid for her to go to medical school in San Francisco, urging her to come back to Honolulu as a doctor.

She wasn't the only one the queen had helped. Laura didn't know how she did it. None of her lands were ever returned to her, and she wasn't a rich woman. One of the retainers told her that the queen paid all the expenses for the son of a man who'd betrayed her at her trial to go to Stanford University. And that she'd given money to others, like Willie Kaae's boy.

Over the years the queen was even cordial to the men of the provisional government and the Republic, who became the government of the Territory when Hawaii was annexed. She didn't accept invitations to their homes, such as to Sanford Dole's famous breakfasts, though occasionally she attended a state affair. A couple of years before, at a reception where the queen was present, Laura was alarmed to see Mr. Thurston proceeding through the receiving line. When he reached the queen, he hesitated, but she extended her hand and said, "I'm very glad to see you here this evening, Mr. Thurston." Those must have been the first words they'd exchanged in almost twenty-five years. Thurston seemed a little surprised. Laura just wondered where the queen found the strength to be so gracious to someone who'd dethroned her and slandered her for so long.

With a sigh, Laura pushed open the wrought-iron gate and walked up to the verandah. She stood looking up at the grand old house, almost expecting Wakeki, with her white-toothed smile, to open the door. But Wakeki was long gone now. Instead, it was Kainoa, who'd come to serve in Liliu's household after Ka`iulani died.

Laura went up the steps, and Kainoa escorted her to the parlor. The queen sat on the sofa near a window, looking out at the garden. Laura approached and curtsied, as she'd always done, and the queen smiled at her. Her face was still smooth, but her wavy hair, tied up in a bun, had turned white.

"Your Majesty," Laura said.

Liliu held out her hand. Laura took it and sat down next to her.

"So, Doctor Akina, how are Will and the girls?"

"Everyone's fine."

The queen regarded her closely. "Everyone?"

How did she always sense what was below the surface, sometimes even before you knew yourself? Perhaps that's why she'd sent the invitation to visit. Laura told her about the letter from David, and Tommy being lost at sea.

The queen listened, holding Laura's hand and shaking her head. She sat silent for a long while. A few times, Laura started to say something, then thought better of it. Finally, the queen picked up a small bell from the table and rang for her retainer. Kainoa came to the parlor door, and Liliu, speaking Hawaiian, asked her to bring something. Laura looked at the queen in surprise.

Kainoa reappeared, a bundle under her arm. The queen shifted in her seat to prepare to stand. Laura stood to help her.

"Come to the garden with me," the queen said.

Laura followed her out the door, and Kainoa came behind them. The queen moved slowly down the steps, one at a time, and over to the flagpole, which stood bare, its ropes tied up since Kalakaua's time. The air was still and warm.

"This Great War convinces me," Liliu said, "that what happened in Hawaii is happening in the whole world. It's being plowed up, things being churned, moved around. People mixed together from so many countries and so many races. It's a new time, Laura. Everything will change quickly now. The old histories are past. A new history is beginning for all of us ... as one people. But we'll suffer until we all forgive."

Laura watched the queen's face, and thought of the kindness she'd shown to those who'd wronged her.

"Remember, I told you about ho'o pono pono, how my people found a way to restore harmony and keep the community together?"

"Yes, you said being in the middle of the ocean, it wasn't so easy to sail away when they were angry with each other."

Liliu gave her a gentle smile. "And it's not so easy for the people of the earth either. Where will they sail away to?"

A slight breeze quivered the ropes tied to the pole. The queen put her hand on Kainoa's bundle. "What I do now doesn't make me any less myself. To give aloha is my nature. It makes me more myself."

The breeze grew stronger, and the metal clasps of the rope dinged against the pole. The trees began to sway. Laura pushed back the hair that blew in her eyes and felt a sudden shiver. Wakeki's long-ago words came back to her — "That no regular wind, that wind calling somebody."

"They never accepted us as their equals in life," Liliu said, "but now, we're equals in death. On earth everything is two; in Heaven it is one."

She lifted her hand and stepped back, nodding to Kainoa to go ahead. The retainer unfolded the bundle, clipping the banner to the clasps on the rope. At another nod from the queen, she pulled hand over hand to hoist an American flag to the top of the pole. The breeze caught it and unfurled it over their heads. The wind whistled and whipped around them, blowing their skirts. The queen turned to Laura.

"I raised a flag too late once, and I've always regretted it. If we feel hatred or resentment, everything turns cold and dark. But we can choose to give aloha, and the power that vanished is restored ... something new can grow." Her eyes shone.

"We have not lost the kingdom." The queen placed her hand on her heart. "The door is here." She closed her eyes, stood silent a moment, and softly spoke a single word, "Aloha."

Laura swore she felt something shift below her feet and above her head. The air shimmered. The queen opened her eyes.

"*Alo* means, 'from my presence, from the center of things.'" In a graceful, continuous gesture, she moved her hand from her heart up past her mouth, extending it out in front of her. "*Ha* is breath, the breath of life."

&

The red fish came up from the sea again. In the corridors at the hospital, the natives whispered, "The queen shall die," long before newspaper headlines proclaimed that she was ill.

Laura went to see her. The garden was crowded with old Hawaiian women and men, softly chanting. In her room, the queen lay against pillows in a four-poster bed, fragile but peaceful. When she saw Laura at the door, she beckoned for her to come close and sit by her side. Then she reached out to cradle Laura's sorrowful face in her hands and gently wipe away her tears. She kissed her forehead and murmured something in her ear. Laura nodded, and put her arms around the queen one last time.

The next day, Lili`uokalani passed away. Her remains were carried from Washington Place to Kawaiahao Church at midnight in the old way, flanked by kahili bearers. Soldiers from the National Guard led the procession, followed by royal torchbearers with the short, feathered scarlet-and-yellow capes of the high chiefs around their shoulders.

In the gleam of flickering kukui-nut torches, an ancient crone in a white holoku followed in halting steps and sang a quavering mele, praising the queen's virtues and the good done by her house.

The streets from Washington Place to the church were lined with people standing silent, their faces — Polynesian, Oriental, European, American — briefly illumined as the torches passed by.

In the flower-filled church, the casket was placed on a koa-wood table near the altar, a royal feathered cloak draped around it. The kahili bearers took up their watch, waving their feathered standards in a solemn tempo above the open coffin.

David and Laura walked together up the aisle to the front of the church. He carried a crown on a velvet pillow. He gave the pillow to Laura, then took the crown in both hands. The queen, her white hair framing her sleeping face, was dressed in a black holoku of silk brocade. David bent over the coffin and gently placed on her head the crown she was never allowed to wear in life.

Thousands of mourners filed past to pay tribute at Kawaiahao Church, then again when the queen lay in state a few days later in the throne room at ʻIolani Palace. The newspapers reported the strange occurrence of a whirlwind that had swept before the procession on the way from Washington Place to the church. It wouldn't have been so strange, they said, except it happened again when the queen's casket was moved to the palace.

The day of the queen's burial, the casket was placed in a polished koa-wood coffin mounted with the royal coat of arms. Her name song, sung at her birth, was gently intoned. More than 200 men with feathered shoulder capes drew the casket through the streets of Honolulu toward the Royal Mausoleum. The royal crown now rode atop the plumed canopy that covered the coffin.

Naval officers in full-dress uniform, ministers of foreign governments in top hats, territorial government officials, and visiting United States congressmen marched behind the casket. Laura recognized that one of the congressmen was the man who'd presented the annexation bill to the United States Senate. She wondered what he must be thinking, as he witnessed the outpouring of love and grief expressed by thousands for the queen. He walked beside Sanford Dole and Lorrin Thurston, now both gray-haired. Mr. Dole, bent and frail, shuffled forward looking straight ahead, supported on Thurston's arm.

Hawaiian societies in full regalia filled the streets to follow the procession up the valley. Men in black wore brilliant feathered capes, some carrying tall kahilis. Women wore black holokus with bright yellow-feathered leis. Some wore purple or white with ribbons bearing Lili`uokalani's own motto, *Onipaa* — "Be steadfast." Others wore feathered helmets of the ancient warriors or carried precious relics of the past.

Laura wore her royal medallion, and walked with Will and David, his wife, Mei Li, and their nieces and nephews — mixtures of Hawaiian, American, Chinese, Japanese, European. Behind them were her cousins, Hannah and Lizzie, with their families — all the children tones of tan and cream. They joined in the procession leaving the palace grounds while motion-picture cameramen perched atop scaffolding to film the scene of blended peoples passing by to pay respects to the last queen.

They reached a crest above the city, and the carriage carrying the royal casket turned into the mausoleum grounds. The crowd flooded in, thronging beneath the spreading trees. Wind swept a shower down from the Pali, swaying the branches. A sudden strong gust snatched the crown from atop the canopy over the casket. It flew up, twirled in the wind, then fell to the ground, and rolled to a stop.

A hush spread over the crowd; in the silence, only a sighing breeze and the patter of raindrops. Then, a lone voice began to sing an old, familiar refrain. The kahili bearers took up the melody and, like a great rising wave, hundreds joined in the chorus of the queen's own song... *Aloha Oe.*

Author's Note

About the Cover

"Poppies" (1890). Painted in Great Britain by Princess Ka`iulani, heir to the Hawaiian throne, at age fifteen.

In 1889, Princess Ka`iulani was sent to school in England. While she was abroad, the descendants of American missionaries in the Hawaiian Islands actively plotted to overthrow the monarchy. Having already forcibly reduced the monarchy's power, they were maneuvering to take over the government completely.

The princess's painting suggests her own inner landscape. She often admitted feeling desperately homesick for her beloved islands; and the bay and coastal mountains, though painted in Great Britain, take on a strong resemblance to the shape of Diamond Head and the curve of Waikiki.

These icons of Ka`iulani's island home fade into the barren background, covered over by Western plants: the red poppy, known for its drowsy, narcotic effect, which can ultimately cause death; and the yellow dandelion, a noxious weed that propagates itself through the soil and the air to choke out other flowers.

Red and yellow are the colors of the royal ali`i, the rulers of Hawaii. Did the princess's art depict how Western influence was usurping that power, and killing the land and its people?

Art is mysterious, and there's no way to know if these images were conscious or unconscious. Princess Ka`iulani left no record of why she painted the picture this way. It is certain, however, that she knew of the Western agitators' intrigues, and her royal family's heroic struggle to save the Hawaiian kingdom.

Mixed Sources

Product group from well-managed forests and other controlled sources

Cert no. SW-COC-002283
www.fsc.org
© 1996 Forest Stewardship Council

X